Enticed

"Masterful . . . fabulous."   *—Fallen Angel Reviews*

"The characters are complex, the romance and sex [are] hot—hot—hot."
—*Romance Reviews Today

"Ms. Dante has done it again! . . . A feast for the senses."
—ParaNormal Romance

"Enough heat to scorch my eyebrows."   *—Joyfully Reviewed*

"A triumph for Ms. Dante and a real treat for all fans of erotic romance, mystery, suspense, magic, and face-kicking action."
—Just Erotic Romance Reviews

"Steamy sex scenes, adventure, and elements of paranormal intensity . . . I found this book fascinating."   *—Romance Reader at Heart*

Entangled

"I was absolutely blown away . . . Brava!"   *—Fallen Angel Reviews*

"All I can say is, 'Wow!' . . . Readers are in for a wild ride."
—ParaNormal Romance

"Dante's sizzling romance delves into the world of the metaphysical sliced with eroticism and espionage."   *—Romantic Times*

"A fantastic book, full of magic, mystery, and incredibly hot sex!"
—Joyfully Reviewed

"Paranormal romance filled with sensuality and fire that any reader will enjoy."   *—Paranormal Romance Writers*

"Toe-curling hot . . . absolutely yummy."   *—Just Erotic Romance Reviews*

"Sexy, smart, and touching . . . Prepare to be spellbound."
—Romance Reviews Today

Berkley Heat titles by Kathleen Dante

ENTANGLED
ENTICED
DREAMWALKER
ENDANGERED

Endangered

Kathleen Dante

HEAT I NEW YORK

THE BERKLEY PUBLISHING GROUP
Published by the Penguin Group
Penguin Group (USA) Inc.
375 Hudson Street, New York, New York 10014, USA
Penguin Group (Canada), 90 Eglinton Avenue East, Suite 700, Toronto, Ontario M4P 2Y3, Canada
(a division of Pearson Penguin Canada Inc.)
Penguin Books Ltd., 80 Strand, London WC2R 0RL, England
Penguin Group Ireland, 25 St. Stephen's Green, Dublin 2, Ireland (a division of Penguin Books Ltd.)
Penguin Group (Australia), 250 Camberwell Road, Camberwell, Victoria 3124, Australia
(a division of Pearson Australia Group Pty. Ltd.)
Penguin Books India Pvt. Ltd., 11 Community Centre, Panchsheel Park, New Delhi—110 017, India
Penguin Group (NZ), 67 Apollo Drive, Rosedale, North Shore 0632, New Zealand
(a division of Pearson New Zealand Ltd.)
Penguin Books (South Africa) (Pty.) Ltd., 24 Sturdee Avenue, Rosebank, Johannesburg 2196,
South Africa

Penguin Books Ltd., Registered Offices: 80 Strand, London WC2R 0RL, England

This is an original publication of The Berkley Publishing Group.

Copyright © 2009 by Kathleen Dante.
Cover photograph by Serge Krouglikoff.
Text design by Tiffany Estreicher.

First edition: April 2009

Library of Congress Cataloging-in-Publication Data

Dante, Kathleen.
    Endangered / Kathleen Dante.—1st ed.
        p.   cm.
    ISBN 978-0-425-22607-0 (trade pbk.)
    1. Women detectives—Fiction.   2. Police—Special weapons and tactics units—Fiction.
3. Snipers—Fiction.   4. Serial murderers—Fiction.   I. Title.
    PS3604.A57E57 2009
    813'.6—dc22
                                                                                    2008039453

PRINTED IN THE UNITED STATES OF AMERICA

10 9 8 7 6 5 4 3 2 1

*Thanks to the readers who e-mailed me asking
what's next, to my supportive family for cheering me on,
and to my editor, Leis Pederson, whose insight helped me
tell Rio and Cyn's story better.*

Endangered

PROLOGUE

Three Weeks Earlier

Sprinting after his fellow agent, Rio Rafael hurdled half-seen rocks and bushes along the garden path, cutting corners in a desperate race against time. Another wild run through the night—one with wailing sirens as the surreal soundtrack instead of plaintive meowing—except this time the danger was all too certain. The last time, they'd found Dillon's lady poisoned. This time, she could be stabbed to death and horribly mutilated, like the corpse they'd found.

The shorter man outpaced him, pulling ahead with fear-fueled adrenaline. *¡Cojones!* That was *so* wrong. Dillon wasn't the point man, *damnú air*. Rio was! His friend ignored the order of the Homicide lieutenant panting behind them to leave the situation to the police.

Swearing silently, Rio lengthened his stride to catch up, knowing Dillon wouldn't wait for backup—not when a murderer stalked Jordan's home. To his relief, two cops stood on the porch, suiting up for hard entry. Maybe they had a chance of doing this the right way instead of blindly jumping into the deep end without recon.

Then a cat screamed defiance, his shrill battle cry ripping through the night.

"*No.*" Dillon dove for the door, slapped the lock panel to shut down its wards, and thrust it open.

Shouldering past the frantic mage, Rio swept the entry for hostiles, training his gun at the shadows. No way was Dillon getting jumped on his watch.

Debris littered the hall, but nothing moved. Nothing crouched on the stairs or hid by the doorway to the living room.

"Clear. Go!" He stepped aside to avoid trampling by his fellow agent. Dillon had barely waited for his okay, sprinting toward the sounds of combat.

Keeping an eye on the shadows, Rio followed for once, trusting his friend's greater familiarity with the house's layout. Pottery crunched underfoot, raising a pungent whiff of green.

In the dark studio, anonymous figures struggled. Keeping his gun pointed at the ceiling, Rio stopped beside Dillon, straining at the shadows for a target.

A magelight bloomed in midair, revealing Jordan pinned over a table with Timothy clinging to the back of her knife-wielding attacker. The big cat's body blocked any clear shot.

Rio swore, furiously debating whether to take the shot anyway.

The murderer flung Timothy away, sending the snarling cat rebounding off a cabinet into ominous silence. The motion lowered the masked figure's profile; Jordan's rigid arms held back the knife, but they and her twisting body gave cover to her attacker.

A bullet could hit either one.

Someone screamed.

Then the knife descended.

Decision point. Rio—

Magic washed over him in a skin-prickling flash of violet power, transforming the struggle for survival into gasping sculpture.

"Police! Don't move!" several voices shouted from behind. Rather redundant, but Rio wasn't about to quibble. The cops quickly secured the murderer, permitting Dillon to lift his spell.

It left Jordan lying on the desk, her arms covered with angry slashes, blood dripping off her neck from the carotid. Rio's heart skipped. Were they too late anyway?

"Get me a medic," Dillon ordered as he rushed to his lady's side. He ran his hands over her, his shoulders relaxing as his examination wound down. Whatever Jordan's injuries were, it seemed they weren't life-threatening, only gory, and she wasn't having any trouble breathing—which was more than Rio could say for the cat.

Holstering his gun under his jacket—hopefully before the cops noticed—Rio broke off to check on Timothy. The cat sprawled in a boneless heap, his black-and-white fur liberally crisscrossed with red. A light touch revealed he was only unconscious and had no obvious broken bones. Despite all the blood, nothing gushed with the strength of arterial damage.

As Rio knelt over him, Timothy's muscles tensed, one paw weakly clawing the floor. A faint snarl came from the battered animal, still defiant.

"Shhh, it's okay. She's safe." Rio offered a finger to sniff, then stroked the valiant cat behind a big ear, while calling some of the medics over; there were enough to see to both victims. At Dillon's worried frown, Rio gave his friend the high sign, sure that immediate healing would see Timothy well.

His friend slumped against the table, his eyes closing in relief, his arms so tight around Jordan a knife probably couldn't slip between them. Shuddering, Dillon gave her a watery smile as she cupped her bloodied hands over his cheeks, which were pale beneath his tan.

Fear and desperation were still etched on his features, disbelief at the miracle of Jordan's survival warring with intense need. There could be no doubt about the depth of the other man's feelings for her.

Rio had to look away. The raw emotion on Dillon's face was too revealing, too intimate for him to witness. The averted tragedy was too close to home.

He didn't understand why it felt that way. Dillon was his friend, but that didn't explain why Rio's gut continued to churn now that the danger was past.

Then it hit him like a pile driver to the solar plexus: a realization so great it froze his lungs.

That could be him—him and Cyn—with even more harrowing results. He couldn't assume that, whenever he came waltzing back to see her, Cyn would be here, safe and sound, eager for more fun and games. Her job was just as dangerous as his, if not more so; in her assignment with the police tac team, she faced violent criminals on a daily basis.

Knowing full well the wild curves Fate could throw a guy, Rio realized he couldn't take his time with Cyn for granted. And he discovered she meant more to him than just a fun, reliable, convenient lay.

She was more. Much more.

And if he didn't want to lose her, he'd better do something about it. Just playing games was no longer enough.

CHAPTER ONE

Ignoring the lingering stench of burnt chemicals, Cyn—Detective Sergeant Cynarra Malva, to sticklers for formality—ran her hands over her body armor, checking for singe marks and anything else that might weaken the protective silver runes painted on the black Kevlar. Finding none, she folded down its ridiculous one-size-fits-all pauldrons that on her smaller frame evoked a fantasy warlord silhouette and hung the black vest in her narrow locker, ready for the next callout. Disgruntlement twisted her face into a grimace. While not all missions were outright successes, this one in particular left a bitter taste in her mouth.

Two doors down, a locker slammed shut, propelled by Hardesty's large mitt. It was followed by a resounding *thunk* when he threw his considerable bulk backward against the metal panel. With his bearlike physique, he managed to rock the bank of lockers.

Expecting an outburst of some sort, Cyn didn't react to the sounds. A start would have undermined her reputation for calm.

New to Tactical and, at twenty-three, the youngest in the team, Jethro Hardesty hadn't yet learned to take setbacks in stride, although part of it might just be his usual intensity. "Those shitheads are laughing at us."

"No shit? Don't hold it in, Jet. Tell us how you really feel," gibed Rick Danzinger as he straddled the bench running the length of the aisle separating the two banks of lockers, his muscular thighs aggressively spread. Only the fact that the assistant team leader had addressed Hardesty by his nickname suggested any levity. Not that Danzinger directed his biting sarcasm in Cyn's direction much; he was too aware of her higher rank.

Hardesty flushed, perhaps realizing his lack of control didn't reflect well on him.

Kelvin Jung looked up with hooded eyes, his thin lips turned down at the corners, his black hedge of fashionably spiky gelled locks positively bristling his repugnance. "They've got it down to a science: threat, money, deflagration spell, go." His hands clenched around his wand, knuckles momentarily going white; a good combat mage and countersniper, that was the only other sign of unhappiness he allowed himself.

A new gang had hit town a fortnight past and gone on a crime spree, hitting small businesses. This was the second heist just this week and the fifth to date—and there were still three days left before the week was over. It wouldn't have mattered so much if the motive were simple robbery, but the perps didn't care who got hurt, using extreme force to get whatever they wanted.

This last call had bombed—literally—with the gang getting away faster than grease through a goose. Her tac team had arrived only in time to contain the fire from the deflagration spell—not exactly the best use of their combat magics, but they'd been the ones on the ground.

Cyn kept silent, along with the rest of the men. She might be a sergeant with Homicide, but here she was just one of the team—and one of the part-time members at that; that was the way she liked it, despite the brass's recent efforts to convince her to make her participation full-time. It wasn't her place to comment. If she opened her mouth now, she might say something she'd regret later. However, she understood the feeling; frustration also left her shoulders tight.

Under the guise of pushing damp, black and white strands of hair out of her face, she sent a sidelong glance at her team leader and fellow sergeant, Fernao Antillia, who, it turned out, was watching her with eyes of polished granite—waiting to see if she'd horn in on his territory, no doubt. Closing her own locker, she broke eye contact, in no mood for a pissing contest she didn't want to win.

"They'll slip up," Fernao finally stated, his dark face hard and determined. "They always do. Then we'll get them."

"Or they'll move on to fresher hunting grounds," countered Danzinger. The assistant team leader was built like a pit bull terrier, his shoulders bunching and rippling as he wiped down his wand with an oiled rag, taking care to get the crannies of its intricate carving. The short blond had gotten the closest to the blaze, actually diving into the building to save a civilian trapped inside; he smelled like it, too, despite a shower.

"Or that," Fernao conceded, standing up to prop his hands on his still-narrow hips, the motion drawing her attention to his flat belly.

Cyn schooled her face into an expression of mild interest; her noticing that little detail about her team leader didn't bear thinking about. Her libido was seriously out of whack. Fellow cops were nowhere on her list of potential lovers—especially married cops.

The senior sergeant, though, cut an impressive figure with his arms akimbo, a deep scowl on his mahogany face. "In which case, languishing here like"—there was an almost imperceptible hesitation in Fernao's spiel as his gaze darted to Cyn before he continued, with probably a more politically correct substitution—"old aunties won't change anything."

Everyone else, including Cyn, stared at their team leader.

"Languish?" she repeated, suspecting the younger men wouldn't even dare breathe the word.

"I can't believe he said that," someone muttered in a tone too low to identify.

"Hey, I went to college, too."

The stunned silence stretched out.

"The wife reads those sorts of books. Great for expanding the vocabulary, you know," Fernao blustered.

The room broke out in snickers, distracting them from their earlier disgust. The sight of all eight hard male bodies flexing rhythmically kindled a different tension in Cyn.

It really was too bad Rio wasn't in town. She'd have welcomed a bout of hot sex to unwind, a little slap and tickle to burn off her tension. Not that she was going to look for relief in-house; it was Rio or no one for her, or at least no one in the department. No way was she dipping her toes in that pool, no matter how intriguing it might seem. Work was work, and sex was fun and games, and she wasn't about to mix the two. Just the thought of the complications of having a fellow cop as a lover gave her hives.

Normally, civilians were intimidated when they found out what she did. Cops, on the other hand, generally preferred women who'd bat their lashes at them, not someone who could go toe-to-toe with them on the mat—or so she'd found. The rare exceptions were so focused on the job that they couldn't talk about anything else.

Unlike Rio.

And unlike him, all the men in the room wore an aura of toughness around them like a cloak, one that on first or even second glance seemed to be missing from her Latin lover; though that wasn't an entirely accurate description of Rio, him being half Irish and half Argentine. His mixed heritage wasn't obvious, except in his name—Riordan—which somehow had been shortened to Rio; however, it had produced a man who was extremely easy on the eyes. If someone had battered his sharp cheekbones or flattened his straight nose, Rio might have managed to look rugged. As it was, his features were too fine to be described as anything else but beautiful. Hardly an adjective one associated with toughness.

But although her sometime lover was a civilian, her job didn't seem to bother him at all. It also didn't hurt that he could make her body sing like a finely tuned instrument.

Thinking of him brought to mind his last visit. Usually their time together was fun and games, both of them too conscious of the implicit contract of nothing serious. Normally, sex meant lots of teasing and laughter.

However, this last good-bye, just before he'd left, had been insane—frenzied and tempestuous. She could still feel his hands on her, caressing her, could feel their pressure and intensity: urgent, stroking and fondling her to a fever pitch. Cyn swallowed down the improper desire that rose at the memory of Rio's blistering lovemaking. His touch had been possessive, his need for her almost ravenous. He'd been fierce, even driven, taking her with a ferocity that bordered on violence.

Nothing at all like her easygoing lover of previous visits.

Then he'd returned to his secretive world of private security—though she had her doubts about that. Rio Rafael showed indications of being an operator, one of the rare few who lived in the shadows of black ops. She might not be military police any longer, but she could still read the signs.

She gave a mental shrug. So long as he didn't break the law in her town, she could ignore her suspicions. Being in black ops didn't make him less of a lover and was probably one of the reasons why he wasn't intimidated by her. Certainly, if the way Rio had taken her that last time was anything to go by, there was no risk of him suddenly feeling threatened by her job.

Cyn shivered at the memory of his leave-taking, missing Rio all the more; then she forced it to the back of her mind. She refused to become one of those women who pined for their lovers when they were gone. It was just sex; great sex, admittedly—but simply sex, for all that.

Snapping back to the present, she looked around, hoping no one noticed her distraction. Her team seemed almost normal, occupied with postmission details. The extreme testosterone that had filled the air was temporarily banished.

Cyn shrugged into her leather jacket, making certain her sleeve covered the wand strapped to her forearm. She still had some hours left in her shift, which meant her desk in Homicide awaited her return. There were cases waiting to be solved and murderers to be caught.

Planting her feet, Cyn pulled, the hundred-pound weight at the end of the line rising smoothly as she extended her arm and leaned forward, using her body as leverage. She held it at full extension for a count of six, ignoring the burning strain on her muscles, then slowly let it slide back down. As the weight clinked on its rest, she exhaled softly, shifted her feet, then mirrored the pull with her other arm. She repeated the exercise methodically, alternating sides over and over, having long accepted the necessity of the mind-numbing routine.

Resistance training was imperative for mages who had to work with high-powered spells, the weights substituting for the invisible but palpable density of serious magic. At those levels, spell control meant strength and coordination, so any master mage worth her salt made sure she was in top physical condition. Cyn might not be in the league of adepts, but since her life and those of her teammates depended on it, she exercised religiously.

Unfortunately, working out left the mind free to wander at will. Commencing yet another set of exercises she knew by heart did little to occupy Cyn's thoughts.

And hers wanted to dwell on her absent lover.

The grunts from the other stations of the department's weight room faded away as the torrid memory of Rio's last good-bye returned to the forefront of Cyn's mind. She couldn't leave it alone. What was it about his leave-taking that bothered her so much?

Rio had met her at the door, already packed and ready to go, but a welcome sight nevertheless, after a long night working a murder scene. All he'd said was that he had to fly out immediately, but he'd waited for her to come home to say good-bye.

Of course, after that, they hadn't done much talking . . . unless you counted gasps and groans and demands for *more* and *harder* and *deeper.* They hadn't made it to the bed, and if she'd had a rug in her apartment, she'd probably have had rug burn to show for their impatience.

She fought down a blush at the thought of their frenzied lovemaking but couldn't suppress the thrum of desire that resonated in her bones. She couldn't blame it all on Rio; he might have been wild to take her that night, but she'd been just as wild to be taken. And boy, had he taken her!

He'd been silent, almost grim. She'd thought it a reaction to the mutilated corpse they'd found—something he might not be accustomed to seeing up close and personal, despite his probable line of work—and dismissed it as natural; even she had been shaken, and it hadn't been her first murder victim or hacked-up corpse. It had seemed only right that he would seek release through sex.

His hands and mouth had been all over her, as though trying to impress her into his mind to drive out the horrific memory. Fervid caresses and kisses hot enough to scorch her senses. All the while thrusting into her, filling her, driving her mad with his sensual compulsion.

Until she was out of control and loving it.

She hadn't questioned his urgency or the difference in his lovemaking. Only later, after he'd left, did it occur to her. She'd found the sketch on a paper napkin of her asleep, which was unlike his usual comic doodling. In it she'd appeared soft and sensual—defenseless. Not exactly the way she liked to think of herself. She'd never suspected he viewed her in that light.

"Looks like you've got some serious issues, Sarge." The comment jolted Cyn out of the fog of her thoughts.

What? She glanced to her left, where Jung stood gripping the ends of a rolled towel slung around his neck. She frowned at him, ignoring the toned body gleaming with sweat under the abbreviated, black mesh shirt and skintight cycling shorts he wore and her own breasts still tingling with residual arousal. Truth be told, as good as he looked, he couldn't compare with Rio. "What do you mean?"

In answer, he tipped his chin at the weight, which in her distraction she'd apparently loaded past her normal limit.

"After that fiasco earlier, you don't think I need to work through some issues?" Too bad she couldn't burn off her frustration with a fast, hard romp in bed. It would probably do wonders for her libido—and her mood.

Jung snorted, a bitter smile of agreement flashing across his face. "*Fiasco* flatters us. Any day now, the papers'll start baying for blood." With a recent arrest putting paid to a high-profile bombing, the media was free to focus on the heists to boost ratings. Since Jung worked Robbery, he had a bigger stake than others in the team in ending that crime spree; his ass was closer to the fire.

"Can't say they wouldn't be justified," Cyn gritted out, her delivery only slightly forced as she focused on raising the weight smoothly and masking the effort it took; as one of the youngest sergeants in the department—and female to boot—she couldn't afford any hint of weakness.

"One of these days our luck will run out, and they'll get someone killed. Then it'll be your hot potato, too." His slanted almond eyes lit up at the prospect.

"Gee, Jung, you're such a pessimist. Don't you know we're supposed to believe we can make a difference? It's in the regs." She gave him a tight grin, lowering the weight to its rack with barely a clink. "Repeat after me: they'll make a mistake, and *then* we'll catch them."

He snorted again. "Just mark my words." The dire prediction was accompanied by melodramatically arched brows as the prophet of doom rocked on his heels.

Smiling ruefully at his suddenly cheerful negativity, Cyn shook her head, then continued her set. "I didn't know you're a precog these days."

"You don't need precognition to see that one."

Much as she hated to, Cyn had to agree with him. The gang was just too free with their deflagration spells not to kill someone eventually. Still, she argued the point as she toughed out the rest of her sets; at least the discussion got her mind off Rio and her current lack of a sex life.

The trip home had been accomplished in silence, which wasn't as difficult as it sounded, since Cyn didn't like to use music to drown out her thoughts. Not only would it also drown out sounds that might warn her of an attack, but it smacked of a crutch. No way, nohow, would she lean on one. But even the police band had been quiet, crackling only once during the drive with a routine request for information.

A slow night.

She cautiously entered her second-story walk-up. Alone. She hadn't been in the mood to hang out with the guys over a mug of whatever was on tap—a frequent occurrence lately, something she wasn't sure was good. But given the carnal humming of her body, she didn't think it was wise to immerse herself in all that testosterone and put up with the ritual dick-beating. Most days she didn't notice the jockeying for top dog—growing up with her brothers had next to inured her to it—but tonight she was too aware of the posturing and the sexual undercurrents.

Her small studio apartment greeted Cyn with more silence and stuffy heat, the evening sun streaming through the cracks between her vertical wood blinds to touch her feet. The door closed behind her with a solid *thud*, audible punctuation to her low mood. Activating the wards was automatic, requiring little thought.

After cracking the balky windows open the few miserable inches they allowed in the hopes of catching a breeze, she turned on the small fan she kept on the window ledge to draw in air, then blew out a breath, more than ready to call an end to another day. Even the long session in the weight room hadn't been enough to relax her—tire her, yes, but not like the boneless release of hot, breathless sex.

It was pitiful how much she missed Rio after three measly weeks of absence. Her playful lover who was so much fun in bed—which was probably very different from his game face, if her suspicions were correct.

Cyn's breasts throbbed at the thought of just how much fun they'd had, her nipples tingling in readiness. He'd trained her body well, had gotten her so accustomed to sexual indulgence that doing without felt unnatural.

Definitely pitiful. She fisted her hand around the white lock of her hair in disgust, the sting on her scalp little punishment for her lack of self-discipline. This wasn't even the longest she'd gone without seeing him; there'd been a couple of times he'd disappeared for nearly three months before he'd shown up again, tired, tanned, and so eager for a romp between the sheets that she'd known he hadn't had any of that kind of action while he'd been gone.

It was just sex, darn it all. Cyn spun away from the window to stalk past the love seat and battered coffee table, ignoring the kitchenette in the corner. Admittedly great sex, but just sex, all the same.

Heading for the bedroom, she stripped off her leather jacket, forcing her mind to shift mental gears by debating whether she ought to retire the jacket for the season. Summer was far enough along that leather was too much for the afternoon heat, but she loathed to give up its protection. Eyeing the wards painted on the jacket's satin inner lining, she hung it in her closet, then pulled off the long-sleeved T-shirt she'd worn under it. Maybe she could use it for another week more.

Continuing to strip on autopilot, Cyn freed her wand from its sheath on her forearm, set it on her nightstand along with her department-issue PDA and cell phone, then undid the bands of the sweaty sheath with an unconscious sigh of relief. The rest of her clothes quickly came off, until she stood naked in the middle of the room. She dumped the limp garments on top of the two-and-a-half-week-old pile spilling out of the plastic crate she used as a laundry basket, then ignored the mound since it had yet to reach critical mass.

Bare minutes later, she stood in front of her drawers, her shoulder-length hair nearly dry despite a quick shower, grateful to be clean and sweat-free. The heat was finally dissipating, so she took out fresh panties and her sleep shirt—a slightly outsized one promoting the Place du Casino in Monte Carlo that she'd filched from Rio—and pulled them on, now wishing she had him in her bed instead to keep her company.

Finding her thoughts dwelling once more on Rio made Cyn grimace. Why did she have him on the brain lately? It wasn't as if anything had happened to remind her of him.

She put some distance between her and the bed she'd shared with her lover, but the movement brought her face-to-face with the one piece of furniture she usually kept shut.

And for good reason.

Now she unlocked the plain, white cabinet, drawn by something she couldn't name. Nostalgia? Wish fulfillment? Romanticism? The need to remind herself of what she'd achieved, how far she'd come? Whatever it was, she couldn't deny its silent call.

Cyn opened the double doors that hid her secret hoard of dolls from prying eyes. A collection portraying girl mages of different nationalities—priestesses, shamankas, weather dancers, and the like—complete with feathers and beads, silks and furs, lace and parchment. Standing side-by-side in their traditional finery, the delicate toys filled four shallow shelves. Not the sort of thing someone like her would dote on.

Her one guilty pleasure.

It had all started with her mother, hoping to entice Cyn away from her brothers' rough-and-tumble play. Eleni Malva had been a traditional Greek wife and mother who'd failed to convince her only daughter to follow in her feminine footsteps—save in this one detail.

Reaching through the prickle of the low-level stasis spell that protected the collection from dust, Cyn took down the Tatar shamanka that had been the first of her mother's bribes, remembering how exotic she'd found its cape of imitation bear fur and miniature bear-paw boots, even now still pristine and in next to mint condition. She couldn't remember what the doll had been payoff for, although it definitely hadn't been for the ballroom dancing lessons; those had come later.

The bribes had started soon after the day Cyn had nearly died playing some tag-team game. Not that she'd known at the time how close she'd come to never wrestling with her brothers ever again nor connected the accident to the doll offerings, but hindsight was a great teacher.

Fingering the garments that had so fascinated her childhood self, Cyn couldn't suppress a sigh at the memory of her mother's overprotectiveness that had followed and the lengths Eleni had gone to, to try to coax, then force, her into more ladylike—and presumably safer—activities. That had gone over like solitary confinement and had been just as unwelcome. Her mother's tactics had turned the succeeding years into a bitter struggle for independence. Eleni hadn't approved of Cyn's brief enlistment in the air force and would never have supported her becoming a cop and a detective with Homicide.

"You'd think she'd have recognized a lost cause when she saw one, wouldn't you?" Cyn's joining in her brothers' games would almost have been a given. Since they outnumbered her five to one, Alex, Bion, and her younger siblings had been her first—and sometimes only—options for playmates.

The doll's enigmatic smile didn't change. Had she expected it to?

Shaking her head ruefully at her whimsy, Cyn replaced the shamanka on its shelf beside the others, blaming sexual tension for the odd mood. She must be really tired to be revisiting old frustrations.

Even after Eleni's untimely death, Cyn continued to add to her collection, despite her ambivalence toward it. The exquisite dolls represented almost everything she wasn't and had fought not to become; yet there was something quietly seductive about the dainty, picturesque toys.

And lately she'd had help in her acquisitions.

But that was one more thing Cyn didn't want to think about. Thoughts in that direction only led to frustration and troubled sleep. Since she had no idea when or if Rio would return, dwelling on memories of his last visit would be unproductive.

She ran her fingers through her white lock, all that was left of that near-fatal childhood incident. *You're becoming maudlin, Cyn.* If she couldn't control her thoughts better, she might as well go to bed and get some rest.

Yet even stretched out on the firm mattress, her mind wouldn't leave the matter aside, her thoughts circling back to the difference in Rio's lovemaking. The possessive way he'd held her. His urgency when he'd taken her: hard and driving, but not just the hunger of a man close to release. It was a matter of nuance, yet she couldn't identify the difference. She just knew it was there.

She wasn't sure that she liked the change, but her body held no such compunctions; Rio's lovemaking had brought her bone-melting release, and it didn't mind more of the same.

Cyn fell asleep, pondering just how single-minded her libido could be.

Hours later, she woke to the sound of falling water. For a moment, she thought it was rain splattering against glass and felt a fleeting concern for her windows; they might not open enough for even a child to get in—not without extreme violence applied to their panes—but that protection didn't extend to rain. Then she realized the sound came from her bathroom. The shower was running. Her heart fluttered and took flight. It had to be Rio. She couldn't imagine that a burglar would break into her apartment to take a bath.

She turned over and confirmed her supposition.

A new doll occupied the nightstand, one of a Shinto priestess brandishing a sliver of rice paper painted with black runes. Cyn didn't have anything of its like on her shelves. She picked up the toy, its silk kimono sliding under her fingers with a cool caress. It was a pretty thing with straight black hair and a look of challenge on her bisque face. Another gift from Rio to add to her collection. He took inordinate delight in finding dolls she didn't have.

Cyn smiled involuntarily, struck by the piquancy of a man like Rio buying such a delicate toy. The fact that he took time to shop for a present for her as a memento of his travels touched her heart. That he continued to do so even months after getting her into bed made that organ skip and soar in a way that didn't bear thinking about—not in addition to everything else that had her mind whirling in circles.

Nor did she want to dwell on the outrageous joy she felt at knowing he was just in the next room. She pushed that, too, to the back of her mind, unwilling to venture into treacherous grounds unprepared.

Anyway, it had nothing to do with the moment.

Rio was here, now. But who knew how long he could stay? She

had to make the most of the time she had with him and get in some high-quality loving in the meanwhile.

Eager to burn off her lingering tension, Cyn got out of bed, grabbed the hem of her shirt, and pulled it over her head. Dropping it to the floor, she headed for the bathroom.

CHAPTER TWO

Rio stood under the tepid rush of water, washing shampoo out of his hair and willing his fatigue to drain out with it. The red-eye flight had been late, but he was finally here. It was done. His time with black ops was over, the last interminable mission complete.

He'd always dreaded taking this step, had wondered if he could ever do it: turn his back on the adrenaline, the camaraderie, the sense of a purpose greater than himself. Doing so had been a favorite topic of speculation among his fellow agents, especially lately, during long hours with little to do save get to the objective.

Could he really leave all that behind? Lantis continued to be a source of marvel in the small black ops community precisely for doing so. And now Dillon was taking that step as well.

Rio had never truly imagined anything could become more important to him than his missions, important enough to forsake that brotherhood and the challenges. Of course, he wasn't quite doing that. Not if his plans panned out.

And they would let him make a life with Cyn.

If she'd let him—not exactly a sure thing.

Still, it felt odd to think of retiring his rifle for anything else save target practice.

Closing his eyes, he tipped his head back, lifting his face to the stinging jets. Let his mind empty of all expectations and apprehensions and gave himself up to indulgence in the moment. He'd made his decision. All that was left was the execution.

Warmth enfolded him in liquid comfort, the water barely cooler than fresh blood. During the time he'd been away, summer had set in. And for eighteen endless days he'd missed Cyn with a tooth-grinding intensity that bordered on obsession, wanting to hear the low laugh that meant he'd broken through her regal reserve. Eighteen days spent wondering if she was still alive.

Being incommunicado, unable to call her, had been torture worthy of the lowest circles of hell. The thought of leaving on another mission to save the world from itself was no longer palatable, not at the cost of time with her and the possibility of returning only to learn she'd been weeks dead.

So strange how a chance meeting turned out to be life-changing. When he'd sought Cyn out in that café, he'd simply been looking for a female cop willing to hang on his arm while he took care of business, which had been providing backup for Lantis. He hadn't wanted to ask a civilian, in case the situation went to the crapper. When it turned out she was a member of the police tactical response team, he'd thought he'd hit the jackpot. Little had he suspected the full extent of his good fortune and how much she would come to mean to him.

His parents would love her. Somehow, when he'd put the moves on her last year, he'd chosen just right. Serendipity. Or maybe just Fate. He still couldn't pinpoint when fun and games had become heart-serious.

Letting the warm stream work on him, the patter of falling water filling his ears, he stood there, poised between one life and the next. Waiting.

Waiting for what?

The rings of the shower curtain squealed softly, as though mindful of the lateness of the night. Keeping his face to the jets, Rio waited, knowing what would follow—what he hoped would follow. Had to follow.

Slim arms wound around his waist, strong yet feminine. A very naked torso pressed against his back, with hard points poking him below his shoulder blades; she'd shed her panties and the T-shirt she'd been sleeping in—one of his, he'd noticed. His Cyn wasn't one to be caught bare-ass naked, in case of emergencies. Her hands wandered over him, lazily roaming down and up with the utter confidence of a passionate lover, a single bloodstone ring their only ornament. The piece of jewelry was something she'd taken to wearing just before they'd become lovers, since it housed a contraceptive spell; the fact that she had it on meant her intentions were anything but innocent.

God, he'd missed this. Missed *her*. Not that Rio could tell her that; that wasn't how their relationship worked. And his uncharacteristic neediness didn't sit well with him, either, what with his earlier preference for fun and games. Grappling with the intensity of his feelings, he held his silence.

"Hey." Cyn planted a kiss on his shoulder. "You didn't tell me you were coming."

"I wasn't sure I'd be able to get away until the very last moment." Something inside him loosened at her ready welcome, a coil of barbed steel wire he hadn't realized had been there until it was gone. She hadn't changed in the intervening weeks.

He caught the hand making for his groin and pressed it to his stirring cock. "But give me just a few minutes . . ."

Cyn laughed: that low, indulgent laugh of hers that boded well for the next few hours. "Oh, no, you don't. Not so fast." Despite her protest, her fingers danced over him, her short, blunt nails scraping lightly, teasing him to full erection.

He let her play with him for a while, enjoying her deft manipulation and the nerve-tingling attention she paid to his favorite spots while she rubbed her body against his back. To think he'd gone two and a half weeks without this. Slowly, the turbulent emotions inside him abated, soothed by the easy companionship between them.

The silence stretched out, and still he said nothing, wanting to prolong the perfect moment.

"Why didn't you wake me when you arrived?"

Stifling the pang of regret he felt at the interruption, even for so innocuous a question, Rio twisted around to hold Cyn in the circle of his arms and study her beloved face. "You looked like you needed the rest." When he arrived, she'd been sprawled across the bed in a sopor that hinted of exhaustion.

"You sweet-talking ass. Don't you know you're not supposed to say that to a woman?" She thumped his chest lightly in reproof, a wry twist to her lips, then promptly shifted to a distracting circling of his nipple.

Smiling, Rio responded in kind, taking comfort in the segue into familiar banter. "Oh? And I suppose I should have said something like, 'You looked so cute sleeping, I didn't have the heart to disturb you'?" He tucked in his chin to meet Cyn's narrowed gaze at her eye level, dancing a half step backward to draw her closer to the spray. There was time enough later for changing the rules.

"*Cute?*" If anything, her expression of mock outrage was even more appealing.

Rio grinned. "Yeah, cute." He bowed his head to plant teasing kisses on her powerful gymnast's shoulders. "Absolutely, delectably cute." He ran his hands up her sides, stopping at strategic points to fondle and squeeze.

Cyn purred, arching into his caresses.

With her guard down, he managed to spin her around so that she was under the jets. Her scent immediately rose around him, filling the tight confines of the shower stall with the heady fragrance of carnations.

He knew it was from the soap she used, but after all their time together, he would always associate that spicy perfume with Cyn. Rio breathed deeply, taking the scent into himself. He didn't think he'd ever tire of smelling it. Not surprisingly, he had his usual reaction: already primed by her hands, his cock twitched with eagerness.

"Hey," she sputtered in protest, pushing her soaked hair out of her face. The falling water flattened the tresses, making them cling to her scalp, the pure white lock that sprang from her right temple flowing through the black like a trail of vanilla ice cream over licorice candy—though she was nowhere so cold or pliable. "You're the one taking a shower. I had one earlier."

So saying, Cyn plucked the bar of soap from its dish and worked up a lather with her hands. Then, with a sexy smile of invitation hovering on her lips, she washed his body with broad strokes, lingering here to cup and tease, and there to knead a tight muscle, leaving pleasure to shimmer in her wake.

Rio let her, treading the familiar steps of their carnal dance as though in a dream. This wasn't the first time she'd joined him in the shower, but he never tired of having her hands roving over him, caressing him, staking her claim and confident in her welcome. With the step he'd decided to take before him, the reminder of what he hoped to gain was sufficient persuasion that he'd made the right decision.

A sudden squeeze spiked his balls with desire, shaking him out of his lethargy. "Come here." He pulled her into his arms and claimed her lips, sinking into her heat with hungry passion.

She matched him, kiss for kiss, need for need, murmuring her approval as she locked her arms around his neck. The slick, soapy contact between their torsos added fuel to the flames, mimicking as it did the more intimate friction he craved.

Cyn undulated against him, her nipples blazing twin tracks across his chest and her belly rubbing his hard-on with the relentlessness of a friendly kitten, stropping him from side to side with seductive insinuation. She thrust her agile tongue into his mouth, curling it against his in unmistakable invitation, one that zinged straight to his cock. There was no question what she wanted. If he harbored any doubts, the leg she hitched over his hip put paid to them.

He wanted the same thing, burned for it probably more than she did, a soul-deep thirst he had to quench. It almost hurt to stop her. "Not here."

Time to get out. Every man had his limits, and Rio knew his. Sex up against the slick plastic of the shower stall wasn't advisable for someone with his level of fatigue, and the rest of the cramped bathroom wasn't any better, as he well knew from past experience.

"Why not?" She drew his head back to suck on his tongue, reminding him of just how good it felt to have her go down on him—a scorching memory that threatened to overturn his better judgment.

For a few heartbeats, he couldn't think of any reason; then sanity reasserted itself. "Don't want to drop you." He groaned as her knowledgeable fingers swirled pure delight through his cock and balls. And despite the surge of energy that flooded his veins, that was still a definite possibility. Figuring out the contortions necessary for making love in her cramped bathroom required more physical—and mental—flexibility than he could lay claim to at the moment.

Now impatient with the geologic pace of their progress, Rio hastily rinsed the soap off their bodies and stepped out of the shower, a simple maneuver made a minor feat by his armful of passionate woman and his own disinclination to release her. Fumbling the towel off the hook behind the bathroom door, he patted her dry between searching, hungry kisses, familiarizing himself once more with the body that had haunted his dreams. Two and a half weeks without her had been two weeks too many. He swore to himself he wouldn't be parted from her ever again for so long. It was with great reluctance that he surrendered her lips to complete his self-imposed mission.

"You're quiet," Cyn commented as he got down on one knee to wipe her long legs.

"Still can't believe I managed to get away." His hands slowed involuntarily to better appreciate their bounty, the curves and planes of her firm muscles inviting exploration.

She snorted in amusement for some reason.

More interested in the quivering of her taut abs, he didn't ask for an explanation. His new perspective revealed just how fine her skin was, prompting him to brush his lips across her smooth belly. Rasping his stubble over the same made her suck in her breath with a hiss and a flinch. He grinned to himself, unduly elated by her response; she was still as ticklish as he remembered.

"Rio!"

Before her protest went any further, he bent his head in apology, nuzzling her dark curls and dipping his tongue between the tender folds they concealed.

"Oooh . . ." Catching his hair in a fierce grip, she arched her hips into his caress. "Deeper." Hot cream rewarded him, the sweet saltiness promising a fervid welcome when he finally took her. She shuddered as he gave her what she wanted, her voice breaking on a wordless exclamation. The scent of her musk surrounded him, beckoning, an exotic perfume that evoked memories of torrid hours spent making love.

Knowing what she liked and wanted, he played with her swelling flesh, doing his best to stoke her arousal, drawing her closer to the brink. Because once he was inside her, he probably wouldn't last long.

Cyn danced in his arms, her breathless gasps and sighs sounding better than a choir of angels to his ears. Color gilded the slopes of her breasts and cheeks, turned her pussy lips into delectable cherry-red candy. She was absolutely beautiful in her reckless pursuit of ecstasy. She shuddered when he sucked on her stiff clit, her voice hitching on a low moan.

Fierce triumph filled Rio at her reaction, the cognizance that he'd brought his woman such pleasure a heady brew for a man in his condition. However, this wasn't getting them any closer to her bed. If he didn't do better, they'd end up finding out if the small, wall-mounted lavabo could bear Cyn's weight.

When he made to stand up, she protested, tried to hold him there a little longer. But he steeled his spine and kept that all-important destination in mind.

"Bastard," Cyn said huskily. "I was so close."

Unable to resist, Rio took her mouth in a hard kiss, silencing her and letting her taste her own passion. "Bed." Leaving the towel on the floor, he urged her out of the bathroom, intent on getting her under him, writhing with need and passion.

Beside the nightstand, just short of their destination, Cyn planted her feet. "Not so fast."

A sudden *click* caught Rio by surprise—that and the steel handcuff that circled his wrist, appearing suddenly, almost as if it had been conjured there. He jerked his arm back, but she kept a firm grip on the chain. "What's this for?"

"This time you're not going anywhere," Cyn explained with a catlike smile. "I'm making sure of it."

It took him a second to process her statement, but that was a second he didn't have. By the time his brain was sufficiently clear for him to understand his predicament, she'd gotten a step ahead of him.

The only good thing about the situation was that the shock had cooled him off enough so that his cock was no longer on a hair trigger.

To his chagrin, she countered his struggles easily. Of course, Rio wasn't putting that much effort behind them; he didn't want to hurt her. His plans for the immediate future included making love, not war—nor fighting.

Cyn giggled as she wrestled him onto her bed. Admittedly, he wasn't resisting that part much; after all, that had been his destination from the start. He might even have helped things along a bit, distracted though he was by the carnal friction as their bodies slid and rubbed together.

But that sound and the sight of her hard-tipped breasts bobbing before his face diverted his attention enough that she managed to loop the handcuffs over the metal rail of her bed frame and snap the open cuff shut around his other wrist. "Hey!"

Finding his arms caught, Rio hauled himself closer to the rail to get some maneuvering space.

No two ways about it. His cop fought dirty. The knowledge was inordinately comforting to his black ops heart.

He forced his shoulders to relax, reining in his instinctive desire for freedom. There was no danger here. The mattress cushioned his hips and heels in firm comfort, a far cry from a cold cell.

An exploratory jangle told him getting free would require a little effort on his part and the distraction of his captor. With his flexible joints and narrow hands, he could twist out of the cuffs, but Cyn might stop him . . . unless she was focused on something else. "Okay, I'm sorry I got your hair wet."

One thin, black brow arched in a playful display of regal hauteur, undermined by a damp black lock that clung to her cheek. "This isn't about my hair, you clit-sucking tease," his lover informed him in earnest, saccharine tones.

Oooh, she must really have been at the brink of orgasm when he stopped. The realization gave him a smug sense of satisfaction.

Cyn knelt over him, a warrior queen surveying the spoils of victory. It was exactly that attitude that had drawn him in from the very first. Strength and confidence, all wrapped up in one lithe, muscled package. Of course, back then, he'd thought that meant she was safe. No threat to his heart.

Rio still had difficulty accepting that he'd fallen in love. All told, he and Cyn had spent only three months together ever since he'd introduced himself just over a year ago, but she'd never been far from his mind from then on. That was the way it had always been; he didn't know when his feelings had changed. Love had crept up on him like a thief in the night, stealing his heart when he wasn't looking. But at that very moment—lying before Cyn, at her mercy—it seemed only inevitable; the joke was that it had taken so long for him to realize it.

"It isn't? Turnabout's only fair, you know." He smirked, anticipating having her at his mercy. That long, lean body writhing under his hands, caught up in the throes of passion and pleasure. His cock twitched at the imagery.

"Nuh-uh. My handcuffs, my rules." Her gray eyes swept his body with a look of cunning appraisal. "Besides, it isn't every day I get to bag a desperate criminal on the lam and make him beg to remain my captive."

"Really now?" *Is that how she wants to play it?* Rio raised a brow in challenge. "You're going to have a hard time of it." If this was payback for not letting her come earlier, he might have to do it more often; he'd never realized Cyn had a kinky side to her. Of course, he'd prefer a role reversal. Though his mother had inculcated upon him the equality of the sexes, he was too much his father's son to take to bondage with any degree of equanimity.

Her full lips stretched wide in a smile of pure mischief. "That's what I'm counting on."

He braced himself on the bed, his heartbeat picking up speed at the look on her face. Even if they lived to see a hundred, she'd probably still manage to surprise him. He actually found himself looking forward to the experience.

Cyn's finger tracing the underside of his cock jerked Rio back to the moment at hand. She didn't seem to be in any hurry to make him beg, but he had no intention of making it easy for her. Rio Rafael didn't beg . . . except in dire straits.

Even if he had no argument with her stated aim.

"Such a hardened desperado requires strong measures." She scraped her nails gently over the thin skin of his groin and inner thighs, taking unfair advantage of her knowledge of his weaknesses.

Rio groaned at the pun and the spiraling tension building in his balls. "Low blow." He struggled not to squirm under the light contact, determined to live up to his words.

Chuckling, Cyn lay down, elbowing a space for herself between his legs. The position put her within optimum titillating distance of his family jewels, which was probably exactly what she'd intended. She met his gaze over his taut belly, a smirk lifting the corners of her mouth and a devilish gleam in her gray eyes. "Oooh! Look what I have here."

A shiver raced up his spine at the carnal promise in the scrutiny she gave him. Holy hell, it didn't look like he was going to get much of a rest tonight. His cock gave an eager twitch at the prospect, unfazed by the odds.

Reminding himself that he had to have some self-respect, Rio injected steel into his backbone. "If you think you can take me, just go ahead and try," he taunted her, waving his hard-on like a banner.

Her eyes narrowed to dark slits that promised retribution for his cockiness. But what else did she expect of him?

Rio shot his lover a confident grin, knowing he had to do more before she'd let loose and—hopefully—give him what he deserved.

"Tough guy, huh?" Cyn gathered his balls in an easy grip, catching him by the short hairs.

Wondering how far she'd take the game, he tipped his chin to one side in careless inquiry, feigning blithe unconcern at her unspoken threat.

She pulled gently, adding a finger rubbing the base of his cock to her teasing. The light massage lit off sudden sparks in his groin, calling blood to thicken his hard-on.

"And getting tougher by the second." Rio gasped as his lungs seized on a blaze of pure sensation. Where had she learned to do that? And why hadn't she done it before?

"This is what you get for teasing me." She smiled, like a tigress contemplating helpless prey. Of course, most prey would object to being eaten.

Not in Rio's case. If only she'd get on with it! "You're no slouch in that department yourself."

Her smile widening in triumph, Cyn leaned closer, encroaching on his personal space, tantalizing him with her intentions. Then she swooped down to lash her tongue along the underside of his aching cock, scorching him with wicked pleasure.

Metal jangled as Rio's body rebelled against his control, arching involuntarily under the lavish delight. Good God! His eyes nearly crossed as her heated caress ended with a lazy swirl over his head, the slit exuding pre-come belying his supposed resistance. How was he to hold out if she kept doing that? He swore beneath his breath, not even knowing what he said.

Cyn laughed as she licked him again, toying with his hard-on with alternating strokes. Her free hand came up to clasp his twitching cock, her thumb adding encouragement as it rubbed his turgid length. "I could eat you up. All this meat, right here for the taking."

Gritting his teeth, Rio forced down the spike of pure need that answered her laving. Swearing silently in Spanish, he fought the urge to tell her to suck him. If he didn't restrain himself now, he'd be begging before he knew what hit him. As much as he wanted to be inside her—craved it with an ache that went to his bones—he refused to go down without a fight. Besides, that would cut her game short, and Cyn's attentions, tormenting though they were, felt too good; he didn't want them to end just yet.

"Ready to beg?" she asked archly, almost as if she'd read his mind.

"Just for that? Ha!" He swallowed with difficulty, hoping his determination held out. He tried to summon mental distance to bolster his control, to use some of the professional dispassion he'd cultivated for his missions, but the sensations coursing through his cock were too distracting.

Evidently taking his words for a challenge, she redoubled her efforts, nibbling on his cock as though she truly intended to eat him. Her soft lips slid along his length in hot, honeyed caresses that promised impossible delights. Her tongue flitted over him like a swarm of butterflies seeking nectar: light and evanescent and dazzling beyond belief.

He groaned, his heart bounding in excitement. Her deft manipulation and playful kisses were like gasoline splashed on the bonfire blazing through his body.

Then her mouth engulfed him and blew away all thought.

Heat. Scalding heat and blistering pleasure. Indescribably potent sensations swirled over his cock head. Through it.

Rio went wild. Needing more and deeper, he reached for Cyn and was brought up short. He strained against the steel cuffs that bound him to the bed to no avail. Getting free took more presence of mind than he could muster right then.

Cyn hummed around his cock, a thrum of approval that sent brazen spikes of delight tripping up his spine.

¡Madre de Dios!

His world—his universe—narrowed to her mouth and what it was doing to his cock. He could only be vaguely grateful for the bite of the handcuffs; at least they allowed him to maintain a vestige of control in the face of impossible stimulation.

Her lips closed firmly around him as she took him deep, sucking on his cock as though she wanted to drain him to the last drop. It was more than enough to bring a stone statue to life, much less a red-blooded male like Rio.

Pressure mounted in his balls, building rapidly to the trigger point.

Suddenly, Cyn jerked away, her lips letting him loose. Her fingers did something arcane that brought his onrushing release to a screeching halt, leaving his hard-on bobbing and gleaming in forlorn, aching stiffness. "No, no, no," she chided lightly, her breath lacing his length with unexpected coolness. "You're not getting off that easily."

Shocked back to himself, Rio dragged air into tight lungs. "What the fuck?" He mentally cursed his loss of control. When it came to Cyn, his training and long-nurtured discipline were proving to be rather threadbare; she got to him faster than anyone else.

"I changed my mind." She leopard-crawled up his body, the sinuous motion giving her firm breasts a mesmeric sway. "I think I want all that, right here." Setting her knees on either side of his hips, she hunkered over him, the dominant pose flaunting her pussy with its spread lips flushed a deep red and juicy with her arousal. Displaying the gorgeous flesh to perfection. Tormenting him with a vision of heaven hovering just beyond the tip of his straining cock.

After that abrupt termination, the sight was cruel in the extreme. And a damned effective carrot, in Rio's opinion. When Cyn decided on payback, she stopped at nothing to make it stick, no half measures. He liked that in a woman, particularly in his woman, especially given her dangerous line of work. He liked it even when he was on the wrong end of the stick. Still . . .

"You're evil, woman." And if he wanted to get free, he had to get his act together.

"It takes one to know one," Cyn retorted easily, clearly content with the status quo. She laid her hands on his chest, bending over him in a push-up stance, then lowered her hips, allowing her pussy lips to brush him.

His heart practically leaped out of his chest at the buttery contact. With a low moan, Rio instinctively arched into it, automatically trying to prolong the slick friction. "That ought to be illegal."

Laughing that low, gurgling laugh of hers, she repeated the stroke, gliding in the opposite direction and anointing him with her juices. If she were a cat, he'd have said she was scent-marking her territory, especially when she insisted on doing it over and over again, to hair-raising, nerve-thrilling effect.

Damnú, it made him want to shout to the world his own claim on her. Short of that, he wanted inside her.

But Cyn merely continued to rock over him, her pussy lips Frenching his hard-on and no closer. She ground her mound against him, evidently wanting more pressure on her clit. The scent of her musk strengthened: the perfume of distilled sex, pure seduction and totally intoxicating.

His hunger spurred, Rio slid down the bed to the limits of the handcuffs, trying to get low enough so he could thrust his cock in.

"Ah-ah-ah." She quickly reared up, lifting her wet pussy before he could do anything more. "Not so fast, hotshot! You have to beg first."

"Cyn." He glared at her in demand, more than willing to chew through steel to have her. "When I get free . . ." He twisted his fists against his shackles, fighting the restraints and for some self-control. "I want you, *damnú air*. So much that I'd walk through fire for you. Now, get down here where you belong," he finished in a throaty growl that was all his tense neck muscles would allow.

She considered him thoughtfully for several heartbeats, then licked her lips as she came to a decision. "I guess that will have to do." With a smirk, she eased down, holding him to her slit and taking him into herself. The tight clasp of her slick pussy was almost his undoing, branding his throbbing cock with a heated welcome.

But his beloved witch wasn't done with her teasing.

Still kneeling above him, Cyn held herself away, stopping short of the deep possession he craved. She tormented the sensitive head of his cock with the shallow penetration, fluttering her pussy around him in a torturous display of muscle control.

Rio raised his hips, trying for more of her slick caress. Steel bit into his knuckles as he arched higher, but she lifted herself away, nearly pulling free, then swayed her pelvis in a slow, decadent motion that swirled delight through his cock.

"*Hechicera*," he reproached her breathlessly, straining against his shackles as pleasure detonated in his balls. His control lapsed briefly, and he resorted to his father's tongue when he called her a sorceress, which she had to be to provoke such a wild response from his flesh with so little movement. "This is police brutality."

She only smiled with the smugness of a woman who knew she had the upper hand. "Going to report me?" She punctuated the taunt with a distracting little shimmy he felt clear to his curled toes.

"Maybe," Rio gasped as his bounding heart threatened to leap out of his chest. "If I survive."

With a low chortle, Cyn rolled her hips in another nerve-tingling caress, undulating in place. Closing her eyes, she speared her fingers through her hair as she gave herself up to the moment, a slender goddess of sensual pleasure incarnate.

And still she held herself above him, dipping only the slightest bit to give him a taste of more, then taking it away. Over and again in a soul-stealing dance of hedonism.

Damnú air, he wanted his hands on her. Had to have more of her.

Bracing his feet, Rio thrust up, trying to get deeper into her scalding embrace—and he snagged against the cuffs. Fed up with the restraints, he gave his hands a practiced twist and wrenched them free, his knuckles scraping on the steel rings.

"*¡Finalmente!*" He caught her tight ass and lunged home, driving his cock hilt-deep into the wet clasp of her body. The slick welcome that met him, surrounding him in hot, willing woman, made him hiss with soul-deep relief. Perfect union. So complete he couldn't tell where he ended and Cyn began. This was where he was meant to be.

Above him, Cyn shouted something he couldn't make out, her gray eyes snapping open in surprise and almost black with pleasure. Her hands clutching his shoulders, she writhed in his arms, her motions slamming pleasure straight into his balls with short hammer blows.

Rio arched up, pistoning into her hot flesh, exulting in the fluttering of her pussy around him. Potent delight spilled through his veins, overwhelming his threadbare control. No longer able to hold back, he raced for the promise of ecstasy hovering just over the horizon.

Head flung back, Cyn rode him, her thighs clamped around his hips and pumping with a driving rhythm. Then she stiffened, her gaze turning blank as she lost herself to the fury of her orgasm, shouting his name as she came. The spasmodic ripples of her release milking his cock was the final straw, snapping his control with the suddenness of a sniper shot.

Ecstasy detonated in Rio's balls, blew through him in a shattering blast wave of raw pleasure. His climax was endless, rolling through him like a wild thunderstorm over the plains. Devastating.

Cyn truly was the sorceress he'd named her. Nothing in their previous lovemaking had prepared him for such a release!

The tension in her body ebbed slowly, her back losing its rigid arch, leaving her draped over him like a warm, slick, sweet-smelling blanket for all her sweatiness.

His own incandescent release left Rio boneless, temporarily free of his apprehensions, content to lie beneath his lover. *"Mo muirnín."* The Gaelic words came to his lips without his volition, but they were only the truth: Cyn was his beloved.

"Hmmm?" It was more a purr than a question, despite the inquisitive lilt at the end.

"Ummm," he responded, his brain too fuzzy for explanations. Listening to his racing pulse, he savored the moment and the sense of rightness. This was what he wanted, what was worth giving up black ops for. He just had to convince her to make it permanent.

Cyn snuggled against him, the random flutters of her sex titillating even as his cock softened inside her. "How long can you stay this time?" She petted him possessively, her hand gliding along his flank in short, light strokes that were damn arousing, even in his sated condition.

The question reminded Rio that, unlike previous occasions, he wasn't here for a bit of R & R—something Cyn didn't know yet. Debating how to tell her, he combed his fingers through her damp hair and gathered it with his hands. Drawing on ambient magic, he cast a minor spell with a brief focusing of will, sighing as her spicy carnation scent lightened to near indistinctness when the now-dry tresses slipped through his fingers. It was one of the simple magics he'd had to master for field ops; after all, it didn't do to drip through a terrorist stronghold, leaving a trail of water behind while on a mission of stealth. He'd have preferred to leave her hair alone, but she probably wouldn't appreciate damp sheets in the morning.

She shivered around him, probably a reaction to his use of magic, since the room was warm. "Handy, since you're such a water freak, but you haven't given me an answer." Her lips brushed his chest in a smile as she tucked her head under his chin.

"That's because I don't know yet. You know Dillon's partnering with Lantis?" A former black ops agent, John Atlantis had retired and set up shop as a consultant, developing and testing the security systems of critical defense and civilian installations, those likely to be targeted by terrorists. After what happened at kidTek last month, he'd invited Dillon to join him and expand his company's services.

"Uh-hmm, the L-T's mentioned the possibility of passing some tracking jobs to Depth Security." Nothing in Cyn's languid voice indicated how the suggestion had been received.

His muscles tightened involuntarily, uncertainty returning in spades, pricking at his floating lassitude. "It seems the load's enough to justify hiring another warm body." He kept his voice light to disguise the finality of his decision.

Despite his deliberately casual delivery, she stilled, her nails biting into his hip. "Any warm body in particular?"

"Me."

Chapter Three

Staring blankly at her monitor, Cyn sucked slowly on the chocolate melting on her tongue. *Rio's moving here. To Aurora.* She still wasn't certain how she felt about that development and the implication that he wanted them to spend more time together. Excitement, of course, at the prospect of regular sex; she couldn't deny the pleasant ache that imbued her with jaunty well-being. But she had a niggling suspicion that he wanted more than just their usual fun and games.

But what?

To her chagrin, she'd fled her apartment and the glorious sight of morning light worshipping virile perfection, to avoid facing precisely that question. The temptation of Rio sprawled across her white sheets, blanket kicked away, couldn't overcome the craven urge. Spooned butt to stirring cock, her mixed emotions had driven her from her narrow bed.

A hand appeared at the edge of her vision, reaching into her candy box.

Her arm flashed out automatically, intercepting the would-be poacher just before it reached its objective. "I haven't had coffee yet. Don't get between me and my chocolate."

"Sorry, Sarge."

Taking the apology with the grain of salt it deserved, Cyn snatched up the white box to hold it against her chest, safe from pilferage. If she hadn't been so distracted, she wouldn't have forgotten that nothing was inviolable to the pack of thieves purporting to be homicide detectives that she rode herd on. Waving off the would-be poacher, she returned her attention to the report she was supposed to be completing.

Why was Rio moving here? She'd thought he was with black ops, an operator. Had she been wrong? After her stint with military police, she knew the signs. Rio had registered on her mental radar as an operator when they'd first met, though he'd been working private security at the time.

This was going to change things, make them more complicated; she had no doubt about that. That wasn't necessarily bad, but she wasn't sure it would be good, either. When Rio was just dropping by on R & R, she knew it was just fun and games, nothing serious. Both of them knew what to expect, and the boundaries were well-defined. That was the way she liked it.

Good sex, good times. A chance for her to enjoy herself without wondering when her date would have the Epiphany, as she called it: that moment of truth when the guy realized she didn't just play at being a cop.

There was no danger of that with Rio. He'd known going in that she was a cop through and through. It was the reason he'd approached her last year, after all.

Popping the last decadent piece of chocolate into her mouth, Cyn dumped the empty box into the trash bin, still lost in her thoughts. But for Rio to decide to settle down in Aurora suggested he wanted to get serious—if she wasn't reading him wrong.

For a crazy moment, she imagined waking up every day to the

hunk of gorgeous male who'd taken up most of her bed that morning. Heat pooled in her belly, kindling an answering flame that spread like wildfire throughout her body. Then common sense caught up with her, making her scoff at her self-centered thinking. *It's not always because of you, you know.* Maybe something had changed with his parents . . . or happened on his last mission.

The noise in the bull pen ratcheted up a notch, sufficient to snag Cyn's wandering thoughts.

"Well, wish me luck. I'm off to pry lab results out of Hollingsworth's hands," Lopes announced, a glum expression melodramatically congealed on his thin face.

"Good luck. You'll need it. He'll probably give you the evil eye and have you sign away your firstborn," Ellis predicted from the next desk over.

Cyn suppressed a smile. Hollingsworth wasn't that bad; he was just paranoically protective of the evidence that came into his hands and hated to hand out preliminary results, since they didn't have 99 percent confidence. Obsessive, but a good sort of obsessive. Sure, he gave detectives a hard time, but he was the definition of *thorough* when working a crime scene, and his meticulousness made it difficult for defense lawyers to question the evidence.

"Please! He can *have* my firstborn, the little hellion." Chuan raised her hands in mock supplication.

Cyn snorted at the nonsense, knowing the detective doted on her only child and had a wallet full of pictures of the three-year-old that she showed off, given the slightest excuse.

"Not even Hollingsworth would take your kid, Wendy," Lopes retorted just before he disappeared out the door.

"Hey!" Chuan's almond eyes narrowed to evil slits. Then her phone rang. Muttering to herself, the detective reached out to answer it, returning to work.

Lopes's departure brought an end to Cyn's distraction from her thoughts, and they circled back to Rio's decision to move to

Aurora. Why Aurora in the first place? Sure, on normal days when mage gangs weren't running wild, it was a great city to live in, but it wasn't like he had any strong ties here. Of course, the reason could be as simple as employment opportunities; this was where Depth Security had its office.

A mug of coffee appeared before her nose, cupped between two hands and extended like a peace offering. She scowled, knowing she was speculating ahead of her facts and spinning her wheels. Best to channel some of that mental energy at the reports due by the end of her shift.

"Aw, c'mon, Sarge. It's not that bad," Chuan wheedled amid mutters of "That's it, Wendy. Take one for the team," and similar nonsense. "It's not like I got the dregs of the pot."

Cyn accepted the mug and took a slug of battery acid, suppressing a grimace at the flavor. Rio's penchant for brewed coffee had spoiled her taste buds for the department's tired, much-abused version—another change she could lay at his door. But since it got the blood flowing, she swallowed it down.

"There, isn't that better?"

She glowered at Chuan, in no mood to be handled. "I'll let you live—this time."

The detective backed off, playing innocent, as if she hadn't addressed Cyn the way she probably talked to her son. But the room settled down after that, the rest of the herd breathing a sigh of not-so-well-concealed relief. Cyn's temper was chancy during the times of month she had to deal with the paperwork required for payroll; it was what she hated most about the job and the only thing she regretted about making sergeant.

Duty-bound to make sure her pack got paid, Cyn mustered the caffeine-fueled energy to slog through the requisite reports. Just staring at her screen wasn't going to get them done.

First in line were the time sheets. She nearly groaned. Coughran was late again. If this kept up, she'd have to have another talk with him about his moonlighting.

More than an hour passed before Lopes returned laden with boxes. Hollingsworth must have been in fine form, demanding all the *i*'s and *j*'s dotted and the *t*'s and *f*'s crossed before releasing his precious lab results; now, there was a demon for paperwork—totally unnatural, in Cyn's opinion.

"Is that the kidTek case?" Carmichael, a crime scene tech who was the department's scrying specialist, turned from his discussion with Chuan to scrutinize the vid card on top of the first box Lopes opened.

"Nope, it's not. Why?" Lopes raised inquisitive hazel eyes to the specialist.

"I heard the retrospection was incredible." Carmichael gave him a flinty stare incongruous with his baby face and fine brown curls. "Was it really?"

Catcalls met his question as the detectives took time out to razz one of their own.

At the noise, Cyn looked up from the stacks of printouts squatting on her desk. Any distraction from the mind-numbing paperwork the department expected a sergeant to complete was welcome. "Oh, it was much more than incredible." Almost a month since the retrospection, but the memory of the amount of raw—visible!—power that had been summoned still made the hairs on her arms stand on end. "Forty feet and eleven prisms. The holovid looked solid enough to touch."

The anguished look on Carmichael's face was priceless, especially after he'd gone around gloating about flying to Washington for training; he'd been so smug, she'd been tempted to give him an early start to his flight with a strategically placed boot. "Forty feet? Impossible."

"Check the telemetry on the video." Tipping her seat back, Cyn slowly wagged her head in awe, deliberately twisting the knife. "He pulled so much magic, the spell lines were like thick, purple cables." She brought her hands together, forming a ring, to describe the circumference. "You should've seen it."

"Would have, too, if the lieutenant hadn't put his foot down," Chuan grumbled, a definite pout on her round face.

A low chorus of disgruntled agreement filled the bull pen. Everyone had wanted to watch when they'd heard the magnitude of the proposed retrospection.

"Silence. No mutiny in the ranks," Cyn interjected mildly, amused by their discontent. Some days, it was good to be sergeant.

"You're only saying that because you saw it firsthand," someone—who sounded like Ellis—muttered from the back of the room.

Allowing a smug grin on her face, Cyn thumped one of the stacks of paper on her desk. "Just one of the benefits of having to deal with this stuff." Too bad sleeping in wasn't another, but she took her blessings wherever she could find them.

Rio woke missing Cyn's warmth, his balls aching sweetly from the night's exertions. That had been one hell of a homecoming celebration! He rolled over to bury his face in her pillow and inhaled deeply, soaking his senses in her faint carnation scent. He could almost imagine she was pressed against his side, all nearly six feet of toned muscle and womanly curves of her.

His heart was light, lighter than it had been in weeks, now that he'd taken this final step. Now that he was here. That, above everything else, told him he'd made the right decision.

Now, if only he could convince Cyn to accept the change.

At least he had hope. The wholehearted welcome she'd given him implied she'd missed him almost as much as he had her. He could build on that.

He stretched leisurely, limp cotton sheets sticking to his back. Today promised to be a scorcher. He didn't mind. It was the first day of the rest of his life.

Rio had to laugh at the melodramatic cant of his thoughts.

First day of the rest of my life. But that was precisely what it felt like. And he intended to spend his life with Cyn.

The angle of the sunlight edging through the narrow windows struck him then.

But if you want a job in this brand-new life of yours, my lad, you'd better get a move on.

Surrendering to necessity, he took a last sniff of Cyn's faint scent and, ignoring his cock's stirrings of interest, pushed off the bed.

Rio presented himself at the door of Depth Security a bare half hour later, clean-shaven, his hair still damp from his shower. That panel stood before him clad in satin steel, an unassuming rectangle bearing only the company's logo. Once it opened, his decision would be set in stone. No changing his mind. New life, new job.

Ordinary investigative work on the main, according to Dillon, but Rio had the government clearances required by some of Depth Security's clientele, companies handling classified defense projects. There was also the chance of helping Lantis with on-site security tests: attempting to infiltrate a nuclear facility was one example given. At least his black ops experience wouldn't go to waste.

He'd be among friends and—best of all—in the same town as Cyn. The opportunity to make something permanent of their relationship was worth any amount of trouble.

The steel door slid aside with efficient silence, in keeping with the grave, blue-eyed man who filled the entry. John Atlantis was a near legend in the black ops community for quitting at the top of his game; he had since found a wife and was soon to be a father. Rio hoped some of that success would rub off on him.

"Lantis." Addressing his new boss by the diminutive he was better known as in black ops, Rio tilted his head back to meet that perceptive gaze and nodded in greeting, struck once again by a sense of destiny in motion. No turning back now.

The die was cast.

"Welcome aboard." The taller man shook his hand firmly, the slightest hint of a smile quirking the corners of his mouth, then waved him inside.

Rio went ahead, knowing the way to the inner office from previous visits. He'd never worked with Lantis before the other's retirement, having met him just last year, but he'd helped out on more than one occasion since then.

The intervening three weeks hadn't rendered any changes that he could see. The small entry still had only the Depth Security logo on the wall facing the door and a firethorn sprawling up the one on his right, its espaliered form breaking out in flowers like something from his mother's gardens. Cobalt blue folding doors lined the left side of the corridor to Lantis's office. The opposite had only three closed doors: workroom; unknown; storeroom for *materiae magicae*, the latter none of his business, since he wasn't one for spellcraft, not being a mage. The glowing ceiling kept the light level even and shadow-free.

Beige-on-beige carpet tiles cushioned his steps, bas-relief Celtic patterns woven in providing low-key visual interest. A line of interlacement like a barrier in front of the storeroom suggested the ornamentation was defensive in intent. It made him wonder what else he'd overlooked, hidden among the commonplace.

Not so different from black ops, after all.

The office at the end held the first obvious change: a door now pierced the left-hand wall dominated by large monitors.

"Hey, about time you got here!" The lighthearted greeting diverted Rio's attention from the modification. His trademark grin lighting his face, Dillon met him with a mock punch to the shoulder.

Rio pretended to rock back from the blow, then countered with a gentle fist to the upper arm. "Came as soon as I could."

"Problems?"

"Nah, just the usual." He shook his head. "You know how it

is." He left it at that, knowing they wouldn't press him for details; they understood the demands of operational security. The last mission hadn't been anything unusual—save for his missing Cyn with a vengeance—but still nothing he was free to discuss until it was declassified.

"I'll bet the Old Man wasn't happy."

"You can say that again. He's all set to declare Aurora a no-go area. Something about losing three men to Lantis." Chuckling, Rio turned to the taller man. "Three? What's that about?" He and Dillon only counted as two.

A huff of amusement preceded the answer: "Brian."

"Brian?" Rio looked around, half expecting the named agent to appear. They'd met last year, but he'd never worked with him in the field. The news that another of their number was joining them in Aurora was a surprise, especially since Dillon hadn't mentioned anything of the sort.

Rounding his desk, Lantis smiled briefly as he took his seat. "Not here. He's accepted a post at kidTek. Head of security." The wife's company, which was involved in black ops R & D. It was logical that they'd hire Brian for that post then; those projects were the reason why the company needed people with stratospheric levels of security clearance to conduct proper background checks, hence more business for Depth Security and a job for Rio.

Dillon and Rio settled in the visitor chairs as they exchanged banter and small talk, catching up on mutual friends and acquaintances and the world in general. The chat put him at ease. Here, he was among friends.

"So, any second thoughts?" Lantis interjected the question into a lull in the conversation.

"Not hardly. I'm eager to start." Rio sat back to study Dillon and Lantis. The two had been partners in the field and were extending that association into civilian life. "But besides background checks and the occasional help testing security, what else do you expect from me? Just grunt work?" He'd jumped at the offer when it was made, but he hoped he could contribute more than just muscle, even if it was cerebral muscle.

Dillon grinned. "A non-mage's perspective."

Rio frowned. That didn't sound like much, not like he'd be pulling his weight. He was sure the job offer hadn't been charity, but he'd have felt better if he could contribute more to the company.

"Don't worry. I expect you'll bring in your share of business," Lantis added, his blue eyes narrowed in . . . appreciation? Speculation?

"Yeah? With what?" Rio asked, taken aback and daunted by the expectation. *Bring in business?* That was somewhat more than he'd anticipated.

"Caricatures for sale?"

He frowned at the straight-faced answer. It took him a heartbeat or two to realize Lantis was joshing him. With Dillon he would have known immediately, but the tall man had deadpan down to an art. "Oh, okay. No problem, then."

A guffaw from the junior partner confirmed his supposition.

"Since that's settled, Dillon's and your office is over there." Lantis tipped his chin at the new doorway, a glint of humor in his eyes.

Standing up, Dillon clapped him on the shoulder. "C'mon. I'll show you the coffeemaker, then you can get started on grunt work."

Rio rose to his feet to bump arms with his shorter friend. "So long as it's clear I don't do windows."

"Yeah, yeah. That's what they all say. They're self-cleaning, by the way."

"Oh, before I forget . . ." Lantis took something from a pile of papers on his desk and handed it over.

To his surprise, it was a flyer for a local shooting range. "You shoot?" A silly question; he realized it even before the taller man arched a brow at him. The adept wouldn't have refused the additional edge a gun gave in the field, even with his magical prowess.

However, all Lantis said was "Not at your level. But it doesn't hurt to stay in practice."

"Thanks." Pocketing the flyer, Rio followed Dillon into the next room.

"This is our home away from home." His friend indicated the small office with an extravagant gesture that emphasized the mint condition of the furnishings, or maybe they really were all brand-new. Around half the size of Lantis's own with maybe a sixth of the electronics, it had a second door of reinforced steel, filing cabinets, a long L-shaped table on one side, the arms of which were set up as individual workstations with computers and chairs, like two desks joined at the hip, and a heavy-duty coffeemaker.

Rio headed straight for the latter, knowing that if he wanted coffee made right, he had to prepare it himself. Dillon always made it too weak. Since Lantis had been preoccupied in the past weeks by other matters, he suspected he had his friend to thank for the presence of his drink of choice.

Chuckling, Dillon claimed a chair facing the steel door, behind one of the arms of the table. "Right. Let's get that out of the way, then we can do your security briefing and get to work."

"What's the load like?" Rio went through the motions of preparing coffee on automatic, his attention on his friend.

"Initially, you'll find it rather repetitive."

"Top secret background checks, you said."

"That's it in one. The defense sector's hopping, so there's a bunch of companies eager for that service." Dillon propped his heels on the desk. "But with your contacts, and mine, and Lantis's, who knows what might develop."

That was only as Rio had expected. He doubted there was much call for a sniper in corporate security. "I must admit, I was surprised by your invitation. Thanks for thinking of me, by the way." He flicked the switch on and started the coffeemaker humming, once again struck by the timeliness of the offer. Dillon had contacted him just when he'd decided to get out.

"It was a shot in the dark. In fact, Lantis was the one who thought you'd be receptive. I was surprised you accepted. Last we talked about getting out, you were black ops all the way. Something like they'd have to retire you to get rid of you, wasn't that what you said?"

"Things changed." At Dillon's look of interest, Rio added, "I'm hoping some of Lantis's luck will rub off."

Black eyes widened in understanding and sympathy. "Is that the way of it? You and me both."

The gurgle of liquid derailed that line of discussion as the mouthwatering aroma of brewed coffee wafted from the corner, and the glass carafe began to fill. Perhaps it was superstition, but he didn't want to talk about his pursuit of Cyn so early in his courtship. Why risk tempting Fate?

Schooling his face to blandness, he poured a mugful, adding brown sugar to temper the bitterness. The first sip was a flash of heat on the tongue, strong, dark with just the right kick to it to keep him on his toes, just like he liked his ladies. "Perfect. Let's get to work."

Cyn stepped into Just Desserts, restraining the bounce in her stride that threatened to devolve into skipping schoolgirl excitement. All because of one man. But what a man. She smiled despite herself, amused by her contradictory emotions. *Lunch with Rio!* They'd arranged to meet at the bakery-cum-restaurant as they had numerous times before on his previous visits. Ignoring the temptation of the desserts on display, she threaded the crowded tables, aiming for the glass doors facing the park.

The patio was mostly vacant, except for one corner. Rio held down their usual table, food already waiting. He was efficient that way, knowing her lunch hour was tight. That she didn't mind him ordering for her just meant she was a creature of habit.

At the sight of her lover sitting so patiently, Cyn forgot the questions that had nagged her all morning, warm pleasure at his presence stirring other appetites. Her heart stumbled over that strange jangle of emotions that seeing Rio gave her these days.

She paused to give herself time to recover, but looking at him didn't help. The dark tumble of locks that felt like silk beneath her fingers. Level brows just bushy enough to be masculine without detracting from his beauty. Deep-set eyes the color of dark chocolate and equally tempting. The sensual lips that played a major role in so many of her dreams when he was gone and probably off on a mission. The firm jaw that came to a definite, almost delicate, pointed chin. High cheekbones and a straight, perfect nose. Those features more than anything else gave him an air of refinement. Her Latin lover.

No two ways about it: he was beautiful.

Rio looked up at that instant, his gaze spearing her as though he'd been aware of her presence all along. Smiling, he rose with fluid grace, that pantherlike control that got her so wet without him even trying. Today, his broad shoulders were clothed in sage green but rather more businesslike than usual: a short-sleeved shirt with a button-down collar and chest pocket, worn over black, pin-striped slacks. He even had a sport coat slung over the back of his chair. The sartorial difference was unexpectedly arousing.

Cyn sank into his welcoming kiss with a carnal hunger that couldn't be denied, ignoring the gun under her hand on the small of his back. Their lips clung with the familiarity of long-standing intimacy. A good thing there weren't that many people around to witness the display of affection. He could make her forget herself so easily. That was normally a good thing, since she had a tendency to take herself too seriously, except at times like this.

"Hungry much?" Rio asked after releasing her, his eyes glinting warmly. He sat down after she did, observant of the courtesies; he'd never made the mistake of trying to seat her, but she didn't know if that was his mother's training or simply good instincts on his part.

Cyn stifled a smile, but her face must have given away her amusement, since Rio grinned, interjecting a satisfied "Ha!" as he picked up his pastry.

Empanadas waited on both plates, probably chicken in hers, since he knew what she liked. He was more adventurous. Though the bakery specialized in desserts, pastry was pastry, even when stuffed with savory filling, so they offered a variety. He'd tried the turnovers with everything from vegetarian to lamb to beef with hot chili peppers. The time he tried the latter, his kiss had been spicier for more than the usual reasons.

As she turned to her food, a doodle by his plate arrested her notice. She swiped it immediately, eyes widening involuntarily as she took in the details: a slender woman—her, going by the streak of white in the hair—wearing nothing but the gaping vest of her body armor and striking a provocative pose. Though she wasn't late, he'd been waiting long enough to decorate his napkin; he'd even included the runes.

"You are *so* sick," Cyn announced, aiming for a tone of reproach, but her lips twitched. Keeping him from drawing would be like forcing a man not to breathe. Still, she tucked the napkin away for safekeeping, out of sight of wandering eyes.

He smiled at her, unrepentant, very much the cat who'd gotten the cream. "I'm a guy. Can you blame me?"

With a snort, she turned her attention to her empanadas, and for the next few minutes silence reigned as they fed their stomachs and she feasted her eyes.

Her beautiful lover.

Even eating, Rio looked so suave and self-possessed, a far cry from the intensity that had driven her body wild just the night before. He leaned back in his seat, coffee mug raised to perfectly chiseled lips. "Your guys are on edge. What's up?"

Cyn glanced around. In the short time since she'd arrived, the tables on the patio had filled up, many of the diners law enforcement. True enough, they were on higher alert, an added advertence that ruffled the nerves of the vigilant, like the electric spark that came from rubbing fur the wrong way.

"There've been a rash of heists lately." She told him about the crime spree afflicting the city, relieved to share her frustrations with someone who'd understand yet wasn't connected to the job. She didn't mention anything he couldn't find in the papers, but it was also a warning to put him on his guard, especially if he was staying in town. She didn't know how she felt about the latter yet but couldn't countenance leaving him in ignorance, particularly given what she suspected was his previous line of work. "Unlike a military base, we can't just close down the city."

He took her comment in stride, confirming one of her long-held suspicions. Ex-military, like her. But unlike her, probably black ops, that entirely deniable, top secret branch of SpecOps. That didn't concern her, so long as he was on the up-and-up in Aurora.

Their conversation wended toward less serious topics, touching on nothing of significance, while they satisfied their hunger. Sunlight dappled the patio, dancing as a breeze blew through the trees, rustling leaves and bringing welcome coolness. Savoring the tangy chicken in her pastry, Cyn settled back in her chair, content with the world. It wasn't what they spoke of that was important, merely that they were together. But eventually she had to ask the question that had been nagging her all morning.

"Were you serious?"

Rio gave her a look of inquiry over his upraised empanada.

"When you said you're moving here," she added, picking up her iced coffee to occupy her hands. The ice cubes tinkled musically as beads of sweat crept down the glass's side to dot the table.

She swished the straw, scooping up the froth along the rim as she forced her breathing to remain even.

Just another game, like their affair.

"Have I ever joked about something like that?"

Cyn had to concede that he hadn't. Even at their first meeting when she'd thought he was using a fairly original pickup line, he'd turned out to be serious. "Why?" she finally asked, her heart lodged in her throat. She returned her gaze to his face, wondering how he would answer.

Why now? What had changed? She'd gotten the impression he intended to stick with black ops as long as he could. Now this?

His expression darkened with some nameless emotion. His eyes were . . . haunted? What could have brought that on?

"I realized that's what I wanted." She thought that was all he was going to say, but he added, "It's time I settled down." His eyes warmed then, telling her without words that she figured prominently in his plans for the future.

"And you decided to settle here. In Aurora," Cyn clarified. Her stomach flopped over as she waited for confirmation.

He took his time answering, biting into another empanada and chewing slowly. He stared at her as though her statement had been in code, and he had to decipher its meaning. "Of course, here. Where else?" he countered with a wave at her plate.

It reminded her that her lunch hour was ticking away. She ate, brooding, unable to give the food her usual appreciation. This was the beginning of the end. His decision would change things. It was bound to—and not for the better. A man like Rio didn't settle down with someone like Cyn, however much he might think he wanted to. What they really wanted was the sweet, compliant type they could protect.

If only they could keep on going the way they had been with Rio dropping in every so often. That arrangement didn't force him to face the reality of her job and the fact that she didn't need a man's protection. Intellectually, he might know it and apparently didn't mind; but emotionally, deep down inside, it went against his instincts.

Yet what could she say? They were both free agents. She was in no position to object to his decision.

"There's a boardinghouse on Eighth. I'll be staying there until I find an apartment."

Cyn looked up, startled out of her reverie by his statement. It sounded like his decision was final. She bit her lip, swallowing back a protest at the arrangement and an invitation to bunk with her instead. That would be way too much like cohabitation. She couldn't buy into that. Fun and games were one thing, cohabitation . . . would be setting herself up for a fall. Pretending he could settle down with her was a blank invitation for a world of hurt when it was over.

For the first time, Rio realized that silence could actually hurt. Not that he had cause to feel rejected. This wouldn't be the first time he'd stay elsewhere while in Aurora since he and Cyn had become lovers. Yet for some reason, it appeared he'd harbored hopes she'd invite him to move in with her, unlikely as it was. Foolish of him.

If his father knew, he'd be on the floor laughing fit to bust—or bawling him out for rushing his fences. Valentino Rafael knew better than most that convincing a strong-minded woman to change her mind took time, something Rio should have remembered before getting his hopes up.

Great sex didn't necessarily translate to commitment. Unfortunately.

Patience, lad. This is just another hunt. One with much more at stake, but a hunt all the same. So long as Cyn didn't send him away, he'd have time to court her. *Pace yourself. Don't rush your fences.* Backing her into a corner wouldn't win him anything.

He shunted the conversation toward safer waters. "How much of a danger is that mage gang, really?"

The relief on Cyn's face gave him another twinge he ignored. "They haven't hurt anyone, but not for lack of trying. The free hand they have with deflagration spells—it's only a matter of time before someone's killed."

And that someone could be her. He hadn't missed the fact that she'd responded to several callouts involving the gang. Knowing her, she'd be first in line to defend and protect.

"There's no telling where they'll hit next. They've robbed small businesses, groceries, tailors, high-end gift shops. Middle-class to upscale places." She gave him a pointed look. "Places where you might go."

It warmed his heart to realize she was worried for him.

Rio mentioned Cyn's concerns back at the office, as the three of them discussed the current projects and the targets for the week to come.

"I hadn't realized it's gotten that bad." Lantis exhaled sharply, a veil of weariness drawing fine lines across his sober features for the space of a heartbeat. "I've lost track of events this past month." He stared sightlessly at the papers on his desk, lost in contemplation of painful memory, his mask of cool composure slipping.

"Only understandable." Shooting a disconcerted glance at Dillon, Rio nodded quickly. The reason for the uncharacteristic lapse didn't bear thinking of, now that it was over and done with. It trod too close to his own fears.

Thankfully, Dillon took his cue and propped his elbow on the arm of his visitor chair. "She does have a point, though. You need more than a gun for protection."

A loud snap of fingers drew their attention back to Lantis. "I believe I have something that can help." He pushed back from his desk and rolled to one of the cabinets behind him. "Very timely." On his return, he laid a magazine in front of Rio. "This arrived the other day."

Drawn by the vivid photography, Rio traced the chunky sapphire ring shown in macro on the glossy cover. Sharpshooting with that gaudy piece would be difficult, though three or four worn together would probably make serviceable brass knuckles. "Jewelry? Sorry, not my type."

Lantis huffed, a smile ghosting the corners of his mouth. "Magical countermeasures," he clarified, tapping some fine print on one side. "It's a reliable company." High praise, coming from him. The taller man was an expert in security magics.

"Sweet." Dillon drew out the word as he looked over Rio's shoulder. He flipped to the contents page, then let loose a long, low whistle.

Rio had to agree with the sentiment. The plethora of products and applications in the thick catalog was an eye-opener: amulets with antitheft, antivandalism, or antispying geas; sight veils that—while not quite rendering the wearer invisible—reduced visual profiles enough to help with stealth approaches and surveillance; personal wards that served as a sort of magical body armor; comprehensive protection talismans much like what Lantis had made for his wife; and more he'd never thought of. It had a whole section for talismans camouflaged as jewelry and other personal effects such as watches and belt buckles. He'd used the like before on his black ops missions, but he hadn't realized they were commercially available—if you knew the proper channels.

Lantis had the right of it: a talisman of this sort would help level the playing field against magical attacks. A good thing to have, especially with that gang Cyn mentioned running loose. "Hopefully, they don't require mage skill to activate."

"They shouldn't."

Chapter Four

The weekend stretched before them in an array of glitter, sunlight reflecting off the glass-and-steel high-rises in the heart of the city. Rio counted floors and buildings, measured alleys and streets by eye, automatically calculating lines of fire, of attack and retreat, and planning escape routes. He noted various specialty stores, mom-and-pop groceries, bakeries, department stores, bus routes, subway station access, cell sites. *That covers supplies, transportation, communications. Bottlenecks?* He worked through his mental checklist and didn't find any major problems.

He could live here.

"Okay, fess up. Why am I here?" Cyn gave him a look of forbearance as she strolled beside him in khaki shorts that made the most of her long, strong legs and a cotton jacket over a snug tank top that positively worshipped her breasts. Without letting up on her stare, she nimbly sidestepped a toddler making a break for it. They weren't the only ones taking advantage of the morning before the heat built up.

Rio grinned, feeling at peace with the world. "I'd like your opinion on something, that's all."

She peered up at him skeptically from under lowered lashes, her lips pursed slightly as though she were debating telling him off—or inviting his kiss.

He wondered if she knew how sultry it made her appear. He was tempted to tell her, just to see her flush with outraged pride. Resisting that impulse tested his self-control.

Even after months of seeing each other, she seemed to consider resorting to such feminine wiles an underhanded trick that was beneath her. He still didn't know why. They hadn't spent all that much time in each other's pockets. There'd been months when he'd be off on a mission and unable to contact her, and due to operational security, he couldn't explain where he'd been when he showed up, but she'd understood and welcomed him back without any questions. He afforded her the same respect, but he did wonder why she generally eschewed what she considered conspicuous femininity.

"My opinion, huh? I can't imagine what for." She leaned into his arm, a playful nudge of her shoulder as she gave him a sidelong look, the most she would go to coax an answer.

Rio draped an arm around her shoulders and was delighted when she didn't object to the gesture. "Patience; you'll see soon enough."

Had she ever just walked with a lover? Just strolled without a care in the world? No rush to get to anywhere?

Cyn remembered dates, preludes to sex, really. She hadn't minded at the time. There'd been the inevitable cancellations because of her job. Rio wasn't the first date to be interrupted by work—his work though, that time, and she couldn't say she hadn't been forewarned.

Now that she thought about it, that might have been the reason he'd stood out from the pack. She stole a glance at her lover, marking the watchful eyes scanning their surroundings. A handsome mask, suavity hiding the deadly wolf inside. *Well, one of the reasons.*

Rio stroked her arm, then threaded his fingers between hers, his thumb caressing the back of her hand. A soothing habit of his she'd recently noticed.

She suppressed a shiver of delight. "Where are we going?" Holding hands like this was . . . nice. Normal. The summer sun flashed off the many windows of downtown's high-rises but had yet to reach its enervating maximum. Traffic was light, and a gentle breeze played with her hair.

Seductive. On days like this, one could almost imagine murder didn't happen.

"A friend of Dillon's said there's a vacancy in her building." Rio tipped his head at a modern, glass-and-steel structure coming up. "I thought we'd check it out." He gave her a quick glance and a teasing smile, his melt-in-your-mouth chocolate brown eyes sparkling with mischief. "Maybe you could favor me with your opinion."

Cyn stopped cold and tried to break contact. "You've seen my place," she protested. "I don't do interior decoration."

Keeping possession of her hand, her Latin lover spun around to face her, his smile widening into a diabolical grin. "I meant crime rates, my darling detective."

Her cheeks heated at the correction. "You mean, this district?" She looked around, spotted her younger brother Evan across the street walking his beat with his partner Sullivan and pretended she hadn't; she'd cross that bridge when she got to it and no sooner.

"With the exception of mage gangs gone wild, you're more likely to die of sticker shock here than violence." That high-rise probably came with management staff, not just a super like hers. Of course, with his line of work, he could probably afford it. "It's not highway robbery, but . . ."

Rio's grin vanished as though it had never been, suddenly at condition red. "They've hit here?"

Mentally kicking herself for stirring the waters, Cyn squeezed his hand in apology. Couldn't she let them enjoy a moment of peace without pulling work into it? "Not here exactly. Near the waterfront east of here." She twitched her shoulder in the appropriate direction since he kept possession of the hand she would have used.

He nodded, his easygoing mask once more in evidence, that warrior intensity hidden from casual view. "Good to know." Returning to his place beside her, he gestured with his free hand at the high-rise. "Shall we?"

Building administration was happy to show them the unit, a two-level loft on the twenty-fifth floor with full-length windows. Much larger than her studio apartment with long sight lines and excellent views of the waterfront and the river.

Embarrassingly, the manager thought they were a couple, which was obvious from the way she pitched her soft sell, looking at Cyn whenever she pointed out amenities that most women would consider important to check her reaction.

And Rio did nothing to correct the woman's misimpression; in fact, he seemed to encourage the fiction by keeping an arm around Cyn's waist and his fingers twined with hers.

Having mixed feelings about that, Cyn squirmed inwardly, tempted to kick him. On one hand, he was making it clear he was taken—by her. On the other hand, he was clearly looking at the apartment with an eye to living in it—with her.

As the complaisant little woman?

Not in Rio's lifetime.

Untangling herself from his loverly pose, she wandered over to the windows, hoping to remove herself from the discussion. Unfortunately, the two followed her, the manager extolling the view and nearby facilities.

"There are several parks within walking distance," she added in her genteel murmur, with a discreet glance of admiration at Rio's trim body.

Indeed, Cyn recognized the park adjoining Just Desserts, which placed them a mere two blocks south of the federal courthouse . . . and police headquarters across the square from it. Her libido immediately pointed out that the loft had the advantage of being *much* closer to the station than her apartment was—so close there was no need to drive. *Think of the possibilities!*

She didn't have to. From previous experience, she knew it was thirteen minutes from her desk to her walk-up if she hurried and traffic was light. Half an hour of torrid lovemaking with barely time left for a quick shower, and a mixed-berry power bar on the way back.

To here? Maybe a five-minute stroll, though waiting for an elevator might slow her down. Call it forty-five minutes of afternoon delight. Heat suffused her at the prospect, tingling awareness spreading to her extremities.

Damning her inconvenient libido to perdition, Cyn fought down her arousal, hoping Rio hadn't noticed. The last thing she needed was to encourage his fantasy.

Unfortunately, her libido refused to be suppressed. It insisted on parading one erotic scenario after another before her mind's eye, taking the loft as its setting.

By the time Rio extracted them from the enthusiastic clutches of the manager, she could barely walk straight. It required all her control to keep from hyperventilating.

Think of something else, Cyn!

"Do you really need all those appliances? I mean, seriously. That kitchen, a washing machine and dryer?" It was an apartment better suited to a couple or a small family, not a bachelor.

"Hey, I'm domesticated," Rio protested mildly. "I can do laundry." His eyes held a wicked glint she didn't trust.

"What are you thinking?"

His grin became fixed.

What about doing laundry would a guy like Rio fantasize about? With the knowledge of five brothers to aid her, Cyn took a stab at answering her own question. "You're imagining fiddling with my underwear, aren't you?" She leveled a stern gaze at him, silently ordering him to confess. It was difficult, especially since her panties were embarrassingly damp at the moment.

Rio laughed, boyishly rueful at being found out. "Your *clean* underwear, mind you, fresh and warm from the dryer." He took an exaggeratedly deep breath, then released it in an unrepentant sigh of pleasure. "Housework should have its perks." His arm went back around her shoulders, his hand coming to rest on her biceps.

"Think of it," he murmured. "I get to remember you wearing those tantalizing scraps of cotton with their sexy side slits, and imagine taking them off you all over again."

Sexy? Her tap pants?

Heat shimmered through her, her treacherous libido landing square on the side of her silver-tongued lover in this unconventional battle. He didn't fight fair!

She poked him in the side, her finger scarcely making an impression on muscle. "Be serious. Are you really considering that place? I mean, the rent's even higher than I expected, what with all those appliances." The loft came with high-end models that mixed spells with electronics, ones she never dreamed of using, they were that expensive.

"It'd be worth it. We have better things to do besides wonder if something's made of cotton or Kevlar and what settings will get blood or oil out."

Her mind boggled at the concept of laundering her body armor, which seemed to be what he was thinking. She left that to the professionals. Then his mention of better things registered, throwing her libido into a tizzy that sent tingles down her spine, hardening her nipples, and all the way to her fingertips.

Down, girl!

"And you have to admit, the location's fantastic." His hand

wandered along her arm, an absentminded caress that only served to stoke the flames of her arousal.

"I don't have to admit any such thing." Cyn forced back the guilty memory of her earlier calculations of travel time and walking distance and afternoon delights. He didn't need encouragement.

But that didn't mean she didn't think of it, every so often. Her libido wouldn't let it rest.

Knocking on her door interrupted Cyn's inspection of her closet's contents that Sunday. Ignoring the summons, she debated between two infrequently worn dresses. The black was more suited to the summer heat, with its simpler cut and lightweight silk gauze, but it also had a much shorter skirt. The gold was fancier with all the lace insets on the bodice and long sleeves, stiff and rather heavy. Neither one was really to her taste—her personal preference ran toward pants—but she'd needed them for social obligations and disliked the waste of discarding them after a single use. Tonight's date with Rio meant wearing one—he'd said semiformal attire—and she was torn between coverage and comfort.

Thud-thud-thud. The sound was louder this time, the insistent triple rap indicating her visitor was someone with police training, which, with her schedule, narrowed the field to two out of five likely suspects.

"Wake up, sleepyhead. It's way past noon already," a husky baritone called out.

"C'mon, Sis. We know you're awake." The second voice was lighter, but the intonation was similar enough to be related.

Crap. Both of them. Surrendering to the inevitable, Cyn hung up the dresses and shut her closet. No need to give them ammo for teasing. The knocking repeated even as she headed for the door to answer their summons.

Habit had her laying fingers on the black security panel beside the door, which immediately filled with light. She made a face at the sight that replaced the blank darkness of the glass. Sure enough, Alex, the eldest of her brothers, and Fotis, twin of Evan and the youngest, stood on the other side. No fair bracketing her from both sides—though she shouldn't have been surprised to see them.

On most days off, her brothers tended to show up and hang out at her cramped apartment. Why, she had no idea, especially when Bion had more space in his house, and their sister-in-law would have loved to have them over more often.

Resigning herself to their invasion, Cyn opened the door. "Don't you two have better things to do on your days off?"

They met her grumpy greeting with near identical smiles that—rumor had it—sent many a female cop's heart fluttering. Personally, she didn't see the appeal, but there was no accounting for taste.

"Nope, can't say I do. You?" Alex directed the latter at Fotis after shaking his head in an astonishing display of obliviousness.

"Nuh-uh," that bravo answered with uncustomary succinctness, smiling all the while.

They made a beeline for her kitchenette, undoubtedly drawn by the aroma of freshly brewed coffee, since they homed in on her mugs and poured themselves some. Fotis, the bottomless pit, found where she'd stashed her emergency supply of double choco-late chunk cookies and shared it with Alex.

Shutting the door, she rested her back on it, wondering for the millionth time what she'd done to deserve the regular home invasions. Probably been born the only daughter, she suspected. "Okay, what's up?"

"Is that any way to talk?" her eldest brother chided her, taking full advantage of his primogeniture. "You sound like you don't care to have us over."

She rolled her eyes, her lips twitching upward reluctantly. "You're eating my cookies and drinking my coffee"—made from coffee beans she'd bought especially for Rio—"how much more care do you want?"

"What's wrong with catching up with our favorite sister?" Alex made himself comfortable at the small table, turning one of the chairs around to straddle it. "Good stuff, by the way," he added, raising his mug for clarification.

Fotis mumbled agreement, his mouth too full for words.

Yeah, right. Cyn made a face at the ass-kissing. "Well, whatever you want to ask, spit it out already." She glanced at the clock on the wall. There was time for a brief chat. "Don't get too comfy. I'm headed out."

Fotis gave her cutoffs and ragged shirt with its hacked-off sleeves and foreshortened midriff a dubious look. He knew she would never go out wearing it. "We heard about your callout the other day."

"Just wanted to make sure you're okay," Alex added.

"We didn't even get to engage them." Slumping into a chair beside them, she wrinkled her nose in disgust, more than willing to talk shop. They were all cops; there wasn't much else to talk about, unless it was the latest gossip making the rounds in the department. "The second time last week. They were out so fast, there was no chance of catching up." And the deflagration spell the mage gang used was a nasty but effective distraction. Since it used magic to fuel and accelerate the initial flame, her team had had to neutralize it before they could give chase.

"Too bad there isn't much left of their spell to study," Alex commented. "Something that fast-acting has to use some serious *materiae magicae*, maybe even hazmat. Couldn't be that many sources for it." He would know. He was on the bomb squad.

Normally Cyn saw only the sharp end of the callouts, not the other side, so she was happy to discuss the mage gang's depredations and pick up pointers. One never knew when such information could prove handy.

Fotis injected his views from the perspective of a beat cop

who'd established a network of his own. He might be the youngest, but he was no slouch when it came to police work.

The conversation flowed so easily that time got away from her. When she next thought to check the clock, more than two hours had passed. She winced. So much for the leisurely prep time she'd anticipated. If she didn't get a move on, Rio would get there before she was dressed. Unfortunately, her brothers didn't look like they planned on leaving anytime soon.

"Excuse me." Cyn sprang to her feet and returned to her closet. Allowing impulse to guide her hand, she snatched up the shorter of the two dresses and clean panties, then retreated into the bathroom before her brothers saw them or second thoughts could change her mind. She didn't have time to waste.

The black dress with its halter neck looked skimpier than she remembered once she had it on, but impatience with her unaccustomed indecision kept her from going back out for the other one. It wouldn't have made her feel better, either way. She didn't play up her feminine side at work, and primping still made her uncomfortable, as though she'd sold out to her mother's side; anticipating the inevitable teasing of her brothers only exacerbated the feeling. However, Rio liked it when she did and was demonstrative enough to make the extra steps worth her time, so she put a stranglehold on her embarrassment and made an effort to look nice.

"You guys had better start planning on leaving," Cyn warned through the bathroom door as she did her hair, in the hope that they'd take a hint and leave before she was done. "I'm really headed out."

Unfortunately, Alex and Fotis could be thickheaded at the worst of times. They were still there when she was done.

After her earlier apprehension, her brothers' dumbfounded silence when she emerged was an unexpected balm to her ego.

Not one to waste magic on nonessentials, she'd combed her wavy hair out and used some gunk that smelled nice to bring it under control. As an added benefit, it left her locks "touchably smooth" as Rio put it, and would let him play with it without leaving her looking like she'd just rolled out of bed. She'd also slicked on some lip gloss for tint.

The black dress with its swishy skirt ending at midthigh was the final touch. A far cry from her usual leathers and pantsuits, it was her biggest concession to the occasion—though what occasion, Rio hadn't explained.

Fotis finally whistled, still wide-eyed.

"Talk about heart attack city, Cyn. Who're you going to kill?" Alex quipped.

She ignored them to fish under her bed for the dancing flats she rarely wore. She made a point to keep her nose out of their affairs; she could only hope they'd give her the same courtesy.

"Who's the lucky guy?"

"Someone at work? Have we met him?"

"Is he a mage?"

Cyn straightened abruptly to stare at her younger brother, dumbstruck by the crassitude of his last question. "No, he's not a mage," she retorted when she found her voice, running her fingers through her white streak in irritation. "What does that have to do with anything?"

Where were their questions coming from? She didn't subject them to the third degree about their dates.

Her brothers' blue eyes homed in on the bloodstone ring she wore, its presence a tacit statement of her intentions, and narrowed accusingly.

"Why . . . everything!" Fotis spluttered, gesticulating wildly as if it were a personal affront.

"The way you're acting, he's not just some guy," Alex added, using the cookie in his hand to point at her. "He—"

A knock on her door kept them from embroidering on their theme. The avid light in their gaze told her Rio would have their full attention.

She hurried to the door before either of her brothers took it upon themselves to answer it. A quick check of the security panel, then she welcomed her lover.

The hot desire in Rio's eyes as he took in her getup was everything she could have hoped for, curling her toes as he gave her a thorough and admiring once-over. "Whoa." His smile was absolutely male, promising all sorts of erotic delights to come.

Rio kissed her in greeting, claiming her lips matter-of-factly, as though he had every right—which he did—and with complete disregard for her brothers just a few feet away. Not that he took her for granted. His kiss was breathtakingly carnal, a slow, deep stroking of mouth and tongue that kindled heat in more intimate parts of her body.

By the time he let her up for air, Cyn had almost forgotten about her brothers herself, tempted to forgo the date and just cuff Rio to her bed and have her way with him.

"I hope I'm not too early." Rio had dressed up, but not just to smart casual. When he said semiformal, he hadn't been kidding. He sported a navy cashmere blazer over a white silk shirt and dark dress pants, the contrast in colors playing up his Latin good looks—and lethal to a woman's common sense.

She couldn't tell where he stashed the gun he usually carried in the small of his back. She hadn't felt it when he kissed her and didn't detect any bulges that hinted at a hidden weapon—not that he needed one, with his probable training.

His appreciative gaze swept down her body once more, like a caress, well worth the extra effort dressing up had required.

Cyn smiled, suddenly feeling like the belle of the ball. "Not at all. My brothers were just leaving, weren't you?" She glared dire threats at the two, just in case they harbored thoughts of disagreement. A little detail that Rio couldn't fail to notice, and he didn't, if the quirk of his lips was anything to go by.

Her brothers exited tamely enough—in fact, too tamely for her peace of mind. They were probably plotting mischief, but she would deal with that when it happened. Tonight, she had more important things to think of.

"Alexis. Fotis." She pointed to each brother in turn, performing introductions as briefly as possible, then got her purse and locked the door. Normally, she would have invited Rio in for coffee first, but her brothers might have used that as an excuse to hang around. The last thing she wanted was to mix her family life with her sex life.

"Rio." Reciprocating with his name, her lover nodded in acknowledgment, that slight smile still ghosting his lips. He stood at ease, neither posturing nor self-effacing, just exuding pure confidence in every line of his body.

Ominously silent, Alex and Fotis hung back as Rio escorted her down the stairs. She'd bet they were taking notes to share with the rest of their brothers.

All that fled her mind at the sight of the silver limousine idling at the curb, a uniformed chauffeur getting out to open the rear door. She stared, dumbfounded by it all, the wave of surprised pleasure she felt tinged with misgiving. What occasion could justify such an expense? Rio wasn't that serious, was he? She hoped he wasn't going to propose. He hadn't given her any indication he was entertaining such thoughts, yet what sort of occasion warranted the expense of a limo?

Rio waved off the chauffeur and handed Cyn into the car himself, treating her like a princess. If she hadn't known that he couldn't have had any foreknowledge of her brothers' visit, she'd have thought he'd set this up specifically to floor them. Alex might pride himself on being a ladies' man, but he was nowhere near Rio's league.

The limo's interior surpassed her expectations. Large enough to host an orgy, it had butter-smooth, black leather upholstery that cradled her backside like a lover. Privacy glass on the windows and between the front and rear compartments blocked out strong light and curious eyes. Glowing pinpricks sparkling like faerie dust provided illumination. Mirrors on the ceiling and walls threw dim reflections of the two of them, which only made the whole experience more exotic.

A spicy scent drew her gaze to an elegant steel vase on the bar that held a small bouquet of carnations—her favorite flower—beside two flute glasses filled with champagne; the magnum itself was nestled in an ice bucket. What were they celebrating? Guitar music played softly from hidden speakers—a tango or flamenco or something similar—spinning a dark cocoon of intimacy around them.

Cyn shivered with presentiment. Tonight promised to be un-forgettable.

CHAPTER FIVE

Candlelight glowing behind etched glass, dark wood panels richly carved, and an old-world ambience combined to conjure an air of romance. Crossed swords glinting on the walls added just a hint of danger. Cyn's heart sped, the pulse at her throat fluttering under her skin like a butterfly trying to escape. He'd never splurged this much on a date before.

Rio's choice of restaurants only whetted her curiosity. La Estancia had a reputation as an expensive steakhouse, but she'd never imagined anything like this intimate setting: high-walled booths covered in leather and set up for maximum privacy. The secluded niches reduced other conversations to a genteel murmur barely heard and unintelligible, weaving a net of solitude around them. Even the tables in the middle of the floor had an air of mystery. Discreet service along with the usual grilled meats skewered on swords. She hardly noticed the waiters come and go, so quietly did they perform their functions.

And the food more than lived up to its billing: soft and succulent, practically melting in her mouth. Her brothers would die of envy when they heard about this.

Cyn didn't push for an answer. Rio would tell her what the occasion was when he was good and ready. Knowing that let her relax and enjoy the novelty while he wined and dined her.

Ignoring the waiters making their rounds, Rio watched Cyn sample yet another slice of grilled meat. He'd lost track of what the waiter had said it was, more interested in the way she consumed it, her lips closing around the piece as she first sucked its juices, then took it into her mouth to chew. She made a sound of delight, a low hum of almost sexual pleasure.

For such a controlled woman, Cyn could be unexpectedly expressive. Sometimes he thought he lived for such moments. Normally, they were both very goal-oriented, so getting her to take time to indulge her senses was a joy all its own.

But when she did . . .

She made love to her food, relishing every bite, one of the reasons so many of their dates involved good cuisine. He got hard just watching her, his body thrilling to her evident enjoyment. The look on her face was almost orgasmic.

Would that change with more time spent together? With novelty gone, what would replace it? He dismissed that nonproductive line of thought. It wasn't novelty he was afraid of being without, it was Cyn herself.

"You're not eating." She tilted her head to one side to consider him, her gray eyes gleaming with gentle inquiry. Her hair brushed a strong shoulder left bare by her halter top.

He couldn't help remembering how it felt to have those black waves skimming over his body. His hard-on got even harder, more urgent. He savored the ache, knowing it would be slaked before the night was over. "Just enjoying the view."

A dimple winked at him, flashing almost too quickly to register. "You spoil me, you know."

Little did she realize just how selfish he was being. He shook his head, smiling. "Not at all. You deserve some pampering, now and then. I'm glad to be the one to give it to you."

Another waiter stopped by their table to flourish his sword stacked full of grilled tenderloin.

Rio ate so she wouldn't fuss, barely tasting the soft meat when he wanted something more tender between his lips: female flesh wet with her own cream, the perfume of her arousal filling his head.

He tried to distract himself from his condition, but watching Cyn across the table in her flimsy excuse of a dress did little to help.

It looked like she wore a pair of filmy black scarves, swathed around her body, from her neck to her breasts, leaving her shoulders bare, crisscrossing her belly, then flaring at her hips, loose yet clinging to her gentle curves. The frilly skirt so perfect for dancing ended at midthigh, leaving an endless stretch of slender legs exposed and accessible.

His hands itched to renew their acquaintance, to slip under the flounces to explore her more intimate frills. It would be so easy, and he was sure she wouldn't object.

That was the only thing that stopped him. She wouldn't object. But he had more planned, and if he put his hands on her now, all that would go up in smoke.

Then so much for the special celebration he'd planned.

No, this was Cyn's night, even though she didn't know it yet. He wasn't about to shortchange her.

Rio's balls throbbed in protest, more than ready to spend their load, but he held firm to his resolve. A little denial never hurt a man . . . much.

"That was good." Cyn settled into the soft leather of the limo, replete and feeling vaguely guilty that she'd enjoyed herself so much. It seemed that even she—tough cop though she prided herself to be—was susceptible to a little romance. A bit of candlelight, soft music, some wine and attention, and she was ready to roll into bed.

Of course, Rio had been watching her all night with a look in his eyes that had her motor revving. She knew that look. It promised something spectacular, more than just his usual lovemaking.

What game was he up to?

"We aim to please." Drawing her into his arms, he nuzzled her neck, his body a wall of male strength she wanted thrusting between her thighs already.

It didn't matter that technically they weren't alone. The soft almost-starlight in the limo conjured a world of their own, the mingled scents of fresh carnations and rich leather so removed from normal life they had to be fantasy.

She tilted her head back, inviting more. Her whole body tingled with desire, positively hummed with anticipation, knowing what would follow.

To her disappointment, Rio raised his head. "By the way"— reaching into the side console, he brought out a gaily wrapped box of familiar proportions—"happy birthday."

Birthday? My birthday? Stunned, she tried to remember the date. He was right; it was her birthday.

That was the occasion he meant?

Overwhelmed by the entire production he'd made of the evening, Cyn trailed a shaking finger over the elaborate red ribbon, her insides fluttering with some nameless emotion. Her family had forgotten. Even she had forgotten. Birthdays hadn't been a big thing with the Malvas in years, not since Eleni died, and before then, Cyn's birthdays had been just another line of attack in her mother's campaign to make a lady out of her, so that Cyn preferred to forget the date altogether.

But, though she hadn't told him, Rio had somehow found out . . . and planned this.

"I—" Clutching the gift, she blinked rapidly to stave off illogical tears, her heart in her throat. She hadn't thought she wanted her birthday remembered.

"Hey, it's not supposed to make you cry," he whispered against her lips, just before he gave her a sweet, almost innocent kiss. "Don't open it now. Leave it for later. The night's not over yet."

He poured them both another glass of champagne, then raised his in toast: "To your good health!"

Not over yet? She had to swallow down emotion before she could get her voice to work, taking a sip from her glass to wet her throat. "Oh, you big spender!"

Grinning, Rio stole another kiss then frustratingly refused to take it any further. "There's still more to come. I want your birthday to be memorable."

Cyn grabbed his lapels in mock threat, pulling him close as she straddled him. "You keep this up, and you'll remember it, alright."

This time she was the one who initiated the kiss, taking him deep and long. Mimicking the carnal give-and-take they both wanted. Reminding him of the pleasures that awaited.

He reciprocated wholeheartedly, silken caresses flavored by his last cup of chicory coffee, lush and vaguely chocolaty, and the bite of champagne. Wrapping his arms around her with a groan, a hoarse growl of very male desire, he pressed her to him, rubbing the hard ridge of his erection against her mound.

She gasped at the lightning sizzling her core, sure she'd convinced him. Then he pulled back and whispered, "We're here," and she realized the limo had come to a stop and that he'd managed to keep track of it.

"Stubborn man." Cyn put her clothes to rights, using the ceiling mirror to confirm that none of their activities over the past several minutes showed.

Rio adjusted the fit of his pants, then opened the door. The darkness of the fabric wasn't entirely successful in hiding the strain of his erection. He needed to button his blazer for concealment— to Cyn's secret satisfaction. At least she wasn't the only one suffering from his bullheadedness.

She stepped out of the limo to find herself at the dance club they'd gone to on their very first date. Her heart skipped at the discovery.

Was Rio that sentimental?

The answer, of course, was not necessarily. He might bring her dolls from his missions, but he could be as pragmatic as any operator she'd met during her stint with the air force. She slanted a wary look at him. "You're not backup again, are you?"

He grinned. "Not hardly. Tonight, I'm all yours."

Cyn swallowed down a wave of excitement at his answer, still half tempted to forgo dancing to make the most of the rest of the evening. Only the suspicion of how much effort planning the date had taken kept her silent. She couldn't let it go to waste when he just wanted to make her birthday special.

She didn't know if he had an arrangement with the club's management, but nothing disturbed the romantic atmosphere he'd woven in the limo. Inside, the lights were low, the music slow and sensuous. Full of wailing sax and throbbing bass, the free-flowing melody wound around them, demanding little but hinting at much.

This time around, Rio was different. Without the need to provide backup, he was free to concentrate on Cyn—and what a difference that made! Giving her his undivided attention, he proceeded to make dancing a breathtaking prelude to sex.

He cradled her in his arms, one arm around her shoulders, the other across her waist with a hand riding her butt. Unable to resist the plush nap of his blazer, she kept her hands on his chest and rested her cheek against his neck, suddenly grateful for the lessons her mother had insisted she take.

She reined back her impatience, allowing him to set the pace. For tonight, he could lead and she would follow.

Through one slow number after another, they swayed in place, staking claim to a few square feet of the crowded dance floor. Standing so close, their bodies brushed together with every step, sensual friction that sharpened her carnal hunger. Their legs intermingled, his hard thigh sliding between hers and grinding on her mound, the swing of her short skirt reminding Cyn of her greater accessibility.

The hard ridge of his cock grazed her hip, fleeting and over too quickly—spice for her appetite. Anticipation of the next contact had her holding her breath.

She stepped nearer, rubbing her swelling breasts against him. His hand dipped lower, his fingers riding the crease between her cheeks. A shiver of excitement streaked up her spine, her nipples tingling in response.

Sweet torture. He could lift the front of her skirt and take her on the dance floor, and no one would be the wiser, her libido whispered. She could imagine how it would feel, that scandalous possession. The very idea had heat swirling in her veins, desire a heaviness in her belly, moistening her folds.

And still they danced, Rio turning her in slow circles within their little space, surrounded by haunting music, one slow melody melting into another, stretching out the moment.

Nothing else existed.

This was right.

Cyn sighed, content with the world. There was no rush to finish. They both knew how this would end. The journey was just as delightful as its peak; they'd learned that much from their months as lovers.

But that didn't mean she couldn't tease back.

She leaned into him, trapping his cock against her belly, then rolled her hips, gliding over that delicious ridge. Knowing just how well they fit together didn't dampen her hunger one whit.

Naturally, Rio countered her maneuver. He flexed against her, his hard-on riding up her belly in mimicry of the ultimate intimacy. "You're playing with fire," he whispered into her ear just before he licked its sensitive rim and blew.

The chill contrast sent a frisson of delight through Cyn. Her nipples throbbed, her sex spasming abruptly. Clenching her hands around his lapels, she screwed her eyes shut to better savor the sensations. Her heart picked up speed, carnal heat rising to a fever. "But what a way to go."

He laughed softly, a low, intimate sound that resonated through her body. "Kinky." The kiss that followed was like a whisper across her shoulder, featherlight and fleeting, taunting her with possibilities.

She panted, filling her lungs with his male scent, musk and coffee and the slightest hint of spice. It went straight to her head. He made her willing to be reckless, made her want to leave caution by the wayside. Fun and games. A break from her usual routine and work, without the dread of the Epiphany. "Get me out of here and fuck me before I go out of my mind."

"Yeah?" Rio gave her a look of speculation. The subdued lighting in the club blurred the straight line of his nose and the sensual curve of his lower lip, hid the long black lashes that were wasted on a man.

If he were anyone else, given an invitation like that, he might have tried to talk her into a quickie in the restroom or even some back alley. He might even have driven her wild enough to convince her—right at that moment—that the risk was worth it.

But this was Rio, and he knew better—knew she'd regret giving in to weakness after the moment was past. Maybe it was his black ops training, but he saw risk in the same light she did. So he didn't even try.

That was why Cyn trusted him with such a reckless invitation when she wouldn't another man. "Yeah."

—∞∞∞—

Rio's heart leaped at the raw hunger on Cyn's face, as honest as the woman herself. He quickly got her back to the limo and the privacy inside. When she looked at him like that, his common sense took to the wind. It made him want to promise her anything she wanted, so long as she stayed with him. "Where d'you want to go? Back to your place?"

Cyn slung a shapely leg across his lap, her hands roaming his chest, restless caresses that started his pulse skipping in his veins. "That's too far. How long have we got left with the limo?"

His heart leaped again. Was she thinking what he thought she was thinking? He checked his watch. "Hours. I booked it for the whole night."

She smiled a siren's smile, her fingers undoing the topmost of his shirt's buttons and heading south. "It'd be a shame to waste that money."

Using the intercom, Rio gave the chauffeur instructions with only half of his attention, his body totally focused on what Cyn was doing.

Her mouth glided down his neck, nibbling and sucking, branding and possessive, touching off sparks in his aching cock. "Ummm . . . you smell delicious. Taste good, too."

He was glad she thought so. But if he was delicious, then she was absolutely edible. The musky perfume scenting the air had to mean she was wet and ready. She hadn't been kidding when she ordered him to get her out of the dance club!

Rio sank his fingers in her hair and let his other hand do some exploring of its own. Thankful for her short skirt, he followed the back of her thigh to the hem, then up again.

When he discovered her wet panties, Cyn gave a husky laugh that tripped down his spine and tickled his balls. "That's it," she crooned, licking his ear. "No more torture."

He stroked her through the thin satin, tracing the edges of her pussy lips, teasing them both. "I thought that was foreplay."

"And what would you call this?" She swiveled her pelvis, grinding her mound against his palm and driving his fingertips deeper. If it weren't for her panties, he'd be inside her already. "Hmmm?"

"Turning up the heat? Police action?" he offered, tongue firmly in cheek. The heat of her anointed his hand like a benediction, a perfumed blessing freely given and all the more precious for it.

A gurgle of delight rewarded his suggestions. "And what would you call a quickie, then? A police special?" Cyn dealt with his blazer's buttons, then finished undoing his shirt, intimate laughter amplifying her siren's smile. "You do have a way with words."

It melted something inside him that she could lower her guard with him, show him this flirtatious, less serious side of her, that she'd put up with his public displays of affection and in fact welcomed them.

She pushed his blazer and shirt off his shoulders, then wrestled with his undershirt to bare his chest for her exploration. Her fingers homed in on his flat nipples, circling and scraping short nails over them until they hardened and he shuddered, raw need slashing him like a razor-sharp knife.

Time to level the playing field.

One small hook was all that held the scarves together at her nape. With a simple twist of his fingers, they fell away, spilling her bounty to his hungry gaze. He swore at length and with great fervor, thankful for being born male, since it meant making love to her.

Rio pulled her loose panties to one side and plunged his fingers into her wet, welcoming pussy. She was definitely ready and willing.

Cyn groaned, clenching around him. Thighs, arms, mouth, cunt—all wrapped tight. Her desire couldn't be clearer.

He could take her now. His cock ached to claim her.

But not yet. It would be over too soon.

————∞————

Pleasure swept through Cyn, hot and desperate, conjured with just his hands. He knew how to touch her to drive her wild and had no compunction about putting that knowledge to thorough use, dancing his fingers and thumb over her sensitive flesh.

She came in a flash of ecstasy, the built-up hunger released in a sudden torrent of sensation, an endless string of explosive delight detonating in quick succession. Surprise forced a wordless cry from her, her back arching abruptly at the strength of her orgasm.

But Rio wasn't done. He rained kisses on her, his mouth hot and demanding as he continued to stroke her to greater heights. Licking and sucking, nipping and laving, he stormed her defenses ruthlessly, giving her no chance to recover.

The soft leather under her only added to the stimuli drowning her senses, its rich scent mingled with flowers and sweat and sex. Stars twinkled around her. Seductive guitar riffs caressed her ears. Rio's heat against her. His fingers stroking masterfully, stretching her, pumping her, commanding a response she couldn't control.

Another release came, strong and sweet, a breathless flight through the heavens. Rapture surged over Cyn, washing her senses with wave upon wave of glittering delight. She lost count of how many times Rio brought her to orgasm. One rolled into another until she couldn't tell when one ended and the next one began.

The mirror on the ceiling filled her gaze when she opened her eyes. She was sprawled on the seat, the next thing to naked, her olive skin pale against the black leather. Her dress was bunched around her waist, her breasts bared to his talented lips, her legs spread for the expert manipulation of his hand. Her body undulated from the lash of voluptuous pleasure, writhing and arching in sensual riot.

It was her—yet not her. The reckless enjoyment the woman in the mirror evinced was so foreign to Cyn's concept of herself. She felt like a voyeur peeping through a dark window, watching someone else's debauchery.

The feeling only whet her arousal.

As she stared, Rio took a nipple into his mouth, his fingers delving between her folds. She gasped when she saw him move, anticipation drawing her nerves taut. In the next instant, she lost her breath on a moan of delight as he nibbled gently, the sweet friction on her sensitized flesh stoking the bonfire consuming her body.

But it wasn't enough.

She craved more than his hands on her, more than his mouth consuming her. She yearned to have him between her thighs, thrusting with all his passion.

As wild and uncontrolled as she felt.

Wanting to touch him, Cyn tried to twist around but fell off the seat, knees landing on the limo's plush carpet. She laughed, but the impact didn't really register, distracted as she was by Rio's lips recapturing her breast and drawing deep, the strong suction echoed by the clenching of her core. Luckily, the seat was at her back; otherwise, she would have sunk to the floor as dark delight rippled over her nerve endings.

His hands closed over hers, boxing her in and holding her in place, trapped against the seat. Not that she minded. The woman in the mirrors wasn't her—not really. This was fantasy, a moment out of time. She could indulge herself just this once.

She moaned his name, craving his cock. His agile fingers were no substitute for that hardness inside her.

Rio gave a breathless laugh. "What's your hurry?"

Cyn couldn't find the words to share her fantasy. This night was different. It was that simple and that complicated. The woman in the mirror would let the man do all sorts of things Cyn didn't dare imagine herself allowing.

"I need you to fuck me."

———— ⌘ ————

She kissed him then, her breath soft on Rio's lips. Her mouth was sweeter than usual, tasting of brown sugar and cinnamon from their dessert. She sucked on his tongue, playful swirling inciting them both.

His cock throbbed at her words, at the symbolic penetration in her teasing, demanding appeasement—a wet, snug sheath for its blade.

Enough waiting. Undoing his belt and fly, Rio freed his hard-on, drawing a breath of relief at the sudden lack of constriction. The only pressure he wanted around his cock was Cyn—any way he could have her. Whether hand, mouth, or cunt didn't matter.

But before he could take her, he needed maneuvering room. Spacious though the limo was, the floor between the bar and the seat was a tight fit for two, especially with Cyn on her knees with her back to the seat, and laying her on the floor wasn't an option.

Not tonight.

He turned her around so she bent over the seat, the round cheeks of her ass upraised and tempting. Her panties were no hindrance to his purpose, but he pulled them off anyway before kneeling behind her.

His cock glided along the crease between her buttocks, a cool promise that sizzled his nerve endings. Smooth like living silk to his burning flesh.

Aiming his cock where they both wanted it most, Rio slid in. The first wet kiss of her pussy on his sensitive head was nearly his undoing. Lightning streaked up his spine, a bolt of exquisite pleasure that scorched his brain. Hanging on to the barest shreds of his control, he pressed home.

Cyn thrust her hips back in welcome, submitting to his possession, parting before him like butter yet snug as a well-made glove. He filled her with a slow, delicious stroke that tested his will, a heartbeat away from bulling in. She took him deep, all the way to the hilt.

Their groans sounded as one, a primitive chorus of mutual relief, heartfelt and spontaneous.

Mo muirnín. To have her like this forever, his to love and cherish and protect, was worth almost anything, even giving up black ops. No matter how many times he made love to her, it was always different. There was always something more, but her enthusiastic welcome didn't change. He hoped it never would.

Cyn kept her face turned away from him. No, not away—she was watching their reflection in the mirror. "Fuck me," she urged, her inner flesh squeezing him, fluttering along his length, a slick caress that wreaked sweet havoc along his nerve endings.

Locking his hands on her hips, Rio pulled out then drove deep, setting a brutal rhythm and pumping Cyn the way she wanted. In and out in rapid-fire succession, blasting sensation up his cock and through his veins.

She gasped his name repeatedly, the lilting sounds like music in the humming silence of the darkened interior as she pushed back to meet his thrusts.

He reveled in their union, his heart racing in exultation. It felt so perfect he wanted to stay this way forever.

Cyn clung to the seat as another tidal wave of rapture gathered inside her, rising higher to crash and batter her already scattered senses. "Rio!"

He let himself go, taking his pleasure just as her climax smashed home. Pounding into her with short, savage thrusts, he drove her higher, faster, past all previous experience.

She screamed, heedless of whoever might hear. Surely this

much ecstasy was impossible! Yet her orgasm continued to build, its crest towering, until it finally broke, flinging her among the stars. Transported by the power of her release, she collapsed on the seat, cradled in Rio's arms.

When she returned to herself, it was to the sight of the reckless woman in the mirror looking totally debauched, a secretive smile on her lips.

Not her.

Someone else.

Cyn clung to the illusion. Not her. She wasn't so reckless.

"Damn, is that the time?" Untangling their limbs, Rio pressed the intercom button and instructed the chauffeur to head for her address.

Catching a glimpse of his watch, she swallowed the objections that tried to rise. O'dark hundred. As much as she wished the night would never end, she had to go to work in the morning. She rose on her knees, the movement dislodging his cock. Her inner muscles clenched as he slowly slid out of her body, the gentle drag lighting off another wave of aftershocks. She missed him already.

Her body hummed with satisfaction, her head swimming with the scent of sweaty sex, virile male, and soft leather. A wonderful end to an unforgettable birthday.

Silence settled between them, neither feeling the need to fill it with empty words. They straightened their clothes on the drive home, then cuddled together, their bodies still resonating with pleasure.

The chauffeur opened the door, professionally blank-faced as if he had no idea what they'd been up to in the hours since they left the dance club.

Rio stepped out first, with the fluid conservation of motion that made him appear so graceful. He extended a hand to help her out, an automatic courtesy she'd come to expect from him. His touch was firm, ready to provide support should she need it.

Clutching his gift and the bouquet of carnations in her other hand, Cyn slid out, reluctantly abandoning the silver limousine with its soft leather and sweet memories. Luckily, her legs remained under her, despite the weakness of her knees.

The bright streetlights after the dark interior of the limo jolted some of the lassitude from her body, a dash of cold water to the senses, the cocoon beginning to unravel. Here were prying eyes and wagging tongues, violent hearts and dangerous magic.

Welcome back to the real world.

Rio murmured something to the chauffeur she didn't catch with her attention on scanning the deserted street for hostiles. Nothing moved in the shadows, but that was no guarantee of safety. The late hour was an invitation to unsavory characters, though no lowlifes were in evidence.

Staying on her left, Rio walked her up to her apartment, maintaining a vigilance equal to her own. He kept an arm around her waist but thoughtfully left her wand hand free. Protective yet not overly so. A nice balance. She couldn't imagine any of her previous lovers even making the effort.

Nothing emerged from the shadows to menace them. Safety should have been anticlimactic, except it allowed the return of the romantic bliss of earlier.

"Enjoy yourself?" He held her in a loose embrace, his fingers laced behind her back a gentle weight pulling her close.

"You know I did." How could there be any doubt? Her body still hummed, the memory of him inside her and her release evoking another shudder of delight. "Thank you."

Rio kissed her cheek. "Don't forget, lunch tomorrow." The door clicked shut with him still on the other side before she realized he was leaving. He hadn't even tried to talk her into letting him stay.

A pang of loss caught Cyn all unawares. Silliness, of course. Why withhold an invitation to move in with her if she wanted him to spend all his nights in her bed? Yet try as she might to rationalize away the sense of abandonment she felt, the illogical reaction still remained.

Leaving Rio's gifts on her bed, she stripped reluctantly, her body tingling with the memory of pleasure. Her dress held the smell of sex and male, sweat and leather. She sniffed it, tempted to keep it as it was as a memento of that night. *Sentimental idiot.* She dumped it on top of the mound of laundry and forced herself to take a shower.

Soaping away the evidence of the night did nothing for her peace of mind. Her skin was hypersensitive to the slightest pressure, breaking out in shivers of delight with every pass of the washcloth, another reminder that she had been well and truly laid.

She thrust the thought away that if Rio had moved in with her, the evening wouldn't be over yet. There would have been cuddling and laughter.

Still, when she finally flopped on her bed, she wasn't in the mood to sleep, and hugging her pillow did nothing to assuage the feeling of isolation.

Cyn tried to convince herself it was lust that had her reaching for Rio and the reason for the disappointment she felt when crisp wrapping paper and delicate petals, not hard male pecs, met her seeking hand. Simply lust, nothing more. Familiar and comfortable. Nothing to worry about. Really.

Too bad she didn't get much practice lying.

The satin ribbon rustled as she picked up the gift, its many slender loops shimmering in the yellow half-light from the window. Silver paper crackled, its embossed patterns a slick texture to her questing fingertips. Never had she received anything so elaborately wrapped; Rio had given as much thought to that as he had to their date.

Setting aside the ribbon for safekeeping, she removed the wrapping slowly, taking care not to rip the paper, and discovered another girl mage doll for her collection—as she'd expected—a

Minoan priestess complete with multitiered skirt, bronze head-
dress and armbands, and short-sleeved bodice jacket framing
exposed bisque breasts.

Was he trying to tell her something?

As a traditional symbol of feminine power, a better one probably couldn't be found. But was his message an appeal to tradition
or the attraction of power?

Chapter Six

"Could be faster, but good job," Fernao concluded judiciously, his mahogany face drawn into stern lines—which was a load of crap, as Cyn well knew, since they'd nearly matched their fastest time for the forced entry exercise, but that was part of the game. "Okay, we're done here for today."

Tension cleared in one sharp exhalation as the team relaxed. Only the next day's sparring was left, then they'd be done with training for the month. They all understood the need to keep their skills honed, but the battery of exercises they normally went through sometimes felt like punishment.

"You know, we'd have been faster if it weren't for your lead foot," Jung teased Hardesty, as they left the low building that housed the training center's offices where they'd been reviewing the video of their last exercise.

The newbie took it in good humor. "That lead foot is what breaks doors down. You should be thankful I have it. If we had to use yours, we'd still be tapping on the door!" His clap on the countersniper's shoulder sent the smaller man staggering.

Laughter rose at Hardesty's rejoinder, loud and companionable. At five eight with a rangy build, Jung was the lightest in the team.

The newbie was fitting in nicely. It wasn't the same as working with Hawkins, especially with Danzinger still feeling his way as assistant team leader and therefore as tetchy as a cat in a room full of strange dogs, but he was making a place for himself.

"No way," Jung retorted, having recovered his balance. "I'd use an ancient *gi* technique and have it down with one kick."

Hardesty missed a step then had to step lively to catch up. "Are you serious?"

Cyn couldn't fault him for his double take. The countersniper could joke about his Korean heritage with the straightest of faces, and certain schools did teach mages to harness their personal energies to channel power into physical strikes, especially the traditional ones represented by some of the dolls in her collection.

"Of course!" Gesturing dramatically, Jung danced a few stylized moves that may—or may not—have been the opening steps for a spell.

Before anyone could call his bluff, a sharp burst of siren jolted them out of their ease. Adrenaline flowed at the sound. Easy grins vanished as mission faces went on. They picked up their heels to double-time back to the team van, where Brunilda Torres, the team driver, stood pumping her arm at them to make haste. She climbed behind the wheel as they piled into the back, Danzinger counting heads, while Fernao swung up in front. Keefe and Renfrew, the team's tactical medics from the fire department, were the last aboard.

"Go!" The slamming of the rear door accompanied the assistant team leader's exclamation.

Bru poured on the gas, her foot heavier than usual. She took the turn off the training grounds with siren wailing, and if there was a song in her heart, it was probably Wagner's "Ride of the Valkyries." The woman should have been a race car driver.

Everyone in the back leaned forward to eavesdrop as Fernao reported in.

According to Dispatch, the mage gang was robbing a jewelry shop in the South Docks Mall, and McDaniel wanted them to intercept, if possible. Since the team had been out at the training center, they were halfway to the wharf already, instead of all the way back at the station. Plus, they could take the highway and exit at the riverbank, instead of fighting through downtown traffic. The gang had finally made their first mistake.

Along the way, they picked up a couple of patrol cars as escort. The road opened up before them as traffic moved aside with alacrity—only to be expected with a big-ass black van barreling along, firing on all cylinders, and sirens howling.

Still, they had to go faster.

Bru slid into the emergency lane. Once the van was centered, Fernao triggered the lane's magic. Fueled by the wicce line running parallel to the highway, the spell took the van airborne, hurtling them faster than rubber tires could carry them.

Hopefully, fast enough to intercept the gang.

Wind whistled at the speed of their passage, replacing the roar of the diesel engine that had dropped to an idling growl. The bench vibrated under Cyn's legs, as though impatient. The rattle of their equipment increased, the team van not exactly the most aerodynamic of vehicles.

She took a deep breath to rein in her exhilaration. A few others had a similar reaction to the imminence of action, but not all. Hardesty fingered the rune against fire painted on the left shoulder of his vest. Just nerves, she judged, since he wasn't fussing with any of the other silver runes. No one could blame him, given this gang's penchant for deflagration spells.

"You rub that off, it'll do you no good," Danzinger warned,

pinning a gimlet eye on the youngest tac team member. Hardesty snatched his hand away, tucking it by his side as his ears turned a painful red.

Busy with their own preparations, the other men ignored the byplay, Moxham almost somnolent at the end of the opposite bench. The copper-skinned Violent Crimes detective had his green eyes closed, probably meditating or reviewing what they knew of the gang's previous heists.

A shudder, a screech, and the renewed roar of the engine announced their departure from the emergency lane and the approaching exit ramp, the stench of hot rubber assaulting their nostrils. They ignored the sensations as routine. The tires would probably have to be replaced after the mission, but that was none of their concern; the perps were.

They rolled into the South Docks with the siren off to avoid spooking their prey. But their caution was for naught. As the mall came into sight, several people laden with black garbage bags exited the store in question at a purposeful run toward a clump of vehicles.

Cyn craned her neck for a better view of the mage gang over Bru's and Fernao's shoulders. From the glimpse she'd caught, nothing about the perps stood out, besides those bulging bags they clutched. They looked ordinary, but appearances were deceptive.

"There! Keep after them," the other sergeant barked, stabbing a finger at a brown panel truck bugging out, his dark face tight with aggression. Barely enough warning for Cyn to brace herself.

The van swerved, almost sending the rest of the tac team tumbling. "What the—?"

A deflagration spell exploded, the blast wave rocking the van further. The patrol cars behind them peeled off to handle the situation, but Bru pressed on. They weren't going to lose the perps now.

Bru called in the incident in her piping soprano, added that they were in pursuit, then shoved the mike at Fernao. He completed the report in an impatient growl.

The mage gang's truck veered for the highway with Bru hot on its tail, the two vehicles descending on the busy three-lane thoroughfare like stooping falcons. Its course didn't give the tac team any advantage. This time they couldn't take the emergency lane. Going that fast risked overshooting whichever exit the truck took to get off the highway.

The long chase weighed on the team's patience. They could only sit tight while Bru muscled the van after the perps, riding the wheel like a witch. It went against the grain to do nothing, particularly when they didn't have much else to think about besides the past weeks' misses and the radio's sketchy, sporadic reports of multiple casualties, ones they might have prevented if they'd only been faster or if they'd stayed behind. The enclosed rear section of the tac team's van meant most couldn't see the truck they were chasing, just stare at each other while Bru's maneuvers threatened to toss them off their benches.

Worse, the gang's driver was using the truck's smaller size and the traffic to his advantage, snaking in and out across all three lanes regardless of safety, taking insane chances. His tactics were opening up his lead—that much they could deduce from Fernao's salty mutters. Sitting beside Bru, the senior sergeant wasn't a happy man.

The rest of the tac team weren't any happier.

Testosterone filled the air, and Cyn wasn't immune to it. That was the only explanation possible for her opening her mouth. "Simon, can you cast a homer?"

Fernao speared a probing look at her over his shoulder at the question, but she couldn't think about that now. Simon Rao was Patrol, but she knew he'd been working on his tracking spells. It wasn't her specialty, and they'd never trained for anything like this wild pursuit—an oversight McDaniel would probably address in future sessions—but surely it wouldn't hurt to make the attempt. They couldn't let this chance slip through their fingers.

"I can try." There was some jostling of men as Rao moved up

the bench to sit across from her, where he'd have a view of the panel truck weaving through the afternoon traffic.

Holding his wand with both hands, he closed his eyes, the muscles at the corners of his narrow jaw tensing. As ambient magic gathered around him in a nerve-tickling puff of power, he brandished his wand in lazy loops, a slow-motion knife dance that wove the summoned energies into a pattern of purpose, each stroke elegant and precise—and next to miraculous given the swaying of the van.

Cyn peered at the glimmer of lines etched in the air. The homer was a thing of delicate beauty, not at all her type of spell, but she wasn't the one casting it. Hopefully, it would work.

Opening his eyes, Rao made a gesture of release, aiming his construct at the fleeing truck, then sat back, a furrow of concentration between his thick black brows. "Got it."

And not a moment too soon.

The truck shot up an exit ramp, fighting for speed.

Bru swerved to follow, rapidly downshifting to give the roaring engine more power. The van squealed into a sudden turn, nearly launching everyone on Cyn's bench into the air. Only their grips on the hanging straps saved them. Across the aisle, Renfrew grabbed Rao's pauldron to stabilize him, the medic being the closest to the preoccupied mage.

Rao muttered an imprecation as he fought to maintain his spell. "Keep us steady, woman."

"I'm trying. This isn't exactly the freeway, you know," Bru shot back, not one to take criticism quietly. She overtook another car to close the distance to their quarry, leaning on the horn on top of the siren's wail.

The chase wound through increasingly smaller streets as the truck fled the city, literally heading for the hills.

"They're turning off," Rao muttered.

Cyn craned her head to look over Fernao's shoulder. Sure enough, when they topped the rise, the road ahead was clear.

"Right." The team leader pointed to a dirt road disappearing behind a stand of trees.

Tires squealing, Bru muscled the van onto the track. Equipment rattled and clattered as they lurched into the woods.

With her view of the pursuit limited, Cyn found herself focusing on sound. Undergrowth crunched under the tires. Shrubs or branches thwacked the sides of van. Gravel pinged on the undercarriage.

If the gang was headed for their lair, small wonder an air search couldn't find them. The trees provided excellent coverage. And in this off-road environment, the smaller panel truck had the advantage. The van's width and weight meant Bru couldn't go charging after it.

"They're getting out of range," Rao warned, his mouth thin, neck tendons corded with the strain of maintaining the spell in the pitching van.

A muttered imprecation answered him. There was a burst of speed, then—

Bang!

The sudden noise had everyone in the back pulling out their wands. But they soon realized it wasn't an attack: one of the tires had blown. Bru's "We're stuck" was followed by an impressive string of vituperation.

Fernao didn't waste time cursing. "Everyone out." Stopped as they were, they'd be sitting ducks for another deflagration spell. The truck's route might be part of an ambush. They couldn't assume they were safe just because the target was getting out of the range of Rao's spell.

They piled out with alacrity, grabbing equipment, Jung automatically shouldering his rifle. In long-range attacks, a bullet was still faster than casting a spell—and it was simpler. Over the radio, the dispatcher reported a delay for air support in calm, staccato tones. If they lost the gang's trail, the odds were against finding it again. That certainty gave an added snap to their response, another goad spurring them to haste.

Only Bru wasn't moving at double time. But then, as the driver, she had to remain behind anyway to secure the van.

Heat engulfed them, a rude slap after the van's superb air-conditioning, conjuring beads of sweat on their faces, but that was a nuisance easily ignored.

"According to the county map, this"—Fernao jerked his chin to indicate the dirt road—"ends at the river, about a mile from our location. It's possible we've found their hideout, so standard approach."

He turned to Rao. "Simon, how're you doing?"

"I can keep up, don't worry. Better, they've stopped."

Heartened by the news, they formed up into two short columns with the medics at the tail and set off in pursuit.

The track led deeper into the trees, the dry earth muffling their footsteps. Before the van disappeared from sight, a yellow ward encircled the crippled vehicle. One less thing to worry about. Bru would be safe while she waited for backup and a replacement tire to arrive.

Once under shade, the heat eased slightly. Without the deafening roar of the van's diesel engine and the chatter from the radio, the world seemed almost silent. A few steps farther, and chirps and twitters started, the cheerful sounds ironic, given their mission.

It was very different from the last time Cyn strode through a forest. Once again, she felt out of place, but this time tension knotted her shoulders to an unusual degree. *How strange.* She hadn't been this uneasy working point with Rio. At some subconscious level, she'd recognized his woodcraft and accepted his lead; she couldn't say the same for her teammates.

On the tail of that thought came hollow pops, sharp and sudden, like gunfire to her straining senses. Her heart jumped. Everyone froze, heads swiveling for the source of danger.

"Damn acorns," Danzinger whispered sheepishly, lifting his offending boot off a mess of crushed nuts.

Quiet snorts answered him, the tension easing at the straightforward explanation. But it only validated Cyn's misgivings. Rio wouldn't have made such a simple mistake. An unfair comparison, but only the truth.

Sticking to the middle of the dirt road to avoid the acorns beside the track, they pushed on, clustered around Rao. "They're on the move," he warned, most of his attention still on his homer.

"Back this way?" Fernao gestured Cyn and Hardesty on, to back Jung and Moxham, who were on point.

"No, they're opening the gap."

They moved on.

Several yards farther, the trees thinned to reveal wooden structures topped by vine-draped, moss-ridden chimney stacks. Victims of a recession decades past, the ramshackle buildings moldering in the clearing looked pitiful in the afternoon light. Formerly the focus of industry, the sawmill now stood gutted, its lumberyard long emptied and overgrown with scraggly shrubs.

And deserted.

Rao swore under his breath. As one, they turned to him with varied expressions of inquiry: frowns, raised brows, pursed lips, steady stares. He answered them all with a disgusted shake of his head. "I lost them."

"It's more than we'd had." The senior sergeant directed his comment at the entire team, his brown eyes flinty, warning that any discord was unacceptable.

"Jet, you're with Cyn."

Cyn heard the assignment with a sinking sense of inevitability. *Thanks a lot, Fernao.* Just because she was an extra sergeant on the team . . . On the other hand, it could be a backhanded compliment or a passive-aggressive tactic to dissuade her from switching to full time with the teams.

Or both.

Never let it be said that Fernao Antillia wasn't efficient.

The team leader assigned them to point. Normally, she had nothing against the position. She'd worked point before with various partners. However, today the newbie was hot to trot.

Before they'd gone twenty feet, Cyn was wishing she could put a leash on Hardesty, who'd apparently forgotten the concept of teamwork and caution or was deliberately disregarding the risk. Either way, she made a mental note to have a long talk with Fernao afterward.

By the first building, the trail veered north, blazing a path along one side of the brambly field. Hardesty seemed to consider the open space a safehold and broke into a sprint.

"Slow down, darn it," she hissed at the cockhound ranging ahead. "If you get me killed, my brothers will make the rest of your short life hell on earth."

Attention glued to the tire tracks dug into the dirt, Hardesty didn't seem to register her threat, pressing forward as if the shrubs didn't exist. Unfortunately, she couldn't say the same; the stringy branches whipped back into position with sufficient force to raise painful welts on anyone stupid enough to attempt to stick close to the newbie—namely one Detective Sergeant Cynarra Malva. "They're getting away."

"Quit thinking with your dick and use your brain," Cyn growled, frustration adding an undertone of sincere menace. If he continued to bull through the shrubs and past the weather-beaten ruins without so much as a glance to check for ambush, she'd—

Something *changed*.

Her hand whipped up, instinctively interposing her wand.

Booby trap!

Even as Cyn hurriedly cast shields around herself and Hardesty, a blast lifted her off her feet and slammed her into a pile of fallen timber. She lost her breath but held the wards, channeling more magic into her spell as flying shrapnel struck. The power fought her control. It shouldn't have but—

"Darn it, Jet, quit struggling!"

Hardesty quit struggling, but he wasn't the only one in motion.

"Cyn!" Fernao's prolonged bellow made it easy to track his rapid approach.

"Careful! It's booby-trapped!"

"Are you—" The tac team leader appeared around the corner of the building and took in the sight of two of his team hanging in the air, blue wards misted around them. He continued in a lower volume: "Well, of course, you're alright."

"Shit." Hardesty's eyes were glued to the wood shards below him, some as long and thick as his arm. Maybe his life flashing before his eyes would make him think twice about charging headlong into danger.

Cyn banished the spell, ignoring a muscle pang and the heavy *thud-thud* of Hardesty's landing as she dropped to her feet just short of the beam they'd crashed into and broken. So much for catching the perps. Unless they got lucky, the gang would just disappear—until they struck again.

Fernao stalked up to her carefully, dark eyes probing. "Damn, I was hoping you'd make him think twice about charging ahead," he muttered, as though he'd read her mind, his tone apologetic.

"Because I'm a woman?" The only one on the team.

"Something like that. Also, you have the best chance of surviving whatever gets thrown at us." An acknowledgment of her expertise in combat magics.

She'd figured as much and couldn't hold it against him. Hardesty probably would have pushed harder if he'd been paired with one of the men. Still, she couldn't help snorting. "He gets me killed, I'll hex him like there's no tomorrow."

"I'll help." Waving Keefe over, Fernao stepped away to check on Hardesty.

Cyn left the newbie to the senior sergeant, automatically checking the rest of the team, which had arrived on Fernao's heels. Jung hugged a niche, back against a wall, his rifle raised, busy surveying their surroundings for snipers. Wand up, Rao was doing the same across the track. Two lean shadows glinting silver, tensed for danger. At least they remembered their training.

Danzinger knelt by the sprung trap. Armored body wrapped in magic, he probed the area with a cautious hand. "They had time to set up. This wasn't the work of a few minutes, leastwise I hope not. I'd hate to go up against a mage who could pull this out of his hat."

"Hold still, will you?" Keefe caught her shoulder, hissing in exasperation when Cyn tried to shrug him off. "You don't know if you've taken any damage. Let me do my job." Luckily, his huskier cousin and partner was hovering around Hardesty, so she didn't have to contend with a double-team, but the threat was there.

With some reluctance, Cyn allowed the blond medic to run his hands over her, a prickle of energy making her insides shimmy in a most disconcerting manner. Her back twinged in complaint. With adrenaline petering away, she was starting to register some pain. Obviously, she hadn't escaped that blast unscathed.

"No broken bones. No obvious internal injury. You'll know you hit something, but otherwise, you're fit to continue," Keefe finally concluded. He'd been thorough in his examination, taking his time. He knew as well as she did that there was no way Fernao would let the team go charging forward, now that they knew the gang had invested in booby traps.

A motor sounded in the distance, lower and hoarser than the van's diesel or the truck's gasoline engine. They all turned to listen. The steady throbbing faded even as it reached them.

"That's probably them. They're gone." Fernao verbalized everyone's fear. There was no way they could catch the mage gang now, with them beyond Rao's range.

Doggedly hoping he was wrong, they crept their way down the dirt road through the outpour of sunshine to the very end. The tire tracks led to the shoreline, no farther, with no panel truck in sight. Somehow the gang had gotten away.

"They escaped over the water," Hardesty announced as he propped his hands on his armored hips, a human tank in black. "We must have been right at their heels."

Fernao frowned at him. "You sure? How?"

"See here." The newbie pointed to some depressions on the sand swirling with muddy water. "They had something waiting. Low, big, wide enough to carry the truck. And see this? It was here long enough for silt to build up."

Cyn blinked at the flood of information. She'd forgotten that Hardesty was on the river patrol with Bion, too focused on his performance with the tac team.

"Flat-bottomed. Shallow draft. A barge?" Fernao guessed.

"Could be."

Pulling out his phone, the other sergeant called in a BOLO for a barge carrying a panel truck, but they didn't hold out much hope for success. The mage gang seemed to stay two steps ahead of them, even when the tac team was right on their tail, and there were lots of hiding places along the river.

She walked to the shore to study the marks in the sand. The mud hadn't had time to settle, the gang had decamped that recently. Glaring at the swiftly running water, she fought down a sense of impotence. They'd done everything right, had been within striking distance of the mage gang, and yet . . .

"Smooth. We were this close, and they still slipped through." Stretching out his hand downriver with fingers spread at chest height, Jung cast a spell, a delicate tracery more felt than seen. Whatever it was meant to do was moot, since he soon tossed his head in frustration, forcibly enough to shift his gelled spikes a visible fraction of an inch. "Too much turbulence," he muttered to himself.

Some kind of air spell, then. Cyn made a mental note to ask when he was in a better mood. Questioning him now would just get her a half-jesting comment about ancient techniques handed down from his ancestors.

The oppressive weight of her body armor combined with the

heat had runnels of sweat flowing down her sides. Beyond flipping up the face shield of her helmet, she ignored the discomfort, more interested in staying in one piece. A cool breeze from off the river lifted damp tendrils around her face that had escaped her French braid, a welcome but all too brief respite from the hellish onset of summer. If the crime spree was any indication, it was going to be a bad one.

"Maybe they left something behind, something we can use," Hardesty mused aloud, throwing a sidelong glance at Fernao, then looking away. At least he didn't start whistling.

The newbie's attempt at diplomacy was bizarre to see, like a red-faced bear tiptoeing up on a panther, but the others brightened at his suggestion. A personal item could be tracked to its owner through the psychic residuals the object absorbed from physical contact. It would be something to show for their efforts. This latest failure after so much anticipation left them willing to grasp at any hint of accomplishment.

"We should get back."

A wordless protest went up, driven by frustration. The entire team looked ready to mutiny, the medics included.

Danzinger sidled up to the senior sergeant. "We're here already. Jet could be right. Maybe they did leave something behind."

"Like *booby traps*?" Fernao could slather sarcasm with the best of them.

"If we can't identify those, who can?" the assistant team leader argued.

"Can't call in the bomb squad until we find us some bombs," Hardesty chimed in, perking up now that it looked like Fernao was giving his proposal serious consideration.

Jung nodded. "What he said."

The tac team leader looked at Cyn.

She made a wry mouth, not having a strong preference one way or another. She didn't like returning empty-handed, but strictly speaking, they ought to head back to headquarters in case they were needed for another situation. However, making that decision was his job; she didn't want it and didn't want him thinking she did.

"Cyn?" Fernao stared at her then cut his eyes over to Hardesty, reminding her of her earlier difficulty. He was asking if she had problems with fishing for booby traps.

"We're stuck here anyway, until Bru gets that flat changed." She shrugged, leaving him to come to his own conclusions. An ache was starting to bloom at the base of her spine where the vest hadn't cushioned her impact, and she knew that if she didn't keep moving she'd get stiff, but that was neither here nor there. The job came first.

"Okay, but this time, we'll take it slowly." Fernao looked at the newbie meaningfully. "You go off half-cocked, and I'll hang you by the balls off the nearest tree." He raised the van driver on the radio and was assured that the replacement tire hadn't yet arrived.

Cyn was glad to see Hardesty flush; maybe mortification would drive the lesson home. She didn't care to crash into more timber—no matter how rotten—because she was watching his back, thank you very much.

They found a camp amid the ruins, hastily abandoned. Trampled paths showed where people had passed. Instead of using one of the buildings, the gang had cannibalized some of the available lumber to make a low roof and camouflaged it with plants for a rough-and-ready carport open on two sides. Apparently, they'd used nearby sheds for shelter and storage, though they hadn't left much to go on, just canned goods, a pile of trash, and spilled food only now attracting ant scouts. Someone had been waiting in camp, getting a meal ready for the gang's return.

Jung swore bitterly, his rifle held once more at the ready. "We were so close."

They avoided the obvious debris better left to Crime Scene's boys and girls: trash that might yield fingerprints or psychic residuals. They sought the hidden, the covert, the nasty surprises that might be lurking in some crevice.

A shout of triumph said one of the others had found something. Cyn didn't allow it to distract her. They each had their own sections to cover.

The search spread out to the surrounding buildings and into the overgrown lumberyard. Here, their progress slowed to a snail's pace as they combed the bushes for concealed trip wires and more booby traps. The dry branches rustled and scraped as they passed, brown from the heat despite the river's bounty. Their disturbance raised a cloud of stinging insects that—happily—quickly lost interest.

Cyn finished her section without finding anything notable. She was just about to rejoin her team when pale marks in the underbrush, regularly spaced and oddly familiar, snagged her gaze. Something about them sent a frisson of foreboding darting up her spine. Staring hard, she cudgeled her brain to identify the parallel arches of graceful ivory.

What could be . . . ?

As though her brain suddenly found the correct depth of perspective, the image snapped into focus, transforming the abstract lines into something recognizable.

Bones.

She signaled Fernao, pointing her wand at the telltale curves when he reached her.

"What have you got?"

"I'm not sure, but . . . it looks like a rib cage." With some reluctance, Cyn drew ambient magic into her wand and focused her will. The standard diagnostic spell, a simple casting every homicide detective had to master to make grade, confirmed what intuition whispered. "Human."

He muttered a pungent curse, and she couldn't blame him; in fact, she agreed with the sentiment.

This callout just got more complicated.

Chapter Seven

By the time the crime scene techs arrived, with Hollingsworth leading the charge, Cyn's back was aching in earnest, graduating beyond the occasional pang to actual biting soreness. It was bad enough that she greeted their return to headquarters with relief. She hadn't planned on hanging around the office past end of shift, because she'd wanted time to prepare for her date with Rio, but now her back rendered that option moot.

Sitting was torment.

She walked home, unable to face the prospect of sitting behind a wheel. Even walking hurt, each step jarring wretched muscle. She rode the pain, shoving it from the forefront of her mind and holding it distant. Just another data point.

Despite the shortcuts that shaved entire city blocks from her route, the trip took forever, an exercise in self-control, tempted as she was to scream. By the time she made it upstairs to her apartment, she had to face the fact that the agony wasn't about to fade within the next hour or so.

Cyn tried stretching, just to see how bad it was. Her back locked up, muscles spasming in protest. She hissed, breathing through clenched teeth, screwing her eyes shut against the tears that welled up despite herself. It was worse than she'd thought.

She called Rio's cell phone to break the bad news.

"Hey, don't think I can make it tonight." Cyn had to force out the bitter admission when he answered. She hated to give in to weakness but didn't feel up to primping and pretending to enjoy herself.

"Something wrong?" The gentle concern in Rio's voice was a balm to her senses that conversely fanned the flames of her frustration. It wasn't just sex—though she tried not to think beyond that—it was his understanding. She could discuss the job, everything including the violence, without him being shocked and getting all overprotective. However, right then, she just wanted his arms around her, someone to lean on who wouldn't try to wrap her in cotton batting.

"Nah, just strained my back, I think. I won't be any good to-night." *Darn it.* She could only hope Hardesty was suffering as much as she was, that gung ho cockhound.

"Is there anything I can do?"

"Give me a rain check?"

"For you, always. You don't even have to ask."

Somehow he knew just the right thing to say to make her smile. By the time they said their good-byes, she was resigned to the situation.

A warm shower eased the pain somewhat, so it only felt like sharp claws instead of a hot poker. Maybe if she babied her back tonight, it'd be gone tomorrow. She hated seeing a healer for something so minor as a strained muscle; Keefe hadn't detected anything major.

A shadow in the fogged-up mirror made her stop to wipe the steam off and get a second, longer look. *Oh, argh.* She was bruised but good. A dark splotch snaked around her lower back where she'd hit that big beam. The purpling was bordered by a broad swath of red, probably due to the ceramic plates in her vest distributing the force of impact. It wasn't pretty.

Darn Hardesty, anyway. Just when Rio was in town for some regular loving. With some difficulty, she pulled her nightshirt over her head and made ready for bed.

Cyn sighed and stepped out of the bathroom, toweling her hair despite the pain raising her arms caused. Her back didn't like the motions, but she couldn't stand sleeping on a wet pillow and didn't know that spell Rio had used. The sight that greeted her gave her pause: Rio lounged on her bed, clad in slacks and a moss green polo shirt, patiently tossing a small bottle from hand to hand. "I said—"

Flipping up a hand, he cut her argument short, taking in her attire in a glance. "I know what you said. But I figured that meant you wouldn't eat, either." He got up and nodded at the small table in her kitchenette where boxes of takeout sat steaming the air with savory aromas. It was a mark of her distraction that she hadn't noticed them until then.

Her stomach growled a belated welcome.

Cyn grimaced, acceding the point. He knew her so well. Since Fotis and Alex had finished off her stash of cookies, she'd intended to go straight to bed.

"After that, I thought a massage?" Rio raised the bottle.

"No drugs?"

He smiled, not offended by her suspicious question. "Just oil, don't worry."

She acquiesced, hurting too much to make an issue of his coming over. It was just that he rarely displayed this protective side of himself, so she didn't know how to behave. She couldn't take umbrage when he'd never indicated in any way that he considered her less capable; his easy acceptance of her job was one of the things that attracted her in the first place.

Supper barely registered. Sitting on the edge of her chair so she wouldn't forget and lean back, Cyn forced herself to eat but couldn't have cared less what she ate. It was hot, and it silenced her increasingly vocal stomach. Good enough. She spooned food straight out of the box, ignoring the spikes of pain the simple motion drove into her back.

Rio fussed over her, claiming her towel to finish drying her hair, then combing it smooth and otherwise keeping his hands busy. His attentions felt heavenly.

Maybe too heavenly. The offered ease was seductive, tempting her to surrender herself into his care. "You don't have to do that, you know. I can dry it later."

"Just raising your arms hurts. Think I can't see that?" He continued working through the locks, though he'd rendered them tangle-free already.

Treating her like one of her dolls.

The thought didn't provoke the outrage it should have. He made her feel cherished—treasured. *Nuh-uh, don't go there, Cyn. You're setting yourself up for a fall. Black ops, remember?*

"Shhh . . . just relax and finish your food."

"You're just playing now," she protested halfheartedly. The gentle strokes on her scalp were hypnotic, wearing down her resistance like water dripping on rock and just as insidious, routing her headache before it could start pounding.

Rio chuckled, a deep, intimate sound full of male satisfaction. "Guilty as charged. I'm imagining all this stuff gliding over me."

Cyn nearly groaned. Why did he have to share that? Now, she'd have difficulty getting that picture out of her head! She could see him in cuffs, locking him to her bed, while she trailed her hair all over his hard body, could smell the musk of his arousal from memory. Her breath hitched on a thrum of excitement. Her back twinged in protest. "Masochist!" At that point, she didn't know if she meant him or herself.

"Nah, it just gives me something to look forward to. Maybe next time." He nuzzled her neck, sending another shiver of futile desire flashing through her. "Go get ready for bed."

When she stepped out of the bathroom once more, Rio had put away the food and dealt with the dirty utensils. Either he was as neat as she was, or he respected her preference for neatness. The thoughtfulness of his gesture still managed to touch her.

"Let me see." He had to help her get her shirt off; she'd stiffened up in the short time since her shower.

"It's just a bruise."

"Not if you're hurting this much."

Rio hissed when he got a good look at her back. "What the hell happened?" he demanded in a growl a full octave lower than his normal speaking voice.

Cyn smiled inwardly at his reaction. *Typical male.* As if she were made of porcelain. But illogical though his outrage was, it was touching. "Forget it. Hardesty's a newbie. It comes with the territory."

He raised cold brown eyes to her, a distant look that in any other man would have chilled her heart; instead, she was absurdly warmed by his reaction. "He hit you?"

"No!" she exclaimed, startled by the question. "Newbie tripped a booby trap. I got a ward up, but it still sent us flying." Though she downplayed the danger, the way his face darkened, she might as well have spared herself the effort. Of course, with his black ops experience, he could probably read between the lines. She gave it up; more protests would only make it sound worse.

Naked, she sat on the bed and gingerly worked her way to the middle. Rio helped her onto her side then her front, his manner solicitous and just this side of mollycoddling, but she was sore enough to overlook his treatment.

"I don't have to like it."

"Believe me, I wasn't thrilled, either. But it was his first real fuckup, so it's understandable. If he does it again, I'll kick his butt myself."

The hard mask he wore cracked, one corner of his mouth quirking up, then he snickered. "I'd pay good money to watch."

"Pervert," she accused affectionately into her pillow, glad the coldness in his eyes was gone. The last thing she wanted was him beating up on Hardesty, as much as the newbie needed some common sense pounded into his head.

Rio maneuvered around her, taking extreme care not to jostle her—not that he was a bed hog, but normally the mattress squeaked under his weight. Now, there was barely any sound or motion to indicate his presence; only his strengthening heat bore testament to his approach.

Warm oil drizzled on her back and down her spine in a sooth-ing glide more sensed than felt. The scent of sweet almonds brought to mind Just Desserts and the many meals they'd shared there, sometimes followed by afternoon delight. Cyn groaned softly. All her thoughts seemed set on tripping over her libido tonight—and her in no condition to act on it!

Rio worked the oil into her skin with gentle strokes, starting at her neck and over her shoulders, unerringly finding the tightness in her muscles as though they were his own and drawing the pain away. He pressed down, teasing out the kinks with deft fingers.

She moaned in delight as the knots slipped loose under his knowing hands. She hadn't realized how stiffly she'd held herself until her tension eased.

"*Damnú*," he breathed, the profanity sounding like prayer. "Do you know how sexy that sounds?" His fingers coaxed a whim-per from her, and she couldn't muster the energy to be embar-rassed at herself. The soreness dissolved, melting away and leaving syrupy bliss behind.

"You're good." A major understatement on her part. Rio might not be a healer, but what he was doing with his hands was nothing short of miraculous.

He took extra care with her lower back, skimming over the bruise so lightly it felt like he was tracing featherlight patterns with aromatic oil. Going round and round and round, over and over. Calling heat and sensual awareness, then focusing them where his touch lingered. Hypnotic.

Between one heartbeat and the next, Cyn was floating, her aches receding in the distance, her muscles like warm wax, all soft and pliant. She purred her approval, more than willing to bask in the comfort he gave her.

The kiss Rio pressed on her neck only added to her euphoria.

"Better?"

"You can't imagine how much." She snuggled into her pillow, enjoying his hands on her body. This was one of the things she liked best about being his lover, the quiet intimacy as much as the exhilarating passion. He excelled at both.

With her guard down and no discomfort to occupy her attention, her mind wandered off, taking a path she'd been avoiding: the imminent change in their relationship. She had to face up to it, what with the hints Rio had been dropping and his quitting his former line of work and moving to Aurora.

Why had he done it, and why now? They had a good thing going. Why couldn't he be satisfied with what they had? Why change it—except for the prospect of more and regular sex? She couldn't believe he was serious about settling down with her. The statistics for men from his line of work were against it; they married compliant women, domesticated, someone like her mother or sister-in-law. The barefoot-and-pregnant stereotype was so pervasive because it had the numbers to back it. A twinge of old pain stirred at the thought, a thin ghost of former anguish and easily ignored.

The chances of Rio bucking the trend? Highly improbable. Might as well wish for the moon.

"You falling asleep on me?" The murmured question drifted up from thigh level where her lover was doing his darnedest to reduce her to a puddle of relaxation. She was halfway there already, the pain from the bruising banished.

"Can you blame me? You've got magic hands," Cyn purred, settling deeper into her pillow. She'd never felt so pampered. Sleep beckoned, irresistible.

His lips brushed the back of her thigh, drawing a shiver of

awareness she hadn't thought herself capable of in her current state. "Just the hands?" The butterfly-light caresses drifted to her other leg, eliciting another wave of delight.

Rio kneaded her butt and thighs and lower, all the way to her toes, reducing the rest of her to bonelessness. Cyn would have told him that wasn't necessary, except his attentions felt too good to give up.

The problem was, she still wanted him, wanted him more, after his thorough massage, desire a throbbing heaviness in her womb. "Rio?"

"Don't worry, I'm still here." He pressed a kiss on her hip, brief and undemanding. But the touch that followed wasn't: a hard finger skimmed her damp folds provocatively, coaxing cream from her body but not seeking entrance. Deliberate temptation. The promise of it sent a shiver through her, anticipation rearing its head, sensual heat spreading to her nerve endings.

"That's not a massage anymore. What are you up to?"

More kisses, farther down, tracing the curve of her cheek and moving inward, stealing her breath. "Just testing the waters, so to speak." His finger found her clit and circled it slowly. Round and round and round. Inexorable. Playing with the turgid nub and inciting a response she was helpless to withhold.

Warm air stirred her curls, tickled her wet flesh. An insubstantial kiss made explosive by its very unexpectedness. Cyn quivered, need spiking in her veins.

"Hmmm . . . could be better, I suppose." Rio's clinical diagnosis would have been more convincing if he weren't plying his thumb along her slit to nerve-jangling effect. The tease.

Not that she minded.

Smiling into her pillow, she pressed down, taking him the slightest bit into her, and choked back a groan at the resulting friction. "You're going to fuck me better?" *Please?* She could hardly move, but her libido didn't care about such niceties.

"Why not? Orgasm's analgesic—endorphins and all that stuff.

Nature's pain relievers." He continued to stroke her, fanning the carnal heat stirring in her belly, a spark of interest that promised flames with just a little more encouragement.

But she couldn't muster the strength to move an inch, much less something more energetic. He'd banished her pain. Unfortunately for her, maintaining her facade of strength had taken everything else she had. After his massage, she had nothing left in reserve.

Cyn sighed. "I want you, but I'm too limp to do anything about it." *Darn it.*

"That's okay. I've more than enough energy for both of us." He tucked a pillow under her, raising her hips, then continued his caresses, obviously content with his pace. None of the reckless rush of previous times nor the laughter of their games, just this . . . heady indulgence of the senses. A slow, deliberate seduction, building her arousal with his hands and lips, with the utmost regard for her comfort.

Deft fingers delved into her channel, plumbing and stretching her delicate inner flesh, finding and fluttering over her hot buttons—and he knew them all from long experience. He stoked her desire to a fever, a breathless heat fomenting unspeakable hunger. A need that went to the bone.

The depths of that need forced a moan from her lips, a wordless cry for release. Nothing else mattered, nothing but the hunger stealing her wits and inundating her body.

Velvet softness brushed Cyn's thighs, then something blunt prodded her slit, seeking entry. Rio, she realized, as his thighs settled around hers, his forearms beside her shoulders. At some point, he'd stripped off his clothes.

He pressed into her, welcome pressure parting her hungry sheath, the flare of his cock head rasping inner muscles more than ready for him. She sighed, a different knot of tension inside her unraveling at the contact. Hard and hot and all male.

Rio worked his cock deeper with short, careful thrusts that

whet her desire to razor sharpness. "*Damnú*, you're tighter this way." His breath heated her neck. The imprecation sent a thrill through her; normally, he stuck to English and kept his language clean. Gaelic meant his control was shredding.

With a grunt, he slid all the way home, snug against her womb, his hard abs pressed to her cheeks, their juices spilling down her thighs, the scent of sweat and sex heavy in the air.

Stuffed to overflowing, Cyn gasped at the sheer overload of sensation. She could feel every inch of him, a thick blade filling her emptiness, so deep she couldn't tell where he ended. All her awareness spiraled inward, focused on his possession. Need coiled in her core, drawing tighter. Waiting for what had to follow.

The mattress shook as he panted, his arms quivering as he held himself above her, their only contact below the waist. His heat surrounded her, penetrated her, but he was ever so careful not to put any weight on her. The bulging muscles beside her pillow attested to his efforts, the sight seductive as hell.

Something about all that male power harnessed for her pleasure made her melt. She clenched around him, savoring his hard cock inside her, tangible proof of his desire. This much at least was hers. For now.

Rio groaned, a guttural sound replete with urgency. "Don't move. I won't last if you do."

Gratifying though it was, his estimation of her energy level was overly optimistic. She didn't think she could lift a finger, despite her insistent libido. Yet it felt decadent to just lie there and accept his caresses, to be so passive in lovemaking. Forbidden, somehow—as though she were violating a nameless taboo.

He withdrew slowly, reluctantly, his cock dragging against her clinging flesh. Pulling out and farther and more. An eternity of erotic suspense. Just when it seemed he would slip free, he reversed direction, pushing back in with equally breath-stealing slowness. Time and again. Lingering over each delicious, voluptuous stroke.

Cyn moaned as her hunger built, captive to the carnal need he evoked in her, the heaviness in her loins demanding release. She urged him on, squeezing him with her inner muscles, the most she could do in her languor, her body weighed down by honeyed bliss. "This can't be that great for you."

"Are you kidding? This is almost as good as tying you up!" He nuzzled her nape and nibbled on her shoulder, his jaw prickly with stubble.

She laughed, unable to help herself. Only he would make an observation like that at a time like this. "Finish me, darn you. I'm almost there!"

Still Rio took his time, slow and steady, rocking in then out, a gentle, inexorable tide unlike any of their previous lovemaking, until she thought she would burst into flames. "Now! Finish me now. I can't take any more."

He ground his pelvis against her, sheathing his cock to the hilt in a surge of velvet power. With that one last push, he tipped her over the edge into a breathless orgasm, sweet ecstasy splashing her senses. All tension spilled free, her body soaring with pleasure, pain a tattered memory fading into oblivion. He took his release after, his low growl of completion the final touch to her contentment.

"You're a dangerous man," Cyn purred, unable to muster the energy to raise her head as he shifted to the bed beside her.

Rio stroked her butt, a shameless smile curving his lips. "But you knew that already."

"It bears repeating." Her eyelids drifted shut, too heavy to keep up.

Gentle lips brushed her cheek. "Go to sleep. I'll be by in the morning, in case you need help dressing."

She carried his reassurance with her into healing rest.

CHAPTER EIGHT

Morning brought with it a different perspective. Prompted by a buoyant feeling of well-being, Cyn decided charitably that Hardesty didn't deserve to have his balls shoved all the way up to his ears. Kicked to his belly would be fine. Her back still protested any radical movement, but Rio had awakened her with another sensual massage, so everything else was right in the world.

She turned her smile to the wonderful man keeping pace beside her. "I really feel fine, you know. There's no need to escort me as if I'll collapse along the way." She rolled her eyes at the improbability, absently noting the cruiser rolling past on the street, its sudden deceleration and the craned heads of its occupants. The rubberneckers. She didn't recognize them offhand but suspected the same couldn't be said of the reverse.

"Okay, I confess." Rio raised his empty hands in surrender. "I have other business with the police besides your delightful companionship." He shot her a knowing look sidelong, the corner of his mouth tilted up suggestively, reminding her of what had followed his morning massage and inciting a reminiscent quiver of orgastic delight in her core.

She nearly blushed. Luckily, her jacket hid the tingling points of her now-hard nipples. The rogue! Getting her worked up with a whole day's work still ahead of her. She bumped a shoulder against his arm in reproach, but he simply laughed.

What business did he have at headquarters? It had to have something to do with Depth Security. He was dressed in what she'd come to realize was his version of business casual: a polo shirt the color of old oxblood tucked into chinos and a tan sport coat on top. The collar of his shirt was even buttoned down with blue goldstone pins, instead of the usual buttons. Definitely not his normal attire when visiting her between missions.

At the steps to the main entrance, Rio turned to her, his face wiped clean of humor. "Sure you'll be okay?"

Smiling indulgently, Cyn rubbed the crease between his brows, unable to resist his sincere concern despite their lack of privacy. "Don't worry. I'll see a healer if the pain returns." Her pride might suffer, but she'd be damned if she'd risk her team by not being at 100 percent.

They parted ways at the lobby, he to his mysterious business, if business it was, and she to thread the crowded corridors to Homicide. Luckily, she wasn't handling roll call today, because it took most of the remaining distance to wipe the silly smile off her face and get her mind on business and off the snug fit of Rio's pants over his backside.

"The lieutenant wants you in his office," Lopes murmured over his monster mug as he walked back from the coffeemaker, his eyes still at half-mast. He needed a few slugs of caffeine to wake up fully, so much so that they kidded he ought to just mainline the stuff.

Cyn paused in hanging her jacket on the back of her chair to shoot a questioning look at the detective. She hadn't even had time to turn on her computer and read the previous shifts' reports. The early summons smacked of unusual developments.

Lopes simply shrugged his ignorance before continuing to his desk. One might think the detective didn't have a curious bone in his body.

Making a beeline for the far side of the bull pen, she mentally reviewed the load of her team. Ellis had just closed a case, reducing her load to three. Chuan was working on a couple of cold cases. The Danvers murder was open-and-shut, nothing to worry about. Everyone else was chugging along, and overtime was down from last month. There was no reason for a meeting before the usual end-of-week one-on-one. She rapped on Derwent's door perfunctorily and stuck her head in. "L-T?"

The pot behind his desk was half empty. He'd come in early, then, long enough to be on his second mug of coffee. He waved her in brusquely, his hand curved around the unlit pipe that had replaced his cigarettes a few years ago. It was a bad sign that he was fiddling with it.

What was this about? Cyn's mind raced, trying to remember any gossip that involved the squad and coming up blank. She hated getting caught flat-footed.

Case files splayed across the Homicide commander's desk, the names unreadable in that quick stolen glance before she trained her eyes back on his tired face. His random dip into the waters? Derwent did that sometimes, just pulled up a few to see what was happening and what was coming in. His way of keeping a finger on the pulse of the city. But it was still no reason for the break in schedule . . . unless he'd noticed something unusual? Something about her squad she'd missed?

She took a seat at his nod, her curiosity on overdrive.

He tapped his pipe on the topmost folder, a slow one-two that seemed more meditative than irritated. "Those bodies you found on that callout with Tactical."

It wasn't a question, so Cyn said nothing, keeping an expression of alert inquiry on her face.

"You found them; they're yours." Derwent pushed the files to her, the rasp of cardboard over the textured hard plastic of his desk filling the silence.

But that was standard procedure. Why did this case merit a one-on-one?

Her gaze drifted down to the folders—the unusually skinny folders; even this early in an investigation they should have been thicker—then snagged on the names on them. Even upside down, they were easy enough to decipher, now that she had time to read. *"Jane Does?"* A neck muscle twinged when she snapped her head up to stare at the Homicide commander. "For real?" They rarely needed to resort to the anonym in this day and age of modern forensics. A simple scry was usually all it took to establish identity.

Derwent's scowl deepened, his knuckles going white around the pipe's bowl. "The bodies were expurgated. We were lucky to get psyprints—and they aren't the best."

"Sanitized." Cyn's gut tightened, a spike of adrenaline sending her heart pounding. *The power required!* It probably took at least a master mage to successfully pull off the sort of spells that could wipe all the psychic traces of personality, someone abreast with current forensic thaumaturgy. No wonder it snagged the L-T's attention. "Any connection to the gang?"

"Doesn't look related." He drummed his fingers on his desk, blunt, discolored nails clicking on the cherrywood-patterned plastic. "From what the crime scene techs could tell, the gang went nowhere near our corpses. Just sheer luck you stumbled over them." His mouth twisted sardonically above his full, gray beard. "So they're all yours."

"Thank you *so much*." She meant it, too, despite the sarcasm she injected in her voice. A case like this was a challenge to sink her teeth into. The perfect murder—if it was a murder. No victim meant no crime. It would be up to her to prove it one way or the other.

———— ∞ ————

Police headquarters was a maze of disparate buildings that bore witness to previous city councils' lack of long-term planning—or at least their limited budgets. The concrete, granite, and glass of the main building ran smack-dab into more traditional brick structures at different points and on different levels, lending it all an ad hoc appearance. Luckily for Rio, there'd been a map at the entrance, and his memory for visual details served him well. That and a mental compass got him to his destination without the embarrassment of having to ask for directions.

"Can we help you?" From the description he'd gotten, the stocky, older man with a shorn head of pale blond hair and a hand flat on the secretary's desk had to be Lieutenant Thorsen McDaniel, the head of Aurora PD's Tactical Unit. Precisely the man he was looking for.

Rio held up the shooting range manager's business card in reverse to show the intriguing note scrawled on its previously blank back. "I think the phrase is *requested and required.*"

McDaniel, if it was he, snorted in appreciation. "Not quite that bad." He jerked his head toward the inner office, the signage on its door confirming Rio's supposition of his identity. "Coffee?"

"No, thanks." Rio had heard enough stories from Cyn to know to refuse the tar that masqueraded as his favorite beverage. He followed McDaniel into the office, closing the door on the secretary's bright-eyed look of interest at the older man's instruction.

"Riordan Rafael." McDaniel finally broke the silence after they were both seated, burring Rio's first name the way his Irish mother did, pronouncing it as two syllables, with the robust tenor of a trained singer. Hopefully, he wouldn't do it too often. She resorted to his full name only when she was mad at him; it used to be his first indication that he was in hot water. "You look familiar."

Content to let the cop get to the point in his own time, Rio waited out the thoughtful silence.

"That kidnapping last year, I remember now. You did good." A smile split McDaniel's broad features momentarily, then he gave a brisk nod as though he'd come to a decision. "You've been setting new records at the shooting range, I'm told. The long-distance range, in particular."

Possibly, except Rio hadn't filed his scores with the range officials. "I couldn't say." He kept his answer noncommittal. The first rule when confronted with official interest was *volunteer nothing*. Sound advice until he knew where this conversation was headed.

"There's nothing in the record books, but they have eyes. Unofficially, you waxed my countersnipers' scores without breaking a sweat."

When Rio merely raised his brows in inquiry, the older man grinned, crow's-feet fanning out from the corners of pale blue gray eyes, his expression unexpectedly collegial. "I have a proposal for you."

McDaniel's offer was simple. On a constant lookout for training opportunities for his tac teams, he'd had difficulty finding one with a sniper scenario. So he'd decided to come up with his own, which was where Rio came in as the proposed aggressor. The police lieutenant had wanted to meet Rio and personally assess his suitability before floating the idea. Clearly, Rio made the grade.

Had Lantis known of the shooting range's connection with the police? That was the sort of thing the adept would find useful and might have been a factor in his recommendation of the facility to Rio. Though he was a few years retired from black ops, Lantis still didn't miss much.

Rio didn't commit to anything, wanting to clear it with Lantis and Dillon first. He doubted they'd object, but it was only professional to put it before them. When he accepted the job at Depth Security, he'd accepted their authority. While McDaniel's attractive offer might count as fresh business, it could conflict with existing projects, and he wasn't ready to freelance this early in his civilian career. The lieutenant was understanding enough not to press for immediate agreement.

Cyn's brother, Alex, was waiting in ambush on the way out, sauntering from a vacant cubicle to block his path as soon as McDaniel was out of sight. "Rio, isn't it? What was that about?" It wasn't a demand, the question sounding almost idle, but the expression on his face didn't match his tone.

A quick glance showed absolutely no one paying attention to them, everyone else ostensibly busy at their desks, but he got the impression that more than one set of ears were pricked. "Why don't you ask your commander?"

"You're the one I'm asking." Alex met his gaze squarely, his dark blue eyes wary.

"If McDaniel wants you to know, he'll tell you." Rio sidestepped the man, unwilling to debate the matter.

"You'd better not be making trouble for Cyn."

The low-voiced statement stopped him in his tracks, dumbfounded by the implicit accusation. He shot an incredulous stare at the frowning cop, tempted to lay him out cold for the insolence. "You're lucky you're her brother."

"What other reason would you have for coming here?"

As if he was dumb enough to fall for that. Did that actually work as an interrogation technique? He shook his head, in no mood to put up with the other man's hostility. "Quit insulting me and just say what's on your mind."

Alex flushed beneath his tan, even his ears turning red. "Look, I'm sure you're a great guy and all, but face it, Cyn's a mage and a cop. You're not. A civilian wouldn't understand the danger she faces or the demands magic places on her. You're out of your league," the cop informed him in complete earnestness.

Rio nearly laughed at the ignorance inherent in such a statement. He might not have the experience of a cop, but he was hardly wet behind the ears. Far from it. "That's for her to decide, don't you think?"

"You think you know what it's like, that you can handle it. You're not the first to think that. And I really doubt you'll be the last. It might not matter to a pretty boy like you, but Cyn doesn't need that kind of hurt." Having had his say, Alex marched off scowling, leaving Rio to stew over his statement.

Not be the last? Hell, he had every intention of being with Cyn till the very end, magic be damned. Rio stifled a growl. In sniper school, it didn't matter if you weren't a mage, only self-control and marksmanship—the ability to stalk prey and take them out with minimum fuss. Dispassion trained to the nth degree.

How ironic it wasn't his mage ability that now brought him to McDaniel's attention yet the very lack made others dismiss his suit out of hand. If there was any justice in the world, Alex would have a part in the proposed training. Rio would enjoy having him in his sights and pulling the trigger.

He left quietly, forcing his body not to betray his anger yet unable to silence his bitter thoughts.

Basic thaumaturgy was an innate ability. Anyone could tap the ambient magic permeating the world, enough to activate lights, unlock doors, and other simple tasks, but not so much that they could rely on it entirely. Thus technology was born.

But a large minority could do much more: weave intricate spells and channel power through body and will; they could, in effect, perform miracles that the less gifted strove to duplicate with technology. A trained mage was practically guaranteed a career. High adepts guided the interstate railways that ran on wicce lines, flew the planes connecting major junctions, built bridges and most major civil works, and headlined the billion and one other operations that depended on magic.

Mage talent was an automatic leg up in the military. Unfortunately, it looked like it was the same with the police.

And Rio didn't have it.

Though everyone could wield magic to a greater or lesser extent, his ability happened to fall in the lesser end of the spectrum—so low he didn't qualify as a mage. If he applied himself, he could have achieved borderline mageship, but he didn't have the inclination to pursue it. His interests lay elsewhere, and he excelled in them. But that knowledge did nothing to soothe his irritation.

To be fair, he could see where Alex and the others were coming from. They were Cyn's brothers, and like any tight-knit family, they only wanted what was best for her. Having the example of his own parents, he couldn't fault them for that. In their minds, the best meant a mage; so-called pretty boys need not apply. But just because that was what they wanted didn't mean he was going to go along with the program. Damned if he was going to step aside to make them feel better.

Cyn was his, and he wasn't giving her up.

A soft growl of delectation sounded from the next desk where Sharyn Ellis was leaning out of her chair, her neck craned, dark green eyes rounded as she stared through the department's glass door and out the corridor's glass outer wall. "Eye candy at ten o'clock. Dang, what I'd give to get my hands on some of that."

Cyn checked the indicated direction to see broad shoulders clad in a dark red polo shirt tapering to a lean waist and long, strong legs, an erect carriage, and confident stride. His police business apparently concluded, Rio crossed the parking lot swiftly, sport coat in hand, looking neither left nor right, the fluid motion of a hunting cat in every step. The late morning light showed his sculpted features in utmost favor. The epitome of masculine beauty.

Mine. Unrealistic of her to think so, and it couldn't last, but for now it was only the truth.

She took a moment to savor the view and her visceral response. "Hands off. He's taken." Her back was starting to stiffen, the growing ache adding a snap to her words.

The blond detective leaned farther forward, practically drooling, and she wasn't the only one; a flock of females were gathered in the hallway, noses pressed to the glass like kids outside a candy shop. "No way. A guy who looks like that? It's open season all the time." She purred the words predatorily. The large bloodstone clipped on an earlobe glinted, a blatant advertisement of availability.

Quashing her annoyance at the insinuation, Cyn returned her attention to the case file in front of her and its meager contents. That was just Ellis being herself. "I'm serious. He's taken." She might not expect anything permanent to come of her relationship with Rio, but while they were lovers, she refused to share.

"Can't blame a girl for dreaming."

"So long as that's all you do." She continued down the forensics report with its listing of negative results. Small wonder the process was referred to as sanitization; the corpses were so clean it was almost as though the vics had never been born, much less lived more than a score of years. She made a note to double-check that their stats had been forwarded to Missing Persons.

"Why?" The lilting question suggested that the detective wasn't taking her hints seriously.

"Otherwise"—Cyn canted her head to make eye contact—"I'll have to go tactical on your ass."

"You—" Ellis blinked rapidly, fluttering her darkened, extended lashes, as she processed the information. "He's yours?" the other woman finally whispered.

"Yes." Satisfied that she'd made her point, Cyn surveyed the bull pen for potential trouble. The interview rooms along one wall were in use. A couple of detectives were hanging around the coffeemaker in quiet conversation. Lopes had his chair tilted back, his heels propped on his desk as he read a report, but that was par for the course. Everything normal. She turned back to Ellis. "Now get back to work."

The blonde finally took the hint and focused on her own files, relieving Cyn of the need to stomp ass.

Flap, flap, flap. Cyn dealt out the psyprints of the victims like playing cards, spreading them side by side on her desk. The images lacked clarity, since they were drawn from lingering psychic traces, and the deaths had apparently lacked the impact of emotional trauma—strange, that—but until the victims were identified, the psyprints and physical records were all she had to work with.

Caucasian females, all brunettes, aged in the twenties, living height of approximately five eleven, in apparent good health at time of death. Cause and manner of death currently undetermined. Times of death estimated from two to ten years prior to discovery. No fabric remains found in the vicinity.

Their killer had hung around—or perhaps returned to the location to dispose of his victims. *And buried them naked?*

She settled back to read, to familiarize herself with the pieces of the puzzle. Because that's what it was. Solving a murder was a challenge, and she was good at it—the main reason she hadn't accepted the overtures of Tactical. This made all the paperwork worthwhile, though there were days when she wondered why she'd applied for sergeant.

Much later, a whisper cut through her concentration. "Don't tell me. He's a mage, isn't he? Some people have all the luck," Ellis muttered. The irrepressible woman resumed her prattle right where she'd left off. Her tenacity was one of the reasons the blonde was a good detective, but some days it took a great deal of self-control not to strangle her.

Luckily for Ellis, Cyn's attention was elsewhere. "No, actually he's not," she answered absently, staring at the psyprints. Were there any identifying marks at all? The victims looked similar enough to be sisters: fair skin, dark hair, light-colored eyes, tall, slender. Granted, part of the semblance could be due to the blurriness of the psyprints, but she had a bad feeling about this. If Forensics was right, and they'd died years apart, chances were she'd stumbled over a dumping ground.

"He's . . . not?"

"He's not." She made a note to herself to check Missing Persons. Maybe someone somewhere was looking for one of them.

"What a pity."

That brought Cyn's head up. "What does that mean?"

Ellis stared back blankly, as though she didn't have two working brain cells to rub together. "Well, if he was a mage, he'd be perfect, wouldn't he?"

"What does mageship have to do with anything?"

"You can't imagine the Marvelous Malva Men won't object." Feigning shock, the blonde pressed her hand to her chest, moss green eyes rounded, camel-long lashes nearly touching her plucked brows.

"Rio's my lover, not theirs. What they think doesn't enter into it." If only her brothers would keep their opinions to themselves. But that wasn't something Cyn was willing to blurt out for the consumption of the gossip mill.

She stacked the papers of the last file, aligning the edges with a *thump* of finality on her desk, her wretched back complaining at the sudden motion. Too bad that was all she could do to the Jane Doe cases for now.

Except for the sanitization and the lack of clothing or the remains thereof, nothing indicated foul play. They could have been three women who by sheer coincidence just happened to expire in the same general area. Their burial? From the descriptions of the skeletons' positions, they'd been shallow—too shallow to have been the remains of some forgotten graveyard—but nothing ruled out siltation due to the river's spring floods.

Unless the ME came up with more, she had other cases that

took priority. As intriguing as the case was, she couldn't drop everything else to focus solely on it.

Now, if only the rest of the world would quit sticking their noses into her life and let her do her job.

CHAPTER NINE

The universe must have heard Cyn's plea, because the hours passed without any further interruptions. But by noon, her spine was so stiff from bending over her desk that Cyn half expected to creak at the joints. Pain zinged up her back with every movement. She forced herself not to stagger as she made her way to Tactical for training. She had a rep to protect.

Luckily, the clinic was next door to her destination, and the duty healer was back from an early lunch. The healing itself took less than a minute—a matter of laying hands while the healer manipulated Cyn's personal energy back into balance. It took much longer for the healer to convince herself that there was nothing else wrong with Cyn's body. She poked and prodded Cyn all the while asking about previous treatments. When the tingling was over, the pain and bruising were gone, and the healer was smiling a little too knowingly—woman to woman—enough for Cyn to wonder if she'd picked up the orgastic aftershock the memory of Rio's care had evoked.

It left a bad taste in Cyn's mouth that she'd given in to convenience for so minor an injury. To her mind, such attentions ought to be limited to major trauma like arterial blood and guts and compound fractures. Unfortunately for Hardesty, her irritation gave her second thoughts about not shoving his balls to his ears.

The scheduled training included full-bore sparring, which suited Cyn just fine. She was in the mood to kick some newbie ass. Breathing in slowly—painlessly—she reined in her annoyance. Control was important. While she wanted to give Hardesty a reaming he wouldn't forget, sparring wasn't a battle to the death. Full-bore didn't mean no holds barred; certain spells were still off-limits, though not as many as civilians might imagine, since the lowlifes the tac teams handled didn't play nice.

Most of her teammates were present by the time Cyn arrived, Jung slipping in just as she opened her locker. Being almost late didn't help her mood, either.

"You okay?" Already suited up, Renfrew looked her over with a professional eye as she pulled on her sparring armor. While the tactical medics didn't practice combat magics, they trained with the rest of the team on defense.

"No problem." Cyn tightened the straps of her own vest to make sure it hung right. Essentially the duplicate of her body armor, the stiff suit weighed the same and had the same protective runes but not the ballistic ceramic plates that made the operational armor so expensive.

When the time came for sparring, Fernao paired her with Hardesty as she'd expected; he'd been using her to break in the newbie, to teach him to temper his gung ho approach with a bit of forethought. The matchup wasn't as lopsided as it might seem to a casual onlooker. Though Hardesty outweighed her by at least a hundred pounds, she had agility, guile, and experience on her side. Plus sheer bloody-mindedness.

They faced off on one of the blue mats in the hall like dozens of police mages had done in the history of the Tactical Unit. In armor, Hardesty looked twice his size, the black Kevlar aggrandizing his bulk, a human tank on steroids.

Both of them took their time testing the waters, circling each other, the wards active in the mat making her feet prickle in their boots. Neither one was in any hurry to go on the offensive—a success in her opinion—the newbie had learned that much from previous sessions. He moved easily, obviously having taken advantage of the healer's services himself.

Hardesty's first spells were probes. Nuisances, really. She didn't bother countering them, avoiding when she could, leaving them to the armor when she couldn't. That's what the runes on them were for. It left her free to watch his shoulders and eyes for the signals that telegraphed his intent, that revealed he'd committed to an attack.

Cyn rode the eddies of power as the other pairs clashed on the adjacent mats, her annoyance a distant presence at the back of her mind. Holding her wand steady, she called power to her, weaving it with her will, the customary elation that accompanied it a familiar hazard. She kept her acrobatics to a minimum, magic being unforgiving of untoward gestures; besides, that wasn't the purpose of today's session.

He frowned, florid splotches spreading across his broad cheekbones as she sidestepped his latest sally, this one a pulse twist—a minor pressure spell to throw an opponent off balance—less than a distraction to someone who knew how to compensate. Frustration was eating at him. He tried to close in, to corner her. Wind flurries. Flash bangs. Haze veils. But no fire spells. He hadn't used them much before, playing to his strengths; but now he avoided them altogether. There was something there, something she could exploit.

Sweat trickled down her neck. The power she'd called fought for release, attracted by the magics her teammates cast. The edges of her wand bit into her palm as she forced the recalcitrant energies to her will.

His eye twitched, a nervous tic she didn't think Hardesty knew he had. His right shoulder dipped. *Now.* The split-second warning gave her just enough time to complete the spell she held in readiness and disrupt his next.

Her turn.

Cyn didn't waste her focus on minor combat magics, letting loose with a forcebolt, then a fire whip as a chaser. Midlevel spells. Just a sharp one-two punch to test his reactions. She could have blitzed him with a major hex; she'd done so the first few times Fernao had paired her with Hardesty, when the newbie'd tried to tackle her. However, the purpose of the sparring match wasn't a decisive defeat but practice in the vagaries of battle.

This time she got a reaction. A small one. His eyes flared wide, suddenly showing stark whites—shock all out of proportion to her attack.

Aha! Fire.

Hardesty managed to interpose a shield, but she'd shaken his composure. His bobble was almost imperceptible, but she trusted her instincts.

Cyn seized the advantage and pressed the attack, lashing out again with a fire whip. Would he be able to recover? That was his challenge, and she wasn't in any mood to make it easy for him.

Wind swirled, short-lived. She siphoned its power into her own spell.

He ran at her, holding his shield before him like a battering ram. She lunged out of the way, blasting the newbie as he passed, then snapping her left leg up and back to plant a boot on his backside for good measure. He should know better than to try that with her.

Someone groaned from the sidelines as Hardesty stumbled on. The other matches must have ended, she realized, since the turbulence in the ambient magic was easing off. Not her concern. It only meant she'd have less difficulty controlling her spells.

Staggering to a halt, he spun around to face her, favoring the leg her blast had hit. Despite her kick, he managed to remain on his feet. He raised his wand, struggling for focus.

Time to force the pace.

Keeping her distance so the newbie couldn't use his reach or strength advantage, she snapped blue white fireballs at him, testing his nerve and distracting him while she completed the complex gestures for her next strike. She couldn't go toe-to-toe with him without losing; in hand-to-hand, speed and agility only went so far, so she had no intention of playing that game.

There. Magic flooded through her in an electric rush of power as she set the spell and released it. Another forcebolt, but this one with a twist.

He dove for the mat, dropping his guard as a vortex of roaring flames rushed at him. Didn't even attempt a counter.

Cyn whipped her wand to the floor, redirecting the attack after him as she set up her next strike.

Hardesty yelped.

Score!

Counterspells bloomed, extinguishing the flames.

She throttled the magic she'd tapped, power roaring through her body as it protested her restraint. *Breathe! Another.* Finally, she managed to ground the sparkling energy, feeling it drain through her soles, fatigue rushing in to fill the vacuum.

"Damn, Sarge, you're lethal today." Jung stared at her from the edge of the practice mat, his slanted black eyes the next thing to round.

Rao worked his jaw, a glum set to his mouth. "Jet let his fear do the thinking. All those deflagration spells are getting to him. She merely took advantage of it."

Cyn walked to the edge of the mat, then bowed to the middle. Ignoring Hardesty still sprawled where she'd caught him, she stepped off, accepted a towel from Moxham, and wiped the sweat dripping down her face. "Got it in one. Have to break him of that before it's too late."

"Good point," Fernao commented, joining them. "How'd you know?"

She shrugged, watching Keefe and Renfrew approach Hardesty out of the corner of her eye. "Just guessed. He's been nervy." She spread her fingers, then absently shook them, working out the tension of spellcasting. They were starting to ache, now that the match was over. Some of the midlevel spells were like pulling saltwater taffy without any candy to show for the effort.

The team leader nodded. "We'll work on it."

With the help of the medics, Hardesty finally stood up, looking none too steady on his feet.

"Doesn't look so gung ho now, does he?" Jung murmured.

"Now, now. You were in his shoes once," Fernao chided, though Cyn suspected he agreed with the sentiment.

"Oh, I thank the ancestors every night for Hawkins's promotion. If he hadn't been, I'd still be the newbie." This was accompanied by a sanctimonious expression on the countersniper's face that fooled no one.

Exchanging sardonic looks, Rao and Cyn bit back their amusement. Jung was bad enough without encouragement.

Fernao just hung his head, shaking it in mock despair. "Now, what I want to know is, how the hell did you do that flame attack?" he demanded, planting his fists on his hips as he stared at Cyn.

"Yeah!" Five other voices chorused.

She looked at Hardesty clinging to the shoulders of the medics on either side. "You okay?"

"Yeah," he repeated, shamefaced. "I thought I had it together, then you threw that last spell at me—and I lost it." He gave her an indignant glare. "What the hell *was* that? I've never seen anything like it."

"A balefire-forcebolt combo." Cyn shrugged, downplaying the result. "Just something I thought up."

"A *what*?"

"Balefire? You conjured balefire just like that?"

"Just thought up?"

"And combined them on the fly?"

The questions tumbled one over another in increasing volume. She blinked under the weight of their stares. "The theory is sound. No reason why it shouldn't work."

"Cyn, *balefire*?" Fernao's frown deepened. Balefire was military magic and incredibly destructive; of course, just because the military thought it up didn't mean it stayed with them. Just like most contraband, military magic had a way of turning up in the wrong hands. If there was a chance of crooks using balefire, it wouldn't hurt the team to face it in training and learn how to counter it.

With a smile, she waved away his concern. "I held back; don't worry." Many of the spells in the team's arsenal of combat magics were deadly if cast at full power; while balefire had notoriety, they used others of near-equal lethality in full-bore sparring all the time. It was nothing the hall's safety magics couldn't handle.

"Still . . ." His eyes turned distant, Fernao clearly giving his objection further thought. He apparently reached the same conclusion she had, since he didn't say anything more than "Huh."

"Can we block it?" A worried scowl settled on Danzinger's face. "I don't think the armor's rated for balefire."

The others followed his worried stare at Hardesty's vest. A few of its silver runes had tarnished, the first stage of burn-through.

She nodded. "Given sufficient power, the standard police-line ward used in crime scenes can withstand balefire."

"That's not something we can cast in a hurry," Rao pointed out. "The talisman might be standard issue for Patrol and CSU, but it's not part of our turnout gear."

"Anything else will only slow it." Crossing her legs, Cyn lowered herself to the floor, sitting tailor-style, since it looked like she was in for a long discussion. The team copied her, arranging themselves in a semicircle around her.

"Balefire is one of the harder spells to block," she continued. "You'd need absolute concentration to maintain a wand-cast ward." Precious few people were capable of such focus, and it was harder in the tac teams where eliminating situational awareness went against the grain, since it could get you or a teammate killed in combat.

The remainder of the session was monopolized by defensive techniques against balefire—at least the preliminaries. In their line of work, survival came first. Cyn found herself diagramming energy flows and finger positions on a whiteboard Danzinger scrounged up from somewhere. And if Fernao didn't like her taking the lead in training, he kept it to himself.

"Sergeant Malva? Cynarra?"

The unexpected use of her full name stopped Cyn in midstride on her way back to Homicide.

A muscular man in short sleeves and blue slacks that showed his physique to advantage stepped out of the human river flowing through the corridors of police headquarters. A few inches taller than her with auburn hair, brown eyes, and broad cheekbones, nothing about his average Caucasian features made him stand out from the other men walking around them. Certainly nothing to compare to Rio.

With her mind on the new case waiting back at her desk, it took Cyn a second to recognize Brett Hollingsworth, one of the senior crime scene investigators at Forensics, he of the reputation for tight-assed adherence to regulations. "Yes?"

"I heard our Jane Does landed on your lap."

That was an odd way of phrasing it, as if her getting the case was a stroke of good luck instead of standard procedure, but combined with the slight smile on his thin lips, she wasn't sure if it was just his version of a joke. Maybe he actually had a sense of humor. "You heard right."

She resumed walking. If he wanted to talk to her, he could keep up or schedule a meet.

Hollingsworth kept pace easily. "Couldn't help but be interested. Not every day we see something like this—unidentified." A slow swing of his head punctuated the straightforward statement with wonderment.

Ah, morbid professional curiosity. Well, she couldn't blame him. Such cases were extremely rare. She'd only heard of two others before, and that was during her stint with military police. Effective sanitization—to the point that forensic thaumaturgy couldn't establish identity—took specialized knowledge and probably extensive training. "Any thoughts?"

"Has to be a mage, naturally." He hooked his thumbs on his pockets, blunt fingers tapping his thighs in a complicated dance beat. "The way it was done—neat." There was an undertone of admiration to the observation.

She nodded absently in agreement. "Knows his work."

"You think it's a man?"

Cyn shot a sidewise glance at Hollingsworth and found him watching her intently, the gold glints in his irises giving him an aquiline look at odds with his average features. "Aren't most serial killers?"

"I'm sure you would know," he observed in a mild tone free of inflection and so devoid of nuance she wondered if it hid some criticism. Of course, she might simply be hypersensitive, too conscious of her status as the youngest sergeant on the force and female to boot.

It wasn't as though she didn't have cause.

But then she'd always been a suspicious bitch. Just another reason why she'd been drawn to Homicide.

CHAPTER TEN

The first thing Alex and Fotis did when Cyn opened her door to them the next Saturday was give her a searching once-over. She shouldn't have been surprised, since her middle brothers, Bion, Mitri, and Evan, had already stuck their heads into Homicide under one pretext or another during the week. Why would the eldest and youngest do any different? Still, their concern both warmed and irritated her. While she appreciated the care implicit in their scrutiny, did they really think a minor bump like that would break her?

Repressing her reaction, she stepped back to allow them inside, resigned to their presence.

Her brothers entered cautiously, their shoulders tense, bodies held in readiness. For what? The two were acting as if her apartment were hostile territory—or a fresh crime scene. Their gazes swept the small living room and kitchenette in one corner, lingering on the bathroom door and the divider screening off her neatly made bed.

She crossed her arms, waiting for them to finish their inspection. Something told her it wasn't the dust on her shelves that merited their attention.

Finally, Alex pulled out one of the chairs in her kitchenette, turning it around to straddle the seat. Fotis hitched his butt on the counter, slouching naturally as if his tension had never been.

Had they been looking for Rio? Or for evidence that he'd stayed over? As if she'd leave her sex life on display. They might overlook their lovers' discarded underwear lying around their apartments; she wasn't like that.

Miffed at their nosiness, Cyn snorted inwardly, tempted to clout them a good one. "Well?"

"Well, what?" Alex deposited a box on the table like a peace offering. "Here, have some," he insisted, folding back the lid to reveal more than a dozen doughnuts. "You look like you could use it."

Even that did little to soothe her, though she did pluck a gooey ring from the colorful mass of sugar overload. No point in letting the calories go to waste.

"Coffee?" Fotis asked hopefully, giving her wide blue puppy-dog eyes. The mooch.

"You know where it's kept," she pointed out around a mouthful of bribe, in no mood to cater to their whims. In her opinion, too many women fawned over her brothers, letting them get away with murder—figuratively speaking. It made them spoiled.

"Ah, c'mon, Cyn. Don't be that way."

She chewed stolidly, planting her butt firmly in the other chair across from Alex. Fotis took the hint with a long-suffering sigh of forbearance and made his own coffee, a weak brew by the anemic aroma that filtered into the room, but the practice would do him good.

"So, what's up with that guy?" Fishing a mug out of her dishwasher, her younger brother kept his eyes on the slowly filling carafe, transparent in his nonchalance.

"What guy?" Cyn asked, all innocence, not about to cooperate in the interrogation she could see coming at her.

"Rio, of course," Fotis blurted out, nearly spilling coffee on the counter as he filled his mug. "He's the guy you've been hanging out with since last year, right?"

"What do you see in him?" Alex demanded, setting an arm across his chest and hooking a hand on the opposite biceps, as he raised a doughnut to his mouth. "He drops in and out of your life, and you just let him."

And that was precisely how she liked it. Cyn shook her head, holding her silence. She hadn't realized they were keeping close tabs on her social life.

Irritation flashed over Fotis's face as he speared his fingers through the mop of black curls on his crown. "Okay, he's pretty, but a pretty boy like him wouldn't know anything about the job. He wouldn't know how to handle it."

Except Rio was black ops. He'd probably seen worse.

Crossing her arms, Cyn smirked, suppressing the annoyance she felt at Fotis's dismissive tone. *Pretty boy?* So what if Rio was gorgeous? There was more to him than that!

"You're just jealous. Rio could teach you a thing or two about pleasing women. *He* knows how to treat a woman right." It was a deliberate diversion. She didn't want to talk about her relationship with Rio, knowing her brothers wouldn't understand.

They'd had no difficulty getting what they wanted from the very start. Unlike her, they'd entered police academy straight out of college complete with both parents' blessings. She'd enlisted in the military to get out from under their mother's disapproval; that stint gave her a different perspective on certain things.

"Speaking of treating women right," Alex interjected between vicious chomps into his doughnut, "what was that about?"

"Huh?"

"That limo thing," Fotis explained, pausing with his mug

halfway to his lips, a furrow between his thick brows. "Does he do that all the time?"

Cyn couldn't prevent a blush, the memory of just how well Rio had treated her in the limo heating her body. "No, just for my birthday." Which everyone but he had forgotten. The fact that he'd made a point of celebrating it continued to give her the most absurd thrill.

Her brothers' faces went blank, the thought of making a lover's birthday extra special apparently a foreign concept. They exchanged glances, totally clueless, then shrugged.

"You need someone who'll be there when the times get tough," Alex opined with all the sagacity of his almost four years' seniority, just before licking orange frosting off his fingers. "That's more important than . . ." He flapped his hand in the air, as though he were shooing off a stray cat, clearly dismissing Rio's thoughtful gesture as idiosyncrasy.

She made a face at the eldest of her brothers. "Like you do?" she asked sweetly. Alex had made it clear on more than one occasion that he considered himself too young to settle down.

"No, like Bion does."

Cyn's mouth tightened at the indirect reference to their fecund sister-in-law, who'd met their late mother's exceedingly traditional standards of womanhood. Who probably wouldn't keep a doll collection like hers hidden like a guilty secret. Eleni had accepted Bion's wife with open arms.

"Think of it this way," Fotis interjected, "you won't have to worry about Dad going all, 'Cynarra Malva, *what* were you thinking?'" He pitched his voice an octave lower, mimicking Theron's growl.

Alex waved him aside impatiently, then added: "You need to be more careful."

"Says the one with the bomb squad." Cyn raised a skeptical brow at her older brother. "At least I get to fight back."

He scowled, resting his arms on the chair back and his chin

on his crossed wrists. "I'd be happier if you weren't halfway into Tactical. I heard what happened last Tuesday. Not good. You could have been killed." As the team leader of the Hazardous Device team, also known as the bomb squad, Alex was a full-time member of Tactical.

"Yeah, well, I told Hardesty you guys would make his life miserable, but he didn't seem to think much of that threat."

Rummaging through her kitchenette's cabinets, Fotis mumbled something scatological, his face darkening in affront. He found the triple chocolate chip cookies she'd bought the other day, extracting his find with a fierce smile that boded ill for Hardesty and her supply of nibbles.

Alex rolled his eyes. "And speaking of Tactical, that Rio of yours was talking with McDaniel earlier this week. What's a guy like him have to do with McDaniel?"

Rio's police business had been with Tactical's commander? Cyn licked chocolate frosting off her fingers as she pondered that tidbit.

"Well?"

"No law against that. Did you ask him?"

Her elder brother flushed guiltily.

Sunlight streamed through the high windows, bathing the walls a cheerful yellow and picking out isolated dust motes dancing in the air. Beyond the thick safety glass, downtown Aurora wavered through a heat haze, the clustered outlines of distant buildings turning indistinct. Indoors, however, was pleasantly cool, courtesy of air-conditioning powered by a spell beyond the scope of his college thaumaturgy courses.

The apartment was empty, as could only be expected with the ink barely dry on the lease. Rio hadn't even had time to ask his parents to forward the stuff he'd dumped with them over the years. All he had were the contents of the bags at his feet.

Leaning his back on the cool wall, he surveyed the wide-open space, unbroken by even a stick of furniture, his first apartment in years. It didn't look like much at the moment, though like a blank sheet of paper, the potential for better was there. Gray carpet, white walls, tall windows—those windows in what would be the living room swept to the upper level, giving him a bird's-eye view of downtown. He gave them an absent nod of approval. The kitchen behind him was efficiently laid out and stuffed with appliances, including the washer and dryer Cyn had seen fit to comment on.

His feelings at the change after years of living out of a suitcase—or a rucksack, which was more often than not what happened—were mixed. The prospect of shopping for things to fill the space brought a grimace to his mouth, though the chance to stamp his personality on his surroundings, perhaps adding something of him and Cyn here, made his heart skip with anticipation. He had a good idea what he wanted, but he wanted it with her.

He imagined his meager possessions spread out in the loft and started compiling a mental list of necessities, with a gun safe for his rifles at the very top. One thing was for sure, the furniture he bought would have to be sturdy; anything less wouldn't withstand the rigors of all the sex he planned on having with Cyn.

Pushing off the wall, Rio took his bags in hand and ran up the stairs in the living room two steps at a time, the thought of his Amazon helping him test furniture chasing away potential glumness. He laughed softly. Not that there was a chance in hell of convincing her to put out in the middle of a store—his cop would never do anything so scandalous—but a guy could dream! And if his imagination was a mite explicit, there was no law against that.

His phone rang in his pocket, a not-unexpected occurrence since he'd informed his parents of his plan for the day. He set down his bags to answer it, his train of thought automatically shifting to a less lascivious track.

"Well?" The question was so heavily laden with maternal expectation, he had to smile. He could imagine Siobhan's blue eyes sparkling with barely restrained curiosity like her asters heavy with morning dew and shimmering in sunshine.

"You can clear out the spare bedroom now, Ma."

"And not a moment too soon, Riordan. I was about to tell your da to build another room to house all your bric-a-brac," she commented with acerbic affection, her lilting accent softened by decades spent outside her homeland.

"No need for that," he assured her, grinning, though his father would have argued with him. There were few things Valentino Rafael enjoyed more than swinging a hammer, especially if Siobhan was working alongside. "I've got room to spare."

Rio reacquainted himself with said room while he passed on the details she needed to arrange the shipment of his worldly belongings and answered the tangents his mother always asked. The upper level comprised the bedroom overlooking the living room, the bathroom on one side, and a walk-in closet opposite. Its view was even better, truly that of an aerie. But it was just as empty as below.

That, too, would change.

Anticipation had his heart picking up its pace. Soon he'd have something tangible to offer Cyn, despite what her brothers might think. Something more than the occasional visit and a romp in bed. Something like what his parents had.

A life together.

He wanted forever.

Roll call took forever, even though Cyn did most of the talking. Today, she had less patience for procedure. Over the weekend the system had finally coughed up a response to her query from the Feds, and she was eager to see what she had. The e-mail waited in her in-box, the tiny blinking icon whetting her avid curiosity, but she hadn't had time to peruse its contents. Doling out the tips that had trickled in from the hotline became an exercise in restraint.

Even word from the night shift sergeant that the mage gang's latest heist had turned deadly, as Jung had predicted, evoked only a spike of concern followed by a measure of guilty relief she'd been off duty when it finally happened.

Hoping the e-mail meant a lead, she greeted the end of the routine meeting with delight. Unless he was some kind of prodigy, the killer of her Jane Does must have had practice in order to pull off the sanitization so flawlessly, so expertly. Surely there were more victims. Her mind ran wild with speculation as she headed back to her desk.

By the time Cyn got through the dryly worded e-mail, though, her mood was decidedly sour.

The news wasn't pretty. Psychically sanitized corpses were so rare that only three other cases were publicly known, all several years old and closed, the perpetrators either dead or behind bars. The Feds had nothing to offer on her Jane Does save professional interest.

Her contacts with military police were even less forthcoming. The two cases she remembered from her stint with the air force had been classified so deep the powers that be refused to divulge its code.

A dead end. Literally.

Cyn could only hope it didn't mean her killer was in the service.

More and more, it was beginning to look like she'd have to push for a facial reconstruction of the vics. With the psyprints inconclusive and precious few psychic traces to work with, the procedure was the last fallback for forensics. Unfortunately, it was as much art as science, and since there was little call for such services in most cases, the city would have to commission a state-accredited specialist. It could take weeks to bear fruit.

But with the sanitization pointing to foul play, she had a hunch Derwent would throw his weight behind her request.

Another avenue of investigation proved too fruitful. Missing

Persons turned up a surprising number of tall brunettes with light eyes in their twenties to early thirties reported as missing, and that was just for the current year, not even half over, and within the tristate area. She'd set the search limit at twelve years, based on forensics' best guesstimate for the earliest burial.

However, Cyn couldn't assume the women were locals, so she'd queried the national database, consequently increasing her load thirtyfold. Unfortunately, that was as far as she could go, pending a forensic reconstruction of the vics' features. The psy-prints were just too imprecise to use as a match.

With a heavy heart, she'd set aside the Jane Does' files, but they continued to nag at her, demanding she consider other avenues for investigation. *But what?* The former ownership and employee records of the sawmill hadn't resulted in any missing females in the correct age group.

Persistence was usually the name of the game when it came to investigating murder. As with almost everything related to police work—especially the paperwork required to keep the department running—sheer stubborn bullheadedness was needed to make any progress. Luckily, that was something Cyn had in plenty.

Unfortunately, it seemed to be something her latest trio of possible murder vics had, too.

Their vague images haunted her, as she slogged through the routine follow-ups for her other cases, hovering in the back of her mind like restless ghosts. Jane Does. Someone had worked hard to erase their identities. Thorough, cautious, controlled, and yet somehow personal. Their killer hadn't just taken their lives but had also stripped them of their names and histories, had made it as though they'd never been, then discarded them like so much trash.

Unable to deny the nagging itch in her head, Cyn returned to what she'd mentally dubbed "the dumping ground." Unlike most of the abandoned sawmill, the site bore signs of recent human activity. The mage gang hadn't touched the area, but the same couldn't be said for Forensics. The brush was cleared around a large trough roughly eight by twenty feet, scoured clean for any clue. Shoe prints radiated from it, trampled on freshly broken soil. Everything that could be overturned had been overturned; though replaced, the surrounding rocks and planks had an air of disarray.

What would Rio make of it? There she went again, thinking of him. Though it was a fair question. With his artist's eye—a hunter's eye—her lover didn't necessarily see the same things she did.

Did she really expect to find something that escaped Crime Scene's boys and girls? While the spell to detect human bones made their job a little easier, they didn't rely solely on magic, and Hollingsworth ran a tight ship.

But still . . .

Crouching at the edge of the excavation, she studied its crumbling walls bristly with hacked roots. The first skeleton had led to the discovery of the second and third, the latter pierced and held by the plant life. They'd been buried in a row, side-by-side, laid out neatly as if in a cemetery. Precisely spaced. Undisturbed by wildlife. And apparently as naked as the day they were born—nothing besides the bones had been found.

It pissed her off.

Cyn stood up, conscious of the forest pressing at the edges of the clearing. What had drawn the murderer here? Was the sawmill significant or simply convenient? Had he driven up or taken the river, which was navigable for several miles farther? Was he connected to the mage gang, or was it serendipity that had them using the same site?

So many questions and no answers. She sighed. She was spinning her mental wheels, wasting time better spent on other cases or on administrative work. She had no names, not even a sure crime, except for the illegal disposal of human remains.

Just three mysterious deaths.

And the certainty in her gut that the sanitization was part of the MO of a serial killer.

———⟞∞∞⟝———

Cyn was preoccupied over lunch, paying her food little of the attention Rio found so damnably arousing. She'd received the news of his change of address with a polite show of interest, but it was obvious to him her mind was elsewhere. He had to admit that his own wasn't entirely focused on her, either. Halfway through the meal, he'd developed a mental itch behind his neck and couldn't pinpoint the cause, like a gnat he couldn't swat.

He persevered, maintaining his air of normalcy, presenting a box of gooey fudge like the treat he knew it to be. He'd intended it as a surprise for later, but it was a bribe she rarely indulged in, and he knew she couldn't resist.

"That's Double Jeopardy!" Cyn stared at the dark squares, the prospect of dessert helping her throw off her distraction.

"Got it in one." He smiled, reassured by her hedonic voracity. The day she had no appetite for sweets would probably be an emergency. Everything was back to normal.

A flash of color out of the corner of his eye made his pulse skip.

Rio stole a glance at the other diners on the patio, wondering what had once again set off his hindbrain. The vague alarm marred his enjoyment of Cyn's voluptuous pleasure as she consumed dessert. It wasn't so much life-threatening danger as an inkling of jeopardy, a feeling of exposure, the need to get under cover. Nothing he saw explained the twitching of the back of his neck. No unattended packages. No unexplainable shadows. No suspicious-looking characters with mysterious bulges. No subsonic tremors or prickles of magic.

And Cyn didn't evince any concern, so the latter was definitely out of the question. She'd surely sense that before he would.

The clinking of metal on china continued to fill the air, blending pleasantly with the ebb and flow of conversations and the birdcalls from the park. The so-civilized normalcy of it all mocked his battle-honed instincts. It wasn't as though he had point and was responsible for picking a safe path through a minefield for his team.

Perhaps he just hadn't fully acclimated to civilian life? Or had he gotten so hooked on the adrenaline rush that he was dreaming up excuses to justify feeling it?

"You're not eating. Something wrong?" Cyn eyed him curiously as she set down her glass.

"I wish there were," he confessed ruefully, feeling his cheeks warm as he turned his attention back to his plate. Then he wouldn't feel sheepish at jumping at shadows.

"Hmmm?" She stared at him, full lips puckered around the tines of her fork, an erotic picture reminding him of his new priorities.

He exhaled sharply, trying to dismiss his unease. "Guess I'm not quite comfortable with the easy life yet. Takes some getting used to."

Try though he might, Rio couldn't recapture his enjoyment of time spent with Cyn. His gut continued to nag him, like an itch between the shoulder blades. By the time they finished their meal and stood to leave, his mood had gone south. And instead of merely stepping off the patio to cut through the park, he followed Cyn to the door leading back inside, his instincts urging him to watch her back.

Another flash.

There it was again.

Like a ghost, a man's image floated before him, a reflection off the bakery's picture window dappled with sunshine. Bright hair, fair skin, his strangely familiar features wrapped Rio in troubling déjà vu.

Rio touched Cyn's elbow as he reached past her to open the

door. "That guy by himself over there in the corner"—he rolled his eyes in the direction he meant—"do you know him?"

She peeked over his shoulder. "Hollingsworth? He's a crime scene tech. Why?"

He stole a last look at the man consuming his lunch in blissful ignorance of the disquiet his presence engendered in Rio. Nothing in his demeanor distinguished him from the other civilians who patronized Just Desserts. "I thought I recognized him from somewhere."

"Police headquarters?"

It was possible, yet somehow that didn't sound quite right. Trying to throw off the vague unease that continued to hover at the edge of his awareness, Rio gave Cyn a self-deprecating smile. "That must be it."

Just Desserts' proximity to police headquarters was one of the reasons he and Cyn met there so frequently for lunch. It was only logical that other cops would patronize it for similar reasons. So why did his gut object to the presence in the restaurant of a crime scene tech to whom he'd never been introduced?

CHAPTER ELEVEN

Eagerness sped Cyn's feet, cutting minutes from her original estimate. This was the first chance she'd had to take advantage of the location of Rio's new apartment. Work had kept her away, so she hadn't seen him for a few days, and after the madhouse that was the department this morning, she needed an hour to herself, personal time to let off some steam. With her body aching for her lover, the ride up in the elevator was interminable.

Inwardly she had to laugh at her impatience. She was like an addict craving another fix. A mature, responsible woman—and a cop, at that! If her brothers knew, she'd never hear the end of it.

Though if Eleni Malva had lived to see her . . .

She shrugged off the thought of her mother's hypothetical approval, unwilling to spoil her happiness. Best to let sleeping dogs lie.

"Rio?" Heart pumping with eagerness, she shut the door to the apartment and engaged the lock by reflex, her thoughts centered on making the most of her short lunch break.

"Here." Her lover's voice came from the kitchen, along with the smell of detergent.

Cyn rounded the dividing wall to find him standing in front of the washing machine, wearing only his pants and apparently about to lose those as well. From the full load she could see, he'd run out of clean clothes and was forced to do laundry.

"Excellent timing." He grinned at her, his hands busy unbuttoning his fly, leaving it to gape promisingly. "You're just in time for me to demonstrate my domestic skills."

"Oh." Her racing libido came to a crashing halt heavy in her belly, tangled in disappointment. While she approved of his undress, he clearly had other things in mind.

But then he reached for her. "Here, let me have that."

Rio made short work of stripping Cyn of her clothes, reducing her to the wand in its holster on her forearm and the bloodstone ring on her hand, then finished off with his pants and the gun in its holster strapped to his ankle to stand before her unabashedly naked.

She couldn't protest, since that was precisely how she wanted him. Golden skin with nary a tan line, smooth chest, ripples of sleek muscle flowing one into another, the dark trail of hair that started below his navel leading her eyes inevitably to the heavy cock framed by strong thighs. Under her avid gaze, it hardened, rearing up straight and proud, thick and flushed, the vein on its underside pulsing.

The sight made her wet. A shiver of desire tingled through her in electric response, sparking her nerves with need. If Ellis and the other women on the force knew what they were missing, she'd have a fight on her hands. "Wha—?"

Rio dumped the whole pile of laundry in the washing machine and started it churning before she got out more than that, invisible eddies of power breezing past her into the appliance. "See how convenient it is?"

Despite the potent distraction before her, Cyn stared aghast at her now-wet clothes. "I don't have time . . ." She'd be late getting back. As much as the L-T might condone her tardiness, *she'd* know she'd abused Derwent's trust, something she preferred to avoid, conscious as she was of her status as one of the youngest sergeants on the force. Worse, her squad would suspect and might try to pull the same on her.

"Don't sweat it." He gave her a complacent smile, a twinkle in his dark chocolate eyes. "It'll be done before we are."

Just like that, he derailed her objections.

Cyn's incorrigible libido leaped at the hint of pleasures to come. "That fast?"

"You mean you don't think I can last that long?" Rio raised a brow at her as he pulled her into his arms, his big body like a heater set on high, nudging her to the melting point. "I'm hurt." His artist's hands drifted down and squeezed her butt.

Alarm flared. He couldn't mean . . . ? Her heart jittered, torn between excitement and trepidation. If he intended to stretch out their lovemaking, she'd definitely have difficulty getting back on time.

He chuckled. "It's alright. I won't make you late."

Cyn scowled at him in mock disapproval, her arms rising to curl around his neck. "Tease." Pulling his head down, she pressed her body against him, delighting in his male vigor. He had no give in him—literally and figuratively. He didn't back away from her demands and wasn't daunted by her strength.

Pure seductive confidence.

So different from her previous lovers, they of her short-lived, much-regretted affairs. Ordinary civilians who hadn't understood her calling.

Here was a man who didn't mind that she was a cop.

That got to her faster than anything, turned her insides liquid with desire.

Rio took her mouth, the tip of his tongue tracing the seam of her lips, coaxing them open with gentle flicks. Her Latin lover had more smooth moves on him than she could count.

Sighing, she welcomed him, her body softening in readiness. She met his probe with one of her own, initiating a carnal duel. The taste of coffee greeted her questing tongue, the smoky flavor adding a bittersweet aspect to the intimate exchange.

He growled approval, his fingers digging into her butt and squeezing gently as he lifted her onto her tiptoes and up against his cock.

As if drawn by that scorching contact, heat pooled in her belly, building steadily and stealing her breath. She could feel her channel moisten, her folds prickling as they swelled and spread in readiness. Though the outcome was certain, she never tired of it. Couldn't imagine ever tiring of it.

All that male power.

All hers.

For her pleasure.

She pressed in, rubbing herself against his thick, inspiring length. Velvet and satin. Hard muscle and thin skin and that delicious confidence.

All man.

Rio.

Arching into her caresses, he groaned softly. "You're in a hurry today." He planted kisses along her neck, each one sending delight zinging unerringly to her core.

Need blazed, her nipples tightening into aching nubs. Cream trickled down her thighs, twin lines of heat that scented the air with her arousal. How could he be so controlled when she felt like she was coming apart?

Cyn clung to his shoulders and tilted her head to give him better access. "You haven't seen hurry yet," she countered, hooking a leg over his hip. The result was an improvement, though less than perfect. Her swollen folds grazed his length, but not the tip, delicious heat on her cream but no penetration. Remembering how he felt inside her, she yearned for more.

"Patience." He rocked his pelvis, his cock gliding over her slick flesh—but no deeper. He repeated the tormenting motion several times, adding a flourish to his thrusts now and then, obviously in no hurry to enter her.

If Rio intended to drive her out of her mind, he was off to a great start. Any more of that, and she'd come before he even entered her.

She growled in frustration. As good as the intimate stroking felt, she wanted him inside her, fucking her for everything he was worth—and that was a lot, as she well knew. The hunger that had built up in her rush from the station was boiling over, scalding hot and demanding appeasement. "Quit fooling around!"

"What a demanding woman." Rio grinned down at her, his brown eyes sparkling with deviltry. "Your wish is my command."

At his urging, she hooked her other leg over his hip as well, locking her ankles behind him, supported by his hands under her butt. With her higher position, his blunt cock head nudged her slit. *Finally!* She moaned as he worked his cock in with short jabs that lit fireballs in her womb. This was what she'd been craving all morning; the seductive knowledge that she'd have it come lunch break had had her nearly squirming at her desk, the promise of a little afternoon delight distracting her from her cases.

He delved into her steadily, his hard length rubbing her channel, sweet friction promising more to come. She bore down on him, glorying in the pressure of his cock inside her.

"Holy—" He staggered, his back hitting the wall.

The jolt drove him impossibly deeper.

"*Damnú*, you feel so good." Rio panted, the warm puffs tickling her ear.

"So do you." Cyn clenched her inner muscles around him again, squeezing him intimately. He was so thick inside her, stretching her channel with delicious power. She could feel every inch of him, the flare of his cock head rasping against her tender membranes. There was so much of him, filling her to the brim and reaching halfway to her heart.

But she wanted more, wanted him moving inside her the way only he could.

Knowing Rio wouldn't let her fall, she flexed her legs, lifted herself up to draw him out, then lowered herself back down, trusting him to bear her weight. *Sweet glory!* Fire surged through her veins, borne on a wave of dark delight.

She did it again, riding him faster. Her position ground her clit between them, brought amazing pressure on her mound. Her heart thundered in her ears, a call to action she couldn't ignore. She pumped faster, chasing the orgasm she could sense gathering in the horizon.

"*Hechicera*." He clamped his hands on her hips, slowing her rhythm. He bucked under her, his hips rocking to a beat of his own. "Slow down."

"No." Cyn raised herself again, continuing to ride him even when he knelt, rising and falling on his hard flesh in a single-minded drive for completion. Need coalesced into a white-hot brand searing her body.

He turned and laid her out on her back, his big body blocking the light.

"Rio!" She cried his name in protest, clawing at his shoulders, fisting her hands in his hair for fear he'd slow down. She couldn't wait! Couldn't bear it if she had to wait.

Desire boiled through her body, impatient for release, a geyser building up to eruption. Soon.

"It's okay. I can do you better this way." He surged between her thighs, pumping deep, steadily in and in, then out and out, until he was almost loose, then returning. Over and over again. Driving her breathlessly, inevitably toward glorious release. "That's it. Go for it, *mo muirnín*," he crooned, each syllable a caress.

"Harder!"

He took her at her word, stepping up his pace to near violence. Short, battering thrusts that forced the air from her lungs and jolted her body, melting all thought. Again and again and . . .

A slow triple beep sounded.

She ignored it, the tight coil of need fracturing before his pounding encouragement. All her senses centered on the conflagration building between her thighs, her whole world narrowing to that one point.

And again.

Yes. Please!

She screamed in relief as a whirlwind of torrid sensation rampaged through her body. Heat and pleasure and lightning combined into an overwhelming cascade of rapture. Her climax shattered her senses into a hundred thousand fragments that went on and on, an endless torrent of ecstasy sweeping her in a tidal wave of abandon.

The loss of Rio's weight on her roused Cyn from her stupor. She opened her eyes to find him unloading the washing machine as though he hadn't just screwed her boneless. Her lover was an amazing man.

Lying on the floor, she watched him transfer damp clothes to the dryer with efficient, practiced motions and marveled at his energy. She herself was still floating from an excess of endorphins, spent from her release. How he could even lift a finger, she had no idea. "You're unbelievable."

"How so?" Rio asked with his broad back to her, his tight buns flexing as he bent and shifted, muscles moving in perfect harmony.

"You can move," Cyn sighed, the answer taking her last drop of energy.

He chuckled, a low male sound full of wordless delight and that dark knowledge that he'd satisfied his woman.

Her body thrilled to his elation, blood rushing back south to swell her tender folds. Her thighs clenched reflexively at the exquisite sensation. How could she want him again so soon? But she did.

Not wanting to add to his already ebullient confidence, Cyn rolled over to hide her response, grinding her mound against the floor to soothe the renewed ache. "You were wrong."

"About what?"

"You said that would be done before we were."

The dryer beeped as Rio pushed some buttons, apparently ignoring her statement. Then he gave her an all-too-knowing grin over his shoulder. "We're not done yet. I've been saving up."

She had to laugh at his mock earnestness. This was the way they were supposed to be, lighthearted, just fun and games. Today and now, leaving tomorrow to take care of itself.

With a final beep, the dryer started.

Cyn's nerves prickled as ambient magic swirled toward the appliance, drawn by its activated spells. Her womb clenched in response, triggering another spate of orgastic aftershocks through her body.

"Let's get you up here. The floor can't be all that comfortable." Rio picked her up and sat her on top of the shuddering appliance, the easy strength inherent in the feat overshadowed by the sweet chaos he unleashed.

Being so close to the focus of power was carnal overload. The vibration under her legs only magnified the electrifying sensations tripping along her nerves. "Oooh!"

Smiling, he stepped between her thighs and pulled her forward to meet his thrust, his stiff cock still wet with her juices. "Now, where were we?" He worked his way deeper into her swollen channel, burying himself to the hilt. "Oh, yeah. Here." Pulling her thighs wide, he proceeded to pound into her, resuming the wonderfully brutal shafting that had sent her senses reeling.

She cursed fervently, unmindful of what she said. He felt so much larger against her sensitized flesh. With him holding her open, she couldn't control how much of him she took—and she loved it.

Rio stormed her senses, a whirlwind of furious pleasure, of power unleashed. Slamming into her over and over. Demanding everything she had to give. Demanding surrender.

Cyn met him, exulting in the violence of his possession. Strength for strength. Need for need. Claim for claim. Here was a man who took her as she was.

Her world came down to him and the wildfire he conjured in her veins.

"Oh, man. Oh—" She gulped for breath, the ineffable pressure building inside her reducing her to incoherence. "Rio!" Her shout rang out in the sudden silence broken only by a quiet beeping.

"See? It's done already." He rode her sweet spot, wringing yet more pleasure from her willing body.

Cyn clung to him, helpless to resist his masterful assault on her senses. Especially here, he knew what she enjoyed and exploited that knowledge ruthlessly. She gave herself up to the tempest, riding the wild man between her thighs until the storm broke in an abrupt explosion of raw ecstasy.

Rio came just as she did, driving deep and shouting her name in the throes of rapture, the heat of his release fanning the flames of her orgasm. She'd missed this: the power of him frenzied and out of control, going wild in her arms and dropping all masks.

When she finally returned to herself, she wasn't sure she'd survived the experience. Her thoughts refused to hang together, wandering off into a muddle. Holy hell, she'd never imagined lunch could be so . . .

"Hechicera mía."

The murmured phrase sounded awfully possessive, but she was too busy trying to force her brain to calculate whether she'd have time for a quick shower after she recovered and still make it back to the station on time. She'd have to run, but it didn't matter. With the way her body was humming, nothing could ruin her day.

———— ⟨∞⟩ ————

Out of respect for Cyn's schedule, Rio refrained from joining her in the shower. It was enough to know she was here, that she'd made the effort to spend this time with him and in doing so, risked censure for tardiness.

Leaning against the sink, he took her carnation scent into himself, breathed it in with simple pleasure. She'd found the soap he'd bought her—that specialty one she liked so much—and it had been a pain and a half figuring out where she bought it without her knowing. It smelled different on her, something about the combination of its perfume and her essence that produced olfactory magic.

He didn't have much time to savor the scent though. She was done in a matter of minutes. *Oh, well. There will be other times.* That certainty had him smiling involuntarily.

"Keep your hands to yourself, buster. I don't like that look on your face," Cyn warned as she stepped out of the shower, a warrior goddess come to life. As she reached for a towel, she pulled her hair out of the knot she'd twisted it into to keep it dry on top of her head, leaving it to slither free and drape around her shoulders in waves of black silk. The gesture, so unself-consciously feminine, natural as breathing, nearly lost him his train of thought.

"Just waiting for my turn."

"Uh-huh." Her gaze dropped to below his waist, where his cock had bestirred itself to show proper respect. "Right." Her vigorous application of terry cloth to body made her high breasts jiggle enticingly.

"So sue me. I'm a guy. We think about sex at least every other second." Rio passed her her freshly laundered clothes. The very domesticity of taking them out of the dryer had given him a thrill that even cleaning the evidence of their activities off the appliance hadn't squelched—far from it, in fact. He was careful to keep that emotion from showing; any hint of it was bound to send her running in the opposite direction.

"Two brains and only one track," Cyn muttered to her towel.

"Complaining?"

She snorted, failing to hide a delighted smirk as she finished drying herself.

He watched his lover pull on her panties. Plain white cotton tap pants, her underwear was deceptively utilitarian. Stealthily seductive. He knew she liked them for the lack of constriction, but he loved their loose fit, the way the soft fabric draped over her ass, the artless sensuality of it.

Whatever he had to do to convince Cyn of the rightness of his decision, he'd do it—anything to keep what they had.

"There you are." The greeting snapped Cyn out of autopilot and back to the mob that was shift change. Crisp midnight blue cotton slacks filled her vision, matched by knife-sharp creases and mirror-shined black leather.

Cyn looked up quickly, surprised to see Bion immaculate in all his starched, start-of-shift splendor. The second eldest of her brothers was the one she saw the least because of their clashing schedules. Besides his assignment to the river patrol, he was a part-time member of Tactical, on the swing shift with Hawkins, while she was day shift. Too, she preferred not to visit him at home in order to avoid alone time with her so-perfect sister-in-law. To be here now, he'd made an unprecedented effort to come to headquarters early and track her down.

Giving in to the inevitable, she stepped out of the main flow, forcing a smile of welcome on her face. "Hey, what's up?" Hopefully the frown he wore was due to one of their brothers, not her nieces or—heaven forbid—his wife.

"I've been hearing talk."

Her stomach sank. "Talk? About what?"

His gray eyes narrowed in irritation. "Don't play dumb, Cyn. That guy you're seeing. It sounds like you're getting serious."

"What makes you say that?"

"I have my sources."

She mentally flipped through the usual suspects and took a stab. "Evan."

Bion's wince confirmed her guess, but he forged on, relentless in his self-appointed mission. "You were seen checking out apartments together. I'd call that *getting serious*. Well, are you?"

Cyn bit her lip, accustomed to candidness with her brothers, but normally they didn't discuss her love life. She wanted to deny everything. *It's just fun and games, right?* Unfortunately, something inside disagreed, wishing she could have Rio for always.

For lack of an answer, she continued heading for the doors.

"Cyn?" Bion shot a glance at her across his shoulder as he matched her pace. "It's a simple question."

"He just wanted my opinion."

"Uh-huh."

She gritted her teeth at the pronounced doubt in his voice. "He did." She'd ended up seeing the inside of five potential rentals over that weekend, though none of the others were as convenient as the loft; she could see its high-rise through the doors, towering above the trees in the park.

The warmth of the afternoon came as a rude slap after the spell-maintained coolness of police headquarters. Ignoring the change in temperature, Cyn descended the front steps in double time to get away from the crowd and likely gossipmongers, and made for the park's shade.

Gripping her elbow, Bion stopped her short of the crosswalk. "That's the first step, you know. He's reeling you in."

"He has to catch me first." She shrugged free of his hold,

wishing her brother hadn't chosen to pursue the matter. Her irrepressible libido insisted on remembering the numerous times Rio had caught her . . . and what followed.

"Well, you don't look like you're trying that hard to avoid being caught."

She nearly blushed at Bion's phrasing, which echoed her thoughts. Luckily, no one else appeared to be within hearing range. She glared at him instead, fed up with his meddling. "So what if I enjoy his company? It's great sex, fantastic sex. What does that have to do with anything?"

He frowned at her bluntness. "You need someone who can protect you—or at least understand what you're doing—not some pretty boy civilian who can barely cast a spell."

Pretty boy? Anger stirred at hearing Bion echo Fotis. The twins must have shot their mouths off at some fraternal caucus she hadn't been invited to.

Cyn speared her fingers through her hair and fisted them, the minor pain when she pulled doing little to relieve her irritation. Bion had always been the most traditional of her brothers, but he'd never extended his babying to her before. "What is it with you and Alex these days? You're starting to sound like Eleni did." And her contentious maternal relations were something Cyn didn't want to go into, years too late to change the outcome.

"Call it hindsight. Now that I'm a father, I see things differently." Bion's smile turned crooked, his smoky gaze locked on her clenched hand and the white strands trapped there. "You nearly died that time. We were children then and didn't understand, but if that happened to one of my girls, I'd have freaked out. It's no wonder Mom did."

She grimaced at the reminder of the childhood accident that had landed her in the hospital and lit off a silent war that had ended only with their mother's premature death. They said she must have brained herself on one of the pavers in the garden. Cyn didn't remember the specifics, only that she'd been roughhousing with her brothers as usual; after healing, the hair on the spot she'd hit grew out white, and for a while Mitri, Evan, and Fotis teased her about having a head as hard as a rock. But Eleni Malva had gone overprotective with a vengeance, demanding that Cyn limit herself to "ladylike" activities. Cyn had had to join the air force to become a cop. By the time she got out, it had been too late to mend fences, even if she'd wanted to.

"We just want you safe—or at least as safe as we can get you." Her brother shrugged. "Since there's no way we can talk you into quitting the force—and if you did, I know a few cops who'd want my head—that means a mage for a boyfriend."

Except Cyn didn't want a mage. She wanted Rio, who was black ops and probably better trained to protect himself than her brothers were. And who—like Bion and the majority of the men in their dangerous line of work—would want a feminine, compliant, domesticated woman if he was really serious about settling down.

But that was her mother's and sister-in-law's path.

Not hers.

She'd been trying to avoid thinking of that.

CHAPTER TWELVE

A quick forcebolt disarmed the last of the perps, small-time thugs trying their hand at armed robbery. It was another straightforward mission, just the latest magical assault in a spike of copycats inspired by the success of the mage gang, but the almost daily callouts were starting to wear on the team, and the extended shifts they were pulling didn't help.

As a result, frustration had Cyn throwing more power into her spell than was perhaps absolutely necessary. The blast went on to knock the perp into a wall; if she rattled some teeth and brain cells, that was just too bad. Maybe it would shake some sense into him.

Even if she'd done worse, no one would blame her. After one of the more violent copycats had landed four of third shift's tac team on medical leave, the brass wasn't taking chances. Tactical had orders to use maximum force as warranted.

This was warranted.

While Hardesty secured the thug she'd disarmed, Danzinger

double-checked the rest of the team, then signaled all clear. They left cleanup to Patrol, more than ready to call it a day, Cyn especially, since it was technically her day off.

It was a quiet team that piled into the van with none of the usual postmission euphoria. She caught Fernao studying them with furrowed brows, no doubt worried about how they were holding up; she would be, in his shoes. They were due for a break, but the tempo of callouts made one unlikely, not while third shift was undermanned and off the roster. Until the next group completed the tactical training course, they were stuck pulling long hours.

Once they were back at headquarters stripping off body armor, Danzinger apparently took it upon himself to lift the team's spirits—or at least provide a temporary distraction. Gripping the ends of the towel slung around his neck, he leaned on the bank of lockers, looking smug. "Brett's been asking about you." He angled his head toward Cyn, making it clear he was addressing her.

Brett . . . Hollingsworth?

She frowned at the assistant team leader, taking in his shit-eating grin with puzzlement. "Asking what?"

Danzinger gave a careless shrug. "Oh, likes, dislikes, favorite drink, that kind of stuff."

Peeling off her heavy Kevlar vest, she narrowed her eyes at him, in no mood to be the butt of some joke. "And this amuses you because . . . ?"

Around them the rest of the team divested themselves of their gear, the faster few already headed for the showers. The others dawdled within earshot.

"It's unprecedented, that's why. Brett's never even hinted at any interest in a woman—and here he is, asking about you," Danzinger practically crowed. If his grin got any bigger, his head would split into two. Which wouldn't necessarily be a bad thing, in Cyn's opinion.

She had to stare, unable to credit what she was hearing. "Are we talking about the same guy? Tight-assed CS tech? Lives for his job? That Hollingsworth?"

"Hey, Brett's a great guy." Danzinger's protest was muffled by the towel as he wiped sweat off his face. "So, are you going to give him a chance? A night out on the town?"

Cyn shook her head in exasperation at the sophomoric glee in his voice as he swayed in place, miming slow dancing. "My guy wouldn't approve." Her phrasing gave her a pause. She'd never quite thought of Rio in those terms before, as hers with all the permanence it implied. In the past, they were just . . . not fuck buddies, but not exactly steadies, either. Whenever Rio had left on one of his missions, he never promised to return to her—he couldn't—and suspecting what she did of his line of work, she hadn't expected him to make such a commitment. Now, she couldn't deny that the situation had changed. While they were together, Rio really was her guy.

Her rejoinder wiped the amusement from the assistant team leader's face. He froze, mouth shriveled up as though he'd bitten into a lemon. "You mean that pretty boy Rafael."

Irritation flared at the obvious disdain. *What's up with that?* It wasn't as if the assistant team leader were one of her brothers; he wasn't even what she'd consider a close friend. So where did he get off, sticking his nose into her love life?

Fernao and Jung hung back, with Moxham just beyond them. Everyone else had already left for the men's showers. That didn't make this discussion any less public. Gossip, like coffee, was the lifeblood of the department.

Still clad in black body armor, Danzinger crossed his arms, his pose bringing to mind a bad-tempered fire hydrant. "Just what do you see in that pretty boy anyway? Besides his looks, that is. He's a civilian. He's no mage—"

"He's no boy, either, I assure you." She scowled, irritated on Rio's behalf by their continued use of the term, especially since she suspected that in a straight-up one-on-one fight, Rio would flatten

Danzinger's ass, mage or not. Fotis had a lot to answer for, for spreading that term around. "Where does mageship come into it?"

The assistant team leader rolled his eyes at her. "Rafael wouldn't understand the demands of the job."

Cyn straightened her back to look down at him, taking full advantage of the one-inch difference in their heights. "And Hollingsworth would?" Tempted to rip into the sanctimonious ass, she snapped flat her vest, the *crack* of stiff Kevlar failing to relieve her irritation. "If you like him so much, *you* date him."

In the stunned silence, she hung the armor in her locker, then stalked off for the women's showers, deliberately turning her eyes from Fernao's wince.

"Me!" Danzinger eventually sputtered behind her, sounding like a tea kettle about to explode.

She ignored him, furious at his interference. Who did he think he was, looking down his nose at Rio? He had no right. So he didn't approve. He could stuff his disapproval and smoke it for all she cared.

A brisk shower failed to cool Cyn's temper. The sight of Rio perched on one of the granite planters in front of headquarters, scribbling on his pad as he patiently waited for her, only fanned her indignation hotter. Cops eyed him with casual dismissal, men who should know better; the women who gave him a second glance clearly had sex on the brain. Several of the latter had their noses pressed to the windows very much like kids outside a candy shop. People saw his face and body and looked no further.

Sunlight played on his dark hair and across his broad shoulders. It must have dazzled supposedly trained observers that his vigilance and ready posture escaped their notice.

He wore cargo pants, soft khaki that she knew cupped his backside faithfully, then turned baggy, hiding corded thighs and probably loose enough to high-kick in. But the muscle shirt bared biceps that took serious effort to develop; he didn't get those lounging around a gym.

Pretty boy, ha! How could they be so blind? And why should anyone object to her relationship with him simply because he wasn't a mage?

"Hey." With a warm smile of welcome, Rio stood up, tucking his pencil and pad into one of his pants' many pockets, bringing with him a whiff of gunpowder, there and gone like faint cologne. "Today that bad?"

She shrugged, downplaying her bad mood. "Just long. You know how it is."

A troubled expression flashed across his face as he turned away, his eyes tracking the pedestrian traffic flowing around them. "Yeah, now that you mention it, I do." Evidently he'd noticed the looks he'd been getting, too.

Ignoring the rapt attention of the dozens of women lining the windows of police headquarters behind them, Cyn studied the red muscle shirt that displayed his well-developed arms to perfection. The day was more than warm enough to justify it, but she suspected comfort wasn't the point—or at least not the only point. "That only makes it worse, you know."

His lips quirked, the sardonic gleam in his dark chocolate eyes confirming her guess. "If they're going to dismiss me as just another pretty face, they might as well add a nice body to it."

Rio draped his right arm around her shoulders. For all that the warm weight felt natural, the casual gesture was probably a flag for bull-baiting.

She couldn't deny he had basis for his resentment. Her brothers couldn't be bothered to give him the benefit of the doubt. And now her teammates were sticking their oars in. He was due.

Giving in to instinct, Cyn hooked her hand on his waist and was surprised to find the small of his back devoid of weapons. Rio must have tucked his gun somewhere else today. She allowed herself to lean into him. It might look unprofessional, but she'd clocked off for the day. And darned if she didn't want all those slavering women to know she had prior claim, no matter how temporary it might be. With her body pressed to his side, it should be obvious to anyone paying attention that they were a couple. And if it communicated to her lover that she didn't share her brothers' opinion of him, all the better.

"How was shift?" Rio tugged a damp strand of hair. "Another callout?" Clearly he'd deduced a slow day wouldn't have required a shower.

"A bunch of small-time copycats, this time."

Walking with him like this held an appeal all its own. With every step, the companionable brush of their hips and thighs was innocent foreplay, made more titillating for being in public. The hard wall of his torso brushing the side of her breast recalled more intimate liberties.

Cyn swallowed against a burst of arousal, suddenly impatient to have him to herself. She wanted to forget about mage gangs and serial killers and crimes of passion that had nothing to do with jumping Rio's bones right here in the parking area. She needed a reminder of all the good that was in the world—and intended to get it as soon as possible.

Thank goodness Rio had decided to take the loft.

By the time they'd covered the intervening blocks to his condo, her libido was simmering, kept on a slow boil by the innocuous contact between their bodies. He didn't do anything overt, but even the weight of his hand on her shoulder took on erotic significance during the long walk, the subtle shifts in pressure of his fingers playing her like a fine instrument. The inevitable delay to deactivate his wards sent frissons of anticipation tingling through her body, the waves homing in on her nipples and clit, like a neural stim spell set to pleasure.

The emptiness of the lower level barely registered, Cyn was that aroused. She raced him up the stairs, determined to use a bed for once. But the sight that met her eyes brought her up short. She stopped so suddenly that Rio almost ran into her and had to wrap his arms around her to keep from falling over.

A ragged sleeping bag was spread out on the floor in solitary splendor, its camouflage print somehow blending in with the gray carpet. She laughed at the incongruity of it, leaning back into his embrace as mirth shook her.

He laughed with her, his chest quaking against her back, undaunted by her sudden amusement. "What?"

Giggling, she gestured at the absence of furniture. Such an utterly bachelor thing to do! When she finally got herself under control, she asked, "How long do you plan on camping out?"

Releasing her, Rio sat on the sleeping bag, clasping his arms around his knees. "I was waiting for when you had some time free." A smile lit his eyes, matching the one on his lips, as though his answer was the most natural thing in the world.

Her stomach lurched. He wanted her along when he shopped for furniture?

"I'd call that getting serious. Well, are you?" Bion's comment echoed in her head, almost smug the second time around.

"You want my opinion on *furniture*?!" Cyn took an involuntary step back. Blood drained from her cheeks, leaving them cold and stiff. The rest of her felt as if she'd plunged into ice water, sex suddenly the farthest thing from her mind.

He stared up at her, his face a study of bemusement. "You don't have to look like that. It's just furniture. A bed, chairs, that sort of thing. No big deal."

"Yeah? Well, if it's just furniture, why haven't you already bought some?"

"I wanted your input." Rio gave a forced laugh, his brows knitting with growing confusion. "I mean, you'll be sleeping in the bed, after all."

Thoughtful of him, but that was beside the point. He didn't understand what he was asking of her.

She turned to the rail, grabbing it to prevent her hands from flailing. The empty living room below suddenly loomed large in her field of vision, the gray carpet like a slurry of cement or quicksand ready to pull her under. Her heart pounded in her ears, a panicky beat all out of keeping with the discussion. "Look, when we became lovers, we agreed it would just be fun and games. Now you want us to shop for furniture together? And don't you dare say I know the local shops better. I bought my stuff from thrift stores."

"You—"

"I'm not the domestic type, okay? If you're looking for Helen Homemaker, you're looking at the wrong woman."

Rio caught her hands. "Hey, hey! Who said I was looking for the domestic type?"

"That's what all you guys look for. Even . . ."

Greg.

She stared at Rio in shock, her jaw dropping as the conclusion to her tirade registered. *Greg?!* She'd thought herself over that long-ago disillusionment. She didn't even remember what he looked like anymore, but clearly the rejection still stung. He'd been an operator, too. Air force SpecOps.

And the reason she'd finally come back to Aurora. He and the woman he'd married.

"Who?"

"Nobody important. Just someone I knew long ago." Just a guy who'd hammered home the lesson her family had taught her. Men like Greg and Rio didn't settle down with women like Cyn.

CHAPTER THIRTEEN

"I'll be out of contact. If you need me, use voice mail." Standing in the doorway connecting the offices, Lantis shrugged on his coat and patted his pockets as he made the announcement. Though it was just early afternoon, he was apparently preparing to leave the office.

His train of thought disrupted, Rio raised his brows in bemusement. A glance at Dillon found his friend bland-faced and awaiting further details. While as senior partner in the firm the tall man wasn't answerable to them, he usually did them the courtesy of informing them of business appointments.

"Hospital," Lantis explained. "Kiera's weekly checkup."

The pregnant wife. Rio nodded comprehension. In light of his fears for Cyn, he found himself with greater sympathy for Lantis. The previous month's bombing must have been a harrowing nightmare.

"You're there often enough, you might as well be checked in," Dillon joked, his trademark grin back in place.

"Heaven forbid." Lantis smiled briefly as he shot his cuffs. "It's good networking. You never know when we might need a trauma healer."

After he left, Dillon lost his grin, looking unwontedly sober. "She could give birth any day now. It's early yet, but they say twins can be very early."

Rio blinked at the unsolicited detail. Having children—personal issue—wasn't exactly a common topic in black ops. His first impulse was instinctive terror and immediate rejection of the possibility. But once introduced, the notion wouldn't go away, floating at the corners of his mind. He'd never given much thought to children, but now he found he wasn't averse to the idea of one—with Cyn. A daughter with her gray eyes. Although his father would probably prefer a grandson first.

And just like that, he found himself daydreaming of one of each and seeing Cyn round with his child.

Dillon cleared his throat in a blatant call for attention. "Found something interesting?"

Fighting back a flush, Rio glared at Dillon, putting the blame squarely on his shoulders for getting him off track. "Nothing."

"What's that look for?"

"You just had to mention kids." He tossed his head to throw off those thoughts. *Back to work.* But as he turned back to the reports before him, he couldn't suppress a niggle of envy at the way his friends' love lives were proceeding.

With Cyn . . .

"Kids?"

Steadfastly ignoring the playful glint in the other man's eyes, Rio hunkered down, returning to the reports he'd forgotten while weaving his castles in the air. "Shut up."

Surprisingly enough, Dillon did, allowing him to focus on work. Weeding through the various documents gave him a sense of satisfaction, of challenging himself and succeeding. Quite different from the silence that met a good shot. It masked the passage of time as he lost himself in the little details that circumscribed personnel risk in a corporate world.

The wail of a fire engine rising then falling in the distance roused Rio from his hours-long study of the background reports in front of him. Dillon had left for the day, gone home to his lady. Too bad he couldn't say the same. Cyn was working long hours lately, putting in a lot of overtime, acting distant. He couldn't deny there was a need, not with all the activity reported over the police scanner. But he'd thought by moving to Aurora they'd . . .

He shook his head, frustrated that his thoughts had circled back to that. His early hopes seemed further off and even more nebulous. He could almost feel his chance for a life with Cyn slipping away.

Sure, she said she was busy, that her cases were piling up and she had reports to finish, but she had to sleep sometime. He missed the way she snuggled her firm curves against him.

Four days, and he'd seen her only twice: a hasty lunch when she'd been in the area, gyros from a corner stand, food she usually avoided; and a furtive quickie at his place—without getting any farther than the door. It had seemed normal enough at the time; he'd thought she'd put that misunderstanding behind her, and anyway, they'd had difficulty keeping their hands off each other, so they hadn't exactly spent the time talking. But now that he thought about it, she'd even used the lower-level bathroom off the hall to clean up, as though avoiding his condo's vacant interior.

Rio stood up to stretch his legs, his brain feeling like snot, his back stiff as an oak board. Too many nights behind a desk waiting for her to call was making him soft. He could only hope McDaniel's plan panned out. He could use the exercise.

With that in mind, he moved to the small space in front of the desk. It was tight but would suffice for the moment. He did a kata in slow motion, the way he'd been trained, to limber his muscles, the quiet office conducive to reflection.

Mentioning furniture shopping had been a mistake, a tactical error of the worst sort. She wasn't arguing with him, just digging in her heels, resisting his overtures to deepen their relationship. She seemed to have some wrong-headed idea he didn't know his own mind, just because some guy . . . what? *Walked out on her? Led her on?*

His muscles tightened at the thought, torn between the urge to hunt down Cyn's Nobody Important to beat him up for hurting Cyn and the certainty he ought to give thanks that she was free of the idiot. He stopped, controlling his breaths to force out the tension. It took longer than he liked, but once he was calm again, he resumed his kata, reaching deep inside for stillness. A good sniper didn't let his emotions control him.

This wasn't anything words would fix. Only experience would convince Cyn of his sincerity. He had to buy time, enough for her to realize he wasn't like that idiot from her past.

Hopefully, his latest move would calm the waters. They couldn't go forward if she was constantly poised for flight. A tactical withdrawal seemed advisable, especially if he wanted to avoid an encore of that interminable two and a half weeks of missing her.

His phone rang, the tone Cyn's.

Let her be done for the day. No more excuses.

An awkward silence fell between them as Cyn and Rio rode the elevator up to his loft—awkward on Cyn's part because she had no idea how to avoid facing the emptiness of his rooms and the unspoken expectations it represented. She could almost hear the questions Rio restrained, an invisible third party slinking behind her back.

By the time the doors slid apart to reveal the twenty-fifth-floor lobby, she still didn't know how to prevent the next few minutes from devolving into an argument. As Rio dealt with his security spells, an unnatural shade of bright red emerged from the adjacent apartment. The attention-grabbing and probably colored hair came with a small, slender body—she wouldn't reach Cyn's chin—very much like a doll come to life, garbed in a sleeveless minidress with convenient peekaboo details revealing fair skin. The slinky cream fabric was caught by a ribbon at her hip and ended well short of midthigh. As she turned for the elevator, she noticed them—or at least one of them.

"Well, hello there," the petite redhead purred, her hazel eyes lapping up the view. "You're Rio, right?" She arched her back, the pose throwing her slight bosom into prominence and raising her hemline a couple of indiscreet inches.

Rio took in the sight. Cyn bet herself he could draw her down to the lace shadow of her bra under the sheer fabric; the flirt wore the kind of lingerie Cyn personally eschewed. Now, it belatedly occurred to Cyn to wonder if he liked seeing that sort of frippery on a woman. Sure, he'd called her tap pants sexy, but he had to have been kidding her. She couldn't imagine anything further from sexy than plain white cotton underwear.

Wanting to tell off the little tramp who made her feel ungainly, tall, and unfeminine, Cyn bit her tongue before she said something impolite.

"Right." Rio returned her smile. "You have me at a disadvantage."

The redhead extended a delicate hand. "Shanna Jones. Dillon said you took the apartment."

"Ah! You're the friend who told him about the vacancy." Rio's smile warmed as he took that hand in his. "I'm grateful for your help."

Cyn gave the other woman a longer look, wondering if there had been something else behind the tip besides helpfulness.

The way she beamed at Rio said she wasn't averse to doing

more than help, quite the opposite in fact. "Uh-hmm, I'm glad it worked out for you."

"It's perfect. Thanks." Rio's arm tightened around Cyn's waist, his thumb stroking her back soothingly.

She suffered through introductions with the little redhead, who barely acknowledged her, so focused was she on Rio.

Luckily, Shanna had an appointment, or Cyn might have been tempted to claw her eyes out. She took her leave prettily enough, but Cyn wasn't fooled. This wasn't the last they'd see of her.

Shrugging off her jacket, Cyn fought to control her expression. Too bad she couldn't kick the flirt's ass for looking . . . or thinking about what came naturally.

"What's wrong?"

Apparently she hadn't wiped the scowl off her face fast enough. He'd seen it. "She was coming on to you."

Rio gave her a charmingly baffled look. "She was just being friendly."

Cyn hung her jacket in the hall closet to give her hands something to do, her motions stiff with an irritation she couldn't suppress. She hadn't intended to come in, but to get this far and then turn around would make her look like a jealous shrew. "A woman like that doesn't know how to be just friends with a man."

"That's rather harsh, don't you think?"

She snorted, remembering how his neighbor's gaze had clung to Rio's backside. That look had held more speculation than mere appreciation. "Realistic, I'd say."

Bending down to take her shoes off, Cyn froze.

Furniture crouched in the middle of the living room. A couch, a coffee table, and a lamp sat on a colorful area rug that hadn't been there the other day.

Freeing her feet in a daze, she stared before mustering the gumption to check out the new arrivals. The lamp and coffee table were ordinary enough; the former an optical plastic luminaire thick enough to serve as a quarterstaff parked in a granite block like a slender icicle stuck to stone, the latter a heavy wooden rectangle squatting on bowlegs.

The couch was something else altogether: one end flowed over an actual log—she could count the tree rings—then sprouted seat backs, armrests, and legs like a stylized fungus in various shades of brown. The cushions, however, were like a feather bed under her hand, an invitation to sink in and snuggle.

Her first good look at it roused mixed feelings. Certainly, she was relieved Rio hadn't persisted in soliciting her opinion; on the other hand, she couldn't help but wonder what outrageous criteria he'd applied in choosing that massive piece of leather and lumber. Probably something to do with sex. She'd missed sharing that.

Closer inspection revealed the couch to be a sectional sofa comprised of a chaise longue, a two-seater, an expansive corner unit, a three-seater, and a large ottoman, which must have been how the thing had fit through the door. But clumped together, the overall effect was still of a monster fungus, something that might have been at home in a bog.

Cyn had to stifle a laugh. "Where did you get this?"

"There's a furniture showroom in the building across from the office." He thumped the log proprietarily, a loud smack that didn't budge the chaise. At least it was sturdy, even if a touch weird-looking.

"Expensive."

"Not really," Rio demurred. "They were changing the display." The shop must have been overjoyed to get the set off their hands, but she could see how its organic shape might appeal to him—if she squinted hard enough.

"What do you think?" His eyes gleamed with enthusiasm, like a boy showing off his pet frog.

"I think I need a shower before I answer that."

The gleam brightened, if that was even possible. Something

about her evasion tickled his fancy. "It's comfy," he offered, as though that detail improved the couch's outlandish design.

"I'll bet." Retreating up the steps, Cyn couldn't tear her gaze from the mutant brown mushroom; the greater distance only heightened the similarity as the details that identified it as furniture were lost from sight. Rio perched on the log and actually appeared smaller by contrast. She was so distracted she nearly walked into the obstacle by the stairhead.

A snort of amusement from below said her lover hadn't missed her sudden stop. "Notice something?" he lilted.

More furniture had mysteriously appeared. This time, a bed and a nightstand. A sleigh bed large enough to sleep three without any problem with a wood headboard and footboard so thick they could probably stop bullets. Someone had fixed it up in matching burgundy red linens with a familiar sheen.

With one stroke, she confirmed her suspicions. Cool smoothness, seduction to her fingertips. Silk.

Most civilians would consider it an extravagance, but she knew better. In this age of modern thaumaturgy, protection could come in the prettiest packages. Silk was one of the few natural substances that could resist magic. Its thaumaturgic properties made it very useful in applications that required insulation from spells or psychic emanations.

For an operator—even a retired one like Rio—its appeal as bedding was probably irresistible, since sleep left a person next to defenseless. And it didn't hurt that silk felt indescribably sensuous against bare skin. "Yeah, there's one posh bunker up here."

The presence of the bed was a peace offering, not that they'd been fighting, but definitely a sign that Rio had backed off a little. *Alright, so maybe it's a bribe.* She wasn't above petty bribery of this sort, so long as she wasn't the one offering sex.

It was just sex, after all.

Call it an incentive, if it'll make you feel better, her libido whispered.

"Want a test ride?" An arm slipped around her waist, pulling her against Rio; the hard-on that greeted her butt made his meaning obvious. He'd come up the stairs so silently she hadn't heard him, a predator on the prowl, all male heat along the length of her back. Yet he feathered a kiss along her neck, tingling softness that beguiled, not demanded.

Cyn shivered, a thrum of arousal answering, low and sweet in her belly. Her body clearly had no qualms about the proper response to his invitation. "Since you put it that way . . ." Smiling to herself, she turned in his embrace, looped her hands around his neck, then backed up toward the bed. "You just talked me into it."

She'd missed him. She could admit that much, if only to herself.

Chapter Fourteen

An aromatic whiff of cherry pipe tobacco reached Cyn, the first indication she got of the L-T's presence. "Here's another one for you." Derwent dropped a case file on her desk. "Kraus caught it last week," he added, naming a detective on the evening shift. "But it fits with your three."

My three? She pushed back from her desk, mentally reviewing her cases to decipher his statement. "Sanitized?"

He nodded, his face grim. "But this time the body's next to fresh."

Another Jane Doe. Something inside her stilled at the news, that waiting readiness she normally felt before combat. "How fresh?"

The L-T leaned against Cyn's desk, for once looking every year of his forty-nine, his burly shoulders slumped, gathering his thoughts with a slow deliberation that was ominous in a man she knew to be decisive and at times exceedingly blunt. "Maybe just a few days old, maybe longer."

Though her fingers itched to open the file, she resisted the temptation, since he seemed to want to talk. "In this heat?"

"It was found in the abandoned meat packing plant on Westinghouse and Twentieth. A bunch of kids playing hooky were exploring the lockers to cool off. The stasis spells staved off decomposition."

The hairs on her arms stood on end. The killer was still in town? "Might not be the same perp. Any mage worth his salt would've sensed the spells were active."

"Someone else who can do that? Here? No, I think he's taunting us." Derwent glared at the file, adding under his breath, "Sometimes this job sucks."

"L-T?" She frowned, not sure he meant for her to hear that.

His jaw worked beneath his grizzled beard, a tic appearing at the corner of his eye. "The vic looked like my daughter. For a second there, I thought it was Trine." Derwent's back straightened, the pall of disquiet around him vanishing as though a figment of her imagination, once more the gruff commander of Homicide. "Your case. Find the bastard, Cyn." He thumped her desk in emphasis, then stomped off, clearly a man unhappy with the world at the moment.

She flipped open the case file, preferring that over the soft copy on the network. The photo of the corpse was at the very top. The resemblance to the L-T's youngest was uncanny. She knew her face well from the photos on his desk and his comparisons between their appearances. Trine Derwent could have passed for Cyn's sister, but unlike Cyn, she was a model who graced the covers of various fashion magazines on a semiregular basis.

Small wonder he was spooked.

Laid beside the blurry psyprints of the Jane Does found at the sawmill, the latest was clearly of the same physical type. There was no denying the similarity. If her killer wasn't the same guy who did the three, it was a darned good copycat.

She reviewed Kraus's notes of the call, the normal noises of the bull pen fading from the forefront of her mind.

The teenage boys who'd discovered the body had seriously compromised the site and the body. Initially believing that the corpse was some sort of grotesque joke, they'd reacted as typical adolescents, leaving their prints all over the vic's body, and had admitted as much to Kraus. Their fresher psychic residuals would be stronger, possibly obscuring some trace of the killer—and the odds of finding anything hadn't been that high to begin with, if the L-T's hunch was correct. The boys hadn't had much else to add, despite enjoying the novelty of police attention.

The body had been naked at the time of discovery. No personal effects or clothing had been found in the vicinity. Due to the stasis spells, time of death was undetermined, though Cyn suspected it was fairly recent. The killer must have heard of the discovery of the three Jane Does. Why else dump the body in a meat locker, unless he was—as surmised—taunting them?

Pending the ME's report, cause of death was tentatively listed as strangulation. Pattern bruising and abrasions on the neck indicated a rope had been used. *Garrote.* The body bore marks of systematic torture, antemortem, conducted over an extended period, long enough for bruises and scabs to form. Indications of sexual assault, also antemortem, although no seminal fluid had been found.

At least this Jane Doe should be easier to identify.

Cyn suppressed a shiver at the possibility that this vic was just the latest in a string of murders. Her only consolation was that he apparently went years between kills.

However, the sanitization argued for a controlled, methodical killer: a mage with knowledge of police procedure or one with military background. And if he was typical of his kind, he'd be on the lookout for his next victim.

Probably in Aurora.

Preserved by power, the tang of fresh blood rode the air in the meat locker, a coppery sweetness on the tongue that clutched at the throat. Large steel hooks dangled from the ceiling, bereft of purpose, still awaiting the slabs of beef that would never come again. Metal rang underfoot, damp but unfrozen. There was no need for ice here.

Cyn pulled her jacket snug, the chill generated by the chamber's stasis spell a welcome change from the summer heat outside. Magic prickled her arms, a low-level buzz she could feel in the back of her skull. Management hadn't bothered to hire an adept to take down the spells in the lockers when they shuttered the meat packing plant, the penny-pinching bastards. Small wonder they'd declared bankruptcy.

Her magelight banished the shadows, casting an unforgiving glare on the detritus of evidence collection. Shoe prints of various sizes and treads. Smudges of fingerprint powder mingled with splotches of bright red. The white chalk outline of the corpse's placement and position.

Except for those, the meat locker looked little changed from when it was first put into operation. No rust bubbled the white paint of the walls. Blood had dripped but not set into the floor—hard to do when the stasis spells kept it from drying out and getting tacky.

Her breath misted in her face as she paced around the echoing space, wondering what she'd expected to find.

She'd viewed the crime scene video. The vic had been sprawled on her side. Discarded, not neatly laid out like her first three Jane Does. She didn't have to read the forensic report to notice the absence of signs of restraint. The vic had either been drugged or held down by magic.

Put to the question, Cyn would have bet on magic. Given the extent of the mutilation, the bruises, and evidence of partial healing, the murderer had dragged out the final act over a number of hours, if not days. Probably enjoyed it, too.

Which argued for him keeping the vic conscious and aware,

therefore mostly undrugged. Thus, magic to hold her down. Even a masochist would have had difficulty staying still enough for the straightness of certain wounds.

But whatever the murderer had done, Cyn wouldn't find it here.

Here, there was nothing. This was another dumping ground. The forensic report had been clear about that. The techs hadn't detected any significant psychic residuals prior to the witnesses' shock of discovery. The vic had been killed elsewhere; otherwise her torture would have stained the walls with pain. Which meant they had nothing to anchor a retrospection, even if interference from the stasis spells hadn't made one impossible.

In fact, they had nothing to show for their efforts besides another very dead Jane Doe.

It looked like the L-T had the right of it. The killer was wagging his ass at them, daring them to catch him. Arrogant, that. But that very arrogance was a mistake. Now they had a face to hang a name to.

One that looked queasily similar to the L-T's daughter.

Docile wasn't a word Rio usually associated with Cyn, but it wasn't far off the mark for her behavior all evening. She'd been quiet, distracted, picking at the food he'd ordered. And she hadn't made any comment when he led her back to her apartment instead of his loft. Granted, her apartment was closer to the restaurant, but he'd expected something more than demure agreeability.

"Are you okay?" Locking the door behind them, he touched the back of his hand to her forehead. Her temperature felt normal, so why the lack of appetite?

She reared away, sputtering with laughter. "Of course, I am. What's makes you think I'm not?"

"Let's just say you barely ate enough to keep a kitten in fur."

Then there was the fact that she'd refused dessert. That by itself was cause for worry. "Who are you and what have you done with Cyn?" Rio asked semiseriously.

"Oh, you!" She came alive in his embrace, twining her arms around his neck and pulling him down to claim a kiss. Her tongue was tart from the stout she'd sipped over dinner, teasing his with white-lightning licks that sizzled all the way down to his cock.

He went steel-hard in an instant, reflexive obedience to her unexpected summons. When she sucked on his bottom lip, the sensation resonated below the waist, almost as if she'd taken more than that into her mouth. His eyes nearly rolled back at the explosion of carnal heat. *Damnú air,* she knew exactly how to get to him.

Despite his kidding, Rio had never been a hostage to his hormones. But Cyn made a mockery of his control, sweeping him away on a roller-coaster ride of sensation.

Their clothes fell by the wayside, victims to impatience, to hands that grabbed and skimmed and pulled. He kicked off his shoes with equal haste, on fire for her even after all this time. Luckily her bed was just a few short steps away; given how hot she had him, he might have taken her against the door.

When they tumbled on the bed mere seconds later, they were naked and sweaty and intent on getting sweatier. The carnation scent of her went to his head. Her hands were all over him, callused palms rough, possessive, touching and teasing. Hungry. Her lips weren't far behind, exploring his body as though it were virgin territory declared open for conquest, rousing his blood to fever heights.

Rio pulled her under him, spreading her thighs and mounting her with little finesse.

To his shock, she was tight—tighter than usual. Not dry, but not the slick welcome he was accustomed to, either. Had he misread her?

As if in answer, Cyn pulled him deeper, her legs locking

around his hips. She squeezed Rio with her inner muscles, fluttering over his length in a heart-stopping, soul-searing rhythm. Pushing his buttons with single-minded deliberation. Shredding his control and driving him to the edge.

A sorceress dancing a spell of ecstasy. *Hechicera mía.* His sorceress. Except he got the feeling she wasn't completely with him. Not quite just going through the motions, but not in the moment, either.

He took her breasts between his hands and nuzzled them, their hard tips irresistible. A murmur of approval greeted his first lick, but her arms didn't come up to press his lips closer nor did she offer her breasts for his sucking—something she usually enjoyed and encouraged.

Enthusiasm was there, but she was holding back.

Pleasure thrummed through his cock, the part of him that was simple-minded in its priorities, demanding ecstasy and relief for his aching balls. Nothing was more important.

Cyn arched under Rio, urging him to take his release.

Except he couldn't.

Lovemaking to him was a two-way street, and it grated him on a primitive level that she wasn't letting him be a full partner in this dance. Taking turns during their games was one thing; this was another thing entirely. Lopsided. Something was bothering her, was preventing her from going with the flow, and he couldn't bring himself to overlook her mood and finish alone.

Rio stopped, gritting his teeth against overwhelming temptation when she continued to flutter around him seductively. Finding her sharp, silver gaze unclouded by passion confirmed his suspicions. "This is supposed to be pleasure, not duty."

Flopping down on the pillows, Cyn made a face of disgust and sighed. "I'm no good tonight."

He disengaged their bodies, his cock protesting the motion with every thick, throbbing inch of him. If they were to have a serious discussion, he couldn't afford the distraction. "Obviously."

She scowled at him, all regal indignation in one svelte package despite her nudity. "Meaning?"

"The way you were throwing yourself on the grenade."

"*What?*"

"Sacrificing yourself. Lying back and thinking of England. You know, honor, duty, country." He settled on his side and propped himself up on an elbow, forcing himself to ignore his aching hard-on and breathe. Clearing the air was more important than getting his ashes hauled.

Cyn promptly rolled over, giving him her back. The silent treatment from a woman who he'd have sworn didn't know how to play that game. He found he didn't care for it.

"Hey, don't be like that." Rio brushed a kiss on her shoulder, undemanding—hopefully, understanding. It was probably underhanded to use sex that way, but he wasn't about to surrender such a useful weapon in his arsenal. "So you're distracted. What's up?"

He tried not to mind the uncommunicative expanse of creamy skin. Surely it merely meant that whatever was bothering Cyn was *really* bothering her. She wasn't one to hold grudges unfairly. They'd talk it through and clear the air. He stroked her back, taking solace from the silken contact. At least she hadn't ordered him from her bed.

A weary sigh signaled capitulation even before she turned to face him. "Sorry."

"I wasn't asking for an apology." Rio gave her a wry smile, his hand settling on her belly to rub her there absently. He wasn't trying to arouse her despite his hard-on—it was just one of those things he did to occupy his hands—but this time she was acutely conscious of the habit.

Guilty conscience?

Too right. She wasn't used to leaving him wanting. After all, this was supposed to be fun and games. If she couldn't give him that much, his oh-so-friendly neighbor was waiting in the wings, ready to take over.

A jolt of sudden fire snapped her out of her reverie, her clit suddenly hard and throbbing with awareness.

"Hey, earth to Cyn. Was it something I said?" He met her gaze steadily, his dark chocolate eyes guileless despite the peccant finger between her folds.

Cyn blushed that he'd had to resort to such extreme measures to regain her wandering attention. "No, it wasn't." She snuggled against him in silent apology, conscious of his semierect cock pressed to her hip. "It's just work." She sighed involuntarily. "As usual."

"Um-hmm." He withdrew his hand from the juncture of her thighs, transferring it to her back. "What about work?"

Chewing her lip, she debated whether to tell him or not. In the past, she wouldn't have hesitated. He'd presented an unbiased sounding board to bounce her thoughts off. Now that he was making noises about settling down, she wasn't so sure sharing details about the job was wise. Surely talking about the gory details would only remind him that she wasn't one of those traditional women focused on hearth and home. She'd lose him eventually, but why speed that day's coming?

On the other hand, he knew something rankled her, and the job was the easiest reason to give him. Anything else raised the specter of argument, which she preferred to avoid while her nudity put her at a disadvantage.

"No callouts lately."

Cyn blinked at the change in subject but welcomed the reprieve. "Nothing major. Either the mage gang's left town, or they're lying low." Even the copycats had petered out. She had mixed feelings about that. The latter meant the gang would strike again, but also meant another chance at stopping them.

Then Rio's tone registered. It had been a statement, not a question. "How'd you know?"

"The police band, of course."

Keeping tabs on her? She mentally snorted at herself. *Self-centered much?* Rio was black ops; of course he'd keep tabs on the local security situation. Did she expect otherwise after she'd made a point of warning him?

"It's just been a few days."

"Since it's not the mage gang, should I start guessing?"

Cyn shook her head. "You've probably heard already. Those murder victims found near the gang's camp?"

"What about them?"

"It looks like they weren't the last." A heavy glumness lodged in her stomach, the sensual mood well and truly broken.

"A serial killer?"

She shrugged, reluctant to expand on her statement. Tomorrow would come soon enough, then it would be back to work and the case. Just then, she realized that Rio had been her refuge for the past year, the one person with whom she could just forget the job and be herself. He understood the stresses but wasn't connected to work. Even when she discussed her cases with him, he hadn't treated her as a cop first and a woman second. With him, there was none of the politics, no jockeying for the upper hand. Having him around let the pressure off.

But now, those very discussions might drive him away.

"It's got me in knots," Cyn explained apologetically, hoping he'd let her leave it at that.

He gave her a long look that she returned with silence, banking on his black ops background for understanding. A long moment later, he nodded, granting her a reprieve. "Got you in knots, huh? Anywhere in particular?" His fingers dug firmly into her butt, squeezing and spreading her cheeks, circular kneading that jolted her clit unerringly.

But tonight had been enough of a disaster. She wasn't about to court a repeat performance.

Rio could understand Cyn's position. Need to know and all that. It was the same in black ops. He just didn't buy into it. Sure, there might be details she couldn't talk about; he had the same with his missions. But if a case was weighing on her so much that it sidelined her healthy libido, she needed to talk.

However, getting a strong woman like her to unburden herself wasn't as simple as asking about it. That wouldn't work with Cyn. She wasn't one to discuss her problems readily. He needed to take a roundabout approach.

Luckily, that wasn't an onerous duty.

Taut cheeks flexed under his hands as he squeezed gently, the skin silken and resilient, the muscle beneath a trifle more tense. He knew she'd think he was offering a massage, but he intended much more. It was simply another mission, intelligence gathering of the most important sort.

Cyn gave a reluctant laugh. "Not there." She laid her head on her folded arms, more relaxed now that it was clear he didn't expect her to perform.

Sliding out from beside her, he pushed up to sit on his heels and consider the challenge he'd set for himself. "Lower?" Her thighs were firm, their long, lithe muscles drawing his eyes inexorably upward to the wet curls at their juncture.

Rio resisted the temptation as ungentlemanly; there was a time for everything, but now wasn't the time to indulge the rogue in him. He focused on playful kneading, working his way down to her calves and feet.

A weak giggle rewarded his teasing. "Silly, not there, either," she chided, but only after he'd reached her toes.

"Up here, then." Straddling her body, he discovered the knots she'd mentioned, her shoulders still tense, despite his efforts. He let silence fall between them as he concentrated on his massage.

Only when he felt the easing in her muscles did he return to the original topic. "So, there's been another one?" The papers hadn't said much about the unnamed murder victims, preferring to castigate the police over the mage gang's continued crime spree.

She nodded briefly, fingers digging into her pillow.

"What's so different with this one?"

"The corpse was fresh," Cyn muttered.

"Fresh?" he repeated, wondering if he'd heard her right.

One smooth shoulder rose in a definite shrug. "Well, maybe not *fresh* fresh, but bloody fresh. We're not sure when the vic was killed, but the killer dumped her in a meat locker with active stasis spells." Her dark head tilted up; a gray eye peered back at him, troubled. "He mutilated her antemortem."

A flash of red made Rio pause, blood bright before his mind's eye, bitter memory wed to the color. He had many to keep him company: the times his team had been too late. He didn't mind his kills—they were legitimate targets—but the victims they'd failed to save continued to haunt his sleep.

"Hit close to home, huh?" He kept his tone conversational as he resumed his massage, bringing his weight to bear on the pockets of tension that were left. Expressing shock would only drive her to silence when she needed to unburden herself. He attacked the holdouts, kneading her body into pliancy.

"You can't imagine how close." Cyn sighed into her arms. "She's the spitting image of the L-T's youngest. Gave us a shock. To look at, she could have been my sister."

He froze at her words. The latest victim looked like Cyn?

"Rio?" A sleepy eye slitted open, puzzlement lightening it to silver.

With a pained smile, he turned her over, shunting his worry to the back of his mind for later. Demanding all the details would only ruin all his hard work. He continued on her front, massaging firm muscle and skimming her breasts with their dusky nipples pouting with promise.

Not yet.

Maybe not tonight.

Now was for comfort, a chance to show Cyn he could deal with her job. That there were other benefits to a permanent relationship with him besides sex. Not that he'd turn down sex if she made advances now. But he wasn't going to be the one to raise the issue.

"He's thumbing his nose at us," Cyn muttered, offering the comment without his prompting, her thoughts clearly still centered on work.

Rio stretched out beside her, then drew her into his arms, relieved that his hard-on had finally subsided. "So you'll make him regret it."

"Such confidence." Despite the asperity in her voice, she snuggled closer, her soft breasts pillowed against his ribs. "We don't even know the vics' names."

They didn't? He reined in the questions on the tip of his tongue. After all the effort he'd put into getting Cyn to relax, he wasn't about to undo the results with a barrage of whys and hows. "I know you. You won't give up until the murderer's caught."

"There's always another one." She hitched a leg over his, thankfully not so high that he couldn't ignore the contact. The hand stroking his chest was more of a challenge.

He chuckled at her rare petulance and its contrast to her sensual actions. "Admit it, you enjoy tracking down murderers and throwing them behind bars. You're not stopping now."

Chapter Fifteen

An entire night in Rio's arms with no sex whatsoever had Cyn waking with mixed feelings. On one hand, there was relief that he'd respected her mood. On the other, the whole taking-care-of-her bit smacked of the traditional me-male-you-weak-female routine, which had her hackles rising.

Yet he hadn't gotten any release and didn't seem to mind. Despite his hard-on and his normally revved-up sex drive, he hadn't suggested a hand job—or he'd taken care of it himself.

Was this the start of the end? The shift to buddies and friends?

Luckily—or perhaps not—Rio wasn't around to ask when she stepped out of the shower. An early meeting, according to the doodle-free note he'd left on her bed; but after last night, she had to wonder. Her suspicions didn't make for comfortable thoughts as she drove to police headquarters.

A white letter-size envelope bearing the logo of an artist's studio lay in her in-tray when Cyn got to her desk, distracting her from her conflicted emotions. Ignoring the mannerly tumult of shift change, she set down her travel mug full of Rio's coffee to heft the packet and consider the Do Not Fold warning printed in large letters on both sides.

What now?

She ripped the flap open and tilted the envelope over her desk. A sheaf of photographs slid out, offering glimpses of a mounted head and torso. The facial reconstruction had arrived weeks earlier than scheduled, she realized with a rush of excitement, possibly as a result of the Feds' interest. Plucking the accompanying report from the pile, she spread the photos across her desk, eager to see the results. Now she could make some progress on the Jane Doe case.

The first glance through was a shock. She sucked in air, struck by their similarity to her newest vic and the L-T's youngest. The reconstructions used flesh-colored clay, glass eyes, and wigs to life-like effect. Though the artist wouldn't have been given copies of the psyprints so as not to influence the results, the wigs used were dark, and the fashionable hairstyles a close match. Probably just inspired guesswork on the part of the artist, since the majority of the population did have brown or black hair. But logic was no match for her back brain, which half expected to see sweat on the sober faces. Only the eyes were off, a standard brown instead of some light color.

Cyn ignored the chill ruffling her arms. Visceral reactions had no place in an investigation. She scanned the photographs and uploaded them into the system, set her computer to cross-checking the images against those of the hits she'd gotten from Missing Persons, then settled back to read the report provided. The search wouldn't spit out a conclusive match—more than five years working Homicide had taught her not to expect the impossible—but it would filter the candidates for her Jane Does, hopefully to a manageable number.

Unsurprisingly, the forensic anthropologist who'd handled the reconstructions agreed with the psychometric specialist who'd created the psyprints. Citing skull architectures and going into extensive, eye-glazing technical detail, the conclusion was that her Jane Does had been adult Caucasian females in good health with no indications of injury or illness to account for death.

A shadow fell across the thick report. Ready to escape the dry references to bone density and cranial ridges, she looked up and found Hollingsworth standing behind her, subjecting the photographs on her lap to intense scrutiny. "Help you?"

"You're a hard woman to pin down." He smiled, blunting the edge of his words, his brown eyes glinting gold. Unfortunately for him, the curve of his thin lips was a marked contrast to Rio's; with his reputation for no nonsense, she didn't buy the bonhomie he projected.

Conscious of the surreptitious glances being cast their way, Cyn set down the report and raised her brows skeptically. "Considering all the paperwork weighing me down, I find that hard to believe."

"True, nonetheless."

The noise in the bull pen dropped perceptibly, enough that she could hear Lopes's cajolery at the far end. She was painfully aware of the pricking of interested ears; it was almost as bad as heavy breathing. "So, here I am. What do you want?"

"You shouldn't give openings like that, you know." Hollingsworth's grin took on a distinctly masculine cast, adding an almost flirtatious nuance to his statement. Or perhaps that was just Danzinger's comments coloring her perception?

Using all the acting skills she'd cultivated in years on the job, Cyn locked down her expression to polite inquiry, mentally damning the assistant team leader for his meddlesome insinuations. "No, seriously."

He wagged his head in playful—*Playful?!*—dismay. "Nothing much, really. I thought we might do lunch sometime?"

Lunch? It seemed Danzinger hadn't been kidding her about Hollingsworth's interest. She wasn't sure how to take the change in the normally business-only crime scene tech.

Sorry, taken, was her knee-jerk response, which was only true . . . but was she going to remain taken? She bit back the refusal at the tip of her tongue. "You just want to talk about the Jane Does."

"Can you blame me?" He smiled, the expression giving his average features a boyish appeal. "How often do I get a beautiful woman investigating a mysterious death, much less a case like that?"

She returned his smile automatically, wishing she responded to him as strongly as she did to Rio. It would make life so much simpler if she could just go with the flow; certainly it would make her brothers happier. Unfortunately, all she could manage was intellectual appreciation for what was undoubtedly a nice smile. "You tell me."

"Never before. You're unique."

"Cyn." Derwent marched past, his face dark with temper, waving her toward his office.

"Whoops, sorry." Grabbing the excuse to avoid outright rejection, she stood up, sweeping the papers on her lap together and following in the Homicide commander's wake. In this mood, the L-T wouldn't brook foot-dragging.

Derwent had her shut the door and pull the blinds when she joined him, his jaw clenched so tight his molars had to be aching. "His Honor's gotten wind of the Jane Does and is freaking out."

The L-T leaned back, resting his weight on his palms on the desk. His expression was disgruntled—only to be expected after a royal chewing-out by a mayor who'd run for office on a Tough on Crime platform that was more bark than bite, then proceeded to gut appropriations intended to upgrade police equipment.

Cyn suppressed a wince. While Derwent didn't suffer fools gladly, he normally reined in his temper better than this. She didn't want to imagine what the mayor had said to get him so worked up.

"Tell me there's good news."

Knowing he didn't mean progress on the squad's other open cases, she still hesitated to show him the photos.

"Well?"

"Sit down." She took her own advice and planted her butt in one of the creaking visitor chairs.

He frowned at her but followed suit. "I'm sitting."

"These came in this morning." Cyn handed him the photos of the facial reconstructions she'd automatically gathered when she'd stood up.

A hiss said their similarity to his youngest hadn't escaped notice. "This is good news?" Derwent stared at her, grizzled brows beetled in perplexity.

"They're early. The system's going through my Missing Persons list as we speak. It's a step forward." She relaxed as he ruffled his beard thoughtfully, his shoulders easing down, his temper once more under control. For both of them, work was always a palliative. Focusing on death and murder made their own problems seem inconsequential in comparison.

Back in her apartment that evening, Cyn found herself second-guessing her dismissal of Hollingsworth's invitation. As she changed out of her work clothes, her collection of mage dolls drew her eye—the shamankas with their feathers and furs, the priestesses with their silks and parchment, all perfectly coiffed and pretty—bringing back to mind the comparison she'd drawn between Rio and the crime scene tech. Was it just looks that made Rio stand out from the rest? Was there some basis after all to her brothers' gibes calling Rio her pretty boy? Was she so shallow?

Surely not.

Cyn stared at the exquisite dolls, unable to deny the fascination. While she might notice the fine craftsmanship and the intricate details, she knew herself well enough—was honest enough—to admit that it was the cute factor that kept her from giving them away. Little had changed from when Eleni bribed her with the very first doll. She'd been taken with their daintiness and beauty and wanted to keep them to herself.

Like Rio?

The thought made her snort. Her Latin lover had more to offer than a beautiful face and well-toned body, no matter what her brothers thought. A sense of humor, a sharp mind, steady nerves, and a willingness to risk himself for others.

And appreciation of her strength.

But appreciation didn't mean that was what he wanted in a woman for the long term. Most men of his type preferred someone who'd lean on *their* strength and make them feel more manly, someone to be protected and cherished—not someone like her who couldn't pretend. She'd seen it in her father with her mother, in Bion's eventual choice for a wife, even in her other brothers' dating preferences.

And she'd seen it in the air force where she'd thought she'd escaped conventional expectations. With Greg.

She took out the Shinto and Minoan priestesses, the latest evidence of Rio's thoughtfulness, proof that he hadn't forgotten her, even when he'd left for parts unknown. He treated adding to her collection like a treasure hunt, a game because they'd agreed to fun and games.

But now he wanted more, and she wanted things to remain the same. Was that so wrong? Yet could she blame him if he sought that "more" in another woman's arms when she didn't want to risk eventual rejection, didn't want to gamble that he would be the exception to the rule?

The cryptic smiles on the tiny faces, forever unchanging, gave no reassurance. They didn't have to worry about men who preferred softness to overt strength.

Returning the dolls to their shelves, Cyn shut the closet doors, cutting off that line of thought before she was tempted to wallow in self-pity. If she wanted to do that, she might as well go down to the nearest cop bar and drown her sorrows. Maybe even take up Hollingsworth on his surprising invitation.

She stiffened her spine. While she and Rio remained lovers, she intended to make the most of it. No moping around about what couldn't be.

Chapter Sixteen

Cyn was on the couch when Rio got home, lying on her side like a mermaid on a bed of kelp, studying a fan of documents on the cushions in front of her. The pose made her body curve delightfully, emphasizing feminine valleys and peaks that his hands itched to explore. Even better, her sleep shirt had ridden up, one panel of her tap pants draped back to bare a rounded cheek. The sight blew out the cobwebs of his frustrating day.

She rolled over as he opened the coat closet with a weary sigh, a smile of commiseration on her full lips. "Bad day?"

"Not anymore." He'd been embroiled in one wrangle after another, coaxing balky contacts for information and wrestling with red tape, culminating with the notification that his shipment of personal stuff had gone missing. But coming home to this made all the aggravation worthwhile.

His answer brought a charming blush to her cheeks, a chink in her regal mien that lightened his heart. Good to know this vulnerability was a two-way street.

"What are you working on?" He shrugged off his summer-weight sport coat, a minor concession to business attire he'd made to hide his gun, and savored the sudden coolness on his back.

"That Jane Doe case I told you about."

"The serial killer?"

"Yeah, what with all the month-end paperwork, I haven't been able to get back to it, so I took it home." Her offhand use of *home* was a surprise and delight.

Rio smiled to himself as he hung his coat in the closet beside hers. The fact that she felt comfortable enough to bring work to his place was progress. And to be lounging around in her sleep shirt? Even better! She'd since relaxed after he'd leased furniture on his own.

Cyn kept several sets of clothes in the loft these days. Little by little she was behaving as if they were living together, although she still had her apartment. He didn't mind the gradual transition.

"How's it going?" Lifting her feet, he sat down in the space he'd cleared then settled them on his lap. It felt so domestic discussing her work like this, another milestone in his quest to shift their relationship to more permanent grounds.

She gave him a wide smile. "We had a break today. The facial reconstructions arrived earlier than expected." She waved at the papers spread before her.

Photographs and psyprints of what appeared to be head shots. Rio bent forward for a better angle.

"To look at, she could have been my sister."

Apprehension touched his spine with ice. The similarities between the victims' features and Cyn's were undeniable. And the serial killer was operating in the area?

Only the knowledge that Cyn could hold her own in battle kept him from reacting. "What makes these Jane Does more difficult than your usual cases?"

"A lot of the homicides we get are open and shut, crimes of

passion, domestic violence, plain stupidity. These . . . they were sanitized. The only such cases I'm familiar with were . . ." Her eyes widened, their gray turning bright silver as her pupils contracted.

"What?"

"When I was still military police." Cyn frowned at him speculatively. "Have you heard of spells for sanitization? I mean, *before* this case?"

In black ops?

This was the first time she'd referred to his job—his former job. From her intonation and roundabout phrasing, it was clear she suspected he was black ops. It was just as clear that she wasn't asking to satisfy idle curiosity.

He wasn't surprised she'd made the connection. Black ops did use sanitization spells to disappear people, especially if they wanted to infiltrate an organization, say a terrorist cell, by taking the target's place or to sow chaos and dissent by making it seem the money guy had taken the treasury with him on the lam. It was a specialized form of wetwork that guaranteed the remains of the target—should they be found—couldn't be identified, not even from psychic residuals.

"Yes," Rio admitted reluctantly, stretching the word into two syllables as he quickly reviewed past missions. His briefing on such spells wasn't classified—at least not as far as he knew. If the knowledge was pertinent to her investigation, he couldn't withhold it in good conscience.

Turning back to her papers, Cyn drummed her fingers, her full lips pouting as she thought. Then she peeked at him from under her lashes. "Can you . . . ?" The diffidence in her voice said she wouldn't pursue the topic if he refused to discuss it. If he cited need-to-know or security considerations, she'd respect his wishes. That tilted his decision in her favor.

He raised a hand. "Give me a minute to change"—and figure out how much he could tell her—"then we can talk."

The brightening of her eyes was all he needed. He took the

stairs to the bedroom by twos. As he shed his shirt and pants in quick succession, he refreshed his memory on the portions of his record that weren't classified and how to phrase his answers without violating operational security.

Rio descended the stairs barefoot, wearing only a pair of denim cutoffs and flaunting a distracting expanse of golden male flesh and the faint line of dark hair low on his belly trailing south. The lamplight practically worshiped his muscles, throwing highlights and soft shadows that emphasized the slabs and furrows of his chest and abs.

Cyn swallowed with difficulty, her libido stirring despite her best efforts. Heat bloomed throughout her body as she fought not to stare, suppressing a shiver as tingles of excitement spread down her arms. All that virility threatened to wipe the questions from her mind.

But this was a rare opportunity that might not come again. She had to make the most of it.

He settled on the ottoman, legs spread, and leaned toward her, resting his forearms on his thighs. The pose threw his broad shoulders into prominence, his biceps and smooth pectorals bulging with power.

Close enough to touch.

And, boy, did she want to touch!

She forced her brain back to work, activating her PDA to take notes. "So, spells for sanitizing corpses."

"What about them?" He watched her, the look in his deep-set eyes unreadable.

"You've heard of them?"

"Yes."

Cyn bit her lip at his monosyllabic answer. Not exactly a hostile interview, but not forthcoming, either. She needed more than that. Deciding to lay her cards on the table, she asked him bluntly, "What can you tell me about them?"

"Probably not as much as you'd like. I'm no mage, so I'm not familiar with the technical aspects of it." His gaze turned distant, as though he was seeing something else or some other time, then dropped to his hands. "In theory, there are two ways to sanitize a corpse. One requires several adepts working together to . . . erase the psychic residuals associated with the body. It's faster—relatively—but power-intensive."

She remembered Dillon's retrospection and the raw magic he'd summoned, tapping a major wicce line more than a mile away. She'd also heard that Atlantis was a high adept; he was probably of the same caliber, power-wise. The two men struck her as black ops, or former operators; they had the moves. She'd looked up Depth Security after last year's excitement and all the hush-hush about its clients pointed to Rio's involvement with them being business as usual. Could the two of them working together pull off a sanitization? It wasn't unknown for serial killers to work as a team.

Of course, maybe she was just being a suspicious bitch. Atlantis's history in Aurora went back less than four years to when he'd set up shop in the city—much too late for her Jane Does. Besides, if they killed anyone, she suspected their victim would just disappear, or it would be made to look like an accident.

So not them, but a team of murdering adepts? As a start for a profile, it might work. "How many is *several*?"

Picking up the artist's tablet he usually kept close at hand, he slid the pencil from its rings and sketched a quick seven-pointed star centered on what looked like a body. "One at each corner." The fluid execution—no hesitation, no fumbling—told her he'd drawn it from memory.

Seven was stretching it for team killers, but seven wasn't necessarily the minimum required to cast the spell. Rio had noted

Kathleen Dante

that he wasn't a mage; all he could tell her was what he knew or had witnessed. "And the other way?"

"Theoretically, it can be done by just one, but it apparently takes some time." A look she couldn't decipher darkened his face. "They say prolonged torture can exhaust a victim's personal energies, until the link to the body can be . . . dissolved. It's a matter of wearing down the will. It's not infallible, though. There are ways of resisting . . ." He bent over his hands, the pose almost prayerful, as his voice trailed off into thought.

A chill went through Cyn, her heart skipping a beat. Was Rio referring to anti-interrogation techniques? Had he been trained for such a contingency? She tried to remember her questions were in furtherance of a murder investigation, but she couldn't avoid the thought of the dangers he'd faced—and accepted—in black ops.

At least as a civilian he wouldn't have to contend with that sort of enemy action; there were other dangers, but probably not torture. She tried to take comfort in that.

"Sorry, got off track." He focused on her again. "I'm told that such a spell would require a lot of finesse, but not so much power that one mage couldn't handle it."

Forcing her mind back to business, she reviewed what he'd shared. The latter was more in keeping with serial killers. "You're *told*?"

A corner of his mouth tilted up reluctantly, the smile not reaching his eyes. "I never saw it done myself, so, yes, *I'm told*."

Her stomach knotted around itself. This case just got better and better. It had been bad enough when she'd thought the systematic torture and mutilation had been the killer getting his kicks. To think that he'd done it with the intent of casting a sanitization spell? Somehow that level of premeditation made it worse.

Chapter Seventeen

A high-pitched titter from over the cubicle wall behind the bank of hard plastic chairs drew Rio's attention. The references to Cyn held it. There wasn't much else to occupy him as he sat waiting for Lieutenant McDaniel, the Tactical Unit commander, to see him. The offices were deserted, whether for training or some other reason, he couldn't tell, but he'd encountered only a few people along the way, none of whom had been Alex Malva—for which he was grateful.

"Did you see him?" the titterer asked. "Cyn's stud?"

"That cutie was him?"

"In the flesh. Can you believe he's for real?"

He rolled his eyes in disgust. Normally he didn't mind being underestimated because of his face—he'd used that to his advantage to make his job easier on several missions—but for Cyn's coworkers to do so disparaged her judgment, implying as it did that she looked no further than the surface. Surely they knew better?

"Some women are just born lucky, I swear." There was a swishing sound like hair brushing nylon—maybe a head shaking. "She already has that stud of hers; now Brett is chasing her, too."

"Oh, to have Cyn's problems." Another titter.

"But think of what that means."

"What?"

"That yummy hunk will be up for grabs soon."

The secretary guarding McDaniel's lair nodded at him, indicating the lieutenant was free, and he was to enter. He stood up, eager to escape the irritating chatter.

"How does that follow?"

"Have you ever known Brett not to get what he sets his sights on? The man's an overachiever."

Brett? Who the hell is Brett? Rio quietly stepped away from the voices. He'd thought Cyn was just automatically resisting any change to their relationship. He hadn't considered there might be other agents in play.

McDaniel's quiet greeting came as a balm to his temper. Here at least was one cop who didn't dismiss him as just another pretty face. As soon as he was seated, the lieutenant handed him the card and visitor's tag that would serve as his entrée to the training center. No nonsense and straight to the point.

"Comfortable with the equipment?" McDaniel had lent him the training marker for the exercise to give him a chance to familiarize himself with its idiosyncrasies.

"It will do." Rio flipped the hard plastic end over end, his fingers restless. "You have a setup in mind?"

"Binge shooter. Give them a few chances to catch you, then pull out, if you can." Pale blue gray eyes drilled at him, probing for weakness. "There's a bonus if they don't catch you."

A challenge, put bluntly. The man knew how to up the stakes. If only the men under his command were similarly astute. But they would learn; he'd make sure of it.

Rio grinned, his pulse slowing as training kicked in. "A pleasure doing business with you."

Excitement filled the van as they drove to the training center with Fernao briefing them on the fly. A sniper scenario. Random fire with a civilian down. That was a new one and a change from the normal monthly training, which usually devolved into speed tests. None of the other teams had mentioned going up against a sniper in their sessions, so they would be the first.

Aggression rode the air, and Cyn wasn't immune to the challenge. Adrenaline flowed, a quickening of her pulse and a sharpening of her senses. Here was something fresh to test herself against, something other than the renewed rash of copycats and the continued depredations of the mage gang.

Bru pulled over beside a truck, its bulk giving them additional cover as they piled out. Hardesty and Danzinger took point, first securing the back of the truck.

The site looked normal enough. Parked vehicles. The usual buildings for an urban training scenario. No actual bystanders; the sidewalks were peopled by holovid projections and dummies, but that couldn't be helped.

Reports crackled over their headsets, directing them to the intersection and the next street over. As they moved forward, screaming civilians fled past, the holovid unsettlingly vivid. Hardesty swore, his wand upraised.

"There!" The medics sprinted for a body liberally splashed with red, sprawled over the curb. The victim dummy looked uncomfortably real as Keefe and Renfrew bent over it, supposedly attempting first aid.

"Talk to me, Clay." Jung had his rifle up as he scanned his area. It looked like the real deal but was actually a training marker that shot nonlethal rounds.

"Nothing," Moxham gritted out. He gestured at Cyn to take over spotting duty while he tried a detection spell.

A low, muffled *puff* sounded, too soft to isolate, especially with the noise bouncing off glass, brick, stone, and steel. Too much background heat for a hidden body to stand out.

"Ugh." Orange paint bloomed at the base of Fernao's throat, just above his body armor, sparking red as the training charm reacted to the mix of chemical and perspiration to register the hit. The tac team leader dropped down, obedient to the scenario. "Damn, that stings."

Moxham cursed softly. "We have a live one."

"What does that mean?" Jung's monotone didn't sound happy.

"It means McDaniel found us a real sniper. I got fuck all from that shot." Moxham's spell should have picked up spikes in emotion; if the sniper wasn't radiating, Moxham would have to cast a more difficult one for sonics to find him. "It's like there's no one out there."

Snatching up his first aid kit, Keefe sprinted for Fernao, then seemed to stumble. When he landed beside their prone team leader, they saw an orange splotch on his neck. Renfrew was slumped over the "victim," likewise out of commission.

Cyn hurriedly cast a shield around her and Jung. It wasn't her best spell, but she had nothing to attack. She didn't have a clue where the shots had come from. "Clay."

Kneeling behind the car where he'd taken cover, Moxham gestured, the stronger magic he called making the hair on her arms stand on end. "Still—" He grunted, then sat down, turning around to rest his back on the car. "Ouch, I'm dead." Orange paint dripped off his chin, below the faceplate, the red sparks looking almost pestilent against his copper skin.

Which meant—

"That way." She pointed Jung in the direction the shot had to have come from, based on Moxham's position when he'd been hit and the angle of the spatter. "Good work, Clay."

Groaning, Moxham rolled his green eyes, taking the gibe in the spirit it was offered.

However, despite the best efforts of the survivors—and Danzinger really tried—they couldn't isolate the sniper. Another shot rang out from a different direction, downing Rao; the sniper had managed to change locations without giving himself away. Then no more followed.

Fifteen excruciating minutes later, McDaniel called the exercise, allowing the "casualties" to recover.

"Who the hell was that?" Hardesty blurted out the question at the topmost of their minds as soon as they were all gathered outside the training center's offices. They looked around, fully expecting the sniper to show himself as the aggressors in previous training scenarios had done.

The Tactical commander dismissed the question with a quick hand slash. "Not yet. Not until you're doing better than that."

"That was—"

"A disaster." Fernao quieted Danzinger with a hand on the shoulder. "And realistic. Embarrassing but realistic. That's why we train." He turned to McDaniel. "I take it that was just a start."

A stern look answered him. "The first of many."

The inquest ran long as they huddled before the monitors playing and replaying the video of the exercise, driven by the determination to avoid a repeat. The evening was well along before Fernao called it a day. The discussion extended into dinner, since everyone felt there were more lessons to be learned if they kept at it long enough; possibly the medics were the only ones not to request a copy of the video.

Cyn smiled when they finally went their separate ways, inexplicably content with the day's training, despite their appalling performance. The bond of mutual embarrassment. There was no denying her team was pulling together to overcome their failure. If she had to have someone to guard her back, at least it was this bunch of overachievers.

---oᴔᴔᴑ---

"You're getting dour in your old age," Dillon observed from his position catty-corner to Rio's, the stack of files in front of him inexorably shifting from *pending* to *done*. "I thought you said the exercise went well."

Rio blinked up from the record he'd been staring at for the past several minutes, chagrined to realize he hadn't absorbed a single detail. "Yeah, it did."

"So if it's not work, what is it? Trouble in paradise?"

"More like a poacher."

"Do tell," Dillon prompted immediately, bright-eyed and so clearly unfazed by his obscure reply that Rio had to smile. "And does this poacher have a name?"

"Brett, surname unknown. Apparently a coworker."

"Should be simple enough." The clatter of keys accompanied the comment.

"Hey!" He'd restrained himself from using office resources to conduct a personal search, mindful of their trust, not counting the success of the first sniping session for McDaniel as sufficient reason to take advantage. Their security clearances gave them access to top secret federal databases; it was the only way they could conduct thorough background checks for corporations handling classified information and sensitive defense projects, including some for black ops. He wasn't about to ask for favors for so minor a matter.

"I'm a partner; I can do these things." A dismissive wave and a careless grin flashed his way. "Ah, here we go. Told you it's simple."

"You *bladhmaire*." Rio shook his head in laughing disbelief, his mother's tongue flowing spontaneously. Dillon looked every inch the braggart he'd named him.

"That's no way to talk. You want to see this or not?"

He quickly walked over before his friend changed his mind.

Good intelligence was always welcome, no matter how it was sourced. "Give."

Pointing a finger at his screen, Dillon leaned back, giving him room to read. "Only one Brett connected with Aurora PD." He'd accessed a site listing police personnel records.

"Brett Hollingsworth?" Rio scanned the page with growing unease. The accompanying picture was an unexpected match to a face in his memory: the same man he'd pointed out to Cyn at Just Desserts. His mind racing with speculation, he retired to his arm of their desk, twirling his pencil idly like a majorette's baton. Keeping his hands occupied helped him think better, and he needed that additional edge to beat back his misgivings.

"Problem?" Dillon had propped his heels on the desk while he'd been lost in thought.

"I don't like it."

"He's putting the moves on your lady." His friend wagged a remonstrative pen at him. "Of course, you don't like it."

"That's beside the point." Frowning at the nonchalant response, Rio mimed a parry with his pencil, then a riposte. Just because everything was fine between Dillon and Jordan was no reason for him to make light of Rio's concerns.

"Sorry." Taking his heels off the desk, Dillon sat up and swiveled to face him. "What—exactly—about Hollingsworth is triggering your alarms?" He rested his arms on top of his papers, giving Rio his undivided attention.

That much predatory intensity was a mixed blessing. Being its focus was rather disconcerting. "That's the thing: I don't know." Tilting his head back, Rio closed his eyes, trying to muster his thoughts into a coherent, sensible whole. "I keep seeing him lately. Not just hanging around Cyn, but talking to her. In the crowd. Out of the corner of my eye. Like background static. Nothing exceptionable." One face blending with many when he was with Cyn. A walk. A back. The tilt of a head. Watching stillness in the shadows.

That time at Just Desserts had simply been one of the more notable instances.

Opening his eyes, Rio rubbed his face in frustration. "I don't know. Just a gut feeling. Could be I'm jumping at shadows."

Dillon shifted his hard gaze slightly, past Rio.

"I, for one, wouldn't discount intuition." Lantis stood in the doorway connecting their offices, a mug in hand, looking like he'd been there for some time. He raised the mug in directive, sending the aroma of hot chocolate wafting toward Rio. "Ask around. Do some research. At the very least, you'll get some practice out of it."

Outright permission to indulge his suspicious mind. Rio smiled, his mood much improved.

Hours later, he waved a hand over the box of Chinese takeout, focusing his will to activate the self-heating spell inked on the underside of the white cardboard. As much as he'd been given permission to use company resources to investigate Hollingsworth's background, he couldn't justify to himself doing so to the detriment of his other—paying—responsibilities. He cleared his daily quota of background checks before taking full advantage.

Long after Dillon and Lantis had left for the day, Rio worked his sources and contacts ruthlessly, dipping into federal databases and private intelligence networks, extracting what he could in the meantime and sending out feelers for more. From years in black ops, he had friends in low places who knew the back doors into all sorts of setups. For this, he had no qualms about tapping them.

Which was why he was still in the office poring over the bastard's credit report while waiting for Cyn's call. As he read, he doodled on the margin, spitting his rival with ink-born stilettos and centering him in a marksman's reticle, in between bites of mandarin chicken and fried rice.

On the surface, Hollingsworth appeared to live within his means, Rio noted with disappointment. The mage—and the bank that held his mortgage—owned his house, a bungalow in an older residential district. He drove a secondhand sedan, nothing flashy, which he'd bought at one of those property auctions the city held to dispose of unclaimed vehicles. His last vacation had been a low-cost, self-guided mountain trek the previous summer. He preferred to pay cash, didn't run up his credit cards, and apparently balanced his checkbook to a fare-thee-well.

The latest doodle along the margin sprouted a halo, in addition to bat wings, horns, and a barbed tail.

No ostentatious purchases. *Tap.* The stab of his pencil left a dark spot over the *diabhal*'s heart.

No unexplained income. *Tap.*

No windfalls or mysterious benefactors. *Tap.*

Nothing that triggered any financial red flags. It would have been so convenient if it were otherwise, but that didn't mean much. More reports were in the offing. Sooner or later something would pop up . . . if Rio was patient enough.

His cell phone rang, the tune Cyn's. Finally. The postmortem for the exercise must have run long. He smiled, the reminder of a job well done lifting his mood—until his eye fell on the *diabhal* he'd doodled.

Unless the reason for her lateness wasn't the tac team but someone else . . .

It was time to remind his lover he didn't share.

Chapter Eighteen

Cyn stabbed the elevator call button again, guiltily aware she'd called Rio fairly late. But training came first, and after that fiasco, it was only natural that the team wanted to dissect what went wrong and the discussion had run long over pizza and beer. It wasn't as if Rio and she had made plans for tonight, though they'd fallen into the habit of having dinner together.

He should understand.

That belief was cold comfort as she rode the elevator up, and she couldn't help a glance at the redhead's door when she got to Rio's floor, wondering if the flirt had pounced on the opportunity to commiserate with him, maybe even offer some personal attention. *The feminine, compliant sort a man like Rio settles down with, and conveniently close by.* Invidious thought, but one with unexpected potency. Just the suspicion had her temper rising.

She let herself into the apartment and was greeted by shadows. "Rio?" she called out as she hung up her jacket and took off her shoes, renewed doubts clamoring to be heard.

"Over here."

He stood before the bank of windows in his usual cutoffs and tank top, a darkness silhouetted against the streetlights. The city sprawled at his feet, etched in light and shadow, as far as the eye could see. Man-made radiance gilded the monuments to civilization: the federal courthouse with its cadre of Tuscan columns, the solid, sober lines promising dispassionate justice; police headquarters with its modern glass-and-steel facade; the bronze statue of the city's founders in the middle of the square; the dancing fountains across the theaters on Broadway. Farther away, the river stood out as a skein of black outlined by clusters of light. And beyond, the brighter, more garish spellboards advertising the bars and clubs on the south side.

Thousands of lives glittering to challenge the heavens.

Cyn stopped in her tracks, taken aback by the poetic nonsense. She had to be brain-dead from rehashing the session to be thinking in those terms, but she could see why the view would appeal to Rio. "I hope you didn't hold dinner for me."

"I had something earlier."

The banal conversation was soothing with its focus on the commonplace, a familiar refrain between longtime lovers, in a song that had yet to lose its appeal. Then it veered off on a tangent into a minefield.

"Are you seeing Hollingsworth?" He asked the question lightly, as though it wasn't important; but it came out of left field, a complete digression that implied otherwise.

She struggled to process the question, her brain tangling in confusion. First, Danzinger. Now, Rio, too? What kind of gossip was floating around about the crime scene tech and how had it reached Rio? Had one of her brothers somehow planted that idea in his head? If she didn't know better, she'd say he was jealous. Her stupid heart leaped at the impossibility.

"Of course, I am," she retorted, hoping to divert the conversation to safer waters. "He's senior in Forensics. It'd be hard to work a case without seeing him." Which ignored the fact that she'd managed the feat for years—until recently.

Turning from the window, Rio frowned, his disapproval of her facetious rejoinder clear despite the weak light. "That's not what I meant, and you know it." He stalked up to her, all lethal grace and fluid motion, the air around him fairly vibrating with leashed emotion.

A lesser—or wiser—woman might have retreated.

Exhaling sharply, Cyn pushed her hair back and out of her face. "Look, I can't do anything about Hollingsworth dropping by to talk. I can't just blow him off. I have to work with him. If I get his back up for no good reason, you can bet he'll make life difficult in future investigations."

"So long as that's all he does." Rio pulled her into his arms, branding her senses with his presence. The pressure of hard muscle against her breasts. The heat of healthy male. The spice of sweat and coffee.

Her heart raced.

He'd never acted so forcefully with her before, never been so dominant. Not that he treated her with kid gloves, but he'd never gone all machismo on her, either.

Rio's aggressive stance sent an animal thrill of excitement through Cyn. Just like that, he had her aroused to a fever pitch, trembling with the force of her desire. She found herself panting, trying to control her response.

Need swirled in her veins, refusing to be subdued. His feral demeanor had her libido singing with delight. Rio rarely lost control, usually managing to play the gentleman. His blatant possessiveness now was like a spark to oiled rags, igniting her own passion in an instant.

Something inside her rose up in rebellion. She couldn't give in, just like that. She wasn't some fragile flower of femininity waiting for any man to pluck her, to be taken on the floor like some fling—never mind that Rio had done so before with her eager abetment.

Twisting out of his hold, Cyn retreated toward the stairs. "What kind of game do you think you're playing?" Her pulse fluttered in her throat, like a butterfly under her skin struggling to break free. The sensation only compounded the exhilaration that stole her breath.

A predatory smile curved his lips, equal to the glint in his dark eyes. "I haven't decided yet. But one thing it's not is catch and release." He lunged forward, tackling her on the wide second step, the ell in front of the tall windows.

She landed on her rump, in the cage of his arms, the wall cutting off her escape—not that there was any question of where this was headed—but she had no intention of making it easy for him. Momentum carried her flat to her back, pressed breasts to hard chest with a suddenly aggressive male. She reached for his wrist, but he merely transferred his grip, catching hers instead.

Grappling was a lost cause, even without the sensual friction that undermined her resistance. Rio was heavier than she was, and stronger, his position between her spraddled thighs giving her little leverage. Irritated by her helplessness, she tried to buck him off anyway. He subdued her struggles without breaking a sweat, that wolfish expression unchanged. Unless she used magic, there was no way she was getting free—and she couldn't bring herself to use magic on Rio.

A sharp *click* was followed by a hard tug on her wrist and the ring of metal on metal. Before Cyn realized what had happened, her other wrist was given similar treatment. Rio had gotten two sets of handcuffs from somewhere and chained her to the banister, her arms spread as though in oblation.

What the hell?

"What do you think you're doing?"

"Turnabout's only fair, didn't I tell you?" Taking his weight off her, he sat back on his heels with a self-satisfied smirk on his lips and a definite ridge tenting the front of his shorts. All that wrestling had only served to turn him on, the sneaky bastard. "I don't know what's gotten into your head, but I'm not letting you go without a fight."

"Gotten into *my* head?"

Had he been waiting for something like this to happen? Why else would he have handcuffs on hand? Even she couldn't conjure those out of thin air, and Rio wasn't even a mage.

Pulling herself up to a seated position, Cyn tested the cuffs but found little slack. She couldn't spell them open; they looked to be standard-issue police equipment, which were warded against lockpicks and magical interference. He had her right where he wanted her, alright. But she didn't intend to take his high-handed treatment lying down, scrambling to her feet to a more defensive position on the stairs, though kicking him wouldn't help her cause. "What happened to that respect for womanhood your mother taught you?"

Rio raised his brows at her. "I still respect you. I'm just applying a different lesson, here."

"Lesson?" Her heart leaped to her throat at the promise burning in his dark eyes.

"Yeah, something I learned in the army." He breathed against her lips, the sultry heat making them throb with awareness. Pulling a switchblade from his pocket, he flicked it open.

She flinched away, but the banister was a cool presence along the base of her spine, a solid barrier allowing no retreat.

He set warm steel to the collar of her T-shirt.

And sliced down.

Cyn barely felt any pressure, yet the knit cotton parted with frightening ease—the blade was that sharp. Three cuts later, the shirt fell to the steps, helpless to resist the pull of gravity. She swallowed cautiously, a frisson of perverse excitement drawing her nipples into tight, aching buds.

"What lesson?" This was the first time he'd made a direct reference to his military background. Why now?

"They taught me to eat what I catch." The corners of his mouth tilted up in a smile laden with significance, his gaze heating.

Meaning what? she wondered, her heart racing, her body in erotic turmoil. That smile of his ought to require a license as a deadly weapon.

With a quick flick of his fingers, Rio disposed of her bra; thankfully he'd remembered it had hooks that freed the straps and didn't just cut it off. "And it looks like I've caught you, hmmm?"

Cream flooded her sex as she absorbed his meaning, a shudder of liquid desire wracking her body. His mouth on her. Eating her. At that moment, there was nothing she wanted more.

Cyn swallowed with an effort, her throat suddenly tight with longing. How could she resist him when her treacherous libido demanded she give in? Disarmed by her carnal fantasies, she didn't think to put up a fight when he stripped her of the rest of her clothes.

Once he was done, there was no hiding her arousal. She could smell her body's betrayal, musk wafting on the night air as hot cream trickled down her thigh.

Undeniable.

Inescapable.

Gripping the rail for support, she raised her chin, daring him to comment on her weakness. "What's this supposed to prove?"

"You did say you wanted fun and games, didn't you?" Rio stepped back, fierce satisfaction blazing in his eyes. Holding her gaze, he pulled off his tank top, taking his time, his corded muscles bunching and flexing in a deliciously slow-motion striptease. No question what he had in mind.

He bared his smooth chest, the golden skin mere inches away yet tantalizingly beyond her reach. What little light leaked into the room hid its color, but she couldn't forget.

Memory had her breathless. The restraints holding her in

place prevented her from touching him, the heat and the velvet over hard muscle. It made her wild for any contact.

"Tease." The husky voice didn't sound like hers at all. She was supposed to be fighting him off.

"Turnabout, remember? Sauce for the goose, sauce for the gander."

Meaning she'd done it to him his first night back weeks ago, so she couldn't object when he did it to her, too.

A taunting smile curled his lips. "And this gander's definitely having sauce tonight."

A thrill shot through her at his words, heated anticipation stealing her voice. She should demand he release her. It would have been the smart thing to do.

Except Cyn had never imagined that being tied up could arouse her so much. Her body was heavy, languid. Any notion of flight or fight gone. Everything female in her yearned to submit.

To him.

The rasp of his zipper purred in her ears, a threat and a promise. He would take her, this needy woman she'd become. Suck her juices. Claim her like a cherry ripe for picking.

And she'd enjoy it.

Cyn shook her head in denial. This wasn't her, not this weak, complaisant woman trembling with desire.

His cutoffs slipped down his narrow hips in slow motion, the cotton twill reluctant to concede its embrace. But eventually it fell, leaving a hint of lean hip barely seen. A faint sheen profiled his naked length. Because of the heat of the day, Rio had gone commando.

Would he have done so if they'd met for dinner?

She felt a pang of regret for lost opportunity, clenching her thighs against the quiver that speculation inspired, remembering how often she laid her hand on his hip and leg. The chance to tease him knowing only one layer of fabric separated her from him, knowing only his control kept them decent . . .

The lasciviousness of her thoughts failed to shock, so lost was she in her hunger. In her need. In the craving that swept through her all the way to her curled toes.

Rio stepped off the stairs to stand behind her.

She craned her neck around to keep him in sight. What was he up to?

His first salvo took her by surprise: he nibbled on her arm, the contact surprisingly ticklish.

Cyn squirmed as a frisson of delight rippled through her, a quick thrill that had her thighs clamping together in reflex. The cuffs clanked against the rail, proclaiming her response.

Teeth scraped over her shoulder, forcing a gasp through her lips. Chills swept her, raising goose bumps on her arms and sparking fireworks in her belly. He'd never evoked such a reaction from her before with so little effort. Of course, she'd never dreamed of letting him tie her up, either.

He kept his attentions light, kissing his way down her back, the feathering of his lips soft caresses. He stopped short of the rail, and she shivered. His hands along her inner thighs distracted her with a feint upward that stopped short of her aching, throbbing flesh.

If only she could touch him!

A sudden nip on her ass made Cyn squeal, eliciting a spurt of hot cream. "You—" She couldn't think of a threat sufficient for the provocation.

"Oh, yeah. Pure sauce," Rio growled as he reached between her legs to stroke her lower lips, spreading dew over her folds and around her clit, nudging her entrance but no farther. "Delicious." His breath warmed the crease of her ass and the tender skin at the juncture of her thighs. The promise of his mouth on her made her weak with longing.

She panted softly, grasping at the shreds of her control. How could such simple contact reduce her to the point of begging, merely because she was bound?

"Look," Rio ordered, his tone implacable.

Safety glows shimmered on, pale blue along the treads of the stairs, and their images appeared before her, reflected off the high, night-dark window. Her white lock glowed like faerie light, her body gleamed with sweat, but that wasn't what caught her attention.

He stood behind her, the baluster between them, his broad shoulders wider than hers, looking as rapacious as his conquistador forebears must have looked raising sword and wand in conquest. "Oh, yeah. I'm going to enjoy eating you—slowly. But not until you're truly ready."

Cyn swallowed against the excitement his words engendered, the heated promise in his eyes inescapable. He didn't think she was ready? She was about to go up in flames!

Rio cupped her breast, cradling it in his hard palm, and strummed his thumb over her pouting nipple. A featherlight touch she felt all the way to her toes. He did it again, over and over, the rhythmic strokes hypnotic in their effect as wave after electric wave of sparkling sensation washed through her.

She closed her eyes, overcome by her body's response. Her head fell back, too heavy to support. Clenching her hands on the rail, she fought not to moan. Reduced to some helpless, melting female with just his hand!

"Watch." The command was low and intense. Compelling.

Startled, Cyn couldn't help but obey. Her eyes shot open to see his other hand tracing lazy circles down her belly, barely there and all the more explosive for its subtlety. Her nerve endings prickled with awareness.

The picture they made was one of blatant possession, his hands wandering wherever he willed, her body his playground.

Excitement shook her.

Somehow, though she'd thought he'd been busy making love to her, Rio must have noticed her response to the mirror in the limo. The realization set off a pulse of need between her thighs, her clit aching for his touch.

In the window, long fingers traced the line of her side, trailing up her ribs to her straining breasts. A light caress followed, barely felt, as he played to their reflection.

Cyn couldn't look away, even if she wanted to. Only by watching could she tell where he would go next. Anticipation built with each fleeting contact, like soft down across her belly and shoulders, between her breasts, under her arms. An eternity of arousal.

He avoided the more intimate areas, knowing it would drive her crazy. That restraint was a seduction in and of itself. Moving downward, he continued to taunt her, drawing patterns along her legs, behind her knees, around her ankles. His lips seared her nerves, lashing them with exquisite delight.

She shuddered, molten desire a fever in her veins. Her gasps echoed in her ears, a distant harmony to the pounding of her heart, the scent of her excitement inescapable.

When he reached her feet, Rio shifted, rounding the baluster to kneel before her. He should have appeared supplicant, weak. But the hot-eyed look he gave her could only be described as predatory. Here was no man begging for her favors. Not a man asking permission. He was here to claim her—no ifs or buts.

Her legs spread of their own volition, falling apart to leave her open to him. She throbbed: her head, her neck, her arms, between her legs. Her skin felt too tight, her breasts heavy. She burned for his touch with an ache that bordered on pain. Craved it more than her next breath.

His hands closed around her thighs, holding her open. Then, catching her eyes, he bent forward and gave her that most intimate of kisses. His tongue dipped inside, delved into her weeping slit, lavished stroke upon exquisite stroke on the delicate flesh, licking her as though she were a confection to be savored. He nibbled her folds as though he would truly eat her, the rasps searing her nerves with white-hot delight, a fireball to the senses.

No one had ever commanded her body so thoroughly.

Lost to the conflagration consuming her body, she moaned,

arching against his mouth, helpless before his mastery. She forgot everything: handcuffs, objections, control.

Only Rio mattered.

Release beckoned, just out of reach. One stroke, one touch was all it would take to send her over the edge.

Then he stopped.

She nearly died.

"I can't get enough of you." Getting to his feet, Rio leaned forward, pressing her against the rail, his smooth chest rubbing against her tight nipples, his cock dipping deliciously close to her aching mound. He took her mouth, letting her taste herself on his tongue, her salty juices driving home her surrender—etching it into her consciousness. His lips seared her neck, tongue and teeth working together to mark her. "You're so damn sweet, I want to eat you all up."

A thready moan escaped Cyn, her bones melting at the images his words conjured. How much longer did she have to wait before he took her? She burned for him, craved his cock inside her, a ravening hunger only he could satisfy.

Only the rail's support kept her upright. Left on their own, her knees would have betrayed her. She needed him too much, yearned for the sensations only his possession could give.

"Rio?" She panted against the fever ravaging her senses, the need inside her coiled steel-tight, thrumming at the point of violence. "Rio, please."

"That's right. It's me."

As though it could be anyone else!

His arms locked around her as he surged against her, all aggression. Heat and power and pure male. He drove into her, his blunt cock relentless, every inch of him stretching her sensitive inner flesh.

It was too much—and just enough.

The carnal friction catapulted her over the edge, detonated the coiled tension lodged in her core. She choked on a gasp, drowning in a dark wave of primal ecstasy, a tidal bore of indescribable plea-sure. One orgasm after another blasted her senses, brutal delight in an unending surge of rapture, as Rio pounded his way to satisfac-tion.

"You're *my* woman," he growled against her neck much later, his teeth capturing her earlobe for a chastising nip, his corded arms the only thing keeping her on her feet. "Don't you forget that."

Floating with the weightlessness of utter release, Cyn could only wish it were true. But she couldn't believe it, not if it meant becoming someone like her mother and sister-in-law.

Crooning soft praise, he unlocked the cuffs, freeing her to sink to her knees, spent.

She sprawled on the stairs in his arms, heedless of any dis-comfort. Bonelessly euphoric yet utterly shattered.

She'd lost.

Given in.

And reveled in her surrender.

CHAPTER NINETEEN

Her uncharacteristic submission continued to trouble Cyn the next day as she handled the minutiae of shift change on auto. She couldn't explain away the urge that had driven her to allow Rio to do all he'd done. She could have put up more of a fight—if she'd been determined. He wouldn't have kept her tied up if she'd insisted on not playing his game.

So why hadn't she?

Picking up her mug, she took a cautious sip of hot coffee, the regular chaos of the bull pen no distraction from her riotous thoughts.

Had she actually wanted a display of possessiveness? Had she in fact driven Rio into such a display? And what did that say about her vaunted disdain for feminine artifice? Her hair slid down, drawing a veil of white across her face. *You're an arrogant bitch, Cyn.*

Last night had torn the blinders off her eyes. Rio made her want to change, to become someone like her mother—traditional, feminine, dependent, something she'd always sworn would never happen—anything to keep him.

Cyn couldn't deny it any longer, and it scared her spitless. She hated that—hated the sinking sensation it engendered—with a vengeance.

The only alternative would be to break things off before it went any further. Her heart actually clenched at the thought, a pang of distress that made her blink at its strength. Not to have Rio in her bed ever again? Not to wake with him beside her, laugh at his jokes, blush at his doodles, or see him smiling at her from across the table? Even though she knew deep inside that he would eventually realize she wasn't the kind of woman he wanted to spend forever with—just like Greg had—she didn't know if she could bear to give that up without a fight.

But to become someone like her mother?

Work called to her. Even if she couldn't control her emotions, she could do her job—and there was a lot to do.

As Cyn pushed her hair out of her face with a fresh work ethic, Coughran shambled in, late again and very much the worse for wear. The stocky detective looked awful. Wrinkled shirt over worn jeans. Curly brown hair far longer than regulation; the department discouraged the rocker look. Plus the unhealthy dark bags under his bloodshot eyes? He looked like someone coming up for air after a three-day binge. Not a sight to generate confidence in the tax-paying public, regardless of his high clearance rate.

She couldn't keep excusing his tardiness just because she understood his need for a second job to supplement his pay; he was helping a nephew through healer training and lately supporting some relatives who'd lost their business in a fire, one of the first hit in the mage gang's crime spree. Besides overtime, he moonlighted as a bouncer at a waterfront dive frequented by bikers, and she'd figured the connection would have its advantages. But with the mayor breathing down the L-T's neck, she'd prefer the bean counters at City Hall not get more ammo to make problems.

"So, how's the stud?" Ellis asked, batting her feather-thick lashes when Cyn got back from counseling Coughran, usually one of the more distasteful duties associated with making sergeant but today a relief from the tug-of-war of her emotions.

"Coughran?" Forced to view the detective as a man, she blinked in surprise. Rested, he probably cleaned up good, if you liked the stocky, barrel-chested type, but he was too burly for her taste—and a cop, besides. "The usual."

"No, silly. That eye candy of yours." When Cyn narrowed her eyes, the blond detective protested, "Hey, no law against looking!" Then her curiosity must have overcome her sense of self-preservation, because she sighed, "And he is one *fine* sight." Another flutter of lashes accompanied the statement.

"He's fine." In fact, he'd been better than fine, so much better that she was tempted to break her rules—but she didn't want to think about that. Just the reminder sent heat to her cheeks.

Ellis broke out in giggles.

Tempted to hex her, Cyn didn't bother to dignify her amusement with a rebuke, opting instead for mature self-restraint. She could always put the blonde on her shit list later.

Work made ignoring Ellis easier.

The cross-check of the facial reconstruction photos against the hits from Missing Persons had filtered her roster of missing tall brunettes down to several dozen matches. Now it was up to Cyn to reduce them to four.

It was a long shot, but her luck had to turn sometime.

As though in answer to her wishful thinking, her computer chimed. E-mail showed a new message in her in-box. From the size of it, the federal database had come through. Negative findings were minuscule in comparison.

Excitement flowing, she downloaded the attachment and sent

it to the printer, refraining from reading until she had it in color on paper and in her hands.

Five ten. Brown hair. Green eyes. Birthmark on right hip. Dental records. Fingerprints. DNA scan. A perfect match on all counts.

"Ha." Cyn grinned as she scanned the printout. The killer's arrogance had worked to her advantage. She had a name: Tamar Lagidze. The passport image the system coughed up wasn't very complimentary to her latest Jane Doe. Lagidze looked wan and uncomfortable in the photo; of course, once they'd removed her from the meat locker's stasis spells, death hadn't done much for her complexion, either.

According to the Missing Persons report filed by her sister, Lagidze had been a folk dance instructor based in San Francisco and was last seen backpacking in the Cascades more than a year ago during summer break. She hadn't shown up for the start of the fall semester. Two months in which she must have met her killer, right in the middle of a wilderness.

One name less in her roster of missing brunettes. Cyn found Lagidze listed smack in the middle of the alphabetically arranged haystack. Progress.

She updated her murder board, adding Lagidze's name under the vic's photo, beside the psyprints of the remaining Jane Does. One down, three to go.

As she wrote, Hollingsworth walked in, nattily dressed in a navy blue suit that had to be hell in the summer heat, which probably meant a court appearance earlier that morning. His arrival set off a wave of double takes in the noisy bull pen.

"Something new on your Jane Does. The ME sent out for further tests, and the results just arrived." Triumphantly brandishing a folder, he grinned smugly as though he were personally responsible for the ME's decision.

Despite the unwelcome reminder of last night's submission

the crime scene tech's presence represented, Cyn smiled back. It looked like her luck had indeed turned. "I thought they hit a dead end."

"There's this new DNA scrying technique that's supposed to be able to locate genetic relations. Unlike standard spells, it's not dependent on psychic residuals." Dropping the folder on top of her papers, he chuckled. "It was a long shot, but it seems to have gotten *something*."

Maybe Hollingsworth had been responsible for the test.

"Something?" she repeated, flipping the folder open. The chart that confronted her was supremely uninformative, and there were several more under it. She nearly groaned, a throb starting up behind her eyes in misgiving. More dry technical reading.

Reaching over her shoulder, he fished out a map of the U.S. from the stack, one covered with colored splotches mostly in New England. "The spell maps populations that share certain DNA sequences with the sample."

Vague as hell but better than negative. If it worked as advertised, it could help narrow down possibilities, even find family . . . unless, of course, the Jane Doe had been adopted or relocated before her disappearance.

Hollingsworth stared at her expectantly, like a puppy awaiting praise. He stood so close she could feel the heat of his body along her arm and smell his cologne, a woodsy-spicy blend like what Alex used.

"You didn't have to bring them yourself," Cyn protested, conscious of the glances Ellis sneaked at them from beneath extravagant lashes, obviously eavesdropping. No telling what kind of rumors would be circulating by end of shift.

"You caught me," he confessed, raising his hands, palms out, in mock surrender. "I volunteered. Any excuse to see you."

His outlandish statement brought a blush to her cheeks, comforting to her ego after facing the prospect of Rio's ultimate rejection. "Um, thank you. This should help."

"The technique is experimental. It's still in the trial stage, which is how we were able to get this in." Hollingsworth shrugged modestly. "So, anyway, I figured you might want some help wading through the jargon. Maybe over a beer at Hotshots?"

Despite his previous invitation, Cyn hadn't expected him to ask her out again and didn't know how to answer. She couldn't deny the temptation was there. Giving in would ease so many difficulties. Her brothers' objections, for one. Hollingsworth was a more-than-competent mage, and though he, like Rio, was a civilian, he'd been with Aurora PD for more than ten years, so they knew that he knew what the job entailed.

Since he wasn't a cop, she had less to worry about. Unlike with men in special operations—or law enforcement, for that matter—the odds weren't stacked in the favor of traditional femininity.

Also, the billiards hall he named was a favorite with Fotis's crowd; she could be sure there'd be cops around. They'd talk about work—not so much different from when she hung out with her team.

"It's only a friendly drink after shift." Hollingsworth shrugged, a self-deprecating smile on his thin lips.

Why not? It isn't like it's a date. And when things proceeded as she feared and expected with Rio, it might help if she hadn't burned her bridges. Perhaps she was being too critical of the crime scene tech. Just because he wanted to talk shop might not mean that would be all they could talk about. Who knew what hidden depths lay beneath his scrupulous demeanor? It wasn't his fault she kept comparing him to Rio—and not in his favor.

At least with Hollingsworth, she wouldn't be tempted to betray herself, wouldn't want to become a person she'd always sworn she'd never become.

Cyn stilled, uncomfortable with that train of thought. It smacked of cowardice. Running away.

And yet—

"Say Friday?" He eyed her expectantly, a nice, average man

who, despite his current attire, wasn't in Rio's league. And then again, she wasn't really Rio's type, either, and sooner or later he'd realize that.

Then where would she be?

Chapter Twenty

Rio held his pace to that of his fellow pedestrians, blending with the crowd as he hoofed his way back to the office. The slower pace suited him for the moment. There was no hurry. He'd arranged for an extended lunch break to take delivery of his stuff, the boxes his parents had shipped him that were supposed to arrive more than a week ago but had gone missing. Making sure all his personal effects were accounted for hadn't taken as long as he'd expected. Finally, something had gone right.

With the background check he'd been working on completed, he was free to spend his time as he willed, which meant touching base with his contacts when he returned. Maybe something new on that *diabhal* Hollingsworth would turn up.

The morning's shower had cut the summer heat to comfortable levels and washed the dust from the air, so the stroll was pleasant, though his definition of *pleasant* was probably broader than most.

A sign in a window advertising a twentieth anniversary sale

caught his eye, the bold red letters announcing deep discounts on select jewelry. The crowd inside promised sufficient protective coloration to evade hard-selling.

What would it hurt? He wouldn't lose anything by looking.

On a mad impulse, Rio entered the store, saw it wasn't as packed as he'd thought but had enough people to blend into. A quiet chime greeted his entrance, but he managed to avoid drawing the attention of the salesclerks.

He ignored the baubles set out on the counters, the necklaces locked behind glass doors, the gaudy pieces that were practically lethal weapons. That ineffable compulsion that had drawn him in pulled him to a case on the far side of the store with its rings on display. Dozens of engagement and wedding rings glittered on beds of dark blue velvet, dazzling the eye with shimmering facets. With that before him, the steady chime announcing arrivals and departures was almost hypnotic.

Rio zeroed in on a display of platinum bands with gems set flush. They sparkled with promise, an embodiment of the future he craved. He imagined offering one to Cyn, in bed, with all the appropriate sensual buildup and her ardent acceptance wearing only his ring. Offering her firm, lithe body to his worship. Writhing in ecstasy as she surrendered all reserve. His breath hitched as his fantasy ran wild, waking an inconvenient hunger.

Idiot, you're getting ahead of yourself.

Or maybe not. Cyn hadn't blown up at him for cuffing her to the stairs the other day as he half expected her to, despite his bravado. It gave him hope that perhaps she was coming around to accepting the change in their relationship. After all, she hadn't disputed his claim to being the gander to her goose.

He smiled at the whimsical thought.

A discreet chime announced another customer. A couple walked in, and Rio's hackles rose for no obvious reason, a premonition of danger he'd learned to heed. Unable to ignore his instincts, he stole a glance over his shoulder, wondering what it was about them that struck him as off. Dressed in business casual, they blended with the jewelry store's clientele, the woman carrying a bulky purse over her shoulder. Stylish haircuts, good shoes, clean hands—completely unexceptionable.

Another chime.

The fresh influx of people obscured his view of the two, yet there was no letup to the clamor in his gut. On the contrary, not having them in sight only ratcheted up his sense of unease. Something was really off with those two.

Chime.

Shoppers departed, thinning the crowd inside. Many left bearing bags with the jewelry store's name. *Business must be booming.* The thought made his arms prickle.

Rio turned his gaze to the display case along the wall to conceal his interest in the pair. It was imperative to find out what about that ordinary-looking couple was raising his hackles.

Their reflection in the glass told a different story.

The man was heavily stubbled with greasy, light brown hair. That by itself was jarring. A tattoo of a bird taking wing flew across his left cheek, its tail curled toward his ear then along his jaw.

His companion had hard eyes, thin lips, and a strong, combative chin thrust forward as if demanding to have a chip knocked off. Streaky blond hair fell halfway down her back, but more important was the full cap of tangerine phoenix feathers that covered it.

A shamanka and her attendant? Rio's instincts flashed to red alert. He double-checked the exits automatically. The door to the back office was still closed, possibly locked, and blocked by display cases, which left behind him.

Chime.

Reflected in the glass, three more desperate-looking characters stepped into the store, their gazes darting about, never stopping for long. Looking for danger. It was a holdup waiting to happen. He could almost see them reading through their checklist: security, sales staff, cash register, potentially problematic male customers.

Calm dropped across his shoulders, shrouding the world in stillness. His heart beat slowly as training kicked in, its tempered pace familiar.

This was probably the mage gang running wild in Aurora, the one that had nearly gotten Cyn killed with some booby trap. They could be copycats, of course, but either way, they had to be stopped. Now, how to do that without endangering innocent bystanders? That was the problem.

"Nobody move!" The order, when it came, was almost anticlimactic. Where'd they learn that line? Hollywood?

The knives and wands they brandished, however, were no joke. The edges of the blades glinted with the bright promise of sharpened steel. The wands glowed with power; even someone with his limited mage sense could feel the spells waiting to be unleashed. Their jackets must be lined with silk for no one to have noticed the active magic.

"What is this—"

"Quiet." With the flick of a negligent hand, the woman sent a minor fireball at the protesting store manager. It merely melted a spot on a glass case behind the man, but that was sufficient to cow him and the shoppers.

Rio cursed silently. A mob would have put paid to the mage gang. This civilized bunch was helpless.

"You men, over there." The rough command was accompanied by a wave to one side of the store, delivered with an air of confidence, certain of obedience. The woman—the disguised shamanka—appeared to be the leader from the attention the men paid her, and possibly the most dangerous of the gang, due to her liberal use of magic. If anyone was likely to cast the deflagration spell, it was her.

As the indicated customers hurried to obey, Rio took care not to draw the gang's notice as he maneuvered himself to the edge of the crowd, into a position to take action.

"Over there, against the counter. Now!" Another threatening brandish of a wand sent the women scampering. The orders left the middle of the store empty, save for some freestanding display cases. Two of the gang swaggered forward without waiting for instructions. No hesitation. No uncertainty. They knew their part in this heist. The shamanka and her attendant played the threat, while the last man stayed by the door to stand guard.

Rio kept cover as the gang raided the cash register and the displays of minor jewelry. Smart of them. The smaller items would probably be easier to dispose of, while the major pieces were likely to have security spells on them to prevent theft. They demanded money from the crowd, using threats to enforce their will, but that was all. More smartness. They didn't go among their victims and risk someone—Rio, for example—mustering the nerve to take action. It also meant they wouldn't get some much-loved trinket that could be tracked.

Despite their caution, their haul was easily in the high five figures, in his estimation.

But so long as they didn't do anything that actively threatened the innocents around him, he held his peace. He daren't draw his gun. Shooting in this crowd would be the height of recklessness. If he missed, there was no telling what he would hit.

If the gang didn't do anything worse than that fireball, odds were, no one would be hurt. Perhaps they'd simply leave once they had what they were after. But he couldn't depend on that happening, especially if this was the mage gang as he suspected. He had to be ready to act.

After filling the plastic trash bags they'd brought with them, the gang began edging toward the door. If this was the mage gang, they'd lob a deflagration spell just as they left.

Right then, the woman reached into her purse and Rio's gut went into overdrive. *Score.*

For a split second, the mage gang's attention was focused entirely on the shamanka.

This was his chance.

Gambling that surprise would throw the others off balance, Rio closed the distance, into striking range. Magic gave them the upper hand, but it required mental focus. He had to keep the woman occupied enough that she couldn't cast the deflagration spell. It would have been next to impossible against a well-trained black ops agent; hopefully this shamanka wasn't of that caliber. If his attack shook the concentration of any other mages, so much the better.

The nearest man shouted as Rio passed him, ending with a croak after a knife hand to the throat just strong enough to disable. But the thug wasn't important.

She was.

Pivoting on his left foot, Rio slammed his right into the attendant who'd stepped in front of him to protect the shamanka. The man folded over his belly, stumbled back, and crashed into her. A shriek of rage pierced the air, birdlike in its shrillness.

He dodged a punch. As he'd expected, the men reacted instinctively, resorting to fists, not magic.

Spinning around, the guard gaped while the last man fumbled the trash bags he carried, torn between coming to the shamanka's defense and the loot.

Focused on getting to the woman scrambling on the floor, Rio ignored them, hurdling the man he'd kicked. *Neutralize the danger.*

She staggered to her feet just as he reached her, long fingers tracing an arcane pattern in the air.

He slashed a claw hand at her face, an attack few could ignore. With a cry of alarm, she ducked the strike, her hair lashing his arm. His fingers brushed fire.

Pain exploded, shooting up his arm with unexpected strength.

The shamanka screeched, gesturing.

Power slammed into Rio, blasting him back several feet into a display case. The impact drove his breath out, stunning him for a moment—a delay he couldn't afford. Before he recovered his footing, she'd thrown herself out of range, her retreat covered by the others. He forced himself forward anyway, hoping she wouldn't risk hitting one of her own.

Fire bloomed between her hands, flashing into being at triple speed.

Damnú air. *The deflagration spell!*

Ripping off his shirt studs, Rio activated the talismans' defensive spells with sheer will and desperation. He dropped one tinkling on the display case behind him, trusting its shield would cover the innocents beyond it. The other he flung at the shamanka.

Maybe—just maybe—its magic would interfere with hers.

Or deflect the spell, mitigating the blast.

He daren't even hope it would activate close enough that the backlash immolated the shamanka and her gang. Dame Fortune was rarely so kind.

She screamed as the blue goldstone stud spun in the air, glittering in the afternoon sun.

Rio dove for another display case in the middle of the store, ducking his head behind his upraised arm reflexively. The explosion tumbled him through the air, heat rolling over him a split second later.

A fire alarm went off, its wail instantly deafening.

His arm was dead for a heartbeat. Then nerves sprang to outraged life, white-hot pain flashing across the left side of his body. He landed heavily, an ignominious belly flop that added insult to injury.

He ignored the clawing agony, thrust it from his mind as he saw his enemies scrambling to their feet, the shamanka heading for the open door with her attendant close behind. They weren't getting away! He wouldn't let them.

Pushing himself to his knees, he pulled his switchblade.

Alive! You need them alive!

Leaving it folded, he hurled the switchblade at the guy at the door. It wasn't balanced for throwing, but its heavy ironwood handle clocked his target on the forehead with a solid *thunk* that knocked him back.

With a shout of pain, the guy doubled over, grabbing his head and—fortuitously—releasing the door he was holding open for the last gang member, who crashed into him. They went down in a tangle of arms and legs and trash bags, landing against plate glass with loud clunks.

Rio rushed forward, scooping up his switchblade and clouting the first guy for good measure. Fighting for time, he tackled the other one struggling to stand. The impact sent white-hot fire through his nerves, but he couldn't let that stop him. He had to keep them there, pin them down. Every second was a second more for the cops to respond.

A punch landed on his injured shoulder, driving a grunt from Rio. The bastard fought dirty.

He blocked another blow and countered with an elbow strike to the belly.

"Ooof." The pained groan was accompanied by a satisfying gust of curried breath, fresh from lunch. The bastard grabbed Rio's shoulder, clawing at the weakness as they grappled on the floor.

"*Cabrón.*" Swearing, he caught a thick wrist. Locking it against him, he slammed his palm heel into the guy's elbow, breaking the joint.

"Police! Don't move!" The shriek from next to his ear nearly drowned out the shouted order.

About damned time.

Sparkling light sprang into being between Rio and his adversary, wrapping around them like so much taffy and eliminating movement from their options. Police magic, a variant of a spell he'd seen Dillon cast.

Uniformed legs surrounded him.

Then someone moved him.

His arm screamed silent invectives, burnt flesh tearing as he was rolled to his back. "*¡Cojones!*" Rio hissed, fighting back stronger language and the darkness edging his vision.

"*Rafael?!*"

He blacked out before he could identify the idiot and give him a piece of his mind.

"What do you think of that new Greek restaurant on Fifteenth?" Hollingsworth—*Brett,* Cyn reminded herself, though it felt strange to think of him that way—stepped out of the way of the influx of uniformed cops that preceded shift change, a questioning smile on his broad face. The crime scene tech was dressed more formally than usual in a pale blue button-down long-sleeve shirt and navy slacks—the color emphasized the breadth of his shoulders and brought out the red in his auburn hair. But the outfit was not quite his testifying-in-court attire. "I figured we'd try it tonight." He ignored a thumbs-up one of the passing men flashed him.

Oh, no, not home cooking, was Cyn's first thought, followed by, *What happened to "a friendly drink after shift"?* She shoved aside her ungracious reaction. He was making an effort, which was more than she could say for herself. She forced a smile on her lips, feeling like a traitor for inviting the attention of a man other than Rio. "I don't know, can't say I've tried it."

She walked beside him, conscious of his cologne, the subtle blend of citrus and spice making her nose itch.

"It'll be new for both of us then." The open pleasure on his face made her writhe inside, guilt pricking her conscience. She was using him to soften the eventual loss of Rio; if that didn't count as bad faith, she didn't know what did.

Ellis waved at Cyn frantically as she entered Homicide with Brett at her side. Clutching the black handset of Cyn's phone to her chest, the detective's expression radiated an odd mix of triumph and concern, as though she wanted to laugh but feared she'd throw up if she did.

"What's up?" Cyn asked once she was within earshot.

"It's Kelvin. They've caught two members of the mage gang." Ellis had to mean the one responsible for the crime spree in the city, the one with a taste for deflagration spells.

She blinked and checked her cell phone reflexively. There hadn't been a callout. In any case, it wouldn't have come over her office phone and not from Jung, so why was he calling her?

"And?" As much as the news was welcome, Cyn didn't see any reason for the other woman's tension.

The blonde leaned over her desk, fist clenched with white-knuckled intensity as she offered the handset. "That eye candy of yours was injured in the takedown. Kelvin thought . . ."

Cyn went cold. Over a roaring in her ears, she heard Ellis name a hospital. She forced back the darkness around her vision by sheer force of will, forced herself to breathe normally. No time for that.

"What's going on?" Brett's face was hard, anger and frustration etched across its broad planes.

Shaking her head, Cyn left them to pin down Derwent in his office. She didn't know what she said when she made her excuses, more focused on getting to Rio. The L-T waved her away with barely a frown. She rarely took personal time without good reason; hopefully doing so now shouldn't be a problem.

Hollingsworth disappeared at some point, for which she was grateful. She couldn't deal with him at the moment, didn't know how to explain her rush to join another man.

The drive plunged her straight into rush-hour traffic made all the more maddening by her urgency. How badly off was Rio that Jung felt it necessary to call her?

Evan's partner Sullivan was in Emergency, arguing with a medic, when Cyn got to the hospital. He broke off when he saw her. No doubt about it now; her dropping everything to check on Rio would reach her family.

Then Evan stepped out of the restroom, and it was definitely too late to avoid him.

"Your pretty boy's in there getting himself patched up." Sullivan tilted his head toward the treatment rooms, watching her as though faced with some oddity, while her brother worked his way toward them.

Cyn ignored the appellation and his curious eyes, more interested in Rio's condition. Getting into an argument over minor name-calling would only prolong the suspense. "How is he?"

"Okay, I guess." Sullivan ran his hand through his shock of red hair, his hazel eyes green with amazement—unless the color was due to the avocado paint of the walls, a silly thing to notice at a time like this. "It's the damnedest thing. The witnesses all say he took down the perps."

The chill that had encased her heart thawed slightly at the news. Rio was alive and seemingly out of danger. She could take the time to find out what had happened.

"If I'd arrived after it was over, I might have arrested him instead," Evan interjected with a wry twist to his mouth. "He actually faced down a deflagration spell unarmed. Who the hell did he think he was, some freaking superhero?" He hooked his thumbs on his belt, his face screwing in a look of mock exasperation. "He's a civilian, damn it. An innocent bystander. He made it look easy."

She ignored her brother's plaintive foolery to pounce on the key datum. "Rio faced down the deflagration spell?" The risk he'd taken!

Sullivan looked around, checking for eavesdroppers, then nodded at Evan. "Tell her the rest of it."

"He had some heavy-duty protection, but used it to shield the others. Didn't even think twice, to hear them tell it." Her brother held up a silk envelope, the kind they used for magical evidence, complete with signed and dated tags. The sealed plastic bag inside held a blue goldstone pin, what looked like half of a pair she'd seen Rio wearing on his shirts lately.

"Talisman?"

"Yeah, what the hell is he, Sis?" The discomfort on his face suggested his foolery had been at least half serious. God's gift to the police force thought civilians ought to leave the derring-do to cops.

A darned hero is what Rio was. Sudden movement down the hall distracted her before she could blast Evan for his patronizing attitude.

"Sarge, thanks for coming over." Jung trotted over, looking cool and collected in a sage green blazer over a black T-shirt and chinos; his expression, though, betrayed suppressed excitement. "I really think your being here will help."

Huh?

"I'd like to get more info before questioning the two perps in custody. We viewed the store's security video, but Rafael was closer. Maybe he noticed something." He rocked on his heels, then snuck a peek at her. "I think he'll be more forthcoming in your presence."

That was why he called? Jung must think Rio needed handling with kid gloves. Little did he know how far that was from the truth. Cyn stifled a snort, frustration welling up inside her. How fragile did they take Rio for?

Impatient to check her lover's condition for herself, she led Jung back down the hall the way he'd come, sure he'd take over before they got far. She kept her comments to herself. He'd find out soon enough that kid gloves weren't necessary.

Evan and Sullivan tagged along like kindergarteners on a field trip, following them through a few turns and stopping only when Jung waved her into a treatment room.

Rio sat on a gurney, bare-chested, looking irritated and somewhat drawn, disheveled but otherwise unscathed, which was misleading, she knew. Jung said he'd suffered second-degree burns on his left shoulder and arm from the back blast of the deflagration spell, his hair somewhat shorter and ragged on the same side.

According to witnesses, the talismans he'd used had been the only reason no one else had been injured in the blast. The gang's mage had protected most of her fellows—one of the ones who'd gotten away had apparently suffered some burns—but her efforts hadn't been enough to overcome Rio and effect a clean getaway.

Cyn introduced Jung, then stepped back, propping her back against the wall. She knew her presence wasn't necessary but was grateful for the excuse to feast her eyes on her lover. He'd taken such a terrible risk, facing down the gang by himself. But she didn't expect it had occurred to him to do anything else. Not and be the man he was.

Pride in him welled up inside her. It took a while to swallow down her heart and pay attention to the interview.

"Can you remember anything about the others? The ones who got away?"

"I can do better." Rio pulled out the small sketchpad and pencil he always carried, flipped it open, then started drawing. His hand flowed confidently across the blank sheet, filling it first with the tattooed face of an unkempt man, then adding that of a strong-faced woman with fancy headgear.

These weren't his usual doodles.

Interest piqued, Cyn leaned forward to study the detailed swirls of plumage and the stylized bird tattoo. *Phoenix feathers. A shamanka and her acolyte?*

Rio spun the pad around so Jung could see the portraits. "They were the first in. She threw the deflagration spell."

Jung frowned as he picked up the pad. He shot an uncertain glance at Cyn, looking for something. Whatever he got from her expression, he turned back to Rio and asked: "Where were you when you saw them? How did you see this?"

"In front of the display of wedding rings. There's a glass case behind the counter. I saw their reflection there." Rio didn't seem to mind the questions; in fact, he seemed to expect them.

Then his answer registered. *Wedding rings?!*

⤬

The baby-faced cop struggling for equanimity gnawed on his lower lip thoughtfully as he stared at the sketch, a finger tapping the rough paper rhythmically. "You're sure of this?"

"Yes, and there's this." Rio forced his left fist open to show shreds of tangerine vanes tangled with hair, angry blisters oozing where they touched skin: a bad case of contact dermatitis made worse by prolonged exposure to the magic-embedded material. The swollen fingers spasmed, cramping from the effort, muscles tight after hours spent clenched. He hadn't thought anything about the pain at the time, but he must have snagged the shamanka's head-dress during the fight. His nerves twinged as cool air hit the raw wounds.

Jung hissed, extending a hand in reflex and holding it palm down over Rio's. "It's the real thing." He pulled out a plastic pouch and a silk envelope like those Cyn carried for thaumaturgic evidence.

She stood up and headed for the door without a word, her face a regal mask.

Rio raised his pencil to catch her attention as she reached for the knob. "Could you call Dillon or Lantis? Tell them I'll be delayed? That spell killed my phone."

Cyn nodded curtly, then stepped out, moving less gracefully than usual. Was something wrong?

He tried to shrug off her abrupt manner. She'd come to check on him, hadn't she? That implied she cared about him, perhaps more than she was comfortable feeling. On the other hand, maybe it was something else altogether, like a setback with one of her cases.

Using ivory tweezers, Jung transferred the pieces of phoenix feather into the pouch. "That must sting." His thorough probing for the fluffy bits broke open more blisters. "Sorry about that." He sealed the pouch and slid it into the silk envelope.

"This is hers, too." Rio lifted the pale strands of hair, pinching them between his thumb and forefinger, when the cop made to rise.

The mask of imperturbability slipped once more as Jung breathed a fervent curse with hot-eyed hunger. "With that, we can track her anywhere." He looked up to stare at Rio, puzzlement furrowing his brow.

But before he could speak, Cyn returned with a healer in tow. "All done?"

Jung collected the rest of his evidence. "Yeah, all done. Thanks, Sarge."

Tight-lipped, Cyn waved the healer toward Rio, pointing to his injured hand in explanation and leaving the other cop to slip out of the room. When she explained the cause of the blisters, the healer tried to insist he stay overnight for observation; though phoenix feathers were classified as hazardous *materiae magicae*, the side effects were uncertain.

Rio wanted none of that. He already felt like a fraud for hogging a hospital bed when his injuries had been dealt with and said so. Besides, if he was likely to succumb to phoenix poisoning, he'd have died long ago. But that he kept to himself.

"There's nothing wrong with me a little liniment won't fix." A sore hand would make typing difficult, but he didn't need it for the background checks awaiting him at the office.

With some judicious stonewalling on Rio's part, the healer eventually saw reason. He cured the blisters then stalked out in a huff, leaving the skin on Rio's palm tender but whole.

Cyn didn't give him time to savor his victory. "They said you ought to rest. I told Dillon you're taking the rest of the day off." She fingered the burnt tatters of the shirt the healers had cut off his back, not looking at him. By the set of her shoulders, she was steeled for an argument.

He wasn't about to give her one; so long as he was out of the hospital, he wouldn't mind taking a day to recover. But it amused him that she was willing to make decisions concerning his welfare that went beyond mere friendship, despite her insistence on the status quo. Fun and games, this wasn't.

Before Rio could kid her about her highhandedness, Cyn added: "This is hopeless."

His heart skipped a beat. *Hopeless?*

"Here." She proffered a T-shirt faded to an indeterminate shade of gray and apparently worn thin by too many washings, so thin it hadn't made a noticeable bulge in her jacket. "Evan figured you'd need it. There's no way you can wear that." A wave of her hand dismissed his ruined shirt.

Oh. His heart resumed its usual pace as he absorbed her meaning. Generous of her brother to lend it. "You'll have to thank him for me."

She nodded brusque acknowledgment, barely polite.

Rio pulled on the T-shirt gingerly. It was a size too small, but the thin cotton was kind to his newly healed flesh, its weight negligible. "Is something wrong?"

Cyn stopped short of the door, her back stiff. "It can wait."

Shit, she was upset with him.

Chapter Twenty-one

Wedding rings. Rio had been looking at wedding rings?

Hours after that stunning revelation, after helping Rio out with insurance forms, getting him cleared for outpatient status, and driving him to his condo, Cyn still couldn't figure out what he'd been thinking. *Wedding rings?!*

Who was he planning on marrying? Surely not her; she'd given him no reason to believe she was open to the idea.

Was it that little neighbor of his?

Without knowing who he intended the rings for, she had no target for the emotions making her queasy: anger, fear, jealousy, outrage, hope.

Hope?!

"Rio, I saw the news. Are you alright?"

Cyn knew her luck was running bad when the sugary soprano came from behind as they waited for an elevator to arrive. Sure enough, Rio's neighbor sidled up, oozing sympathy and concern, her hair a clash of blues and greens that somehow complemented her cunningly seductive purple business suit.

"It was on the news?" He grimaced, though probably at the publicity rather than from any pain. Black ops avoided media exposure whenever possible, preferring to utilize the press as intelligence instead of feeding them.

That explained Dillon's lack of surprise at her call and immediate acceptance of her description of Rio's condition; he must have caught a similar report. She'd expected him to want to talk to Rio personally, not take her word for it.

"Uh-huh." The flirt bobbed her head, all eyes for Rio. Drinking in every inch of sculpted muscle revealed by Evan's T-shirt, she followed them into the elevator when the doors opened. "Is there anything I can do to help?"

Thus insinuating yourself further into Rio's life?

Cyn forced a smile. "Thanks, but he just needs rest."

"Food? I don't mind cooking."

Of course she didn't. Reining in irritation, Cyn ignored the flutter of lush green lashes directed at Rio that accompanied the offer. "Don't worry. I've got it covered." She showed the bag of Chinese takeout they'd bought on the way home.

The remainder of the ride to the twenty-fifth floor was accomplished in silence, with Rio seemingly oblivious to the undercurrent of tension swirling around him. Intentionally? For whatever reason, he just nodded politely at the flirt as they stepped off the elevator and headed to his apartment.

"What's wrong?" Rio asked as soon as the door was locked behind them.

What could she say? She didn't like that he'd been looking at wedding rings? That she thought he intended to propose to her? Talk about presumptuous! That she suspected he intended to propose to the flirt? Jealousy or insecurity—she didn't know which one was worse.

You're being irrational.

Unfortunately, that didn't change how she felt.

Cyn fled to the living room and its large windows, knowing she did, yet unable to help herself. The apparent peace at street level far below mocked her inner turmoil, as much an illusion as her vaunted control.

She'd frozen when she heard he'd faced down a deflagration spell. *Froze like a ninny.* Thankfully, she hadn't broken down in tears.

Even now, when she remembered the scorched wreck that had been all that remained of Rio's shirt, her insides turned to water. How pitiful was that? So much for the strong, tough cop she pretended to be.

"Cyn?" His hands on her shoulders drew her back to lean into his seductive heat.

Her eyes drifted shut as she soaked her senses in his presence, the heat of him and hard strength. It was times like this when she had difficulty remembering she wasn't anything like her mother. It was so tempting to rest against him, to believe nothing would change. That he would always be there. That he wouldn't want a traditional woman like her nurturing sister-in-law or his petite neighbor.

Only the vague whiff of antiseptic belied that fantasy.

"What's wrong?"

She caught herself before she said something unforgivable. While she might believe that Rio would eventually leave her for a more compliant woman, she didn't want their affair to end any sooner than it had to. And certainly she wasn't going to push him into the arms of his flirtatious neighbor.

So she gave him part of the truth.

"For a moment there, when I heard you faced down that mage gang"—Cyn swallowed back a wave of emotion that threatened to choke her—"I thought you'd gotten yourself killed." She had to blink several times to keep her eyes dry.

His hands slid down and around her waist, pulling her closer, and despite her fears, she let him, her hands coming to rest on his forearms. "For a moment there, I thought I had." Rio snorted, the sharp exhalation stirring the hair at her temple. "I'm lucky your brother didn't finish the job. I think he was tempted."

Cyn should have been relieved he could make a joke of it. Only she wasn't. Her heart still felt like it was stuck in her throat, the prospect of losing him suddenly undeniably real. Whether to his neighbor or simply the Epiphany, it would happen.

But not now.

Not yet.

Yet here she was keeping Rio standing when he was probably famished from all the healing. A sense of failure threatened to rise up and take her. So much for not needing that flirt's help to care for him.

"Let's get some food into you before you die of hunger."

"You won't get any argument from me." He hugged her before releasing her, the affectionate gesture bittersweet.

Back to normal—or what passed as normal—for now.

She turned to the dining nook only to discover it had undergone a transformation since breakfast that morning. Several large, brown, corrugated cardboard boxes crowded the chairs and round table, reducing the area to claustrophobic proportions. The nearest one gaped open, its white straps cut, breaking the support spells embossed in the plastic.

"That shipping company found your stuff?"

"Finally."

Cyn set the food on the table, leaving the small space available to Rio.

"Want some?" he offered, opening a take-out box.

Still wound up with tension, her stomach lurched at the overly sweet aroma of orange chicken. "No, thanks."

Rio ate with the single-minded focus of extreme hunger, another reminder that he'd been injured, that he'd faced down a deflagration spell on his own, with only luck on his side. Without counting the cost.

Another reminder of what kind of man he was.

And the knowledge that men like him chose women like her mother or sister-in-law or the flirt next door.

To derail that train of morosity, Cyn explored the shipping boxes. His clothes had been used in lieu of packing material, stuffed between and around the larger items. In short order, she unearthed a pair of old jump boots worn down at the heels, a horned owl staring out of a partially carved log, some art books, and three rectangular aluminum cases each around three feet long. She pulled out one of the latter after a glance at Rio for permission.

Numerous dings and scratches on its sides attested to violent use. Other than that, its plain exterior gave no hint as to the case's contents. It was locked, sealed with hefty steel charms that by their mere presence warned against tampering.

But Rio simply reached over and deactivated their magic, a display of confidence—in himself or in her?—that wasn't lost on Cyn, then got up to dispose of his trash.

The case opened without further ado, revealing irregularly shaped metal pieces nestled in high-density foam. She blinked at the sight. Whatever she'd thought it would contain, she hadn't expected a rifle—disassembled, but still a rifle. Then it all came together in a flash of intuition: the smell of gunpowder, Rio's police business with McDaniel, his silence about that discussion when he knew she'd be interested . . .

"You're McDaniel's sniper."

We have a live one. Moxham had been right on the money.

"No comment." Despite his noncommittal reply, he gave her a wry half smile of admission.

Confirmation enough.

The confusion of that day at the training center came back to her. The carefully chosen shots. No spikes of emotion. No untoward movement to betray his location. Professional control.

The steadiness of his performance suggested it wasn't out of the ordinary. He'd served as a sniper before. In the field. Black ops. He'd killed in the line of duty. Wetwork.

Silence filled her soul, as though time stopped and the world held its breath while her mind followed that thought to its logical conclusion: someone like the flirt wouldn't be able to handle that side of Rio, probably wouldn't even suspect it existed. He deserved better—a woman who could meet him at all levels.

A woman like her.

Pride and possessiveness unfurled inside Cyn, the embers of hope taking flame. The sultry hunger of a woman who knew her mate.

She wouldn't give him up—not without a fight.

The very air seemed to crackle as Cyn quietly shut his rifle case, moving with a deliberation that had Rio's nape prickling with awareness. The sense of purposeful meandering she'd had was gone, replaced by decision. She stalked toward him, the hunted turned huntress.

Adrenaline surged in response, his heart picking up its pace. Ingrained caution had him slipping crabwise out of the tight confines of the kitchen. Whatever she had in mind, he wanted space to maneuver.

The first inkling he got of her intentions was when her hands dropped to her waistband to release the button there, then pushed her pants down her hips. The descent of the garment barely slowed her. She kicked it and her shoes off as she approached, her eyes dark with hunger. Her tongue darted out to wet her lips, leaving them a glossy pink and fuller.

Rio couldn't help the smile on his face. *Damnú air,* she was

magnificent! He'd expected some sort of reaction to his revelation, but nothing like this—not after she'd acted upset with him.
Cyn pulled herself up against him, her mouth hot and hungry. Her hard-tipped breasts poked his chest, demanding attention.

Another step, and her bare legs were tangled with his, lithe feminine strength under his hands as he automatically reached out to support her. His left hand gave a twinge, forcing him to adjust his hold, but the ache was worth it. Her round, firm ass filled his palms, flexing as she undulated against him, siren-strong and potent enough to bring a stone statue to its knees.

The couch behind his knees cut off his line of retreat, not that he was of a mind to retreat. Despite his surprise at her sudden aggression, his body had no doubts as to the proper response. His lips throbbed from her kisses, the frantic beat repeated in his balls. His cock swelled to readiness, rising so quickly he thought he'd burst out of his fly.

She pressed forward, tipping him onto the couch. He landed with her on his lap, still writhing against him. She wriggled her hands under his borrowed T-shirt, tugging it up so impatiently he feared she'd tear it.

"Careful, that's not mine."

"I'll buy him another one," Cyn growled, the lower register of her voice triggering another thrill of excitement. His Amazon at her fiercest. She could get him so hot just by talking.

Once she got the shirt off, she unzipped his pants, reached in, and freed him of their constraints, her hand squeezing him possessively.

A blast of delight rocketed up his spine, sizzling with erotic promise. He swore fervently, praying for strength not to embarrass himself.

Cyn milked his length, the magic of her touch making a mockery of his control. Her firm grip had him seeing stars, his hips rocking to her command.

He tore at her panties, desperate to feel her on him, the loose cotton shifting aside before his fingers like a wish come true.

Another growl greeted his success. She pushed him on his back and straddled him, her mouth roaming his shoulders and chest and anywhere else she could reach, capturing his nipple between her teeth and nibbling.

Rio laughed, exhilarated by the fury of her passion. Cyn took him without the usual preliminaries, the hot, firm grip of her pussy sudden and shocking, so tight he feared she wasn't ready. But she was wet and getting wetter.

She bit and clawed at him like a tigress marking her mate. If she hadn't kept her nails short, she might have drawn blood. But even in her frenzy, she avoided his left side, still sore from healing.

Cyn started coming almost before he was fully sheathed, the fluttering waves caressing him to greater thickness. It couldn't last. She'd gotten him so worked up it was a miracle he hadn't shot his load prematurely. His balls ached, swollen with need and tucked high.

Locking his hands on her hips, he reared up, his backside losing contact with leather as he pounded into her. She rode him like an Amazon on a bucking stallion, with total confidence, her hard-tipped breasts bouncing before his face. He gave in to temptation, taking a tight bud into his mouth and sucking hard through her thin shirt and thinner bra.

She arched above him, resplendent in her ecstasy. Her scalding orgasm bathed his cock in fervent glory, the fluttering caresses driving him to renewed frenzied motion.

Digging his heels into the floor, Rio thrust upward, the intimate friction fanning the bonfire in his balls. Release came in a white-hot eruption of pleasure, shooting through his cock in searing pulses, emptying him to the root and blasting him out of this world.

Incandescent bliss.

He didn't want it to end.

Feeling like he'd gone ten rounds of Swedish massage and ended with a branding, Rio lay beneath Cyn, his heart pounding fit to wake the dead, tempted to check his ass for ownership marks. He wouldn't have been surprised to find some.

What the hell had just happened here?

Chapter Twenty-two

A guilty sense of goldbricking drove Rio out of his loft to go to work Saturday to make up for Friday's absence. Sure, he was a touch sore, but he'd crawled through jungles and scaled mountains in worse condition; a few hours behind a desk wouldn't kill him. Besides, Cyn was pulling more overtime; between that and Sunday lunch with her family, he wasn't going to see her until Monday, so he had no excuse to stay home.

As he made for his shortcut through one of the nearby parks, he noticed the jewelry store defiantly open for business, new plate glass already installed in the windows, its scorched premises defended by a pair of stern-faced guards, the charred anniversary sale banner swaying bravely in the breeze. Despite the unpromising facade and evidence of construction work, business seemed brisk, with people drifting in then leaving bag-laden with encouraging regularity. Clearly, its patrons hadn't been put off by the attack.

Rio veered toward the shop, drawn by curiosity and a proprietary interest in its welfare. The effusive reception he received took him aback. One of the clerks immediately recognized him, her startled exclamation cutting through the buzz of conversation. When he was identified as the man who'd saved the store, the customers broke out in spontaneous applause, the noise attracting the manager's attention.

Embarrassing though it was, the response encouraged Rio. Perhaps he could make a life with Cyn in Aurora. The thought spurred him back to the display case with the rings that had sparked his interest, despite the intense curiosity aimed in his direction, the proffered handshakes and backslapping and other violations of his personal space.

Just as he remembered, the rings sparkled against the dark blue velvet, platinum bright with promise. A clerk was by his side immediately, offering to show him anything. From her eager smile, he got the uncomfortable impression she would have stripped naked if only he asked.

The manager waved off the clerk, bustling up with an expectant smile on his round face. After a quick glance at their audience, he invited Rio around the counters into his office.

Nonplussed by the continued fuss, Rio grabbed the chance to escape the limelight. If he'd known they'd blow it all out of proportion, he wouldn't have stuck his head in.

"I want to thank you for what you did." The manager pumped his hand as though trying to draw water from a dry well. "If it weren't for your intervention, who knows what would have happened."

Rio recoiled from the blast of goodwill. "I didn't do anything . . ." Flustered, he heard his voice trail off. In fact, most ordinary civilians couldn't have done what he had, yet anyone with his training would have done the same thing. "Nothing special," he concluded lamely.

"Allow me to disagree." Once ensconced behind his desk, the manager rested his clasped hands on its document-covered surface.

"The papers say they're the same mage gang that's terrorizing the city."

Papers? Rio bit back a curse as he took one of the visitor chairs.

"We don't have anything like those talismans you used." The apologetic comment reminded Rio that his shirt studs and switch-blade remained in police custody and brought back the feeling of exposure the talismans' absence had roused while dressing that morning. He'd have to order replacements, and it would take several more days before they arrived. "But you were looking at wedding rings. Is there anything there we can offer?"

"I—" About to disavow any interest, it occurred to Rio that the store probably could use the business, what with the unexpected expense of repair work. Guilt niggled at him. If he'd been faster or had handled the shamanka better, they wouldn't have suffered any damage from the deflagration spell. "I was looking for palladium or platinum rings with no prongs to snag." Platinum would be expensive, but he could afford it. They'd need the durability, especially Cyn with her work with the tac team.

The manager's face lit up at the prospect of a sale. The tray of rings Rio had been perusing was promptly brought in with a minimum of fuss.

Rio picked up a set, running his thumb over the brilliant stones. As he'd hoped, nothing protruded that might catch or scratch. "Are these suitable as talismans?"

"They all are. But if I may, these are particularly suited for carrying spells." He plucked four rings from the tray and with gentle twists broke them into pairs. "By its very nature, the interlocking design of a puzzle ring helps its spells resist corruption. We also have more elaborate models"—he selected a complex-looking ring that collapsed into a jumble of six linked bands—"and all are available in matching his and her rings."

The intricate designs reminiscent of Celtic knotwork appealed to Rio. But it was the suggestion of matching rings that woke something primitive inside him and captured his imagination. A tangible symbol of their relationship, the symmetry therein and—especially—the acknowledgment that Cyn was his and he was hers...

"Thank you. I'd like that." A major understatement. He wanted it with a gut-wrenching ache that took him by surprise.

"Any other preferences?"

"I barely had time to look at rings."

"Aah." The manager nodded understanding, then withdrew some trays from a cabinet behind him. "If you plan on having multiple spells placed, I'd recommend one of these." He offered more rings for Rio's perusal, calmly reassembling the ones he'd taken apart while Rio studied his choices.

Once Rio settled on a set and the stones he wanted, the manager laid a bunch of steel rings on the table between them in a sweet jingle of metal and quickly determined Rio's ring size. Cyn's was more problematic. She didn't wear much jewelry, and the only ring she owned was the bloodstone ring with its contraceptive spell. She never took it off, and he preferred it that way until they decided they were ready to be parents.

The other man fanned out the gauge rings on the steel circlet. "Most women wear between a size six and a size eight," he murmured, isolating five rings in the set, an almost reverent expression on his round face.

Rio fingered one carefully, willing his body to remember the feel of her hands in his, the slender digits and knuckles. Too narrow. He moved to the next size ring, focused on getting it just right.

"Don't worry if they're too large. We can always resize them, and it won't affect the spells."

Easy for him to say, but for Rio it felt like a momentous occasion, as though his whole life hung in the balance. How well did he know Cyn really?

"This." He raised the gauge ring that instinct told him was the right one. "I'd like to have protection spells placed on them," he told the manager as the other man jotted down the size.

"That's . . . an unusual request."

"You can't do it?"

"Certainly we can. It's just that most customers want spells for fidelity or everlasting love. Those or an antitheft geas."

Rio shook his head in bemusement. Some people always wanted the easy way out. Might as well ask for a miracle. "If they need a spell for that, they need professional help, not magic."

Smiling agreement, the manager brought out a folder listing the thaumaturgic options the store offered with their jewelry. "Which ones?"

Rio ticked off the spells he wanted, mentally comparing cost versus his budget and coming up with a month or two of short rations, but it would be worth it. "How much for adding those?"

"Nothing; it's on us."

On them? He blinked. Even one spell was expensive, adding all those . . .

"After what you did, it's the least we can do for you. Against the lives you saved, there's no comparison."

"But—" Rio gestured toward the front of the store and the damage there.

"That's what insurance is for."

He stared at the earnest man, at a loss for words. He hadn't expected anything in return; he'd just done what needed to be done. "Well . . . thank you." What else could he say? He hadn't intended to take advantage of what the other man clearly considered a debt of gratitude; but to back out now would only embarrass them both.

"It'll take a day or so to finish the rings and place the spells. But if you come by Monday morning, they'll be ready."

After the embarrassing applause at the jewelry store, his low-key reception at the office came as a relief. Dillon and Lantis were matter-of-fact about the incident, kidding Rio about his need for danger and the extreme measures he took to alleviate his boredom. They understood that he'd only done what had to be done, no more, no less. However, he was surprised to see them.

"What are you guys doing here on a weekend?"

"I've been ordered not to hover," Lantis admitted, his blue eyes bright with amusement.

"Jordan's busy with a project, so I figured I'd get some work done, then haul Lantis off for some sparring, so he doesn't hover." Dillon grinned at the tall man's raised brow, then mimed a one-two combination of punches. "I'd invite you to join us, but that's probably too strenuous for your condition," he added to Rio.

Rio had to agree. He was still feeling the effects of the healing. Luckily for his peace of mind, the press hadn't tracked him down to Depth Security. He didn't know how long that would last, but in his opinion, the longer he remained incognito, the better. He dove into the background checks with renewed enthusiasm. Delving into credit statements, criminal histories, military service records, and the hundreds of other documents available from public sources and otherwise was much more palatable than contemplating an imminent media frenzy.

Hours later, his phone rang. He answered it absently, still mulling the list of suspicious contacts for his current subject.

"Rafael? I'd like to know, who put you onto that line of investigation?" The lazy drawl didn't hide the speaker's palpable irritation.

Shifting mental gears, Rio sat back and grinned. "Sir!"

His former drill instructor had returned home to Georgia after his medical discharge from the army and now was firmly ensconced in his local county sheriff's department, but Rio hadn't expected to hear from him this soon. Such a quick response usually meant news, and by the gruff salutation, it was the meaty sort Rio could sink his teeth into.

"Don't *sir* me. I still work for a living." A grunt came through loud and clear; civilian life obviously hadn't smoothed away his rough edges. "Now, answer the question."

"A little green-eyed monster told me," he quipped, rolling his eyes at Dillon when the other man looked up from his share of documents, though it was nothing less than the truth.

"Seriously."

"No one. It was just a hunch."

"Fine, be that way." A gusty snort sounded over the handset. "A hunch, huh? Well, then, you'll be interested in this. See what I just sent you. Let me know if you have any more *hunches* afterward." *Click.* The call ended almost as abruptly as it began.

Just then, his e-mail program chimed, notifying him of a new message, one from his former DI. Curiosity piqued, he downloaded and opened the attachment, then began reading.

By the third time Rio pored over the report, he wished he'd taken the time to print out the damned thing; he always worked better with hard copy, and the dry phraseology made him wonder if his eyes were deceiving him. Finally, he called Dillon's attention, waving at his screen in invitation. "Do you get what I'm getting, or am I reading too much into this?"

Leaning over his shoulder, his friend went through the text with nerve-prickling deliberation, reaching over to tap the keyboard to backtrack through the document several times, humming thoughtfully every so often.

"Suspicious, don't you think?"

Dillon waggled a skeptical hand from side to side in a maybe-yes-maybe-no gesture. "Tragic, more likely to provoke sympathy than anything else, and those last two are circumstantial as hell."

"But suspicious."

"Yeah, suspicious, if you're paranoid and a jealous bugger." A quick grin blunted the comment and was followed by a shrug. "Which doesn't necessarily mean it isn't, just because you are."

"It needs digging into." And if there was fire behind the smoke, Rio didn't want Hollingsworth anywhere near Cyn.

CHAPTER TWENTY-THREE

Birds twittered in the trees, the chirps and fluting warbles of the house finches louder than the traffic the next block over. The cheerful songs fit Rio's mood as he cut through the park, heading for his lunch date with Cyn. The velvet-covered jeweler's box was a warm presence against his thigh, the precious rings inside snug in a bed of satin. It was a negligible weight in his pocket, yet to his mind it was so much more. A promise for the future. The embodiment of all his aspirations. Cyn's recent possessive ardor gave him hope that she was coming around.

Then, too, there was the fact that the police were closing in on the mage gang. City Hall had come through with emergency funds for high adepts. From what Cyn told him, they were burning through the blocks set to prevent their locating the shamanka in quick order.

One less danger for her to face.

And he'd had a hand in ending it. Though he knew she'd face others, he still savored the thought.

Life was good, despite the lingering soreness of his left side. Time and rest would fix that, according the healer at the outpatient department when he'd gone in for the mandated checkup. No complications from the phoenix feather.

Rio lengthened his strides, eager to get to the bakery and lunch with his lover. With the park deserted, he didn't have to constrain himself to the slower pace of shorter-legged people, and he welcomed the freedom. He couldn't suppress a smile as he imagined Cyn's acceptance. Sure, she was bound to demur at first, but he didn't think he'd mistaken her feelings for him. Only her fears held her back, and Cyn wasn't a woman to let fear dictate her decisions. Celebrating their engagement would add extra spice to their lovemaking.

A blast of power came out of nowhere. Soundless. Scentless. He had no warning before it crashed into him, throwing him into a tall hedge.

Ambush!

Rio struggled against the force whipping around him.

To no avail.

Magic surrounded him, wrapping his limbs in lines of power. He couldn't move. Fire seared his nerves, overwhelming his system. He tried to scream—and couldn't.

Darkness rushed in.

To her intense disappointment, the patio was empty when Cyn arrived at Just Desserts. The strength of her reaction brought home to her just how much she'd come to depend on Rio being there, waiting for her. She scoffed at herself. He was just running late. There was a first time for everything; it wasn't the end of the world.

Returning to the bakery, she forced her stomach to settle. This was her chance to choose her own lunch—and his. The novelty brought a smile to her lips.

She'd have time to debate with herself what to tell Rio about Sunday lunch when he asked—and he would ask. That had been a strange meal with her family: outbreaks of incomplete arguments just as quickly abandoned; silent discussions between her brothers punctuated by gestures and faces; and Theron frowning at her, keeping his opinions close to the chest. That last was the strangest part. Their father wasn't known for taciturnity.

Thirty minutes later, Cyn didn't know what to make of the situation. Rio still hadn't arrived, nor had he called to say he was delayed.

A babble of conversation rushed into the chirping quiet, accompanied by a fresh whiff of chocolate, butter, and spices. She stole a glance at the door to the bakery and fought down a pang of disappointment at the lanky lawyer type standing in the threshold. Not Rio.

She toyed with her fork, demolishing the innocent square of flaky baklava in its pool of rosewater-flavored syrup while pretending to eat. It wasn't like him to be late. Wondering if his tardiness was due to a certain petite neighbor of his, she pushed the crumbs around the plate, viciously stabbing a clump of pastry that dared survive.

The turnovers she'd bought for Rio sat across the table going dry, the coffee long gone tepid and to his discriminating palate probably undrinkable. A silent testament to his absence.

Had something gone wrong?

Feeling foolish, she called his cell phone. It rang endlessly before dropping her to voice mail. Her stomach turned over queasily. She didn't leave a message.

It was like Greg all over again. First, no-shows, then ignored calls. Silence. Only to find out the jerk had dropped her for another woman—a feminine, compliant woman—and hadn't taken the time or breath to tell her they were through.

Her heart dropped.

Rio . . . Rio wouldn't do that.

Or would he?

That way lay madness. Refusing to consider it, Cyn forced herself to think constructively. Not all operators were like Greg. Something could have happened to Rio's new phone.

Like getting fried by a shamanka's spell?

Unable to sit still, she disposed of the remains of her meal and had Rio's boxed up. With fifteen minutes left to her lunch hour, she might as well go to the source before she drove herself crazy with what-ifs.

Cyn jogged the path through the park, reversing the route Rio would have taken to Just Desserts, though meeting him along the way was unlikely. If he were simply running late, he would have called.

His silence played on her nerves, causing her to check her phone repeatedly. There were no messages from Rio, just one from the Tactical Unit secretary putting her on alert. Her belly tightened. They expected a breakthrough with the mage gang at any time now. By rights, she ought to return to headquarters in case of a callout.

She soothed her conscience with the promise that she'd head straight back once she was sure Rio was alright. Anything that could take down a black ops agent was bound to be a danger to the public, right?

The steel door of Depth Security was before her by the time she'd settled her qualms, and there was nothing left to do but press the call button.

"Yes?" The voice came from a small grille to one side of the door. The speaker had a smooth baritone too low to be Rio's.

"It's Cyn—Detective Sergeant Cynna Malvara." Her meager lunch curdled in her stomach. Her fingers dug into the take-out box, the white cardboard creaking in protest.

"Hang on a moment."

Seconds later the door slid aside to reveal Dillon Gavin— alone. He blinked at her, then looked over her shoulder to scan the hallway. "Where's Rio?" He turned back to her with an easy grin on his lips.

Cyn went still, heard herself ask calmly, "He's not here?"

He waved her inside, sealing the door behind her. "I don't know. I just got back myself."

Dillon led the way to the inner office. She followed cautiously, wary of inadvertently setting off an alarm.

"Lantis, Rio around?"

The tall man rounding the desk had to be John Atlantis. She had only seen him at a distance, but there was no mistaking the towering stature of the husband of one of Aurora's prominent business leaders. "No." He gave Cyn a searching look. "I take it he didn't make it to lunch?" His deep voice matched the one at the door.

Ice crept down her back at the question, a ball of unease that lodged under her heart. "No, he didn't."

"Did he mention planning any side trips?" Dillon perched on the desk, a look of calm inquiry on his mobile face.

Atlantis gave a negative shake of his head. "Lunch was all he said."

Cyn forced back a surge of dismay at the statement, no doubt in her mind it was the truth. If Rio had decided to stand her up to go courting his flirty neighbor, he'd have told his friends; he was straightforward that way, despite what the nagging voice of insecurity in her head said. On the other hand, he hadn't planned that jaunt to the jewelry store that had gotten him hurt. "He's not answering his phone."

The two men traded a look of concern, then Dillon was off the desk and striding to the next room. Cyn tagged along, her unease growing to boulder proportions. If even they thought Rio's being incommunicado unusual, something was really wrong.

The smaller office held an L-shaped table piled high with documents. It was easy to deduce which section was Rio's. His was littered with bits of paper sporting doodles. One report boasted a haloed devil, recognizable even upside down.

Dillon quickly scanned the confusion. "Nothing here." He checked a few spots and apparently found no evidence of Rio's plans, since he returned to Atlantis's office and sent the other man a negatory slash of his hand.

Anxiety was a living, growing thing in Cyn's chest, a suffocating pressure unlike anything she'd felt before. "Can't you track him?" She'd seen Dillon locate a submerged corpse from several miles away; surely a detection spell to find Rio would be simpler.

The two men exchanged glances, then Dillon shrugged apologetically. "I don't have anything of his I can use."

Atlantis frowned, more a narrowing of his blue eyes than anything else. "Remind me to take blood samples for the personnel files. It'll make tracking easier next time."

"I'll do that. In the meantime, there's another way we can find Rio."

"How?" Cyn asked as she watched Dillon check the leather sheath on his forearm and the wand holstered in it.

"Jordan," he answered briefly, sweeping up his jacket and shrugging it on. He headed for the door with Cyn at his heels.

"Wait." The quiet command froze them in their tracks. As one, they spun around to face the tall man. He ignored their questioning stares, intent on his monitor as his fingers flew over the keyboard.

"What?" Dillon's eyes narrowed, the mild concern on his face sliding away, replaced by an aura of danger, a sense of hair-trigger reflexes coming to the fore.

The printer on the side table hummed to life, spitting out sheets of paper in rapid succession.

"Something from Rio's queries. At this point, I think the sergeant should know about it."

Cyn found herself standing in front of the desk with no memory of crossing the room. "What is it?"

Atlantis scooped up the printout and handed it to her. She

scanned the top sheet impatiently. Background information about—

Her eyes flew back to the start; this time she gave the text her complete attention. The gist remained the same, even after reading it through twice.

Pain filled Rio's world. Hardly surprising after he'd let himself be ambushed. Who the hell had gotten a jump on him? A member of that crime gang? Lying on his side, Rio kept his eyes shut and his body limp, exploiting the guise of unconsciousness while he took stock of his situation.

The musty smell of old sawdust mixed faintly with machine oil and grease, almost lost beneath the fresher, more definite odors of soil and animal droppings. Eau de field mouse, if he wasn't mistaken. The air was surprisingly cool.

Quiet. No traffic noises. No birdcalls.

Obviously, he'd been moved.

The rough wood beneath his cheek, weathered and pitted with age, vibrated from heavy, silent steps. Maybe one man.

"Aren't you awake yet?" A hoarse tenor heavy with disgust.

A solid kick landed on his gut, a blast of hurt he didn't need on top of everything else. His body tried to curl up against the pain, but his bonds held him motionless.

¡Cabrón! When he got his hands on the son of a bitch, he'd break the bastard's foot for that.

Another kick followed the first. Clearly the bastard wouldn't be satisfied until he woke Rio. He certainly didn't seem worried about causing internal injury. Who the hell had such a fucking hard-on for him?

Forcing the pain away, Rio slit his eyes open to face his tormentor.

Hollingsworth?!

Chapter Twenty-four

Glaring at the red traffic light, Cyn brought the car to a halt, grateful that driving gave her something to occupy her hands. They'd stopped by headquarters to pick up her assigned vehicle, since she needed guaranteed transportation; Atlantis now followed in his black tank of an SUV. "Hollingsworth? The serial killer?" The papers were pretty damning on the surface.

In the passenger seat, Dillon flipped through the printout, clearly familiar with the material. "Stepsister apparently suicided at seventeen by hanging herself. Brown hair, blue eyes, five ten. Description's similar enough to your victims."

A detail that hadn't slipped by her. She rubbed her temple, tugging on the white lock that sprang from there. "I noticed."

The light changed to green, and she accelerated smoothly, tempted to floor the pedal. Not that she could outrun the demons dogging her heels. To think someone in the department was hiding behind its authority to commit his murders. Someone she knew.

"Matches your description, too, come to think of it."

"That, too." A hard lump settled in Cyn's stomach.

"But that's not really news," he informed her oh so casually, apparently unaware of the impact of his words. "This came in last week."

"It did?" Rio hadn't mentioned anything. The knot in her stomach twisted to Gordian proportions.

"Uh-huh, Rio didn't think it was meaty enough to bring to your attention." Rustling accompanied Dillon's turning of pages. "Here's the meaty stuff: before moving to Aurora, Hollingsworth resided in Athens, Georgia."

She hadn't gotten to that part, too worried about Rio to go through all the papers before leaving for Jordan Kane's. "So?"

"A year or so ago, two corpses were discovered in counties bordering that fair city. Murder victims. Three guesses as to their description, and the first two don't count."

"Dark hair, pale eyes, slender, around five eleven." She didn't even bother to make her statement a question.

"Score."

"But not sanitized." They would have come up in her search of the federal crime database if they were.

"No, *but*"—bent over the papers, he wagged an index finger in the air in emphasis—"someone made an attempt. However, advances in forensic magic found sufficient traces to identify the victims, so they weren't classified as sanitized."

Cyn swore under her breath, unable to suppress a familiar irritation at the shortcomings of the federal database. That little detail would have given direction to her investigation—if it was connected.

"Unfortunately, there are no suspects as of yet. Rio inquired, and tests established time of death to within Hollingsworth's residence in Athens. The second one was killed just prior to his relocation to Aurora."

She checked the rearview mirror and found Atlantis's SUV

behind her, a dark bull looming over the sheep. "That's still circumstantial as hell."

"Why do you think Rio hasn't told you? He knew you'd say that and didn't want to come across as jealous—though I wouldn't blame him if he were." He raised his hand, forestalling her retort. "And, no, I can't say you'd be wrong. But with Rio missing, Lantis figured you ought to be apprised of Rio's suspicions. I can't say he's wrong to do so, either."

And if he was right . . .

Dismissing her fears, Cyn turned to the other question nagging her. "How can Ms. Kane find Rio?" Dillon's lover was a renowned psyprint artist. Cyn didn't see how she could help when Dillon couldn't.

"Jordan's clairvoyant," he reminded her. "All we have to do is ask. Problem is, she's probably in her studio right now, so she won't pick up the phone no matter how long it rings."

"You sure she can?" The forensic specialists Cyn had worked with always needed something associated with their subject to focus their sight, the same reason Dillon had given for not being able to track Rio. As far as she knew, Jordan Kane used her clairvoyance to get around, despite her blindness.

"She's done it before," Dillon replied obliquely.

What does that mean?

He didn't elaborate on his statement; instead, he flipped down the visor to use its mirror to check behind them.

Automatically following his attention, Cyn glanced at the rearview. Atlantis rode their tail, instead of staying a few cars back, not letting anyone between them, almost like a security detail. Paranoia or professional reflex? Or were they deliberately taking defensive measures because of her similarity to the serial killer's victim profile, despite Dillon's seeming insouciance?

She shot a sidelong look at her companion as another possibility occurred to her. Was Dillon riding shotgun and not merely accompanying her to explain the situation to Jordan Kane?

Typical overprotective males.

But were they?

Speculation vied with concern for Rio the rest of the way to the artist's house. The two men hadn't struck her as the chest-beating he-man sort, so why would they take such measures?

Cyn checked her phone once again when they arrived at Jordan Kane's. Still nothing from Rio. Despite her confidence in his capabilities, the absence of any contact was getting to her. What could have happened to him?

Trailing Dillon down the front walk, she paid scant attention to the exuberant garden, merely refreshing her memory of the trees and rocks that presented potential ambush sites, more intent on the house nestled in its green depths.

Atlantis stayed in his SUV. To keep an eye on her car? She tossed her head impatiently. Next she'd be jumping at shadows.

Dillon got them past the security spells with the ease of habit. If she'd had any doubts of his relationship with the artist, his confident entry put them to rest.

A humongous black-and-white cat came bounding down the hall to greet them, prancing at their feet despite his muscular heft and rubbing against their legs in a demand for attention.

"Not now, Tim," her companion told the walking fur coat.

"Dillon? What's wrong?" The soft question heralded Kane's appearance from a room down the hall. The slender woman paused, barefoot, one hand on the door, as she waited for an answer.

"Where's Rio?" he asked instead, closing the distance between them with the cat threading between his legs.

"He's . . ." She frowned, a distant expression sliding across her delicate features. "No place I recognize."

"Describe it," Dillon urged.

"He's lying on a wood floor, rough, unvarnished. Restrained somehow."

"What does that mean?" Cyn whispered to Dillon.

"His position doesn't look natural. Some tendons are tensed." The artist held her hands before her, made a fist, then stroked the fingers of the other along the inside of her wrist. "But I don't see any ropes."

Cyn struggled for composure, dread nibbling at her equanimity. "Magic." That was the one aspect where Rio was vulnerable. But that didn't mean it was Hollingsworth who was responsible. The mage gang could have decided to avenge themselves on Rio for the capture of their members.

"Probably," Dillon agreed, then added to his lover, "He's alive, then."

"Yes!" Open surprise flashed across Kane's face. "You thought he wasn't?"

He ignored the question. "What else do you see?"

"There's a man standing over him."

"Can you—"

"Show us."

Dillon's curt order cut short Cyn's question. She stifled the resentment that tried to rise. He knew the artist better, could direct the questioning more efficiently. The point was to get the information as quickly and accurately as possible. Who got it didn't matter, not when Rio's life was at stake.

Kane spun on her heel, heading back into the room she'd come from, moving faster than Cyn expected for a blind woman, even with her clairvoyance. Dillon gestured for Cyn to precede him inside what had to be the artist's studio, to judge from the high-end psyprinter against one wall beside a large-screen monitor that displayed a male figure dappled by sunlight.

Kane laid her hands on the psyprinter's input plate and the image promptly vanished, leaving a blank screen. She then bowed her head and seemed to lose herself in thought.

The monitor came back to life, vertigo-inducing swirls of brilliant color swooping across the screen. Gradually, it resolved into a vague picture of two figures, one horizontal and the other vertical: Rio lying at the feet of Hollingsworth, if Dillon's suspicion was correct. As it was, it took a leap of faith to see people on the screen; the forms could just as easily be a mountain range, for all Cyn could tell.

With a shake of her head, the artist transferred to a bed of pins that repeated the image on the monitor in relief. She played her hands over the pins, stroking and fingering them like a lover, refining the slopes and emphasizing the valleys. Gradually more detail appeared on the screen. Lines and shadows emerged, as though condensing from thin air.

The process was excruciatingly slow. Cyn had to stop herself from fidgeting at the delay, though her heels started to ache from standing still for so long. Waiting stretched her nerves to singing tension. Time slowed to a crawl as she stared at the monitor, straining for something recognizable.

Kane's progress was circumspect—so much so that it took Cyn a moment before she realized the pixels of the screen formed a distinct picture. Once her mind made the connection, other aspects suddenly sprang into focus: taut tendons and the awkward position, clothes and color, even the grain of the dusty planks.

The two figures were now undeniably Rio and Hollingsworth. Her stomach sank. By itself, the image wouldn't be enough for a conviction, but it was enough for her.

Rio lay on his left side. Cyn felt a pang of sympathetic pain, knowing the muscles there would still be tender from his injury. The image wasn't quite up to the artist's usual photorealistic standards, but it was sufficient to put the crime scene tech on the top of the suspects list, though not for a warrant, if Cyn had to get one.

"Good enough. I'll need a printout." She looked at Dillon to see if he had anything to add, but he seemed lost in the image, absorbing the details, like a hunter who had caught sight of his prey. "Where are they? Can you zoom out, show us the location?"

The artist pressed a button that started the psyprinter humming. Turning to face them, she bit her lip, then shook her head impatiently. "There's too much detail to work up quickly."

That was quick?! She had taken more than an hour.

Cyn opened her mouth to say something—urge the woman to try, beg, plead maybe. Dillon gripped her shoulder, commanding her silence; he obviously thought there was more to come.

"They're in a building here." Jordan Kane held her left index finger straight up, touching empty air. "There're trees all around"— her right hand described a circle around her left. "A bunch of other buildings here"—she gestured to either side of the location. "A river"—a snaky line sketched above the finger. "And an old road"— another line trailing down.

Cyn gasped, recognizing the description of the site.

Rio cursed his luck and the magic that had allowed Hollingsworth to get the drop on him. Now the bastard had the upper hand and his choice of battlefield.

He scanned the room automatically, noting the rude construction that suggested he was somewhere outside the city, looking for anything he could use to his advantage. Exposed rafters, some of the beams still covered with bark. Rough planks for uneven flooring. Near one wall, metal pieces that might have been tools or machine parts: potential weapons, if he got free.

Hell, if he got free, he could use his gun. He'd felt its weight in the holster when the bastard kicked him. Obviously, the mage hadn't considered the possibility that Rio might be armed.

Sunlight slanted across the floor beyond one of the doorways within his view, its reflected glow imperfectly illuminating the large room. The lack of direct light told him he was in an inner chamber. That door was probably the fastest way out . . . if it wasn't trapped.

Hollingsworth snorted derisively, coming to a stop in front of him. "I can tell what you're thinking. Give up. Do you really think a talentless drone like you can escape my magic?"

The question was deliberately targeted at his minimal spell-casting ability, a fact that did nothing to blunt its barb. Rio kept his face blank, refusing to acknowledge the thrust. This wasn't over until one of them was dead—preferably Hollingsworth.

"I'm not letting you get away, and no one will find us here. It's the perfect spot. After all, it's been thoroughly searched already. Several times, in fact. I do have a reputation to maintain. Who would think to look for your corpse here? No one." The mage's mouth thinned in a mirthless smile of triumph.

The knowledge that his instincts hadn't led him astray was of little comfort to Rio. Hindsight wouldn't help if he didn't survive this fuckup. Then there was the meandering monologue; something about it was off in a major way, making the back of his neck itch.

As if the reference to his corpse wasn't enough.

"It's perfect," Hollingsworth repeated, his gaze turning inward, seeing something Rio could only guess at. "You'll disappear, and I'll console the ungrateful bitch. I'll punish her, of course. She shouldn't have left me like that."

Rio went cold, his mind crystal-clear. Cyn was his target?

That scratchy voice dropped to a confiding whisper. "She keeps leaving, but she always comes back. A bit different, but she always comes back."

Comes back?

Hollingsworth was insane. He had to be, to think Cyn was his stepsister returned, for whom else could he mean? And a madman made an unpredictable enemy. Who knew what risks he'd be willing to take to achieve his goals?

"It's her fault, you know. If it hadn't been for her, I'd be a cop, too. Become a detective." The words resonated with passion, broke with bitterness. The pain of a festering wound gone necrotic. "I wouldn't have failed the exam if she hadn't killed herself."

The poor fool didn't seem to realize the illogic of his state-ment. Or did he truly believe his stepsister came back to life?

Nothing in Hollingsworth's demeanor suggested otherwise.

Rio could almost pity the man. Driven to become a police of-ficer, only to flunk the grade. But the moment the mage threat-ened Cyn, he placed himself beyond the pale.

"Now, she's back—that ungrateful bitch with everything that should have been mine. I'm the one who should be a cop. I'm the one who should be a detective, not her! Then to walk away after all I've done. Wasting it on you—" The mage broke off, his chest heav-ing as he glared down at Rio. "I'm going to kill you. Slowly. She'll pay for leaving me, embarrassing me like that. But you'll die first. And when I get her back, she'll know your death was all her fault."

Not if he had anything to say about it.

Rio scowled at the mage. "They'll find you. They'll catch you and cut off your balls."

A rasping laugh answered him, hoarse yet confident, filled with the knowledge of his previous kills. It sent ice through Rio's veins; so had he been tempted to laugh when Alex had called him a civilian to his face.

"You don't understand. That's not the way it works. Emotions are what charges events into inanimate objects. They're the psy-chic residuals a successful retrospection needs. But by the time I'm done, you'll be too weak, too disheartened to project much of anything. You'll just want to die. Then I loop the rope around your neck, which compresses your carotid arteries, and you're dead. No one will find you. No one will know how you died," Hol-lingsworth concluded with another thin smile.

No way. Lantis and Dillon wouldn't stop until they found him. And Cyn? She wouldn't accept his disappearance so tamely. Rio held himself still, refusing to give the madman the satisfaction of seeing him struggle.

"And there's the convenient fact that wood rots." The mage tapped his foot on the floor to emphasize his point. "Especially when exposed to the elements. And after I sanitize your corpse, not even a high-level scry will identify you. So, I'm sorry, you'll really just disappear." His whiny voice dripped with false sympathy.

Irritation twinged at such confidence, but Rio knew better than to contradict the crazy bastard. Black ops had safeguards in place to circumvent complete disappearances, necessary because there were always some who were tempted to turn rogue. Unless Hollingsworth vaporized his body—and his previous kills suggested he didn't think along those lines—Lantis and Dillon would be able to find him, if only his corpse. The question was, would they find Hollingsworth?

But that was negative thinking. He wasn't dead yet.

Unwilling to get a start on his protracted murder, Rio encouraged Hollingsworth to keep talking, hoping that in the meantime, someone would realize he was missing. Preferably Dillon. A nice, quiet extraction would be just the thing right now.

The mage played along, but his ramblings were the stuff of nightmare, leaving no doubt in Rio's mind as to his mental state. From what he let slip, Hollingsworth had wooed then abducted his victims, believing them to be his stepsister returned. He'd kept each in turn as his sex slave until they tried to escape, then he tortured them, ending with death by strangulation as punishment for wanting to leave him.

And he had his eye on Cyn as his next victim.

Cyn studied the psyprint, wondering if she was missing anything. The land the artist described had to be the abandoned sawmill, but which building? Could there be some detail in the picture to identify where Hollingsworth was holding Rio?

Gut instinct said they didn't have time to waste. If the crime scene tech was the serial killer, abducting Rio was a deviation from his MO. Going from female vics to male. It was too . . . reckless. Too abrupt. Killing Rio immediately meant a shift from months between kills to weeks. That wouldn't be mere escalation. What had set him off?

Useless speculation.

She shoved the questions racing through her head to a quiet corner where their gibbering wouldn't distract her. Rio needed help, not answers. If she was to call out the tac team, having the L-T on her side might tilt the scales with McDaniel. Derwent knew Jordan Kane's abilities and respected Dillon's; his argument would likely hold more weight than hers with the commander of the Tactical Unit, especially given her personal involvement.

Listening to Dillon coax more information from his lover with one ear, Cyn flipped open her cell phone and called the Homicide commander. "L-T, I have a situation."

The first cut didn't hurt at first, the damage minor. Just a shallow slice along his biceps. On his right arm. His dominant arm. It didn't register for a second or two.

Then a cool draft smelling of river brushed past, and it *hurt*.

He bit back a hiss, nerves suddenly afire.

The son of a bitch must have dipped the knife in something.

Chapter Twenty-five

Cyn automatically braced herself against the lurching of the team van, her thoughts circling back to Rio's danger. Minutes and hours had passed, spilling through her fingers like running water. It had taken time for Jordan Kane to make the psyprint, more time to convince Derwent, and even more to convince McDaniel. The latter had required a face-to-face back at the station, and even with Derwent arguing her side, it had taken some doing before McDaniel had approved the mission.

Finally they were on their way. She could only hope they wouldn't be too late.

Rio, be alright!

She closed her eyes against another spurt of cold fear, willing it down before it showed.

Blood was drying under his ruined arm. The mess of cuts had exposed sinew. Fear touched him with cold despite the heat.

Even if help came, it might not be in time to save his arm. Wait too long, and nerves and muscles died, and all the healing in the world would do him no good. He'd seen it happen in the field before.

He sucked in air against the fear and shrieking pain, muscles aching from fighting invisible bonds. Damned if he'd let the bastard win.

"Go ahead. Shout. No one will hear you." The knife cut his chest. "No one will miss you."

Fucking mind games.

Cyn's face flashed before his eyes. She'd know something was wrong. When he hadn't shown up for lunch, she'd have known. So would Dillon and Lantis.

He clung to that conviction, using it to wall off pain.

But then the knife came again.

"How good is this info, anyway? It's not even twenty-four hours since Rafael was last seen. How do we know he hasn't simply done a bunk? For all you know, he could just be holed up in some woman's bed."

More questions, this time from Danzinger. Cyn shouldn't have been surprised, yet she was. They implied that the unusual summons—Hawkins's team was now the one on duty and should have gotten the mission—was McDaniel humoring her.

Surely he knew better?

She rather wished she had Jordan Kane's psyprint on hand to silence the assistant team leader. Unfortunately, they'd needed it to convince the Tactical commander. It didn't matter. What was important was that they were on their way. She knew her identification of the site wasn't wrong, whatever the others might think.

"We're just haring off on some fool's errand. Just because that pretty boy is missing doesn't mean a serial killer is responsible. And to suggest that Brett had anything to do with it!" Danzinger shook his blond head dismissively, an incredulous twist to his mouth. "Impossible. Rafael's probably just shacked up somewhere."

Cyn's temper stirred at the assistant team leader's intransigency. He'd rather she be wrong than face the possibility that one of their own had gone bad.

"No way." The surprising disagreement came from Jung on her right. Bracing his legs against the van's motion, he looked up to narrow his almond eyes at Danzinger. "I don't know what he is, but Rafael's no airhead—and he's no pushover, either."

She stared at the countersniper. What had gone on between Rio and Jung at the hospital to merit such a volte-face? She wasn't alone in her surprise; the rest of the team stared at him as well. Even Fernao craned his head around to look.

"He held on to phoenix feathers without flinching. It's only because of him that we're closing in on that mage gang." Jung shot a glare at the rest of the team, his face set in hard lines much like his spiky hair. "Hawkins's team was suiting up when we left. They're going after them."

As a member of Hawkins's team, Bion would be part of that. Cyn suppressed a twinge of concern for her brother. He could handle himself and had backup. Unlike Rio.

Myriad expressions flashed across the other men's faces, some too fast for her to decipher. At least they were listening.

The countersniper returned his glare to Danzinger. "I can't imagine someone who'd dare take on that mage gang single-handed, someone Sarge is dating"—he made a slashing gesture in her direction—"would just . . . do a bunk, as you put it."

"Touching, I'm sure," Danzinger bit out, his ears turning red with temper.

Fighting to keep her astonishment off her face, Cyn ignored the assistant team leader. What had been said at the hospital?

Jung's glare turned withering, pale skin stretched taut across his cheeks, eyes narrowed to ominous slits. Danzinger met it with a scowl, unwilling to back down.

Turning in the front seat, Fernao slung an arm on its back and broke the deadlock with an attention-demanding snap of his fingers, his gaze sweeping the team. "The lieutenant believes there's something there—enough to send us out. That's good enough for me." He frowned at Cyn, but left any doubts he harbored unspoken. "We'll check it out."

Once convinced, McDaniel had been definite in his agreement with Derwent. It probably helped that he remembered Rio from last year. How much of that support was due to his hopes Cyn would transfer to Tactical full-time, she didn't know and didn't care.

Saving Rio was what was important.

Cut after slow, methodical cut blurred into a haze of pain. He floated on torment, numb to escalation, throat tight against his screams. *Cyn.* He held her before his mind's eye, a shield against the pain.

Her temper.

Her regal amusement.

Her incandescent rapture.

He swore to himself he'd hold her again.

The van lurched to a halt none too soon. Fernao had Bru pull over short of the clearing, not wanting to tip their hand. If Hollingsworth didn't know they were coming, they'd have an advantage. "Everyone out."

The team dismounted with less than their usual enthusiasm. Despite Jung's argument, even he dreaded to find confirmation of Hollingsworth's perfidy. They straggled about the van, all out of sorts.

The chirring of insects rose around them, a living wall of sound rising and falling with no obvious source. It was such a normal sound it didn't seem possible anything could be wrong.

Green surrounded them, the hot air welcome after the air-conditioned tension. The bushes had grown bushier in the weeks since she'd last been there, the leaves carpeting the track thicker—and freshly churned by more than just the team van's tires.

Jung hissed, pointing to one side.

A white van with the seal of the Aurora PD was parked in the trees a distance from the track. Its location argued for a deliberate attempt at concealment. From the license tag, it was one of the vans assigned to crime scene techs.

Of course. It was the perfect cover. Hollingsworth could transport anybody in it—even a corpse or four—and no cop would give its appearance a second thought, much less stop it.

"Oh, fuck," Danzinger muttered in a monotone behind her as Fernao waved Moxham and Rao forward to check it out. "It's Brett's."

She swallowed back the vindication she felt at the ID. Rubbing it in wouldn't help her case. They had to work together.

The slamming of car doors drew Cyn's attention from the van. McDaniel had arrived, bringing with him Derwent; Atlantis had pulled up beside the Tactical commander's car, and the two Depth Security agents now stood taking in their surroundings.

Apparently satisfied with his inspection, Atlantis opened the back of his SUV and took out two gray vests—probably Kevlar—dotted with silver periapts shimmering with power. The good stuff, not mere painted runes. They took their body armor seriously. He passed one to Dillon and donned the other, all in silence and moving with familiar efficiency.

She suppressed a pang of envy. Not with the unit's budget. It was reassuring they had so much, since technically they were civilians on a police op.

"Clear," Moxham called out, sheathing his wand to open the

van's doors. The rear compartment was uncharacteristically messy, especially for someone like Hollingsworth. That plus his abduction of Rio hinted at a loss of control that was worrying.

They continued down the dirt track on foot, Jung and Moxham scouting ahead. An ominous silence fell among them, the soft rustling that was their footsteps sounding louder by contrast. Taking the rear, Dillon and Atlantis were like ghosts in comparison, at home in the woods—just like Rio was—so much so that she found herself looking over her shoulder to confirm that they were still there.

A flock of birds took to the sky at their arrival, the sound of beating wings momentarily making soft conversation impossible. Cyn could only hope that Hollingsworth hadn't noticed.

The sawmill was little changed from the first time she saw it. The dirt track was only slightly wider, shrubs on either side trampled by the recent comings and goings necessitated by police investigation. Other than that, it looked the same. What had been the lumberyard was still overgrown with dry, scraggly bushes. The river still flowed along the far side, glints of sunlight dancing on what water could be seen behind the ruins. The ramshackle buildings still crouched in the shadow of the encroaching forest, their grayed planks flecked with remnants of red paint like dried blood in the late afternoon light.

Two dozen wooden structures and Rio was in one of them.

A crunch of dry leaves announced McDaniel's and Derwent's arrivals. With narrowed eyes, the Tactical commander took in the multiple possibilities. "Do we have a better idea of Rafael's location?"

Coming to a silent stop beside them, Dillon pulled his cell phone from a pocket and called his lover. "Can you see me?" he asked almost immediately. The reply must have been in the affirmative because he added: "Where's Rio's location relative to mine?" The conversation continued along those tracks while he refined her answer.

They couldn't attempt a scry at this point. Hollingsworth might have set up defenses to detect magical probes, the sort of thing someone with his paranoically obsessive personality and knowledge of police procedure might do.

Clairvoyance was another thing altogether. Though the results were similar to scrying, Jordan Kane's sight was an inborn ability that didn't depend on magic. In practical application, that meant there was no risk of discovery.

Cyn rocked on her heels while she waited, the tension in her body demanding release. Her teammates were equally restless. Jung stroked his rifle almost compulsively. Rao kept lacing and unlacing his fingers, while Fernao drummed his against his thigh. Danzinger paced, stomping around the clearing like an animated block of granite. Hardesty was rubbing that damned rune again. The medics made another redundant check of their supplies with Moxham hovering by their shoulders. The lieutenants had their heads together, discussing their approach in low tones.

She had to envy Atlantis his calm. He stood utterly still, holding himself in readiness, seemingly immune to worry.

"They're in there." Dillon pointed to a building near the river bend, on the far side of the site. It stood two stories tall with a broad portion on stilts. Part of its roof had fallen in, promising debris and uncertain footing. Broken windows gaped at them like blind eyes in the lowering sun.

The words electrified his listeners. But they weren't what held Cyn's attention. A scowl darkened Dillon's face, a dire gleam in his narrowed black eyes. Its very force clutched at her heart. This wasn't a man to cross lightly.

Something was wrong.

"What is it?" McDaniel demanded.

"Bastard's cutting Rio."

Rage filled Cyn. Pure, incandescent fury that threatened to shatter her control. She wanted nothing more than to rush to Rio's side and tear Hollingsworth apart. Nails biting her palms, she gulped her rage back down, wrestling it into reluctant submission. Losing her head wouldn't help Rio. She had to be ice. Had to act, not react. Going berserk could get him killed.

It was like swallowing molten lava, but she managed.

Derwent and McDaniel exchanged looks. Normally, SOP called for negotiation first, before resorting to a tactical response. The two lieutenants had been debating that very point earlier. Now . . .

"This—" Derwent's sharp wave encompassed the trees and the ruins. "This shows premeditation. You give him warning, he'll kill Rafael."

"No negotiation." McDaniel gave a quick nod of concurrence and a gesture for Cyn's team to get ready.

This time there was no hesitation as they gathered their equipment, Rio's danger adding a snap to otherwise routine actions. His friends each carried a duffel bag in one hand, leaving the other free to fight or cast a spell.

Everyone was silent as they closed the distance to the target building. But when Dillon and Atlantis moved as though to join them for the final approach, McDaniel objected, shaking his head. "From here on in, you don't know any more than my team does. You'll just get in their way."

The set expressions on Atlantis's and Dillon's faces said his argument cut no slack with them. If they were black ops like Rio, she wasn't surprised they didn't buy that reasoning. They knew what they were capable of. Problem was, there was no time to convince the lieutenant that they were more than civilians. Even if she could, it wasn't wise to mix them in with her team without preparation.

Cyn thought fast. How to convince them to hang back? They were Rio's friends and comrades; they'd want to guard his back just as he had theirs.

"Set up a perimeter. If Hollingsworth gets past us, he's all yours." She ignored Fernao's glare; waltzing around his delicate toes as she'd been doing could get Rio killed.

McDaniel nodded reluctant approval, which was all that mattered. As team leader, Fernao would back his decision.

Atlantis gave her a hard look, then crossed his arms. "Agreed."

In less time than any of their specialists could, the two "civilians" cast a tall ward that encircled the entire wooden structure with land to spare. "It will only stop people from getting out," Atlantis informed them. The limitation meant the spell required less power to maintain, but it was still a major undertaking, one sufficient enough to leave McDaniel eyeing them with speculation.

"Good enough." Fernao motioned Jung over to the rest of the team. Without the ward, the countersniper would have been left to cover the approaches in case Hollingsworth tried to escape. While Rao and Moxham might have managed to cast a similar ward, they'd have had to remain behind to maintain it, and Fernao had chosen not to reduce their offensive power that way.

But even with Jung in on the attack, would it be enough?

She studied each member of her team in turn, wondering. Rio's survival depended on how well they performed. Could she trust them to do their utmost, the way Rio's friends would have? Of their own accord, her eyes lingered on Danzinger, Hollingsworth's friend, her doubts taking on a life of their own. Questions on the wisdom of having him in the entry swirled through her mind.

Just keep him where you can see him.

As Cyn set out with her team, Atlantis pulled out his cell phone. "Get me Jamie Rodriguez, please."

Shoving curiosity out of her mind, she focused on the mission: save Rio.

The pain subsided, lifting the fog that had protected his senses. Rio panted through gritted teeth, his jaw frozen in a grimace. Only gradually did he realize the *cabrón* had stopped.

Why?

A vicious kick landed on his side, mashing his arm into the floor. Red starred his vision, black at the edges and sucking him down. He fought to remain conscious. *¡Caray!* Passing out would be bad. Dillon and Lantis could come at any time; he had to be ready.

"There comes a point where anything more is just noise. Diminishing returns. It's not punishment if you can't appreciate the pain," his torturer lectured with clinical disinterest as he stretched leisurely. He spread his arms and rolled his shoulders with a sigh of pleasure. "With a short rest, everything should be fine."

The *cabrón* was an expert. Obviously, he'd used his murders to refine his technique.

This time Rio saw the kick coming. But he still couldn't shift an inch to save himself. And he couldn't suppress a groan when it landed. The constant torture was wearing him down. Even training had its limits.

"That's more like it. Don't think you can escape punishment. I won't let you, not even that way. Before I'm through, you'll beg to die." A chortle of anticipation followed, ending on a strange squeak. "You won't look so pretty by then."

Crazy bastard. He sobbed for breath, choking on dust and renewed pain. The *maleton* would die. He'd make sure of it. "You're not going to win." *Caray*, even talking hurt, but he couldn't let Hollingsworth walk all over him.

High-pitched laughter assaulted his ears. "And what are you going to do? You're not coming back. Only she does that."

The sawmill loomed around them, its tumbledown buildings losing the fight against the forest. What might have once been workers' cabins were thoroughly shrouded in vines and smothered by starlike purple flowers. The broad walkways connecting the larger structures had already collapsed, done in by time. Moss and lichen grew everywhere, restoring a semblance of life to the weathered planks. Feathery ferns rooted in cracks, the vanguard to the bigger assault. This close to the river, the stench of rotting wood was inescapable.

Keeping to the shadows, they closed in on their target. Jordan Kane's information eliminated the bare ground between the stilts; she'd said Rio lay on dusty planks. But that still left a sizable area to search.

Cyn and her team picked their way through the ground floor, broken boards leaving gaps for the unwary. Wood creaked in complaint under their feet, undressed and unvarnished, just raw planks nailed down end on end with little regard for aesthetics. Carpentry at its most basic—and most treacherous.

The setting sun was of little help. The bright red rays streaming through the small windows cast the shadows in greater darkness.

Though the first cavernous room seemed empty, they couldn't just go charging through. They'd encountered booby traps once in pursuit of the mage gang; what more might they encounter with Hollingsworth, who was more familiar with their procedures? If he knew they were on to him, he might have prepared some nasty surprises.

Caution slowed their progress. Cyn's gut hurt from the tension, worry urging her to haste. She couldn't forget that Hollingsworth had killed before—several times and brutally—and Rio had been in his clutches for hours already. Would her lover be his next murder? She clung to Dillon's reassurance that Jordan Kane had seen him alive less than half an hour ago. Surely Rio wouldn't go quietly to his death; they'd have heard something.

Yet there was nothing. It was as silent as the proverbial tomb—not exactly an original comparison but accurate. The ground floor was empty, save for dust, leaf litter, and other rubbish from decades of abandonment, and nests of wild animals sent scurrying by their search.

The team sighed in relief when the sudden noises turned out

to be nothing more than a family of mice and a raccoon making a run for the nearest holes.

But it was too soon to drop their guard.

Entering a deeper twilight, they took a flight of stairs to the second level in tandem, avoiding the uncertain middle of the steps. Even then, some planks groaned under the weight of the heavier men. She held her breath, her senses straining for some clue to Rio's location.

Still nothing.

Darkness met them on the upper floor, the sun having dropped below the treetops during their slow ascent. They were forced to activate infrared hand lights to find their way, pulling night vision goggles over their eyes. The world turned green and oddly flat, the view playing hell with depth perception and providing no peripheral vision whatsoever, but no one complained. They couldn't risk the brilliance of a magelight warning Hollingsworth. Besides, they needed their minds free to concentrate on offensive spells.

The small circles they lit threw the rest of the area into deeper shadow, transfiguring obsolete equipment, more than half a century old and rusting, into grotesque forms. The footing was just as bad as she'd feared. Shattered timber waited to trip an unwary boot, along with debris from the fallen roof and discarded sawhorses broken by time. Small eyes glowed in the darkness, unfriendly curiosity they didn't dare discourage.

"Hisst!"

Everyone's attention snapped forward at the wordless exclamation. One of the lights played over the floor, drawing their gaze to scuff marks in the dust, too large to have been made by any of the animals they'd seen, yet too fresh and too concentrated in one area to have been due to the weeks-old crime scene investigation of the mage gang's camp or the Jane Does.

They were on the right track.

With renewed energy, they surged toward the empty doorway the marks led to, eagerness to take down the department traitor giving their feet speed.

"*Skreeek!*"

CHAPTER TWENTY-SIX

Hollingsworth spun away at a sudden squeal of animal pain. He raised a short wand, its ends glowing red with summoned power. Moving with lethal grace, he danced in place, arms and hands sweeping the air in sinuous motions, obviously casting a spell, though Rio couldn't see any immediate effect.

Feet pounded the floor, the minor vibration of the rough planks under Rio growing stronger. That wasn't Lantis or Dillon. Neither man would make such basic mistakes on a stealth approach. But if it wasn't them—

"Police!"

"Brett! We know you're here."

"Over here!" Rio rasped out before the consequences of drawing a police response occurred to him.

Fear touched his spine with ice. Cyn would be at the forefront of the attack. She had to know Hollingsworth had captured him; why else would the police be there? She wouldn't be anywhere else.

If she got hurt because of him . . .

That was defeatist thinking. He had to trust in her training to see her through . . . and in her team.

Cyn swore silently. *Of all the cursed luck.* They'd lost the element of surprise. Now that Hollingsworth knew they were here, time was of the essence. She readied a spell automatically, training taking over. They'd had so many callouts lately that she knew what the others would do; she could have predicted the moves in her sleep.

Around her, her teammates leaped forward even as Fernao gave the order. Danzinger and Hardesty led, Rao and Moxham cast shields to cover the sides, Jung and she had offense, while the medics took the tail.

Lowering his head, Hardesty charged the doorway—and rebounded off an invisible barrier!

Actinic white arcs lashed out at the newbie, enveloping him in a deadly cocoon of crackling magic. His scream was cut short as Danzinger slammed into him, the assistant team leader's momentum carrying them both out of the spell's reach.

"Shit." She clawed at the goggles, her eyes tearing from the blinding flash. Around her was darkness and silence, no one daring to breathe. Red floated before her eyes, and squeezing them shut didn't help. She could only hope the burst of light hadn't burnt out the optics; mil-spec they weren't.

"Hardesty?" Fernao hissed from somewhere to her right.

"He's fine, but our NVGs are dead." From the shift of his voice, Danzinger had gotten to his feet.

A white spot swept the room beyond—normal illumination, not infrared—as Rao checked for immediate threats. Nothing revealed itself, no killer mage nor hostage. No target in sight. In the gloom, she saw the others had also pulled up their goggles, the newbie shaking his head as he leaned on the wall while the medics checked his and Danzinger's conditions.

Fernao signaled Jung and Moxham to scout for another route forward. There was no time to waste. They couldn't let Hollingsworth refine his defenses.

The stench of ozone followed the sizzle of a lightning strike. A yell in the darkness ended suddenly with the thunder of large bodies landing on wood. The floor transmitted the shock to Rio.

Bo-booom!

Near simultaneous explosions shook the planks, dust puffing up to assault the nostrils. He couldn't see what caused them, just their effect on the *cabrón*.

Hands moving in spellcasting gestures, wand spitting red and orange sparks, Hollingsworth kept up a steady flow of imprecations, his attention on fending off the magical assault. It sounded like Cyn's team was hitting him at multiple points. They were getting closer.

The last thing the bastard needed was a distraction.

Rio grinned through the pain, feeling an unexpectedly cheerful viciousness. "Perfect spot, ha! I told you they'd find me. Only an idiot would have thought otherwise." He taunted Hollingsworth, using the mage's ravings against him. "You're going down, and Cyn's just the woman to do it."

"Shut up!" The mage's leg swung back then forward, the intermittent flashes of light giving the movement a surreal impression of slow motion.

Even with warning, Rio couldn't avoid it, only tense his belly to mitigate the impact. The kick drove the air from his lungs, blasted agony into his mutilated flesh. He gagged, empty stomach rebelling, though it had nothing to lose. Blackness rushed in, tempting him with unconsciousness, sure escape from torment.

No, he couldn't give in! He had to fight. Hollingsworth might have tied his hands, but he had other weapons.

"You can't escape," Rio gasped through the red-hot needles of pain skewering his arm and gut. "They know who you are. You won't be able to relocate this time, not like after Athens. People will know you for what you are: a failure."

"*Athens?* You—"

Thooom! Dust swept the room, borne by a sudden wind. Loud *thwack*s filled the stunned silence, hundreds of them, like wood shards pelting a wall at high speed. Cyn's team must have breached the mage's defenses.

Eyes wide with shock, Hollingsworth spun away.

Another barrier and another empty room. The nested defenses were only to be expected of someone as anal as Hollingsworth, but they were working as intended and slowing them down.

Cyn blasted the jamb, Fernao adding his efforts to hers. The empty room beyond meant there was no risk of shrapnel hitting Rio, and if the barrier was anchored to the frame like the previous ones, brute force would be sufficient to break through. Too, it provided a distraction for Jung and Moxham's scouting. She could only hope the two found another way in.

Danzinger probed the doorway, drawing a virulent orange arc crackling with malice.

Still up.

Hollingsworth continued to ignore him, swaying in place as his fingers flicked through another spell, power coruscating around his hands in garish bursts. A deadly cobra given human form, holding off multiple mages. How long could he keep it up? Just how strong was the *maleton*?

In the flashing lights, Rio imagined he could see some strain on the bastard's face.

This was his chance. Flight or fight, he had to be ready.

Rio tried to assess his condition. His right arm was next to useless, the muscles shredded almost to the bone by Hollingsworth's attentions, though the bastard had deliberately avoided the arteries to drag out his sick game. Even if he didn't count the spell holding him immobile, his body was stiff from hours trapped in one position. His belly hurt, threatening to cramp with every breath, nausea roiling in his gorge.

And he was cold, his pulse fast.

Possibly shocky.

Adrenaline tried to kick in, but his system was long past that point. His prospects didn't look good. Especially if he couldn't get free.

Shackled by unyielding magic, Rio could only listen as battle raged above him. *Damnú air.* Bound and helpless like some tyro who couldn't find his ass with both hands tied behind his back. Pushing the agony to the back of his consciousness, he fought the invisible chains furiously, straining to get free.

In vain.

The spell countered his efforts with equal force. Given how powerful Hollingsworth seemed to be, Rio could exhaust himself long before the spell failed, even if one arm weren't so much dead weight.

Use your brain, Rafael. What would Dillon or Lantis do? Wrong question. They probably had several spells for the situation. Never had Rio felt his lack of talent more keenly. He tried to remember previous missions and how they'd countered magic. Spell versus spell. Spell versus steel. Cast properly, given sufficient power, spells could provide the ultimate protection.

But magic was only as infallible as the caster.

If there was a loophole . . .

Maybe subtle movements weren't out of the question. After all, he could breathe. The spell didn't render him entirely immobile, just bound. If he could just free his arms of its strictures, he might be able to draw his gun.

Maybe, he cautioned himself, reining in his excitement. *Maybe not.* But he had to try.

Another spell rocked the building, its *boom!* lifting the floor and making it shimmy like gelatin. Rafters creaked in protest, showering them with decades' worth of debris. Rio flinched at the downpour, then realized he'd moved. The spell binding him was weakening!

"*No.*" Hollingsworth flung something onto the floor and muttered under his breath. Whatever he did stopped the draft of cool air blowing past, leaving dust to tickle Rio's nostrils. "She won't win. She can't win. She'll never win. I won't let her."

A ward sprang into being. In its faint red light, the *maleton*'s face gleamed, pale and dripping sweat. He cast around, arms flailing, frenzied and wild-eyed with disbelief and something else.

Desperation?

Despair?

The grief of one who sees his world crashing down around his ears?

Whatever it was chilled Rio to the soul.

The mage had slipped over the edge.

Scarlet flared, then a whining ricochet. The hard *thud* of a bullet hitting wood.

Rio searched the darkness, hope leaping to the fore, his heart pounding despite himself. The rules just changed. He wasn't alone. Anyone shooting at the bastard had to be a friend.

"Hollingsworth!"

Jung and another man stood in the doorway Rio had marked as the fastest way out, his exit if he managed to get free. Though he looked, he didn't see Cyn with them, but she couldn't be far behind. The countersniper let loose, firing in semiautomatic bursts, while his companion threw fireballs at Hollingsworth. Both attacks splashed against the ward, all red fury to no effect.

"You won't take me alive. I won't let you!" The *cabrón* reached into his shirt and pulled out a chain. Closing a fist above its silver medallion, he hunched over it prayerfully, as though it bore all the knowledge in the world, his back to Rio.

The metal began to glow.

¡Maleton! Rio swore silently. He had a sick feeling he knew where this was headed. Final strike. He'd seen its work several times in his black ops missions, and the results had been devastating. If Hollingsworth unleashed it, the mage would die, but in doing so, he'd take Cyn and several others with him.

And Jung couldn't stop him. The ward was too strong. The cops' attacks didn't even distract the bastard.

Even with his limited ability, Rio could sense magic growing, the prickling energy making the hair on his arms stand on end. He could almost see the power surrounding Hollingsworth, and it scared him. *Cyn.*

But it also gave him an advantage. With the *maleton's* attention focused on drawing power, his hold on the spell binding Rio seemed to be wavering.

Of course! A final strike sucked in all the ambient magic in the mage's surroundings. Only talismans were proof against its pull. No wonder the binding was weakening.

Now if only Hollingsworth would continue ignoring him . . .

Cursing silently, Rio fought his invisible bonds. A hand finally slid free. It was his left, but that didn't matter; he could shoot nearly as well with it. He reached for his gun and—*Yes!*—it wasn't blocked. The spell was specifically designed to hold living beings.

By reflex, he aimed for the sniper's triangle of head and upper body. Shots there had a good chance of severing major arteries, guaranteeing a quick death.

Except it wouldn't be quick enough.

Even a few seconds of consciousness would be sufficient for Hollingsworth to cast a final strike—which Rio couldn't risk. He had to prevent the mage from releasing the power he'd summoned, even if it meant not killing the *cabrón*.

He shifted the gun sight to the talisman in Hollingsworth's hand, a much smaller target.

Normally, Rio wouldn't have had any difficulty hitting it at so short a range, even with a pistol. But his hand bobbled damnably as his shoulder spasmed, the still-tender flesh protesting the added trauma and resisting his demands. *¡Caray!* His whole right side cramped, a blinding agony he could have done without.

He panted, riding out the pain. *Focus,* damnú air. *You can't let that* maleton *succeed. Think of Cyn!*

Still, his arm quivered, the gun sight jumping around.

Gritting his teeth, Rio fought his body, struggled to find some reserve of energy. Just a little. Just one more time. He had to do this. Now, before it was too late.

The gun sight continued to waver.

Chapter Twenty-seven

A shot rang out, a low, loud bark amid the sizzle of clashing magics. Cyn's heart missed a beat at the sound. *Rio!* It had to be him; Jung's rifle was equipped with a suppressor. Her lover was alive!

She closed her eyes, fighting the enervating tide of relief. He wasn't safe yet.

A split second later, a breathless screech of pain split the night air, full of towering rage and bitter rancor. Hollingsworth must have survived. A storm surge of magic swept them, wild and potent, the electrifying eddies zinging her nerves. Power unleashed. Had he struck at Rio? Maybe killed him?

Just then the barrier across the door collapsed, leaving no time to think or fear.

Hardesty was first through the hole, charging in almost before the barrier dropped, with Danzinger close at his heels. It was risky, even without booby traps. Debris, abandoned equipment or materials, wild animals—any of them could bring the newbie to a crashing halt. The ancient planks underfoot could give way from his stomping.

But speed could mean the difference between life and death—Rio's—and Cyn couldn't bring herself to call for caution. Heedless of the danger, she followed them into the darkness, a hair faster than Fernao and the medics, with Rao taking the rear, guarding their backs.

Luck was on their side for once. No ambush, no traps, no accidents nor screw-ups. They blundered into nothing worse than solid walls and spiderwebs.

Indistinct shadows grew in the hall, cast by a source of light somewhere through the next doorway. Danzinger grabbed Hardesty's shoulder, forcing the newbie to stop and giving the rest of the team a chance to catch up.

Whoosh!

A sudden brightness made the knots in the planks of the facing wall spring into visibility, to stare at her like accusing eyes. Another crackle of power splintered the air. It sounded like an all-out assault, but no way could Rio have been responsible this time, not with magic boiling over.

She stole a peek around the jamb.

Fireballs splashed against a line sparking red in the center of the dark room, one that floated at chest height, possibly a variant of the police wards used in crime scenes. Behind the magical barrier, ignoring Jung's and Moxham's attacks, Hollingsworth stood scowling, a bloody hand held to his chest, the other gesturing awkwardly—but to some effect. Rio writhed at his feet, thick coils of magic contracting around his chest.

The son of a bitch was killing him!

Rage flared, electrifying in its intensity, elemental fury that knew no bounds, that demanded she slay her enemy. Cyn *reached* for power, then unleashed the savage energy that answered her call, adding her efforts to her teammates'.

To no avail.

Heated by clashing magics, the air hissed and popped, solid walls of red flashing where their attacks struck. The barrier withstood it all, behaving exactly like a police ward, which meant Hollingsworth didn't need to concentrate to maintain it. He, on the other hand, was free to counter, lashing out with multiple spells that lit the room like lightning.

She lunged aside, pressure blooming along the path of Hollingsworth's wind-shear strike, too close for comfort. Wood cracked. She risked a glance behind her. Shattered staves clattered to the floor, adding to the uncertain footing.

Damn, he was powerful. How could the department have overlooked his strength?

"Give it up, Brett! This doesn't solve anything." Danzinger sidestepped a forcebolt, his wand whirling up to counterstrike.

Dust fell, visibility deteriorating. She lost sight of Moxham on the other side of the room, and Jung was just a darker outline amid the flickering shadows. At least her target was immobile, otherwise she couldn't let loose for fear of a blue-on-blue; friendly fire was always a risk in melee conditions.

"You're not taking me in." Hollingsworth unleashed a blast at Cyn, so quickly she barely had time to cast a shield. "You ungrateful bitch. This is all your fault."

What the—?

Strike after strike fell in quick succession. The single-minded focus they required was frightening. Even more so being the target of such animosity. She held her ground under the vicious onslaught of power. Hollingsworth had the upper hand, safe behind his ward. But with him concentrating on her, maybe someone else would find an opening.

Fernao signaled the others to spread out.

Magic swirled around her in nerve-ruffling waves. Spell versus counterspell. Attack and counterattack. Heat, wind, fire, and the *boom* of thunder. Flaring shields. Grunts and curses. It ate at her to be so passive, a sitting duck waiting for some lucky shot to burn through.

In one of those frozen tableaux of battle, she caught a glimpse of Rio, unmoving, his very stillness in the middle of the fray chilling her heart. Her lover wasn't one to leave others to fight his battles—especially in a fight for survival.

This couldn't go on. While Hollingsworth held them off, Rio could be dying. They had to get him to a healer.

Cyn's mind raced as she strained to maintain her shield before the fury of Hollingsworth's attacks. If her guess was right, only slow-moving air would get through unhampered—but, like police wards, the barrier had to be anchored on something.

She couldn't let Hollingsworth pin her down, cowering behind a shield like a victim waiting for rescue, keeping her on the defensive. Her strength was combat magic. If she continued to play his game, they'd lose.

Calling power, Cyn sidestepped the next strike, leaving her body armor to deflect what her shield wouldn't stop. The blue white fireballs she launched momentarily lit the dark room with an actinic glare and splashed off his ward. Not that she expected anything more from that salvo. The dazzling light was a diversion to spoil his vision and his balance.

Even as they hit, she lunged away.

One chance. She had to get it right. With both hands, she wove the balefire-forcebolt combo she'd used before, willing all the magic around her into the spell. Air glowed, wreathing her arms with roiling, arcing, exhilarating power. More power than she'd ever summoned in her life.

Snarling, she extended her wand, thrusting spell and all at her target. A blue inferno roared at her command, sizzling through her to ignite everything in its path.

Red flashed in answer.

Engulfed.

Hollingsworth's ward wavered—

But stayed up.

The floor didn't fare as well. Rough planks burst into flames, kindling wood after years of soaking oil and neglect. The combustion lit the room, banished obscuring dust.

"Rick!" Cyn shot a look at Danzinger, the nearest of them to Rio. The assistant team leader nodded back, raising his wand in readiness as he carefully sidestepped a broken sawhorse. She cast her balefire-forcebolt combination again, this time deliberately aiming for the floor.

Foooooom! The blazing vortex of blue power was joined by tongues of red and yellow as fire consumed the planks.

The ward held.

Other spells filled the intervening space as Hollingsworth attacked, and her team blocked and parried. His control had to be at the adept level to be able to juggle so many workings simultaneously—flawlessly. The attacks, the one killing Rio, all that ability could have done so much more. Too bad he hadn't put it to legal use.

Cyn pushed bitterness from her mind. All that mattered was the spell challenging her mastery. She was at the very edge of her capability; she'd never dared use so much.

If she lost control of her magic, Rio would die.

But if she held back, Hollingsworth would win.

And Rio would die.

Neither was acceptable.

She couldn't fail him.

She *would not* fail him.

Reaching for more, she thrust fresh power into her spell, her fingers cramping as she willed it hotter, her body the mortal conduit for primal energies. Wild magic flooded into her, elemental and electrifying, a savage torrent of burning rage beyond anything she'd ever known.

The air roiled with power, filled it with breath-stealing potential.

Lights flashed, the visible portion of clashing magics. Unseen but more dangerous turbulence disrupted the flow of energy, threatening their command over all the spells.

Wreathed in smoke, Hollingsworth stood firm, his defense impregnable. Despite his injury, he continued to duel the tac team, a mask of hate contorting his ordinary features.

The same smoke grabbed at Cyn's throat, hot and arid, acid and ashes on the back of her tongue. She panted, fighting down coughs that could break her focus.

Crack!

The loud sound broke the standoff. Beyond the flames, a hole gaped as a plank fell away.

"No!" Hollingsworth staggered back, arms flailing. Out of control, the spell he was casting tangled in chaos.

This is it. The enemy's first mistake. Now to make sure it was his last.

Like the well-trained team they were, Fernao and the others pushed the offensive, almost as though they'd heard her thought. Their spells struck before Hollingsworth could regain his formidable balance.

She added her own, renewing her cast and setting up the next. The tide was turning; she could sense it. If they could retain the momentum . . .

The ward flickered. Despite the backdrop of smoke and flames, that much was clear.

As more of the floor gave way, the floating red line between her and Hollingsworth vanished.

Now!

Cyn unleashed a spear thrust, throwing all the power at her command at her enemy's chest—the center of mass and the most certain target she could make out in the haze. Magic shot through her, a flash flood of violent energy barely under control.

Hollingsworth fell. Without his magic to hold back the fire, the flames leaped to greater heights, billows of yellow too bright to stand.

Rio!

She flung up her arm reflexively, shielding her face against the flash and gust of searing heat. From behind that meager protection, she saw Danzinger dive into the fire with Hardesty close behind.

Let them be in time.

Please!

Chapter Twenty-eight

Rio came to slung over someone's shoulder, not exactly his favorite position, but he was in no condition to complain. Smoke assaulted his lungs and bone pounded his gut, the discomfort almost distracting him from the agony that was his right arm. All he could see were flashing legs as he bounced painfully in place. His left hand was empty, his gun gone missing at some point.

His rescuer dumped him in some bushes a distance from the burning building. The big guy was puffing from his exertions, but that didn't stop him from checking Rio's condition. His horrified expression didn't bode well. The lapse of control said he was just a kid under all that armor.

Hacking his lungs out, Rio grabbed the kid's vest. "Cyn?"

"She's fine. Who do you think took Brett down?" another man answered, getting down on one knee beside them to conduct his own examination.

That was all Rio wanted to know. Releasing the kid, he concentrated on not puking as his body continued to relieve itself of the smoke he'd inhaled, his throat protesting the effort. The coughing fit sent jagged spears of pain through his arm, the spasms cracking the heat-seared crust over exposed muscle, a potent reminder of what he still stood to lose.

When he could finally breathe with only the occasional cough, the other man parked him in a field station with a healer. Dillon and Lantis descended on him, clad in body armor, the grim set of their faces looking formidable enough to stop an army. They helped him onto a gurney, the motion jostling his arm despite their extreme care.

"Cabrón." Stars splattered the back of his eyelids. Pure agony came roaring back as though it had never left.

Brown eyes above him widened, thick brows arched theatrically high. "I hope you don't mean me."

Blackness claimed Rio before he could respond.

Spent from the confrontation, Cyn's team slumped on the ground a short distance from the blaze, content to let others contain it. The river patrol had arrived while they'd been inside, bringing more than enough bodies to handle the situation without their help. The heat was nearly unbearable, but her team was too tired to move. Even Fernao looked as though only an earthquake would move him.

Hardesty barely flinched as Keefe treated his burns; whatever his issues were with fire, he'd come through when it counted. He would do.

Trembling with adrenaline letdown, her body armor a pile of bricks on her shoulders, Cyn was tempted to join them. After that fight, nothing was more attractive than rest. She'd channeled so much power, her mage sense felt raw, but she didn't think she'd burnt out.

On the other hand, she'd never burnt out before, so she wasn't exactly sure what it was supposed to feel like.

But then Danzinger left the field station. He walked heavily as though slogging through thick mud, his shoulders slumped, his normally pale face black with soot and striped by sweat. The bright magelights around the field station gave the marks zebralike definition.

She lengthened her stride to intercept the assistant team leader, forcing unsteady legs to support her. "Hollingsworth?"

"Don't worry, you got him." Grimacing, Danzinger waved off Renfrew, refusing the other team medic's attention. "Brett's not coming back." His fists clenched and unclenched repeatedly as though he didn't know what to do with them, his mouth twisted with strong emotion.

Of course. He'd considered Hollingsworth a friend. The betrayal of that friendship had to cut to the quick.

Cyn politely ignored his distress, knowing he wouldn't appreciate her noticing. "Thanks for getting Rio out."

"Was the least I could do." Danzinger inhaled sharply. "I—Rafael took a lot of damage."

Her pulse picked up speed. *A lot of damage?* She searched his face, trying to decipher his meaning, to read his blue eyes narrowed with . . . what? Warning? Sympathy? Apology? All of the above?

"But his only thought was of you."

Admiration? That possibility was the hardest to wrap her brain around. It almost distracted her from the sudden warmth in her heart, but not so much that the need to find out more didn't overwhelm her.

Danzinger's hand on her shoulder stopped her as she swung toward the field station. "You okay?"

She eyed it then the assistant team leader quizzically, wondering why he asked.

"You were sizzling tonight. I never imagined you could wield that much magic." Left unspoken was the possibility of burnout.

Removing his hand, he looked aside, discreetly avoiding her gaze and any emotion she might betray.

Mustering her will, Cyn focused on her wand and raised it to display a faint glow. She couldn't do much more against the glare of the magelights, but it sufficed. "A tad charred along the edges. Probably won't be good for much for a few days or so, but . . . I should be fine."

He let her go then.

Dillon nodded at her as she approached, acknowledging her presence, then continued his scan of the area around her, his eyes never stopping at any one spot for long. "You okay?" he asked, his voice soft, unconsciously echoing Danzinger.

Sweat trickled down her brow toward her eye. Cyn swiped at it then grimaced at the black muck coating her hand. "Nothing a shower won't fix. Rio?"

He twitched his shoulder in a motion that only the charitable might call a shrug, the gray Kevlar he wore barely rose. "See for yourself."

Inside the tent, a healer bent over her lover, freeing him from the tatters of a shirt and leaving the empty holster at his back visible. Rio lay on a gurney, unresponsive as his arm was extended and his wounds sluiced clean and debrided. Sweet and pungent clashed as blood and antiseptic filled the air, and soot-laden water dribbled into a tray. The treatment left his injuries all too clear.

Fear shot through her at the sight. Her lungs seized, and for a moment she couldn't feel her legs. The world receded to a dull buzz, her head a hot air balloon about to float away, as her mind tried to deny what she was seeing. But even when she'd first joined Homicide she'd had difficulty with denial, and she couldn't do it now. *A lot of damage? No kidding.* She'd never realized before that Danzinger had a gift for understatement. Of course, he might not have gotten that good a look.

His drawing hand. Cyn suddenly wished she hadn't killed

Hollingsworth so quickly. He hadn't deserved a clean death. He should have suffered. She wanted him to suffer.

Gray filled her vision, glinting with light. It took her a moment to realize Atlantis had blocked her sight of Rio, standing so close his body armor occupied her field of view, its shiny periapts mere inches from her nose. "You don't have to see that," he told her, his voice coming from a distance.

"Rio—" She gulped down a sob. To her horror, her eyes watered, blurring the look of compassion on his still face.

"He's in good hands."

"The best hands possible," someone interjected mildly from behind Atlantis.

"But—" Rapid blinks saved her composure, drying the tears that threatened to fall.

"He's in good hands," Atlantis repeated. "Don't do this to yourself."

The world returned in a rush. A crack and crash and answering shouts. A potent reminder of what was left to be done. This wasn't over until they found Hollingsworth and confirmed Rio's suspicions.

This was a crime scene, and she was a cop. She had a job to do. As much as she wanted to plant herself by Rio's side, she couldn't.

Deep inside, she couldn't stifle a sense of relief.

Rio woke to no pain. The relief he felt from its absence was almost enough to make him pass out again. He clung to consciousness, knowing the lack didn't mean much. He remembered what his arm had looked like. To describe it as raw meat would have been too kind.

"Hold still, I'm working." The robust tenor was clearly not the nasal whine of the *maleton*.

Other details began to register. He was lying on crisp cotton, not dusty wood. Unbound. The rescue hadn't been a dream. Relief threatened to swamp him again, embarrassingly enervating. He must have suffered worse on one of his black ops missions, though he couldn't recall any that fit the bill.

He slitted his eyes to night-dark waters and police boats beached among a mass of logs. *That must have taken some fancy driving to get to shore.*

"You in there, Rio?" A different voice this time, deep and ineffably calm: Lantis.

Rio allowed his eyes to open fully, taking in his position. He lay on his left side on a gurney, still bare-chested and reeking of blood and smoke, his hand hooked up with a length of tubing to a drip bag.

"No, I'm having an out-of-body experience." Snorts met his grouchy reply. He tried to twist around to check his arm but earned a smack on his hip for his trouble.

"I said, *hold still*, damn it."

The rough treatment was reassuring and strangely familiar—maybe the healer had some military experience—whatever the reason, at least it implied he wasn't dying. Just in danger of losing the use of his right arm.

"Has anyone ever told you your bedside manner stinks?" Talking hurt, his throat tight and raw. He sounded like a frog to his own ears, but that was only to be expected after nearly choking and all that coughing.

"You're lucky I do field calls. Now, shut up and let me do my job."

Power and ice swirled through Rio, not magic, per se. Technically, healers didn't use magic; they could barely stand it. What they did do was manipulate their patient's personal energy. He'd been healed before, so he thought he knew what to expect. But this time it felt like an icy hand pulling on him, on something inside him.

Gripping the cotton sheet, he shivered fitfully, unable to suppress a groan as that invisible something snapped back into place, like a dislocated joint reseated. Once again he was helpless, fighting pain.

"That's got it. Now for the tricky part. Hmmm . . ."

Lousy bedside manner.

Rio tried to put what was happening from his mind, but the healer stepped in front of him and set a metal tray by his head. With detached fascination, he watched as shavings of scorched flesh landed in the tray, only the steady pressure on his shoulder telling him they were his. "What are you doing?"

"Convincing your body to heal the wounds, regenerate muscle, nerves, ligaments, you know, the usual stuff," the healer replied absently as the unpleasantly familiar scent of his own blood joined the odor of roasted meat.

Nerves? The reminder that he wasn't out of the woods yet forced him to swallow hard. *Idiot. At least it's just your arm. It could have been your cock, if that bastard had thought of it.* He shuddered, but considering the alternative helped him endure the remainder of the treatment.

"Problem?"

"I missed lunch." *Shut up and get it over with.*

"Shite." An energy bar was thrust at his face, smelling of dried fruit and cinnamon sugar. "Here, get that in you before you go into shock."

Rio complied gratefully, careful not to dislodge the drip tube. It tasted like heaven, though normally he couldn't see how Cyn could subsist on the stuff. Too bad he didn't have coffee to wash it down.

The tac team kept their distance all the while, whether out of consideration or some other reason Rio didn't know and didn't care, focused on what was being done to his body. Yet by the time the healer let him sit up, Cyn still hadn't made an appearance. He tried not to mind, knowing she had her responsibilities, but it hurt, and he worried. He only had Danzinger's word that she was fine. What if she'd actually been injured during his rescue? "Lantis? Cyn—?"

"She's fine. Busy and somewhat sooty, but fine."

"Typical. Nearly gets himself killed and he's sniffing after a woman." The healer turned out to be a curly haired Latino built like a bantam cock, small but scrappy.

Rio arched a brow in challenge. "My woman." With guys like that, you had to make sure the ground rules were stated upfront.

"All better, aren't you." He raised Rio's arm, testing full range of motion. "How's that feel?"

It didn't feel like his arm at all, and Rio said so. The limb shook, aspen-weak. If it didn't get better than that, it would be a long while—if ever—before he could hold a rifle or a pen. He cursed silently, his hopes for a normal life with Cyn taking a nosedive.

The healer waved his hands over the biceps, making a few passes in the air: nothing dramatic, but something inside twinged in response. "Okay, I think that's most of it. Let's see . . ."

Rio sat impatiently through the rest of the healer's examination. His remaining injuries were minor: first-degree burns, some bruising, cracked ribs, a sore throat from the bastard's magical chokehold, and a small wound after the drip tube was removed. On the surface, his arm looked fine, whole and unmarked, completely restored except for the tremors. But would he regain full use of it?

What felt like thousands of sharp needles prickled his fingers, like returning circulation only much worse. The hand felt hot and swollen, too big for its skin, like an overstuffed chorizo that could burst open at any time.

Knowing cops were watching, he kept his face impassive while he waited to hear the worst. He'd be damned if he'd give Cyn's coworkers more ammo for their biases.

The trembling eventually subsided somewhat. He explored his arm cautiously, half afraid the light contact would break skin. "It's still—"

"What did you expect? That was a major injury, and those muscles are brand-new. It doesn't have the conditioning of the rest of you. Plus, you lost muscle mass." The healer slapped down a sling on the gurney. "Use that. Give yourself time to rest and recover, and you can gradually—*gradually*, mind you—work up to your old form."

Rio pressed his shaking arm against his chest. It ached like the very devil. "How long?"

"Two months."

"Two *months*?" He winced as his throat seized. Now that the mutilation was more or less healed, his other injuries were making themselves felt with a vengeance. His left side, still recovering from Friday's trauma, was the worse for wear.

"Even babies have to crawl first, you know. Did you miss what I said about brand-new?" A disgusted shake of the head punctuated the irascible flow of words. "Two months with physical therapy. Come by the hospital next week, after you've rested."

"Two months," Rio repeated, torn between relief at the promised recovery and outrage that it would take his arm so long to get back up to speed. It almost felt like a betrayal for his body to be so weak.

"He'll be there. We'll make sure of it," Lantis assured the healer from the foot of the gurney. Which meant his job, at least, was safe, not that he'd had any doubts on that front.

"Good, now let me finish up." Passing his hands in front of Rio's torso, the healer flinched. "*Shite.*"

"Diego?" Lantis suddenly loomed behind the healer, blue eyes narrowed.

"Back off, mother hen. I need room to work." The healer—who had to be Diego—shook his fingers as though he'd touched a live wire. "Is that a talisman you have there?"

Rio found hard corners where the healer indicated and remembered the rings he'd picked up just that morning; he'd tucked their box in a pocket then forgotten about them because of everything else that had happened. Diego must have grazed the spells on the rings. "Something like that."

"Huh." The healer resumed his examination, more cautious with his gestures. It looked as though he was probing the vicinity of the box, coming at it from different directions until he was satisfied with his findings. "Lucky you had it; otherwise you'd've been in a world of hurt."

Rio stilled, his sore hand closing around the box reflexively. "You mean, I wasn't?"

"You're using your fingers, aren't you? Given he'd cut you to the bone, you should have some nerve damage, but damned if I can find any." The healer propped his arms akimbo, an intrigued scowl on his face. "Must have hurt like hell while it was happening, but if you consider how long you were under the knife, it was all to the good. Otherwise, the neurons would've been dead by the time I got to you, and you'd need graft surgery to fix something like that."

"How's that possible?" Dillon asked from where he stood guard outside the tent.

"Some big-ass spells in there." Diego used his chin to indicate the box under Rio's hand. "Don't ask me, I'm just a healer. I have shite all to do with magic, and that's the way I like it."

Stunned by the revelation, Rio sat on the gurney in silence. The rings were the reason he'd recover full use of his arm? Talk about heavy-duty protection spells. Dame Fortune had been pulling overtime.

"If you would take it off, I can finish up," the healer prompted when Rio continued to stare at his hand.

"Sorry." He pulled the velvet box from his pocket and set it beside him, then gestured for Diego to carry on. The final healing was over almost before it could register. The sudden lack of pain left him reeling, he'd braced himself against it that much.

Lantis caught him by the shoulder, when Rio might have tipped over. "Easy," he murmured as the healer exhaled sharply and stepped back.

"Thanks, Diego." Rio extended a still-trembling hand to the healer.

"No problem." The healer shook it gently. "And it's Jamie. Jamie Rodriguez. Only the big lunk calls me Diego." Shooting a mock glare in Lantis's direction, he thrust the sling at Rio, the implicit order clear.

"Thanks, Jamie," he repeated, correcting himself. Pushy guy, but Lantis apparently trusted him to know what he was doing. Once he'd donned the sling, the healer abandoned him in search of another patient—incidentally giving them a measure of privacy.

Joining them under the tent, Dillon gave the velvet box a quick glance. "Is that what I think it is?"

The small square case sported the jeweler's logo, so the question was only logical. Rio cracked open the box briefly to flash the two a glimpse of the rings in their satin bed.

"Congratulations?" This from Lantis.

"Nothing final yet." Certainly his prospects didn't look too good. Cyn still hadn't come. Did his arm change the way she saw him, or was her job that demanding? He forced the question back, in no condition to ponder it.

Struggling with the ravenous hunger and light-headedness that was the corollary of accelerated healing, Rio fingered the unmarked armor Lantis wore to give his mind something else to think on while he regained his equilibrium. Not even a smudge of dirt on the gray Kevlar. The sight sent a pang of unease through him. They'd stayed back.

"Your Amazon didn't want us charging in," Dillon explained, a glum twist to his mouth, apparently intuiting Rio's thoughts from his face. "Arguing would've only delayed your rescue." His gaze continued to sweep the spell-lit night, still on guard against crazed mages.

"They let us set up a perimeter." Lantis nodded at a shimmering blue ward, twelve feet high, that stretched out of sight in both directions behind the field station. "That was it." The tiny wrinkle between his brows announced profound disgust.

A laugh forced its way out, unbidden. "Thanks." Rio pressed a hand to his tender gut, glad that they hadn't undermined Cyn's position. But if Hollingsworth had taken her down, they'd have gone in, regardless; of that, he had no doubt. "That must have sucked."

Lantis and Dillon shared a dark look. "Civilian life," his shorter friend muttered, his customary grin still missing.

Ah, yes. They all had to live in Aurora and make nice with the cops, especially since Depth Security was in a position to get some business from them. In black ops, they'd simply done their best not to come to the attention of the local police in the first place.

Times have changed.

Rio straightened, dispensing with Lantis's quiet support. No point in displaying weakness to the cops. He pocketed the velvet box with its precious contents.

Now that he was down to simple aches, he could pay more attention to what was going on around him. Magelights glared, miniature suns hovering above the riverside where the field station had been set up, casting merciless brilliance on the trio of beached speedboats he'd seen. To his surprise, he recognized McDaniel and Derwent among the police personnel milling around Jamie Rodriguez.

Shadowy buildings lurked at the edge of the day-bright shore, their dark lines broken by a mound of sullen embers. Given the smoke he'd inhaled, the latter had to be where Hollingsworth tortured him.

The blaze had been put out well before it could spread, but not until the structure had collapsed into itself. Rio couldn't deny his relief that the silent witness to his helplessness had gone up in flames. He didn't like the thought of anyone seeing him like that. With the wood reduced to ashes, even Dillon would be hard-pressed to pick up any psychic residuals.

Digging through the rubble, the cops eventually found the

body of Hollingsworth, burnt almost beyond recognition—and good riddance, in Rio's opinion. He only hoped the bastard had suffered before dying. From the expressions on some searchers' faces, he wasn't alone in those sentiments.

The discovery allowed his friends to lower their guard, since Hollingsworth worked alone. Once the corpse's identity was confirmed, Lantis banished the ward.

That wasn't the end of it, of course. Cops being cops, McDaniel and Derwent insisted on documenting the entire mess now, before the embers had time to go cold.

Watching them have at it, Rio scarfed down several bars of dark chocolate from Lantis's hoard between sips of water, emergency rations the tall man retrieved from his SUV.

"How're you feeling?" Dillon's scrutiny warned him not to pussyfoot.

Rio took a moment to gauge his condition. The bottomless pit inside him had eased to the hollowness of extreme exertion. Unpleasant but survivable. "Better."

"Good. You can take your time getting this inside you, then." The shorter man handed him a battered take-out box containing turnovers and the pitiful-looking remains of a soggy baklava. More sugar and maybe protein to rebuild muscle.

"Where'd this come from?"

"Cyn left it in the SUV. I suspect it's your lunch."

He'd stood her up. *Damnú air.* He added a few more silent damn its for good measure, wishing he had his hands around Hollingsworth's throat. That *maleton* had died too easily.

Dillon and Lantis seemed determined to stay up to the bitter end—at least that was the impression Rio got until a romantic tune he didn't recognize drifted in from nowhere. It was a ring tone, he realized only when Lantis reached into his coat pocket and pulled out a cell phone.

Lantis stepped away to take the call, his broad shoulders stiffening almost imperceptibly, as if he were bracing himself.

Trouble? Hopefully, nothing serious. Rio didn't think he could handle another emergency so soon.

Looking pale beneath his tan, Lantis drew Dillon aside and murmured, "It's time."

The latter's eyes flared wide, his throat working. "Already?"

Their reactions could only mean one thing.

Rio mustered a grin from somewhere, amused at seeing two oh-so-competent former black ops agents visibly unnerved. To think that imminent fatherhood could shake men who hadn't batted an eye when facing death! "Go ahead. I'm fine. I—" McDaniel, in conversation with Derwent, shot Rio a quick glance and raised a hand in summons. "It looks like the cops aren't done with me yet." He waved back acknowledgment, then adjusted his sling to a more comfortable position.

Dillon and Lantis frowned at him, apparently torn in two directions. Did he look that bad?

"Go on. Shoo! Get out of here." He flicked his hand at them to encourage haste. "Drive safely now. And good luck!"

As they took him at his word, Rio stared after them, wondering if a similar dilemma, too, lay in his future. How the stouthearted were brought low.

Made vulnerable.

He traced a hard edge in his pocket, struck by all it represented, for good or for ill. He couldn't have one without the other.

Cyn looked up from her discussion with Fernao to see Dillon and Atlantis take their leave of her lover and drive off in a hurry. Something must have come up. Whatever it was didn't seem to involve Rio, since he remained behind, walking over to join McDaniel and looking harder than his wont. He held his head high, his face expressionless, scarcely recognizable as the pretty boy civilian her brothers had derided. He didn't look her way, didn't smile, just headed straight to the two lieutenants.

"Better you than me."

She eyed the tac team leader askance, surprised by his comment. "What do you mean?"

Fernao watched Rio, a rare daunted expression showing on his face. "That's one proud guy."

True. She could still lose Rio. A shudder rocked her, her heart jittering in her chest. Needing rescue—being rescued by a woman, at that—had to be a blow to his pride.

CHAPTER TWENTY-NINE

Wrapping up the loose ends took a while. Hollingsworth was a legitimate kill, but the department survived on paperwork. Nothing was final until it was documented. That meant long hours of getting Rio's statement, opening up Hollingsworth's house, and the rest of that unspeakable can of worms.

What they found was horrifying. Hollingsworth had converted his basement into a prison for the women he abducted as sex slaves. From his library of videos, he'd kept each one for more than a year before torturing her to death. The obscene terror permeating the walls left even the hardened crime scene techs nauseated, made worse because no one had suspected. His position had rendered him immune to casual police scrutiny, free to cart his victims around without risk in his official vehicle.

The only good news to be had was that Hawkins's tac team had cornered the mage gang at the waterfront: shamanka, tattooed acolyte, remaining gang member, one each, plus two accessories, all now under wraps. The gang had put up a fight, setting fire to the abandoned warehouse they'd holed up in, but this time they hadn't had surprise on their side nor a convenient getaway ready.

Evan had called to crow over that triumph while Bion and his teammates were occupied with mop-up; the waterfront was part of Evan's beat, and he and Sullivan had been in on the takedown. So far, they'd turned up a stash of *materiae magicae* for deflagration spells and even recovered some of the loot from the heists.

Word was, the mage gang was responsible for a string of robberies across four states. Aurora was just the latest—and last—city they'd sacked.

Hollingsworth's case, on the other hand, was a PR nightmare waiting to happen. Only luck—and the fireworks at the waterfront—had kept the media away, thus far. Once the story broke, the feeding frenzy would likely be savage.

At some point, the brass decided to call it a day—or night such as it was—hours after Rio had been released. He'd refused to go to a hospital, accepting only a ride to his condo. Cyn couldn't help but worry.

When she finally clocked off, though Rio's was the logical place to crash, she almost turned away to make the longer drive to her apartment. So long as she didn't see him, she could put off facing his reaction to events. Would her rescuing him be too much for his pride to take?

Avoidance isn't necessarily the coward's way out, a timorous voice whispered at the back of her mind. She was sorely tempted to take its advice. Sidestepping confrontation was how she usually dealt with conflict, emotional aikido in the hope that circumstances would change and spare her the effort. It was how she'd learned to fight Eleni, how she handled Fernao's insecurity and Hollingsworth's advances, how she'd dodged most romantic entanglements, how she'd kept her heart safe.

But this time she couldn't, despite her doubts as to her reception. She needed to see Rio again, needed to know she hadn't just dreamed his rescue. She wouldn't be able to rest until she was sure. If that made her weak, she didn't care.

The loft was dark when she got there, the only light the pale glow from street level coming through the windows; the waning moon had yet to rise. Cyn shut the door behind her, uncertain where to find Rio. Could he be asleep already? Or had he gone else- where? To his neighbor, maybe? The thought was like a fist around her heart. Yet could she blame him if he'd sought comfort there?

Damn right she could.

Before she could build up a head of steam, the lamp flickered to life, a glowing spear of cool white illuminating a lounging fig- ure on the couch and the remains of an enormous meal on the table—a reminder of the extensive healing he'd undergone. "About time you got here. They kept you late."

She couldn't see his face, didn't detect any emotion in his voice. The dispassionate delivery checked the initial surge of relief she felt at his presence. After all this time, were the demands of her job finally getting to him? Her heart skipped a beat. Accord- ing to his statement, Hollingsworth had targeted him because of her; she'd endangered him. Was this an unexpected twist to the Epiphany?

"Rio?" To her embarrassment, her voice quavered, the sight of him blurring as sudden tears threatened to spill over.

"I'd rather hoped to see you sooner." His voice was so even, she couldn't read anything from it.

"I'm sorry. I just couldn't. I can't afford to break down in front of them." Cyn widened her eyes, desperate to stem the tide. If he was going to break things off between them, she didn't want his last memory of her to be of a weeping ninny. She wasn't turning on the waterworks to hang on to a man. If he couldn't accept her as she was, then they had nothing.

He got to his feet in one fluid motion, his arms stretched wide, the right wavering slightly. "Come here. I need to hold you."

Unable to restrain herself, Cyn flew into his embrace. She

hugged him, desperation tightening her arms convulsively around his neck.

Heat and hardness.

Solid muscle and gentle strength.

Coffee and male musk.

Rio.

"I was so scared I'd be too late." She could have lost him. If Hollingsworth had succeeded in his plot . . .

"You're not getting rid of me that easily." Bending down, Rio returned her hug, pressure for pressure, giving her tangible proof of his survival despite the aches he had to be feeling.

"Your arm?" She found smooth skin, seemingly untouched by the day's events, the bloody mess so seared into her memory gone as though it had never been. The healer had been emphatic in his prognosis for a complete recovery, but they always seemed to say that, in the belief that doubts could create a self-fulfilling relapse.

He flexed his arm tentatively. "It needs strengthening, but should be fine with therapy."

The guarded words made her consider the proof of her eyes more carefully, comparing the biceps with its counterpart on his left. It wasn't atrophied—there was no obvious muscle loss or disfiguration—merely less developed in contrast.

A subtle imperfection.

And a reminder of the fortitude he'd displayed in the aftermath. Her teammates couldn't stop talking about it. He'd impressed them.

"Are you going to give it a chance to recover? I mean, the healer said you're supposed to be using a sling."

"Yeah, but I can't make love to you properly with a sling on." The easy confidence in his smile was assurance enough that his time in that bastard's hands hadn't broken the core of him.

Relief punched the air from her lungs. Cyn rained kisses on his beloved face, still unable to believe he was safe. "I nearly lost you." The sight of him writhing at Hollingsworth's feet flashed before her eyes, stopping her heart with an instant of renewed horror.

His arms tightened, pulling her into his heat. "That's what I realized, when Jordan was attacked."

"What?" She arched back to study his face, thrown by the non sequitur.

Rio cupped her cheek, his gaze intent, his brown eyes nearly black. "I could lose you so easily."

"You're the one who was nearly killed today," she protested, her hands fisting on his shoulders.

He snorted. "It's a dangerous job you've chosen. That *maleton* could have gotten lucky. The booby trap left by that mage gang could've killed you. Your job ups the chances of that happening. If not today, some other day." A gentle kiss punctuated his somber statement, the contact almost chaste. "I don't want to waste what time we have together."

Cyn stared up at him in wonderment, remembering the extraordinarily intense lovemaking that had followed when he'd taken his leave of her after the attack on Jordan Kane. He'd made his decision back then? And he still wanted her after she'd rescued him? "Truly?"

"If you need convincing . . ." Rio captured her mouth in a torrid kiss, sucking and nibbling with carnal intent.

She plunged into the kiss with soul-deep relief. She'd been so afraid she'd never have this again. Never touch him. Never feel him. Never hold him. Selfish of her, but there it was.

Rio consumed her, his heat enveloping her, his embrace surrounding her. His hands branded her. His mouth claimed her. Sweet ravishment of her senses. Raw pleasures she could never tire of and had nearly lost.

Cyn returned his attentions kiss for kiss, touch for touch, lick for lick, driving away the specter of his loss in the most physical way possible. Savoring what her senses told her: Rio alive and whole and holding her.

Need woke, a burning in the blood that demanded satisfaction. Too impatient for niceties, she tore the cotton under her hands, baring hard muscle. Small nipples met her palms, dark buttons on his smooth chest. Muscles tensed at her touch, hot and hard and male. Her questing fingers mapped his body, renewing their claim on this virile territory. Hers.

"I want you." That was safe to say, but Cyn didn't want safe. She'd tried playing it safe, and look what happened.

"I'm right here. I'm not going anywhere."

His hands were doing some claiming of their own, dragging up her blouse and diving under to stroke yearning flesh. His touch soothed an inner ache, the primitive fear that his rescue had all been wishful thinking.

They sank into the couch together, paying little heed to the butter-soft leather. Tongues dueled. Bodies arched and thrust. Hands stroked, groped, squeezed, ripped clothes away, madness setting fire to their blood.

Reckless.

Cyn didn't care any longer. She had to have him any way she could, keep him any way possible. If magic could have held his heart, she would have dared it. Her fears didn't matter; she'd just faced the worst of them.

Rio didn't resist when she pushed him on his back, seeming to understand that she needed this—to run her hands over his body, to touch and feel him—to exorcise her fears and believe that he was truly safe. That didn't mean he was docile. He caressed her all over, talented fingers wringing gasps from her lips with each knowing stroke. His own version of magic.

Desire blazed to towering heights, a mutual seduction stoked by torrid kisses and soft sighs. Slabs of muscle rippled under her hands, whole and unblemished, resilient with good health, burning with male heat.

Kneeling, she straddled Rio, both of them already naked. Having him under her didn't lessen his power; she'd never been more aware of it. Hard thighs flexed against her calves, almost scalding to her inner thighs, strong abs rippled under her hands, his thick cock pressed snug against her belly. Even supine, he projected potent control, subordinate only because he allowed it. A man who could accept her strength.

His yielding only excited her more.

Cyn took him into her, moaning at the delicious friction as the ridges of his cock caught at her delicate inner membranes. Hard where she was soft. Male to her female.

Her lover.

Her man.

Pleasure washed through her, sweet beyond reason.

Drinking it all in, she rocked over him, acknowledging her need for this man and finally accepting it. There was nothing wrong with needing Rio. Loving him wouldn't make her weak. He truly didn't want to change her, wouldn't ask her to be less than she could be. Instead, it made her stronger. Gave her another reason to fight for a better world.

"Oh, yes," he groaned, thrusting into her, reaching so deep inside he was halfway to her heart. His hands rose to fondle and cup her breasts, his touch firm yet gentle. Exquisitely controlled.

Rio stared up at her, a fierce look in his eyes, skin taut across his cheekbones, baring his teeth in a grimace of brutal pleasure. Fearsome, but if she wanted safe, she should have stuck with dating accountants. No one seeing him now would mistake him for a pushover.

His urgency thrilled her, but even more than her feminine power was the knowledge that he let her give him this.

They drove together, united in their quest for fulfillment. The slapping of wet flesh, the growls and the moans, the heady scent of raw sex—all combined to heighten their desire.

Cyn rode him harder, faster, lifting herself higher until he was almost free, making the most of his strokes. Taking as she was taken. He filled her completely, so thick she could hardly breathe, steel-hard yet so right he slid into her as though made for her.

Need escalated, thundering higher with the relentless might of a wicce train at full speed, lust and love and hunger rising on a tidal wave of passion roaring toward completion. They couldn't hold out for long.

"*Hechicera.*" His hands clamped on her hips, squeezing her butt possessively. Anchoring her against him, he pounded her in a fury of desperation, his face set in ruthless lines.

Need surged, digging into her with velvet claws. "Rio!" She arched above him, caught in the urgency of her desire. Ecstasy hung just a heartbeat away.

"I'm here. I'm with you."

The breathless words of assurance triggered her release. The dam burst, rapture spilling over in a cataract of ecstasy untrammeled by doubt. It swept Cyn up in wave after glorious wave of consummate pleasure, flinging her to tempestuous heights as Rio arched up, lifting her off her knees and choking out a gasp of his own.

Her release overwhelmed her, leaving her boneless and quivering on top of Rio, her pulse a thrumming in her throat, fluttering as though it would never slow.

For this man above all others.

She couldn't lose him.

Not now.

A gentle hand pushed back her hair, recalling her to herself and her lover. His heart beat beneath her ear, a steady drum all the more comforting for its strong, even rhythm.

"*Mo muirnín.*" The solemn cast of Rio's chocolate brown eyes caught her gaze and held it. She couldn't look away. "*Te amo, hechicera mía.*"

Cyn's heart trembled at the depths of his certainty, the sincerity in his avowal of love. This beautiful man was hers? "Smile when you say that. It's not supposed to be a death sentence, you know."

She couldn't control the quaver of her voice. What woman could in the face of such a declaration?

The corners of those perfectly formed lips of his tilted up in amusement. "I love you. I want to live with you, have children with you, grow old with you. I want the right to fuss over you, and make love with you every night—and twice daily."

She gulped at the enormity of his hopes, dragging air past the tightness in her throat. It took her two attempts to say the words. "I love you, too."

Rio claimed her mouth almost before she finished speaking. His exultant kiss stole her breath then returned it, air for her air. "Was it that difficult? Maybe some practice saying it will help." He smiled down at her, mischief lighting his eyes.

"I'm just overwhelmed, you— You—" Cyn sputtered, unable to find the words she wanted when her heart was doing wild loops in her chest. She finally settled for thumping his shoulder, the left one.

He kissed her again, as though he couldn't help himself, his joy irresistible, the simple touch of lips to lips becoming a celebration of life.

She let him sweep her along, a buoyant sense of inevitability leaving her breathless, now that she'd surrendered to her feelings for him. She melted against him, rejoicing in the solidity of his body, male to her female, the other half of her soul. Her lips clung to his, passion and devotion combined into one searing exchange.

Why had she fought this for so long?

"While you're feeling daring, how about one more question?" Rio reached for something on the side table. "Wear this for me?" He held up a platinum ring in front of her nose, between two fingers. A simple engagement ring that shouldn't have scared her so much, but it did. Marriage was a step she'd never contemplated for herself; the commitment necessary for such a relationship was something she'd always reserved for police work.

Then Cyn looked into his eyes and knew there was only one

answer she could give. She offered her trembling hand, feeling like she'd stepped off a ledge miles above the ground into free fall. Her heart jumped to her throat, hope and terror and happiness wrestling for the upper hand.

Supporting her palm with one hand, Rio slid the ring down her finger, his eyes blazing with emotion.

She could feel strong magic on it, akin to the spells on her body armor, extending a cloak of protection around her. Serious business. He'd gone to a lot of trouble for such a simple piece of jewelry—for her. "A perfect fit." She forgot how to breathe as the diamonds sparkled with seeming sentience. Or maybe that was just her, trembling.

"Of course." He kissed the back of her hand, the tip of his tongue sneaking a surreptitious lick of the tender web at the juncture of her ring and middle fingers.

Cyn gasped as delight streaked up her arm, shattering the sense of unreality that enfolded her. Her Latin lover had a way of getting to the meat of things. "Rio . . ." She licked her lips, her irrepressible libido stirring.

Looking into her eyes, he took a fingertip between his teeth and nibbled, the carnal intent unmistakable.

Her lungs seized, anticipation and trepidation making the ordinary act of breathing difficult. This time would be different. Had to be different. No longer merely lovers having fun, but engaged. No longer novelty.

Would sex lose that allure? The spontaneity? The freedom of being just lovers?

Rio drew her finger into his mouth, licking and sucking suggestively, kindling excitement all out of proportion to his action. As though he were plying his attentions on something much more intimate.

Heat engulfed her. She melted, creaming as she went up in flames. Such a simple gesture, yet he knew her so well. Lightning found her core with explosive results. She shuddered, decadent pleasure tripping along her nerves to curl her toes. "Ooooh . . . that ought to be illegal."

"Heaven forbid." He chuckled, the sound coming from deep in his chest, rich with male delight and satisfaction—that sure, male confidence of a man who had his woman and knew he would have her again. "There's a lot more where that came from."

She didn't mind. She wanted him to have her, after all.

Cyn slung her arm across his shoulders, sinking her fingers into his hair and drawing him down to her lips. "I want it all."

"You've got it. You've got me."

Rio met her kiss with heat and promise, with cherishment and claim all at once. Tenderness and challenge. His hands danced over her body, long fingers tracing patterns known only to him, trailing delight and desire in equal measure. His tongue glided over her neck in velvet seduction, his breath a cool contrast to his warm caress.

Tilting her head to give him greater access, she savored the tingling anticipation of the moment.

They touched, knowledge and desire adding spice to their caresses. They laughed, the intimate laughter of lovers for whom time was of no concern. They rolled on the couch, legs tangling, neither one struggling for the upper hand.

Lost in the heat of their passion.

When Rio parted her thighs and pressed into her, Cyn welcomed him with a sigh of relief. "Yes."

This time, it was a sweet possession, a give-and-take between equals. Slow and sure. No rush. Deliberately fanning the flames, building up to certain release.

Rio settled into a dreamy cadence, rocking them with calm deliberation. Cyn let him, in no hurry to get things over with and lose the comfort of his embrace, the hard thrust of his body sliding into hers.

Their orgasm, when it came, washed over them in slow waves of gentle pleasure, fountaining in ever-higher spurts of rapture. The promise of more and better yet to come.

Replete with sensation, Cyn quivered through the sensual aftershocks, her muscles trembling from yet another sweet climax. Blanketed by male heat, she could only lie there, curled around her lover, too spent to do anything more than breathe.

Sheer heaven. Why had she thought it would be different?

"Mine," Rio growled, the rumble aggressive and somehow territorial. "Now I can say it. *My woman. Mo muirnín.*" He nuzzled her breasts, caressing the upper slopes with gentle lips. "No poaching allowed."

She giggled. He definitely wanted her. How could she doubt a statement like that?

"Think that's funny, huh?"

"No, just that it's so *you.*" Cyn raised her hand, as much to change the subject as admire her ring. Under the lamp, the diamonds glittered at her like stars in the night, the spells on them warm to her finger. "Pretty sure of yourself, weren't you?"

"I had hopes, nothing more." Rio pushed himself up on his forearms and plumped her breasts between his hands. He strummed his thumbs over her nipples, circling and coaxing them back into tight peaks. Her body responded with a frisson of delight, ready for more of his lovemaking, motor revving and faster off the trigger. "This reminds me"—another breath-stealing stroke over the hard nubs—"I have something for your collection."

"Another doll? You can think of that at a time like this?" Cyn panted against her fast-rising hunger, incredulous that even he could do something so practical-minded as that.

He chuckled as he buried his face in her exaggerated cleavage, his stubble rasping the tender flesh. "Precisely because of this. You see, it's a Minoan bull leaper."

She fisted her hands on his hair and pulled back so she could see his expression. "So?" she demanded impatiently.

"You don't remember how they're dressed? Footwear, brace-lets, armlets"—his hands glided over the relevant areas—"and this short front-and-back apron that just covers the crotch." His fingers tripped along her waist and down her inner thighs, stealing her breath. "It reminded me of you." The mischief in his eyes suggested he meant that literally.

Of her?

Suspicion stirred. She narrowed her eyes at him. "Don't tell me you jerked off looking at it."

Rio laughed, his hands squeezing her butt possessively. "I'm not telling. But it really reminded me of you when I saw it in the shop. You know, taking a bull by the horns and all that."

Despite the potent distraction of his tongue lapping a nipple, her heart flipped at his description, at the sincere acceptance inherent in the words. "There's only one horn I'm interested in at the moment, and it's not doing me any good where it is right now." She'd tried to deliver that in a no-nonsense voice, but it came out too huskily to convince.

"You don't scare me. My sorceress. My Amazon. My warrior woman." He punctuated his claims with wet kisses, sliding downward after each one, his tongue swirling teasing circles that had her lungs stuttering and her halfhearted irritation banished.

Cyn dug her fingers into the couch's leather cushions, the warm band around one the only bond that kept her in place, but it was enough to keep her still, accepting his homage.

Poised above her mound, Rio gave her a salaciously meaningful grin. "It's a good thing you're off-duty tomorrow." Clearly, he had plans for tonight, and they didn't include sleep.

She laughed, the lingering trepidation she felt at the major step they'd taken finally vanishing in effervescent delight. The more things changed, the more they stayed the same. She could live with that.